Corporation Wife

A searing novel which opens the doors into the boardrooms and bedrooms of the Organisation men. It takes a revealing look at the women they desire—and the ones they marry—and, above all, at the company they love, honour and obey.

Power is the company's promise to the men it employs, stature to the wives and women it controls; women with too much time on their hands, whose husbands are having an affair with the Corporation . . .

D1584731

CATHERINE GASKIN

Corporation Wife

Collins

FONTANA BOOKS

First published 1960
First issued in Fontana Books 1963
Fifteenth Impression January 1975

© Catherine Gaskin Cornberg 1960

Printed in Great Britain
Collins Clear-Type Press
London and Glasgow

For Sol

Corporation—an artificial person created by legislative act

THE OXFORD DICTIONARY

BOOK ONE

CHAPTER ONE

There were some days in Jeannie Talbot's life when sitting in a school-room appeared to have nothing to do with the essential business of living, days when she needed other air to breathe, and other sounds to hear. These were the days when she simply took off from Burnham Falls High School —sat on the bluff above the freight yards watching the trains shunt in and out, or walked by herself in the woods. She recognised that there were going to be very few more days such as these, because she was seventeen and an adult world was close upon her.

She had settled herself in the midst of an outcrop of granite boulders on the edge of the wood, where the rocks gave her shelter from the light wind, and trapped the warmth of the spring morning. She knew she was trespassing on country-club property, and she didn't give a damn. Jeannie Talbot had lived all her life in Burnham Falls, and Talbots had lived there for a hundred years before her, and she just didn't believe there was anywhere around Burnham Falls she couldn't go without hindrance. She took some satisfaction in the thought that there were such rights which belonged to her without paying for them, because in the Talbot family there was very little evidence of what hard cash would buy.

Jeannie didn't particularly mind the lack of money—it only hit her when she needed a new dress, and couldn't buy it, and even that she forgot about pretty soon. If she had been asked she couldn't have said exactly what it was she wanted that more money might have bought for her. Her father was the town's odd-job man, and her mother hired out as a maid when she was called for. They lived in a neat, crowded house near the shellac factory; she had a sister, Christine, who was three years old.

She supposed that she had to take these days off occasionally because she was like her father, Ted, who hadn't done a full day of indoor work in his life. Jeannie had a sharp, quick mind, and a good measure of her father's pride and independence; she had a sensuous, graceful body, mature

7

to the point of lushness, and rich, golden hair she had inherited from her mother—though in Selma Talbot the richness was fading. Jeannie was the prettiest girl at Burnham Falls High School, was voted the most popular, and she would graduate in June near the head of her class.

She liked to come up here because from this high point among the boulders she could see the town and the whole valley. It was a fine place from which to view her world.

But this was also the start of the cleared land around the Carpenter place, and the start of the acres of daffodils that Joe Carpenter had planted. They were in full bloom now; that was why she had come here to-day. Soon after she had settled herself she had noticed that Harriet, Joe's daughter, had come out of the house, and begun to cut and lay daffodils in a basket. The sight of Harriet did not disturb her; if she kept still Harriet would never look up here, would never notice her.

As she watched Harriet moving in the distance, she debated with herself whether or not she would go down into the town to hear the speeches at noon, and share the free lunch they were handing out. The high school was being let out at eleven thirty so that the students could be present, and the school band was going to play, as well as the Fire Department Band.

But the thousands of daffodils waving lazily before her eyes half-mesmerised her, and soon she forgot about Burnham Falls, and the high school, and about Harriet Carpenter. She lay back against the rock and closed her eyes, feeling the warm granite against her shoulder blades. Her mind drifted into the vague places of the future, the unknown places where she would become a different Jeannie Talbot, one that even she was unable, at this moment, to recognise.

II

In the town they still called it "the Carpenter place," even though her father had been dead for over two years, and there was no longer anyone in the town named Carpenter. Harriet sometimes wondered if Steve minded having the house he lived in called by another man's name, but she doubted it, because Steve only noticed what went on in his laboratory and at Amtec, and he wasn't likely to care what they called the house. It stood on a gentle rise, about half

8

a mile from the edge of the town, with the white paint flaking off the columns of the wide veranda, surrounded by its own five acres of land, and at the back the four hundred acres that belonged to the country club. It was heavily mortgaged, and it belonged to another time.

She laid down her garden shears, and stared reflectively across the stretch of lawn towards the house; she was standing in the long grass where the daffodils grew—with the pale sun full on her face, with the wind from the west swaying the long-stemmed blooms and the feathery branches of the trees. This was the house she had lived in all her life, except for those few years in California, and it was bound in every thread and fibre of her uneventful history. It was part of her, something accepted, and scarcely ever questioned; it represented her father as much as anything a man can leave behind him. Now she wondered if Steve had grown to hate it.

It was the typical large house of the area—built of white frame, of spacious and even graceful proportions, with the faded green shutters opening back from windows that gave a view of the town and the lake, and the rolling, wooded hills beyond. Her grandfather, Henry Carpenter, had built it as a young man, and it was here Henry's only child, her father, Joe, had been born.

Harriet took up the shears again, and for some minutes concentrated on cutting the flowers, piling great masses of them in the basket. Her father had not been an imaginative or exotic gardener, but he had cherished a fondness for the old-fashioned, conventional flowers. Harriet could remember, before the war, when the great stretch of lawn had been mown velvet-smooth right to the edge of the woods; each year since she had come back, the square had shrunk, and the long grass and the alien weeds had crept nearer to the house. The formal border was gone now, long ago overgrown, with only the irrepressible hollyhock and phlox coming back each summer, like old relatives who could recall better times. She still kept up the rose garden in front of the house, and the climbers still embraced the fat pillars of the porch. That was all—the rest of the garden she had lost, just as she was losing the battle with the house itself, with the dust that gathered on the high cornices, with the worn rug on the stairs, with the old-fashioned bathrooms, and the furnace that used too much fuel. When Joe Carpenter had made his addition to his father's modest house

9

he had built generously, with many rooms to accommodate the swirling, restless life of the large family he had wanted. He had had only two children—Harriet and his son, Josiah.

Again Harriet's shears fell idle, and again she straightened and looked towards the house. Her arms dropped limply by her sides. Josh should have been living here now, his own children filling the rooms, and learning from him the secret places of the woods that he had known. But Josh was dead, and his chance to have children was gone—in Australia there was an Army nurse who should have married him, and come here and borne his children. Josh should have been here now instead of Steve.

She turned away from the house, and went on cutting. She picked many more daffodils than she needed to fill the vases, moving with deliberate slowness against the flying minutes, against the inevitable hour of noon.

Inside, the house felt chill, which meant their worn-out furnace was giving trouble again. From the laundry room she heard Nell muttering irritably to herself.

She went upstairs and showered and dressed, and put on her make-up with great care. The new warm, red shade of lipstick suited her, she thought, but she wished that she had something new other than lipstick to wear to-day. It would have been nice to surprise Steve. Then she tugged the skirt of her suit a little to the side, and paused to pat her flat stomach approvingly—at least she still fitted her six-year-old suit. She didn't think she looked thirty-three, and the mother of two boys—or was she glossing over that as well as the suit? Suddenly the thought struck her that she hadn't been to New York for a long time, and what was considered youthful and smart in Burnham Falls was apt to look faded on Fifth Avenue. There would be a lot of women from New York there to-day. She turned away from the mirror hastily, and took up her bag and gloves.

Downstairs she called to Nell.

" I'm going now, Nell! "

The old woman appeared in the kitchen door. She nodded approvingly. " Well, you do look nice, Miss Harriet. You'll be a real credit to your dad to-day. You always have looked nice in that suit. . . . He always knew what was right for you."

Harriet, about to open the back door, turned around and faced Nell. She laid her hand affectionately on the other's

10

shoulder. She said, half-jestingly, " Well, I did make a few decisions for myself . . ."

" Yes—but *that* suit he picked out for you. I remember it perfectly. You both went to New York, and he got that contract. That was the time . . ." She broke off, frowning. " Well . . . it doesn't matter now. People have been quick to forget about Joe Carpenter since the new company came in. But I don't forget. I remember everything."

" *We* don't forget my father, Nell. But the company had to come . . . you know that. We couldn't hang on any longer."

Nell sniffed. " Mr. Carpenter would have found a way to hang on. He always did."

" Not this time," Harriet said; she turned, not wanting to discuss it any further with Nell. She opened the door, then paused. " If Gene and Tim get back before I do, tell them their father has promised to take them over to Sheraton to see about that fishing gear. Don't let them go off somewhere."

Nell nodded. " All right—I'll keep them." She added, " Will hamburgers be all right for supper? I don't expect you'll want much after that fancy lunch they'll give you."

" Hamburgers will be fine," Harriet said. She closed the door, and started along the flagstone walk to the garage.

Nell Talbot had been in the Carpenter house for twenty-six years, and it was true that she remembered everything of even minor importance. She had been the daily help for two years before Claudia Carpenter died, and after that she had moved in to look after Josh and Harriet. She was Ted Talbot's aunt, and the two were the last of a clan that had lived in Burnham Falls for four generations.

Harriet opened the garage doors—the extravagant white frame building that Joe had built to house his two cars, his saddle horse, and the array of gardening equipment he had collected. She smiled when she saw the car. She had explained to the boys the importance of the occasion and they had responded with a burst of family pride. The car had been lovingly polished; its dark surface mirrored every stud and nail in the walls.

She touched the starter, and backed the car out, turning it to face down the drive to the road. For the first time now she had misgivings about using the Rolls to-day—it would have been better to have Steve come and pick her up in the Chevy. Of course the townspeople were used to

11

it—" Joe Carpenter's old Rolls "—but what would the strangers think of the old-fashioned convertible? Joe had seen it in the showroom window on Park Avenue one afternoon back in 1938. He hadn't been able to afford it but he had bought it after only three minutes' hesitation; he had driven it proudly until he died.

The clock on the dashboard told her that she had a few minutes before she need leave; she lighted a cigarette and leaned back, relaxing.

The land that stretched on each side of the house—to the edge of the town on one side, and over to Route 40 on the other—comprised a little more than four hundred acres. In her grandfather's time it had been known as the Carpenter Farm. It had given Henry Carpenter a good living, and sent his son to college. The soil of this New York State farm was stony, and Henry, and his father before him, had had to blast boulders away to grow feed for their cattle; it wasn't an easy living they won from that land. Henry's son, Joe, had little inclination for farming, and he had recognised the era and the competition of the giant farming combines out West; he had no plans to work the land when he should inherit it. Instead he brought his degree in chemistry home from college, and had put it to work. Here in Burnham Falls he had started to manufacture shellac from his own formulas, and his first operation was carried on in one of his father's barns. His product was good, and from the barn he had expanded into a plant, and had become one of the principal suppliers for the New England region. In giving employment to the men of the town, Joe had realised something of an unspoken dream—that the decline of farming in his area should not entirely bring to an end the old way of life. His shellac plant had given employment to the sons of farmers who might have moved away; his weekly pay cheques supported their families. The plant was called the Burnham Falls Shellac Company.

Even in the early, struggling days of the plant, Joe had refused to sell off even an acre of his land to the week-end cottage dwellers from New York who were just beginning to make an appearance. He had held on to all of it, at first only by sacrifice and thrift, and then later because he could afford to hold it. It had been a luxury he had held on to until right at the end—and then he had sold it all in one piece, leaving the house its island of five acres. Over by the stream the woods had been cleared again, copses moulded

12

out of their thickness, earthmovers had come in and shaped the bunkers, sand traps and greens. Now it was the finest golf course in the county. Harriet had never been there. The townspeople welcomed it as a source of business, until they found that the contracts went to suppliers in New York. The local people were hired as help.

To-day the celebration lunch would be held at the club.

The clock on the dashboard ticked gently, and the hands moved up towards twelve. She squashed out her cigarette, and brushed the ash off her skirt. Out here, in the bright sunlight, the suit seemed even more out-of-date than it had been upstairs in her room. She really should have got something new for to-day, and be damned to the expense; she should have done it for Steve's sake, even if the habits of eight or ten years were hard to shake. The suit had been an expensive one—and her father had bought it for her six years ago, as Nell had said. They had been in New York together, and he was celebrating a contract that had just been renewed.

Joe had been shrewd enough to see the effects of the giant combines, of mechanised farming on the small farms of his father's day; but he had not known when his own time had come. In the plant at Burnham Falls he was using much man-power on outdated equipment, and he was paying them too well to leave much surplus to put into new toools and machinery. A businessman, he now bore small resemblance to the young man who had started the shellac factory in his father's barn. He had placed his bid for the renewal of the contract confidently, because he had held it for over twenty years. But his bid had come in too high, and two days after that trip to New York he was told that the contract would not be signed. All that remained from the trip was the suit Harriet was now wearing. Afterwards the bill had come, and they had been a long time paying it.

She slipped the Rolls into gear, and started down the drive to the road.

CHAPTER TWO

Burnham Flats lay in a shallow valley between the gentle, wooded hills that ran down to the edges to two lakes—Lake Burnham and Downside. Lake Burnham was the town's

13

lake, a lively place dotted with summer houses and boat-sheds, where families went to swim on hot Saturday afternoons, and where the townspepole kept their canoes and fishing-boats. It belonged to, and was used by everyone in Burnham Falls, and it was still large enough to serve all their needs. Even so, it was small by comparison to Downside.

Downside stretched for five miles along the upper curve of the valley, a narrow, silent stretch of water fed by many little streams that slipped down the rocky sides of the hills. There were no houses built along the ridges of those hills, and the only road was narrow, curving, and almost totally deserted. The foreshores of Downside, save for a few acres, belonged to the New York Water Supply, which had made the lake a part of its chain of reservoirs to supply the metropolis, sixty miles away. The other important owner was the Catholic Church. The heirs of the millionaire who had built his grey granite mansion as a faithful copy of a German castle, had given Downside to the church when taxes made the place impractical to maintain. It was now a seminary for students for the priesthood.

The earliest records of Burnham Falls were dated 1732. The town itself looked like a hundred, or a thousand other towns that lay north of New York City and on the verge of the New England States, and which shared with them the rocky terrain, the long, frozen winters, the fierce tide of spring that turned too swiftly to summer, and the orange and scarlet falls. The houses were mostly white frame, and their lawns were trim and tended.

The courthouse at Burnham Falls had been built a little after the Revolution. Its beauty of line and proportion was so simple that many people who had lived in Burnham Falls all their lives had never really noticed it; the porticoed front, with its slender columns, was shaded in summer by the tall elms that still remained along this section of Main Street.

Across the lake from the courthouse, piled one on the other up the slope of the hills, were the cottages of the summer visitors. Viewed from here they were not unattractive—the distance and the trees softened the outlines of the boxy little frame bungalows, with the screen porches and the split rail fences, and took away the painful obviousness of their square gardens. Those built since the war had coloured roofs—green, red and blue. To anyone standing on the steps of the courthouse at Burnham Falls, they looked like dabs of bright paint autocratically imposed on a picture of the

14

quiet lake and hills. The summer bungalows did not exactly belong with Burnham Falls, but they were needed. From June to September the population of the town was almost trebled, and many people lived on the proceeds of those months. The storekeepers did not overcharge the summer people purely from motives of greed—but because the winters were long, and they had to make their profits before the bungalows across the lake closed down. They had yet to test fully the damage the supermarket and the shopping centre down the highway could do to them.

Since the full employment of the war years, Burnham Falls had tottered on the verge of decline. It needed more of one kind of person, and less of another—more people to build new houses across the lake, and fewer farmers whose living had dwindled with the importance of agriculture in the area. Burnham Falls needed industry to bring employment to its people, or it needed a fast train service to turn it into a commuter dormitory, instead of just a summer resort. At one time it had believed that Joe Carpenter could keep its young men in jobs, and he had believed it also. But in the end Joe had failed to do this, and the young men had moved away with their families. Singly, Joe Carpenter had not been able to keep Burnham Falls alive.

And so, many eyes had turned curiously to look after Hariet, driving Joe's old Rolls along Main Street. They wondered, a little uncomfortably, if anyone had told her about the sign. It was stretched, big scarlet letters on white cloth, from the portico of the courthouse to one of the elms on the lake shore. It was simple and blunt, and it spoke painfully of the town's need.

BURNHAM FALLS WELCOMES AMTEC INDUSTRIES, INC.

II

Amtec had chosen to introduce itself formally to Burnham Falls in the little square at the back of the courthouse. Harriet, at the time she had glimpsed the sign moving gently in the breeze, had only just begun to comprehend the homely touch that holding the gathering in the town square, instead of the new building up on the hill, would give to the occasion. There would be no ribbon-cutting at the glass and metal doors of the new Amtec Laboratories—though

15

they would be on show for three days to anyone who wanted to visit them. They had actually been functioning after a fashion for about a month, as scientists and technologists had begun to arrive from Amtec's other smaller research centres across the country. In the next few weeks they would be followed by their families.

Main Street, and the two short streets leading to the square, were lined with parked cars, and there was a steady drift of people in that direction. Already Harriet could hear the low, rumbling noise of the crowd. She glanced anxiously at her watch as she nudged the Rolls through the pedestrians, raising her hand now and again to salute someone she recognised as she passed. It was almost noon. Unless she found a parking space quickly she would miss the opening speeches. Right at the edge of the square she saw Jed Wilson take his Ford out of the line of parked cars; thankfully she backed the Rolls into his place. She slid out of the seat, slammed the door, but did not lock it. As she started across the road towards the square she smoothed on her gloves; she noticed then that her hands trembled slightly.

Harriet hesitated as she reached the edge of the worn lawn that surrounded the bandstand. Just about everyone from Barnham Falls was here, she judged, and many people who'd never been in Burnham Falls before. But this wasn't the untidy, good-humoured carnival or political-rally crowd, milling about noisily, or fighting for space on one of the eight wooden benches facing the bandstand. Burnham Falls had never known a meeting like this one before. The little square was packed solidly with folding aluminium chairs, set out in neat blocks.

Suddenly she was aware that Steve was coming towards her down one of the aisles between the chairs—and that she had stood absent-mindedly on the kerb, absorbed in the scene. But even before he came close Harriet could sense his tension. His tall, loosely-jointed body, with its slightly hunched shoulders, was held with unnatural stiffness. He threw a half-smoked cigarette on the grass, and paused to stamp it out; then he came on towards her again. His tension was visible in the frown on his handsome, weary face; it was also in the feel of the hand that he laid too firmly on her arm.

"I thought you weren't going to make it. They're just about ready to start."

She shrugged and tried to smile. "Too much traffic and

16

no parking space—and that big Amtec sign scared me half to death."

Her tone was deliberately light, but she looked at him almost appealingly. She wanted him to understand how she felt about the sign across Main Street; she needed the reassurance of a glance from him, or a further tightening of the grip on her arm. But whatever his concern, it was not, at the moment, for her; he seemed hardly to have heard her. He was leading her forward to a seat, leading her down through the rows of townspeople, many of whom had noticed her arrival, down to a section in the front near the bandstand that seemed to be filled with strange people, and with women wearing hats. Here, she noticed, the aluminium seats were different, more generous in width, with curved, padded backs, and arm-rests. Steve nudged her towards two empty ones at the end of a row. A few faces turned towards them, mostly unfamiliar ones, though she recognised Herb Miller, the Mayor, and Charles Stanley, the Prosecuting Attorney. She smiled warmly at these two; but her first quick glance had marked the chic spring hats and here and there a mink stole among the women, and she was conscious that she had not bothered to put on a hat, because she never wore a hat in Burnham Falls, and that her suit must show every one of its six years. She was a naïve fool to have taken this occasion so much for granted; this wasn't Burnham Falls, this was Amtec. Steve leaned across her and touched the arm of the man on her right.

"Tom! . . . Harriet, this is Tom Harvey, head of market research—and Mrs. Harvey . . . my wife, Harriet."

"How do you do?" Harriet said to both of them. Tom Harvey's wife was a slim, pretty woman, who wore a mustard-coloured hat, and suède gloves that were an exact match; Harriet found herself taking the gloved hand, and being subjected to a swift, complete scrutiny. Her interested look of recognition told Harriet that she probably knew a great deal of the history of the Burnham Falls Shellac Company, and of Joe Carpenter. The eyes of the two women met firmly.

"I'm glad to meet you at last, Mrs. Dexter."

Then, from directly in front of Harriet, a man interrupted them. He turned around, and of his own initiative, held out his hand to Harriet.

"Mrs. Dexter! . . . I'm Arthur Sommers." His round babyish face creased in a smile. "Don't mind my introducing

17

myself—we're all in the same family now, and I've known Steve ever since he joined the company. Steve tells me you were actually brought up in Burnham Falls."

"Oh, yes. . . . Burnham Falls has been here for quite a long time . . . a long time before to-day." Beside her, Steve shifted his position in his chair.

"Well, it's certainly a pretty spot—and I'll bet it's got quite a bit of history attached to it, too. I liked this place the moment I saw it, and I've been telling my wife, Mary, that she and the kids are going to enjoy living here. Mary isn't here to-day . . . we're moving here from New Jersey next week, and there was too much to be done for her to take the day off . . ."

Steve cut in, leaning in towards the group. "Art is going to head up our finance division here, Harriet. He's comptroller."

"Just an old penny-watcher, that's all I am!" His face crinkled with laughter, as if it were an old joke for him. "Hateful—but necessary, Mrs. Dexter. Can't let the boys get so relaxed by these fresh open spaces that they don't watch the costs any more. But say—my wife would like to meet you as soon as she comes up here. You being brought up here—you could tell her all about the neighbourhood, the stores, and so on . . . whatever it is you ladies always want to know about a new place."

"I'd be glad to," Harriet said, "but there isn't so much to know about Burnham Falls—or much to do in it, either."

"There will be," Sommers said genially, but with firmness. "There will be! Just you wait and see the plans Amtec has for Burnham Falls. They'll have all you ladies so busy you won't have time to turn round. There's the new school to get off the ground, for one thing. . . ."

"I thought the country would be paying for the new school . . ." Harriet murmured.

"That's true, but Amtec is bringing in the people who'll be the taxpayers. And it's up to Amtec to see that we get the kind of school we want. . . ." He paused, and then decided to finish out his thought. "The company's had a lot of experience, Mrs. Dexter, and there are a lot of planning and construction experts on the payroll. Amtec expects them to give their time to community work, just like everyone else."

Then Tom Harvey said, "You're darned right, Art! We can only get the things we want here if we're prepared to work

18

for them . . . and for my part, that'll suit me fine. I'll enjoy getting my teeth into some community projects. I've been a cliff-dweller in New York for too long."

Mrs. Harvey said gently, "My two girls are going to enjoy going to school in the country. They go to P.S. 6 now, but they'd rather be in the country. And if the Town Council passes the present plans for the new school, it'll be one of the finest in the State."

"I didn't know the plans were ready," Harriet said.

"We've had them at Amtec for some weeks," Tom Harvey said. "In fact, we recommended the architect who prepared them to the Town Council."

Steve lit another cigarette. "I've only glanced at them," Steve said, "but it looks like a pretty expensive project to me."

"It's going to be a consolidated school," Art Sommers explained. "It's going to join a couple of the towns round here—and after all, we have to take care of the needs of the future population. If we don't get first-class establishments, we can't get the right kind of teachers, either. Amtec, of course, has made it possible for the Council to get the loans. . . ."

He stopped speaking as the Burnham Fire Department Band suddenly struck up. They played rather raggedly, but with great gusto. Harriet realised that they were nervous —incredibly they were nervous, these men who knew almost every face in the crowd except for the group of strangers sitting in the special seats.

Tom Harvey suddenly touched Harriet very lightly on the arm. "Here's E.J.—coming now."

"... and we are proud, very proud indeed, to become corporate citizens of Burnham Falls."

E. J. Harrison had been speaking for some minutes. Along with the others he had listened politely to the Mayor's, Herb Miller's, speech—a brief, enthusiastic speech that had risen to a little crescendo at the end, as he led the applause which accompanied the progress of the Chairman of the Board of Amtec Industries, Incorporated, from his seat to the speaker's place in the centre of the bandstand. Amtec wanted its chairman heard; the public address system was evidenced by only one discreet mike at the speaker's stand, but Amtec engineers had done a very competent job of wiring the whole square. No one would miss the words of E. J. Harrison.

"You here in town know, of course, that about eighteen months ago the operation that used to be known as the Burnham Falls Shellac Company became the newest member of the family of growing companies that make up Amtec Industries. Under the guidance of Amtec, with improved production methods, with the Amtec distribution and sales channels open to it, the plant has considerably increased its volume, its markets, and its manpower. We are determined to continue this trend until Burnham Falls is the biggest producers of shellac in the Eastern States."

Herb Miller again led the applause, but the crowd didn't need urging. This was what it had come to hear about—more production and more jobs.

"The Research Laboratory is working for the United States Defence Department—who have long been one of Amtec's leading customers. Now I am able to announce that we have been granted increased government contracts to manufacture the products of our research—research which in the past has proved to have been vital to our defence. This will require a new and extensive plant, and one that must be capable of being enlarged, as our needs and products increase. It gives me great pleasure to tell you now that Amtec has decided to build this plant in Burnham Falls, and we will want Burnham Falls man-power to run it."

He cut out the applause with an authoritative gesture.

"Ladies and gentlemen—Burnham Falls is going to take its place in the space age!—in the age of missiles and rockets! We are in the process of developing new and improved epoxies and solid fuels—substances that will be used in building and firing the missiles that will keep our country safe from aggression, missiles that will give us control of outer space!"

Wild applause broke out now. Harriet joined in the applause, and she knew that Burnham Falls was being carried away on a wave of patriotic fervour, even though most of the people were hearing about epoxies and solid state fuels for the first time. There was a comfortable thought of prosperity to accompany the patriotism.

". . . And we of Amtec Industries are fully conscious of the responsibilities we owe to any community which we enter. We have brought, and will be bringing, progress to

20

your town. There are two hundred scientists coming to staff the research centre, and with them are coming their wives and families. Amtec has met its responsibilities to these families, by building the development which is known as Amtec Park. We pride ourselves at Amtec that no move of personnel has ever involved hardship."

His voice grew louder, more forceful. " You in Burnham Falls will share the privileges and benefits enjoyed by the thousands of people throughout the United States who work for Amtec. You will share its health plans, its insurance plans, its pension funds. You will know the feeling of security which comes from belonging to an organisation which has the means and the capacity to be a friend and a helper to you."

E. J. Harrison was happy, because these were words which he had said many times before, in many different places.

He went on: " Amtec has made some far-reaching plans. We know that when we build the new plant here, our demands on man-power are going to exceed the supply available to us here in Burnham Falls. This man-power we must bring in from outside. But don't think we're going to throw a housing problem into your laps, or despoil or overcrowd this beautiful town. At the same time we break ground to begin construction of the new plant—which is scheduled for this season—we shall immediately begin construction for housing for the families of the men Amtec will recruit to work in the plant. With this plan in mind we have just completed the purchase of a large tract of land on the western limit of the town, where we will build three hundred homes."

He paused, and the pause was long enough to let the feeling and the picture of the three-hundred house unit take shape, the thought of the fresh money flowing into the cash registers of Burnham Falls, the thought of the children crowding the schools, the automobiles crowding the streets.

" Ladies and gentlemen . . . we believe that in this new extension to your town, in these new families who come to live there, will lie the future life and growth of Burnham Falls.

" We will all be partners in this corporate venture—we will be a team working together to make Burnham Falls, and the United States, a better place to live in."

With great modesty E. J. Harrison left the speaker's stand, and returned to his seat, apparently unhearing of the clap-

21

ping, whistles and cheers that flowed about him. He merely smiled and nodded at the men about him who pressed their congratulations on him; he looked calm and unruffled— a handsome, even distinguished man, Harriet thought, who for a moment had enjoyed playing God.

She leaned towards Steve, and said, under cover of the applause, "Well—I guess Burnham Falls really knows it's alive at last."

Then it happened again. That strange look of wariness and chill came down on his face, a concern not for her, but for what was happening around them. He looked beyond her to Tom Harvey, and then at the solid bulk of Art Sommers in front.

"Quietly! . . . They'll hear you." He groped for his cigarettes, producing the familiar, untidy package that was characteristic of him. "Let's not give them the wrong impression of Burnham Falls on this first day."

Harriet froze in a second of disbelief; she seemed to exist in a little shell of troubled quiet in the midst of that noise. She couldn't look any more at Steve, and didn't even want to. She needed time, a little more time to try to get used to the thought that it was Steve who had just given her—she, Joe Carpenter's daughter—the first lesson in how things were to be for the future in Burnham Falls.

As the crowd broke up, and began to flow towards the parked cars and the stands where the box lunches were being handed out, Harriet suddenly found herself staring into Jeannie Talbot's face. The girl was looking at her questioningly, and Harriet shook herself to attention, aware that she had been looking at her for some seconds without seeing her.

"Hello, Jeannie!" Harriet liked Jeannie Talbot very much. She was Nell's grand-niece, and Harriet had watched her grow up. For a girl who was so pretty, and near the head of her class, there was something strangely unspoiled about Jeannie; she had a sweet, wild quality, like honey with an earthy tang. Jeannie's lips parted in a friendly grin over strong, white teeth.

"Hallo, Mrs. Dexter! Some turn out, isn't it?" Her eyelid came down in a broad, deliberate wink. "I'm going to get myself one of those lunches, and as much ice-cream as I can hold."

Harriet felt herself linked in a swift kinship with this girl,

22

and slightly envious of her air of nonchalance and freedom. "You do that, Jeannie!" she said. "Might as well take everything that's being offered—while it is."

CHAPTER THREE

Clifden Burrell had slipped away from the square as soon as E. J. Harrison had stopped speaking, and consequently he was first in the bar at the River Bend Country Club. He had little use for speeches of the sort just delivered, and a great deal of use for the Canadian whisky that rested briefly now against his throat, and then touched his stomach, where he needed it. When you are sixty-eight years old, he thought, and you've been a widower for fourteen years, and growing a little more sour with each of them, then you may sometimes be forgiven for thinking that the first whisky of the day was a sweeter, more necessary thing than staring at the legs and faces of strange women. All those same legs and faces would presently be crowding the bar, and in the meantime he had his hand cradled round the second whisky, and he could begin to enjoy the prospect.

The bar was dim—chintzy, with hunting scenes. Clifden disliked it intensely; it wasn't a place where a man might get drunk comfortably. Almost as violently he disliked the whole club, and belonged to it only because his membership was almost obligatory as the town's veteran attorney, and because he had to make some small effort to hold together the remnants of what had once been a very good law practice. He disliked the club because it was new, sanitary, and cultivated an air of pioneer America, while it discouraged him from wearing his old clothes there. He also resented it because its handsome greens and fairways had been cut from woods where he and Joe Carpenter had hunted on still, sharp winter mornings, mornings when the ice had crackled under his boots, but Joe's well-trained dogs had remained exquisitely noiseless, their breath clouding in the cold air. Joe had known, of course, that the club would be here when he had sold the land. He had argued that it was better than selling it off in half-acres for week-end bungalows. But Joe, Clif reflected grimly, had not had to see the hunting prints in the bar.

He could hear the cars now, and he moved his position so

23

that he was at the end of the bar, with his back against the wall. He felt grumphy and old, and had to acknowledge that he was both of those things, and he called for another whisky because the arthritic pains in his back and knees were giving him hell. He reckoned that if he stayed at the end of the bar and looked unconcerned, he wouldn't be noticed by any of the Amtec people, and he could get on with his drinking without the necessity for any small talk. He scowled as the first of the crowd entered the bar, and buried his nose in the glass.

Five minutes later he had decided that they were a good-looking bunch of women, all right—smart as paint, some of them, and some of them so young they looked as if they were just out of college, and they had young husbands to match. He figured that possibly all of those favoured two hundred engineers and physicists E. J. Harrison had talked about had been asked to the lunch with their wives. Papa Harrison was giving them and their bright new houses in Amtec Park the big welcome. Belonging to the River Bend Country Club was almost as much a part of their job as showing up each day at the Glass House, Clif figured—but from this day on they would pick up their own tabs. He nodded to them over his whisky—drink up, children, drink up. At the same time he realised that he was enjoying the freshness of their faces —their young faces.

Harriet Dexter came in then, with Steve. Seeing her there in the midst of all the strangers, Clif did a quick reckoning of her age . . . thirty-two or thirty-three . . . he remembered Dorothy had died not long after Harriet had gone out to California to Steve, instead of going to college as Joe had wanted her to. She'd been one of those pretty kids who gave promise of being beautiful when she got past thirty. She'd lived up to that promise, though it wasn't the kind of beauty that knocked you over at first sight. It was a quiet, composed face, with good lines—hair a little darker than it used to be, and showing less of the red tints it had once had—or was it, Clif wondered, just as the result of these damn', dingy lights they'd put in here. Steve's hand was on her elbow, steering her through the crowd, and Clif admitted that he was a good match for Harriet. Steve Dexter's clothes always hung inconclusively on his tall frame, and his tie was apt to be askew; most people stopped noticing that when he talked to them—particularly women.

He watched the two of them closely as the crowd and the

24

smoke thickened in the room. This was the first time Clif had seen either Steve or Harriet at the Club; he guessed that they had joined, not willingly, but because it was expected of them. The membership of the River Bend Country Club would be drawn almost exclusively from two groups—the new Amtec people, and the executive level of the T. J. Water Rubber Company that had set up their Eastern headquarters over at Swanston three years ago. Clif sensed that from now on Steve and Harriet would have to put in command appearances so that all the world could see how the old-timers and the newcomers could mix. From what E. J. Harrison had said in the town square, Amtec, in a polite sort of way, would be running Burnham Falls from here on, and Amtec was to-day officially putting its seal of approval on the River Bend Country Club as a place for its executives to spend their leisure hours. And its executives now included Steve Dexter.

Clif felt rather proud of them both, Steve and Harriet, as he watched their progress from group to group, and the introductions and the handshakes. He felt that they were representing what remained of the old Burnham Falls more than adequately—they were doing it very well. If he and Dorothy had ever had children, he hoped they might have behaved as well as these two. In a sense Joe Carpenter had been the old Burnham Falls, which was to-day disappearing. However inevitable had been the take-over of the small company by the giant one, there still must remain for Steve and Harriet a touch of defeat. They were young, Clif thought, and they had inherited from Joe nothing but trouble and slow decline, and they had deserved better. He was proud of them because it did not show in their faces or manner; they were neither aloof nor over-eager. They did not seem either frightened or defeated, nor did they seem too anxious to please. Steve's eyes were tired, and lacked their customary snap of humour, but none of the newcomers would know that. And there was Harriet, brown-eyed, olive-skinned Harriet, who was almost as beloved of Clif as she had been of Joe, with her gentle smile and the look of warmth that seemed for him to shine clear across the room. Harriet was almost as much the product of Clif's upbringing as of Joe's; that might explain why he loved her, and why he ached over what her feelings were at this moment.

He laid his glass down on the bar, and looked about him for someone to talk to. But when he saw Laura Peters he forgot

25

that he needed to talk. She was worthy of any man's eyes, any man's attention, and Clif gave her both in full measure, as he knew many other people in the room must be doing. She was not tall, but in the matter of figure and colouring she was so spectacular that one didn't notice, at first, whether she was strictly beautiful. Some women understand beauty so well, reverence it so deeply, that they are able to create its attributes without actually having its substance. Clif thought Laura Peters may have been such a woman. Her hair was drab gold, subtly shaded, her clothes were expensive and soft—beige and gold and light-brown colours merging imperceptibly, as only expensive things can do. There was an air of mysterious and complete femininity about Laura Peters, sexual in a deliberately understated fashion. She understood her art very well. There had been enough talk about her for Clif to be able to identify her as the wife of Ed Peters, the new President of the Amtec Laboratories.

Clif didn't own a television set, so her face was not familiar to him, except as it resembled hundreds of faces of fashion models that stared out from the magazines. But he knew something about her, because Burnham Falls had been excited by the news of her coming. Seven years ago she had starred in a play that had run on Broadway for eighteen months, under the name of Laura Carrol. Since then she had been in three flops, and she had done a series of television commercials for Amtec. Clif tried to remember what she had sold—dishwashers or gas stoves—something like that, and he wondered how the public could believe that such a woman as Laura Peters could know anything about either, or might conceivably be pictured, hot and dishevelled, cooking a meal or washing dishes.

Thinking about this, and craning a little to get a better view of her through the crowd, Clif slid his hand back behind him on the bar and started groping for his glass. In raising it, he brushed against someone's sleeve, and he felt the cool liquid spill against his fingers.

He turned to encounter a pair of light-blue eyes in an oddly attractive, but not a pretty face; they were amused, not annoyed.

" I'm very sorry," he said. " It was stupidly clumsy of me." He slipped off the stool, and pulled a handkerchief out of his breast pocket. As he dabbed at the sleeve of her dress he noticed that her hands were little and pretty, with rounded, unpainted nails.

26

"Oh, don't worry," she said. "A few drops of liquor never hurt anyone. I thought it was the traditional way to christen an occasion." Her voice was soft and pleasant.

"Well . . . you're exceedingly gracious about it, ma'am." He gave her a half-bow, knowing that he was old enough to do it, and she still young enough to be pleased by it. "And I *am* truly sorry." She was really absurdly young—or so she seemed to him. She had a fresh, clear face, with little curls of dark hair against white skin. For a hat she wore a straw bow, with a wisp of veil attached.

Then he noticed that her glass was empty. "Can I get you a drink?" he said, gesturing towards it.

She smiled. "No—I'll stay with what I have. Drinks at lunch aren't much in my line. I lost my husband ten minutes ago to several of his bosses, and I'd hate him to come back and find me stumbling. Besides, I don't want to miss a second of all this. . . ." She motioned towards the crowded room. "This is my first look at the Amtec top brass. My husband Tom, has only been with the firm three years, and he's still a very junior physicist." She smiled again, but this time with a touch of diffidence. "I'm awfully sorry—and I expect I should know—are you with the corporation?"

"Don't worry . . . I'm not your husband's boss, and you haven't put your foot in it. My name's Clifden Burrell, and I'm one of what they choose to call 'the old timers' in Burnham Falls. Lawyer by profession. Fisherman by choice."

"Well—I'm Sally Redmond. Tom and I are moving here on Friday—into one of those new houses in Amtec Park." She gave a faint giggle. "I don't mind telling you . . . we've only been married since Christmas, and I'm scared stiff by so much house. Imagine it! . . . The one we've got has three bedrooms. In New York we live in one room and a kitchenette!"

"Obviously Amtec believes in looking to the future. They expect you to settle happily in Burnham Falls, and fill those extra rooms with children. Will your husband be working at the research centre?"

"Yes—it's a promotion for him, and we're very excited about it."

"Do you think you'll like it here?"

Her eyes opened wide. "Why, yes! Shouldn't we like it?"

"Well . . . I just wondered. *I* like Burnham Falls, but I know young people want some excitement . . . since you've

27

lived in New York I wondered how you felt about settling in the country."

She looked at him firmly. " Mr. Burrell, I've had all the excitement I need for the rest of my life when I was working my way through at Columbia. You can't *own* New York—when you can't afford to go to theatres and concerts and expensive restaurants you kind of look forward to having enough space about you to raise some petunias. Children too—Tom and I want a family, but not in one room and a kitchenette."

He nodded, encouraging her to go on talking. A minute ago she had seemed a child, her eyes bright with excitement. But when she had spoken of New York a little edge of disillusionment had appeared briefly, and a little of her lovely, shining youth had gone. When she wasn't smiling she had a rather serious, questioning face; in repose it was almost plain. He decided that he liked her very much, and he was sorry that both she and her husband would consider him of an age that it would be impossible for them ever to be anything but acquaintances. He knew that Tom Redmond would, inevitably, call him " sir."

" Then you like your new house?"

" Yes—yes, very much. It isn't a wonderful house—I mean it doesn't look like anything out of *Architectural Forum*. But it seems pretty wonderful to me. We couldn't afford one of the better ones. Ours is the least expensive model they have, but I expect we'll move up when Tom's been with Amtec longer, and earns more money. You know, Mr. Burrell, the only difference between it and the next-but-one house is the colour of the roof and the front door. I know Tom doesn't care for that part of it too much—but it's got big windows and plenty of closets, and space for a dishwasher. And they haven't cut down the trees—we have seven trees on our lawn, Mr. Burrell, and that's a different view from staring into our neighbour's living room across a light well."

" I suppose after living in the city these things matter very much," he said gently. " I suppose they matter more to a woman than to a man."

" I think they do too—and I don't think it's because we read more house and garden magazines. I think, as a woman, I want to have neighbours. I'm tired of riding up and down in an elevator with the person who lives in the next apartment,

28

and pretending they're invisible. When the mood hits me, I like to talk. . . ." She grinned suddenly. ". . . Just as I'm doing now. I think I'll enjoy having coffee with my neighbours, and keeping a dog, and playing with my babies on the lawn."

" You don't mind living in a place that's called Amtec Park . . . you don't get a Big Brother feeling?"

She shrugged. " Let's not be too sensitive about it. . . . Tom works for Amtec, and without Amtec we wouldn't own our house, or our plot of earth, Mr. Burrell. Amtec is doing an awful lot of things for us that we couldn't do for ourselves. I don't mind our house matching the one next door because it also means there's a medical centre two blocks away—which Amtec also built. When I have my children they'll have a playground to use—you know, wading-pools, sand-pits . . . a workshop and hobby rooms for them when they get older. I don't have to worry about them running out on a highway, because there aren't any highways going through Amtec Park."

She gestured, with her small hands. " This sounds pretty good to me. There's going to be a lot more in Amtec Park than just houses, Mr. Burrell. If the price I have to pay for it is conformity—why then, I'll conform. After all . . ." she laughed a little ". . . Amtec isn't trying to own my soul. I intend to do much more with my life than just grow petunias and conform."

" Oh . . .?" Slowly Clif took up his whisky again. " And what is there for a young woman of intelligence and ambition to do in Burnham Falls?"

She said quickly, " I'm going to write. I'm going to write a novel I've been planning all through college. I think Burnham Falls is going to give me the peace and quiet I need to really get into it. I've got all the notes made. . . ."

Then a flush began to mount in her white skin. " I talk too much," she said. " I told you I wasn't used to drinks at lunchtime. I've never told anyone except Tom—I don't believe in talking about things until they're accomplished. And this is only beginning . . ."

" My dear," he said, " telling your secrets to an old lawyer is like telling them to the grave. They're buried." He raised his glass to her. " It would give me very great pleasure if your plans work out. I hope this town gives you what you're looking for. Good luck to you!"

29

He smiled at her, laid down his glass, and took her arm. "Now, I see they're starting to go into lunch. Let me help you find your table."

At lunch there was only one speech. It was delivered by an ageing Jew, with tired face and strained eyes behind his spectacles, and with a name so famous and so revered in science that it was capable of casting a spell on the people gathered in the room—and so the lunch lacked the heartiness that had been evidenced in the bar.

He made no concessions whatever to Amtec—although he was himself a notable part of the company. He ignored the women in the room, the corporation heads, Amtec Park, the shellac factory, and Burnham Falls. With his words even the glass and aluminium building vanished, and the young and the middle-aged scientists who listened to him felt again that they were dedicated men, removed from, and not even caring for the corporate benefits that surrounded them. He gave their work the importance that E. J. Harrison had failed to do, and they knew their work had to be done, whether it was in the cool, beautiful laboratories up on the hill, or in basements or garages or dirty lofts. For a few seconds he let them see the many men working through the world, struggling with the same problems as they, and they understood their fellowship with them, their eternal involvement, one with the other. He let them see that their struggle was universal, and would go on endlessly. He spoke of truth, and not of profits.

Had it been some years earlier, or the speaker less famous, or had his work not thrown so much weight with the Allies during the war, his words might almost have been taken as treasonable.

Clif found himself quite spontaneously with all the others to applaud the man who now sat quietly in his chair again, looking old and frail.

II

Clif leaned against one of the porch pillars, his hands thrust deep into his pockets; he was feeling slightly more mellow towards Amtec since lunch, and he was consciously grateful for the warmth of the sun on his aching bones. The side porch where he stood faced the parking lot of the

30

club; people were leaving, and he was wryly amused by the elaborate courtesy observable in the ritual. No one swung wildly out of the line of cars, or laid an impatient hand on a horn. The higher echelon were permitted maximum manœuvring space, and the younger members hung back until they were sure their pulling out would not inconvenience anyone. Clif caught a glimpse of Sally Redmond's pointed little face as she sat beside her husband in a green Ford. She was not talking, but to Clif she had the look of someone who is holding back until they can have the freedom of privacy. He remembered she had said she liked to talk. Her husband was a dark, rather serious-looking young man, who filled and backed with extreme neatness and dexterity.

Clif was debating whether or not he would go back into the bar when Harriet's hand fell lightly on his arm. "Clif!"

He turned slowly. "How's my girl?" In the sunlight her clear olive skin reminded him of an old Italian painting; she was smiling, and her eyes were alive. He patted her arm approvingly. "You look great—just great!"

She grimaced. "I'll look lots better when I get a mink stole to match all the others. You just watch, Clif! I'm going to learn all the tricks . . . I'll wear a hat, and have a cocktail party once a month. You'll be proud of me, I promise you. . . ."

He winked at her. "That's my girl! If you can't lick 'em . . ."

They both laughed together, grateful for the relief of each other's presence, and the unspoken words they shared. Steve came out of the club house as they stood there.

"Hi there, Clif!" He was searching for a cigarette, and eventually produced a crumpled packet, which he offered to Harriet and Clif, who both declined it. As Steve lit his own, Clif thought that after eighteen months of working for Amtec, it was remarkable that Steve still looked like a scientist.

Steve inhaled deeply, and jerked his head back. "Great day, isn't it?" It was impossible to tell precisely what he was referring to. Then he said, "I mean, great day for fishing, Clif."

"Oh, come on now, Steve . . . it's been so long since you've been fishing you can't tell what's a great day, and what isn't."

The other nodded, treating the words more seriously than

31

Clif had intended. "Perhaps you're right . . . I don't seem to have given myself a day off in about five years." He gestured, indicating the crowd in the parking lot. "Well, maybe things will be different now. Maybe that shiny hunk of laboratory on the hill will function so beautifully I'll have time to catch up on some sleep, or read a few books . . . or even do nothing." He looked at Harriet. "How'd that be for a change?—just do nothing."

"I don't believe it," she said lightly. "You were born with a problem to solve."

"Well," Clif said, "any time you feel like exchanging it for a fishing-rod, give me a call. I figure the Downside lake is so overstocked with fish it must be just about solid. Hardly anyone from the seminary fishes it, you know . . ."

His words trailed off, because E. J. Harrison and the old man who had addressed the luncheon walked out of the club house, followed by a small, respectful group. With them were Ed Peters and his wife. Under ordinary circumstances Clif would not have stopped talking, but in Burnham Falls the chances of observing a Nobel Prize winner close at hand were remote, and Clif had a veneration for greatness, and wanted to express it. Steve's gaze also was fixed on the slight, aged figure, and his expression, for a second, was one of hunger and near-pleading. His lips opened, but he said nothing.

A Cadillac with a uniformed chauffeur waited at the bottom of the steps. The old man shook hands politely, almost humbly, with those about him, entered the car, and waited for E. J. Harrison, whose car it was, to follow him. Harrison, in turn, shook hands all round, and at a gesture from Ed Peters, Steve and Harriet were motioned into the group, and somehow Clif also found himself shaking Harrison's hand, and even saying something about Burnham Falls being glad to have Amtec. Harrison was smiling and slightly flushed in the face. He lingered over Laura Peters, holding her hand, and telling her that Broadway's loss was Amtec's gain. She made a graceful little reply, and he smiled more broadly. The last hand he held was Ed Peteres'.

"Well, Ed—it's all yours now. We expect great achievements here—and you know, my boy, you can always come to E. J. to talk things over. Any time, my boy—any time."

When the Cadillac drove away there was a momentary pause in the group. They were waiting for Ed Peters to move. He was a slim dark man, of middle height, with a clever, well-controlled face. He looked first towards Clif.

"Nice to have met you . . . Mr. Burrell. I'm happy you could be with us to-day." As Clif replied he was aware of a grudging admiration for Peters, who could remember his name without effort, and appear sincere about being glad that an old-fashioned town lawyer had come to the lunch. He watched closely as Peters took Harriet's hand.

"Mrs. Dexter, I'm afraid we're going to be calling on you for a lot of things. Steve's a very valuable man to us . . . but we're going to need your help, too. So many of us are new in Burnham Falls, and we'll need help from the ones who know the ropes. I know Laura will appreciate . . ."

It would have been hard not to respond to him, and Harriet smiled warmly. He nodded to the men standing about him.

"We'll want to get into the swing of things as quickly as possible . . . see you all at the Laboratories." He saluted them casually, then said to his wife, "I'll get the car, Laura. You wait here."

Steve also walked across the parking lot to get the Rolls, although it was usually Harriet, and not he, who drove it. The Rolls looked strange among all the new models. Peters noticed it, and began to walk towards it. The two men stood together while Peters questioned Steve about it. As Clif watched them, Peters patted the shining bonnet, and bent to look at the dashboard. It was funny to think of Joe's old Rolls suddenly becoming a social asset. Clif turned his attention back to the two women beside him.

Seen close to, he decided that Laura Peters had more than the attributes of a beautiful woman. She really was beautiful, with the indestructible lines of a clear jaw, high cheekbones, and large, well-shaped eyes. She was speaking to Harriet; she had a low-pitched voice, rather husky—a memorable voice, Clif thought. She carried a blond mink stole nonchalantly, gracefully; it was almost the same colour as her dress.

". . . I think I'll like living here," she was saying to Harriet. "I've always wanted to live in the country—ever since I was a little girl." Then she added, smiling, "After all, it's not exactly the wilderness, is it? I mean . . . they don't make it too hard for those of us who'll be a little homesick for city lights. It's only a two-hour drive from New York." She turned to Clif. "Mr. Burrell, I hope all the Amtec activities aren't going to spoil your beautiful countryside for you. Mrs. Dexter says you're a great fisherman, and you've always lived in Burnham Falls."

"I don't think anything can happen now that will surprise me, Mrs. Peters. Burnham Falls needs Amtec here . . . and there are still plenty of lakes left for an old fisherman. Do you come from the East, Mrs. Peters?"

"Yes—that is—no!" She smiled. "Does that sound stupid? I was actually born in Los Angeles, but I've grown used to thinking of New York as being my home."

She broke off, as Ed Peter's honey-beige Cadillac halted at the steps. When you saw Laura Peters beside it you knew the car had been bought to match her hair. "Good-bye, Mr. Burrell. I'd like to hear something about Burnham Falls' history sometime." Then to Harriet she said, "Ed and I are moving in over the week-end—I'd like it if we could get together with you and your husband very soon." She waved to them briefly as she slammed the car door, and Ed Peters raised his hat to Harriet.

Clif wondered if, behind the polite and easy phrases, he hadn't caught a tinge of desperation in her voice when she had spoken of New York as being her home; it had been there only momentarily, and he could have been mistaken. He thought of the one successful play, and the three flops, and he wondered if the move to Burnham Falls represented the end of the dream of Broadway for her. He knew it was none of his business, but still he had no conscience about questioning Harriet about Laura Peters as they stood and watched the big car move away. "How long have they been married?"

"I think Steve told me it was a little over a year . . . she was married before, and so was Ed Peters. He has two daughters who live with them."

"What's Ed Peters' training—is he a physicist?"

"No—he's purely administrative, I think. He moves around among the Amtec subsidiaries."

"Oh—a career boy! Is she still doing commercials for Amtec?"

"I don't think so—though I suppose I should know. I think she did a whole series just before she married Ed Peters. Did you know she was an actress?"

"Is or was? When do you stop being an actress?"

"She's been in a couple of Broadway shows. She was

34

in a show that ran for eighteen months—*The Leaven*. Do you remember it?—about six years ago."

"Who was she married to before?"

Harriet looked at him, eyebrows lifted in surprise. "I've never known you to ask so many questions, Clif. . . . She was married to Lawrence Warde. He got a Pulitzer Prize a couple of years ago."

Clif nodded slowly. "And he wrote *The Leaven* . . . it fits, doesn't it?"

"What fits? . . . Honestly, Clif, I haven't seen you so concerned about a woman since I used to bring my teen-age heartbreaks to you. Come on . . . tell me! What has Laura Peters done to you?"

"I can't help wondering what the hell a woman like Laura Peters is going to do in Burnham Falls."

Harriet broke in. "There's Steve—I've got to go now." On the steps she looked back, and said to him in a low voice, "I wouldn't lose any sleep worrying about Laura Peters if I were you. She doesn't look as if she suffers any hardships."

Then she turned and hurried towards the Rolls.

The parking lot was almost empty, and Clif wanted to go back to the bar; instead he made himself go to his car and get in it. He had no inclination at all to return to any of the things that normally occupied his afternoons. There was the Williams brief to study, and the references to look out—it was the only decent case that had come his way in months, and it was stupid of him to neglect it, because people heard about those things. It was subtle and insidious the way news got about a small town that a man was drinking; it wasn't that he was seen drunk on the streets—in fact, he was never drunk, completely. But people noticed small differences, and sometimes they put it down to the fact that he was growing old, or they knew about his arthritis and guessed he was in pain—but mostly, it seemed, they knew he was drinking. And so he handled less law work, and he noticed, once or twice, that someone had crossed Main Street to avoid meeting him. He was not at all repentant about the amount he drank each day, and he had no intention of altering his habits.

He drove slowly along the road that skirted the golf course, and felt the sudden chill that came down when he entered the thick belt of trees near the gates of the country club. He was out in the sunlight again as he approached the

35

main road. By an effort of will he was able to pass the old Carpenter place without thinking more than fleetingly of Harriet and Joe; he kept his eyes fixed on the daffodils, and even heard himself mutter that they were better this year than he ever remembered them. He glanced backwards over his shoulders for a last look as he rounded the bend, and then had to step on the brake hard to miss a collision with Ted Talbot's old jeep.

Ted looked up morosely from his task of changing a flat tyre.

"Hello there, Ted—nearly ran you down! Didn't see you!"

"Hello, Mr. Burrell." He pushed his peaked cap back on his head. "Can't say it's any surprise you nearly ran me down—you're about the fiftieth car in the last twenty minutes nearly did the same thing." He spat disgustedly. "All I got from most was a blast on the horn."

Clif nodded, and leaned farther out the window. "All coming from the shindig at the country club—just been there myself."

"Yeh," Ted agreed. "I heard about it."

"Did . . .?" Clif broke off because Chrissie Talbot suddenly came round the off-side of the jeep.

"Hello, Chrissie."

"Hello . . ."

Ted swung round. "Now, Chrissie, you get back there. Don't want you gettin' run down." Then he beckoned her, and took a clean handkerchief from his pocket. "Come here a minute, sweetheart—let Daddy wipe your nose."

Chrissie Talbot was golden-haired and doll-like, with delicate features and limbs, and large eyes that were more green than blue, like her sister, Jeannie's. She submitted patiently to Ted's ministrations, but kept her gaze fixed on Clif. She knew Clif well, because in good weather she always accompanied her father on his jobs. She had come to anticipate the candy Clif gave to her every Wednesday, spring to fall, when Ted cut the front and side lawn at Clif's house on Main Street.

Ted put the handkerchief away, and patted the child's fluffy, pale hair.

"I'm sorry, Chrissie," Clif said. "You caught me unawares. No candy to-day."

The child smiled shyly, but said nothing. She rarely had much to say to anyone except her own family. She played contentedly by herself while Ted did his chores, and Clif

36

had watched her and guessed there existed whole worlds in Chrissie's imagination that kept her quietly absorbed. She was an even-tempered, self-contained little girl, who seemed as yet quite unspoiled by the attention she got from the families Ted worked for. She put her thumb in her mouth now, and sucked reflectively.

" She's growing, Ted—she gets taller every time I see her."

" Yeh," Ted said fondly. " She's smart, too, like Jeannie. She'll be four on June seventeenth Jeannie's graduating 'bout the same time. Kids all growin' up—I tell you, I don't know where the years are going to." He shook his head regretfully, but his rugged face relaxed with pride as he contemplated his two daughters.

" Be no time at all before Chrissie's graduating too," Clif acknowledged. Then his tone changed. " Hear the speeches in the square at noon, Ted?"

" Nope! Ain't got no time nor no inclination to listen to their speeches. Man's got to make a livin'."

Clif raised his eyebrows. " I should think Amtec could help you turn a dollar. A lot of new people and houses up in Amtec Park . . . you should do a bit of business up that way."

Ted spat again with more emphasis. " Sons o' bitches!— they've called in their own contractors from Elmbury. Every house pays a flat fee—gets their lawn taken care of, trees and shrubs planted—the lot. They're the same outfit got the job lookin' after the grounds of the research place and the nursery school and the medical centre. They've got a load of equipment and a team of guys. Move in, do the whole place in a day—move out. They've got a year-round contract, and every single house has signed up."

" That's too bad, Ted. I thought the whole idea of the hoopla in the square this morning was to let us know that the town was going to benefit from Amtec's coming here."

" Yeh, that's what I thought too, but them sons o' bitches didn't give me a look in. I ain't got no fancy equipment, and I ain't got no team of guys. . . ."

Clif nodded slowly. " How's business been, Ted? You making out?"

Ted directed a stream of tobacco juice towards the ditch. " Yeh—I'm makin' out all right. They give me pretty steady work out at Downside helpin' the regular gardeners, and they've been givin' me handyman jobs during the winter. That's when it's tough—winter. A man's got to look out for

37

what he can get. I'm sending Jeannie to business school at Elmbury after she graduates, and that costs money." Then his face relaxed again. "But I tell you, Mr. Burrell, that Jeannie . . . she's quite a girl. Gets top marks all the time."

"Yes, Ted, and she's a nice girl, too. A very nice girl." Clif started to draw away. "Good-bye, Chrissie! . . . See you around Ted!"

"Sure thing, Mr. Burrell." Then he suddenly called after him, "Say—Mr. Burrell!"

"Yes?"

"You goin' t'need some new rose bushes put in this month. Them ones o' yours didn't hardly bloom at all last summer. Reckon they was put in before Mrs. Burrell died, and they're most worn out."

Clif gave a slight shrug, more for himself than for Ted. "I don't . . . think so, Ted. When there aren't any women about, a man feels kind of foolish playing round with a garden. Just tend to the lawn, and leave the old rose bushes be."

As he drove on towards the town he knew that he had used Dorothy's death simply as an excuse, a convenient way of saying no to Ted Talbot without further explanations. It was easier to let Ted think that he was a sentimental old man, still grieving for a woman who had died fourteen years ago, than to say outright that you grew indifferent with age, and cynical—so that rose bushes and spring blooms mattered less each year.

From here the road ran without a bend straight into town. Clif thought of the notes on the Williams case lying on his desk, and thought of the discreet, inquiring look Milly Squires would give him when he entered. She would hope he had not been drinking—at least, not enough to show. Milly typed and answered the phone for Clif, and had been doing it since she left school sixteen years ago; when her mother died she would go to New York—that wasn't too far off because Ginny Squires was reported to have cancer. In the meantime Milly got some satisfaction from the mistaken idea that she ran Clif's life, and she thought it rather dreadful that a man she had been brought up to think of with respect, as a pillar of town society, a standard by which to measure honesty and civic responsibility, should undo himself with a drink. She behaved sometimes as if her personal god had been defiled. Clif felt uneasy as a destroyer of ideals; an outright reproof would have been better than

38

her silent sadness and concern for him. He didn't want to go back to Milly Squires this afternoon.

Then suddenly, just past the Downside road he stopped the car. He didn't know whether he was driven to it by the thought of Milly Squires, or because Joe Carpenter had been on his mind all day, but he suddenly slapped into reverse, backed, turned, and set off in the opposite direction, taking the curve of the Downside road too sharply, and hearing his tyres whine in protest. Immediately off the main road were two massive stone pillars, but no gate hung between them, nor had there ever been one there. He didn't trouble to read the notice—he knew it by heart.

DOWNSIDE
Private Road
Keep Out

It had been sheer bluff on the part of the millionaire to place that notice, and the stone pillars. He had been unable to buy back the small properties and right-of-way from the three families who owned waterfront land along the lake before he had come to the district. But most people saw the notice and heeded it. The winding road through the close timber was almost always deserted.

The edge of the Downside lake flashed into view abruptly through the trees. Here the lake lay within the shadow of a high hill, the highest in the whole surrounding countryside. The lake touched the base of the northern side of the hill, and the sun only reached it briefly during the early morning; on the other side of the hill were the summer cottages of the week-enders, facing south across Lake Burnham to the town. The hill was the dividing point between the two lakes—one open and sunny, with the town of Burnham Falls lying gently in its valley, the other cool and narrow, shadowed by the hills. The road to Downside had been cut from the side of the slope; beyond the white guard rail, the drop to the rocky shore of the lake was sharp.

Clif followed the road for a little better than two miles, flashing in and out of sunlight as the trees lightened or thickened. So far he had not caught a glimpse of Downside itself; it was at the farther end of the crescent-shaped lake. But as he topped a rise just on the bend of the lake, it came into view. The green copper turrets might have housed a story-book princess, a bridge of grey granite had been made where none had been needed, and an artificial lake created behind it, where in the summer the water lilies

39

bloomed. The afternoon sun flushed pink on the grey stone. At this point it was nearly two miles distant. Clif braked sharply, as he always did, to look at it before he turned down the dirt road leading to the fishing cabin that had belonged to Joe Carpenter, and now belonged to Harriet.

Each of the three cabins here fronted on the lake, but they were far enough away from each other, and the woods thick enough to completely screen them. Joe's cabin had the best position, for he had been first here, and had bought the rocky land, useless for farming, very cheaply. The house stood on a point right at the bend of the lake, the nearest of the three to Downside, and the only one which had a view of it. It was built solidly of brown timbers and an old slate roof. It was impossible to see it from the road until the break came in the woods—almost at its door.

Clif got out of the car stiffly, taking the flask from the glove compartment with him. He reached down under the stone where the key was always kept; the lock was stiff, and he tried several times before it yielded. While he struggled with the lock, he was aware of nothing so much as the deep silence that hung over the whole lake, and seemed to wrap the hills; a hush lay on the woods, and for a second or so he felt himself holding his breath, as if he expected something to happen.

But nothing happened. The door opened at last, and he stepped inside and was greeted by the smell of dust and disuse —the smell of an unoccupied house. The door gave directly into the main room, a large room with windows running along two sides, and a fieldstone fireplace on the third wall. The fourth wall had a long counter that concealed the stove and sink, and had another door that led to a bathroom and two bedrooms. Joe had built it in 1928 when he had made a killing in the stock market; he had used it most week-ends through the season, and it was to this place, rather than to the house in Burnham Falls, that he had invited Clif and the two men who had remained close friends after college. His housekeeper, Nell Talbot, had never spent a night under this roof in all the years she had worked for him; here Joe did the cooking, and it was he who ordered the furnishings and kept them to a minimum. It was here he sat with his friends before the fire until late at night, with the whisky bottle on the table between them.

Clif had been part of those week-ends, and those nights before the fire, and he remembered how sometimes Joe would

40

hush them to silence when the laughter got too loud, and he would tip-toe with exaggerated motions to the rooms where Harriet and Josh lay asleep. Whoever stayed with Joe in the cottage always slept on one of the sofas, or on a mattress on the floor. The rooms were for Josh and Harriet—until Josh grew old enough to join the group. Harriet had always accepted the maleness of these week-ends with complete unconcern, and even in adolescence had never gone into a stage of coyness. Clif wondered if this was the reason he found it so easy to be with Harriet now.

He sank down on one of the couches facing the windows, and sat staring for some time at the double image of Downside, reflected now in the still water. The long shadows of afternoon edged out on to the lake.

He could remember how it had been when Joe had come out of college with a degree in science, and had got a job with a big chemical manufacturing company in Pennsylvania. He had swung into the job with brash confidence, and had tried to interest the company in a new formula for shellac which he had devised; they had examined it, and passed it up. In 1917 he had joined up and spent a year behind a laboratory bench for the Army; he had never seen France. Then he'd come home to Burnham Falls, borrowed some money from his father and space in a barn, and had set about manufacturing his formula. He had gone on selling trips through New England, sleeping in the back of the Ford to save hotel expenses, and counting the pennies on every meal. He had come through those first years by a hair's breadth—and because the formula was a good one, after all.

When the business was a going concern, he had borrowed money from the bank and bought a hundred-acre farm about three-quarters of a mile on the other side of town, and here he had built his permanent plant. He was now selling his product through most of the New England region, and the business began to show a good profit.

These were the years when Clif and Joe had started to be friends. They had fished together, and hunted together, and Clif had sat with Joe when his wife, Claudia, had been dying.

Clif believed that if Claudia had lived, things might have been very different for Joe Carpenter and the shellac factory —Claudia, intelligent, alert, the daughter of a Boston manu-facturer, who had inherited his shrewdness, might have

41

made that difference. She might have kept Joe's eyes open to the world outside of Burnham Falls, might have seen the trend of what was happening in America, or might have got Harriet and Steve out of the factory before it engulfed them.

But Joe had taken a good profit from the factory, and had spent it on himself and his children. He had seen the depression through not too uncomfortably, and had swung into glowing prosperity towards the end of the thirties, and after the outbreak of the war in Europe. When the States had entered the war, Joe picked up government contracts which had absorbed the whole output of the factory. But the factory did not expand, and with rising wages he was able to buy very little new equipment. When it was obvious that the war in the Pacific would soon be over, Joe had begun casting about among his old friends and acquaintances for new business, and had found it by becoming a supplier of shellac to two chains of stores which spread across the country; he manufactured for them under their own label, and the two contracts had taken care of his total output. He still had no other product.

It was fortunate, Clif thought, that Joe had secured those contracts before Josh was killed, because for more than a year afterwards he had hardly noticed what was happening in his own business; he had spent most of his time here at the lodge, fishing or simply sitting where Clif sat now, staring blankly at the lake and at Downside, empty and deserted, except for a caretaker. He had scarcely seemed to stir from his apathy—not even when Harriet had returned home with Steve, who was convalescing after a wound received in the Pacific, and waiting for his final discharge. The only events that really roused Joe in the years that followed were the births of his two grandsons, Gene and Tim; they were to be all the things Josh had not lived to be.

It seemed obvious, almost as soon as Harriet and Steve came back, that the factory must either be sold, or Steve must help to run it. Clif had been close enough to their troubles to sense very strongly Steve's reluctance, his backward look to California where he had wanted to stay—and perhaps to start his own business. But Steve had had no capital, and Joe had been pathetically grateful for his son-in-law's presence, and his experience as a chemist. They had listened to Joe's pleas, taken a half-share in the business, and tried to forget about California.

42

It was then Steve started his fight for another product, for diversification, for an attempt to find new capital, for a way to use his ability other than supervising the manufacture of shellac. After a year in which he had spent more than half his time unsuccessfully trying to secure capital, Steve had finally returned to Burnham Falls and in desperation had set up his own laboratory. He spent every cent he could spare, and every hour that could be snatched away from the factory to work on formulas for vinyl products, seeking in them an answer to the narrowing market for shellac, which was being used less and less as the new finishes and veneers for furniture were developed, and as aluminium began to replace wood. With the formulas in his pocket, he went out to get capital to manufacture them, and found that the giants in the plastic and vinyl industry had cornered the market for investment in that direction, and that no one was interested in backing the efforts of a lone chemist working in a tiny laboratory. He lacked money for further research, for the equipment and help he needed; with the formulas incomplete and unproven he was unable even to sell them to the big vinyl manufacturers. They lay on his desk unused until he read in the scientific journals that one or other of the plastic or vinyl fabricators had finally found the answers to the problems he had researched. Then the formulas became worthless, simply a crude imitation of what was already known and in use.

And while Steve worked in the laboratory, Joe's market for shellac was hit by a price squeeze. The young men who had joined the merchandising companies Joe supplied at the end of the war, were now rising towards top management. They were feeling their muscle, and seeking new ways to cut costs, to make the profits keep up with the rise in the price of labour. Joe, along with others, faced an ultimatum —either to reduce costs to his customers, or to lose his contracts. When he appealed to his friends in the companies against the narrow margin of profit, he encountered the unexpressed but obvious fear among them of the younger men who were pushing hard and talking loud against outdated business methods and sentimental softness. Against the fear of the younger men who would take their jobs, Joe's appeals had no weight.

At this point there came the offer to sell out and become a subsidiary of one of the companies he was supplying, retaining management, but not ownership of the factory.

43

For a time he played with the idea, and Harriet waited for him to acknowledge that the day of the small factory was almost over, as he had known in his father's time that the day of the small farmer was over.

But he had decided not to sell the factory, still clinging to the belief that business would improve, and unable to bear the thought of working for anyone but himself. Labour costs were rising, and his profits dropped back to just slightly above the break-even point.

Clif had never understood why Steve, at this time, had not demanded his release from a mundane and dwindling business, a huge uneconomical house, and a father-in-law whose thoughts were back in the twenties. With firms all over the country clamouring for chemists and physicists, he could have taken his family and left behind the obligations and frustrations of Burnham Falls. Instead he chose to remain, and Clif had never been sure if it was a genuine desire to spare Joe's feelings, or the complete and absolute belief that his work in the laboratory would produce something of value, and he must struggle to remain independent until that time came.

Steve went to the factory each day, and on selling trips when necessary, leaving Joe free to fill in his time as he wished. He returned to the house for meals, and spent his evenings and week-ends in the laboratory; any time away from the laboratory he used to read scientific journals and papers. Occasionally he put together enough money to attend a conference; these trips were the only vacations he permitted himself. Invariably he stayed in the cheapest hotels, and Harriet did not accompany him.

The expense of keeping the laboratory supplied and equipped was straining their resources, and Joe, perhaps from a sense of guilt, or perhaps cannily knowing that it was the only way to hold Steve in Burnham Falls, sold off his remaining securities to meet the demands of the laboratory. It was at this time that he sold the four hundred acres of land his father had worked to the country club syndicate.

Clif knew that most of the years since Harriet had come back to Burnham Falls had been a lonely and disillusioning time for her. From his frequent visits to the Carpenter house, he surmised that Harriet's chief concern was in keeping the annoyance of unpaid bills away from Steve and seeing that there was hot food for him at whatever hour he returned from the factory or laboratory.

44

It was spring, two years ago, Clif remembered, when Steve had gone to a conference in Denver to deliver a paper on a solid-state fuel—the result of the research he had been doing since his failure to find anyone to listen to his ideas on vinyls and plastics. The conclusions he reached were new, but soundly based. They caused a storm of argument and discussion, and for two triumphant days Steve tasted the reward of the lonely hours. He even felt exultant enough to call Harriet to tell her about it.

During the conference he had been approached by a representative from the research division of Amtec Industries, who had suggested that he stay in New York for a few days on the way home to have further talks with Harold McNaughton, who was the Amtec vice-president in charge of research and development. Behind the casual words he could sense an eagerness to own and control his formula, and he began to think that at last he might have found the backing he needed. He had been on the point of calling Harriet again to tell her he was going to New York, when she herself called him with the news that Joe had died during the night after a heart attack.

It was Clif who had drawn up Joe's will, and had, of course, read it to Harriet and Steve. It was very simple—apart from a small bequest to Nell Talbot, his estate was equally divided between Harriet and Steve, and he expressed a desire that his thanks be conveyed to "my beloved son-in-law, for his devotion and service."

The estate consisted of the mortgaged house and land, and the run-down factory.

Steve turned at once to pursue Amtec's interest in his solid fuel formula. Clif tried to help steer him through the maze of bargaining and arguments that went on in the months following, but found himself bogged down in a kind of hole of corporate vagueness. Amtec pointed out that Steve's formula was untested, and they hesitated to commit themselves; Steve countered by offering to sell the Burnham Falls Shellac Company to them, demonstrating how easily it could be converted to producing the first components of his fuel. Amtec investigated the company, and pronounced it on the verge of bankruptcy, but at the same time it discovered other things about the situation that Steve had not mentioned—the value of the large acreage which surrounded the factory, the spur of the railway that went to it, the abundance of water, and the cheap, non-union labour.

45

Almost immediately following came the decision of the Board to buy the Burnham Falls Shellac Company, to retain Steve on a salary to continue research for Amtec, to give him stock in Amtec Industries in payment for the factory, while they assumed its liabilities; the agreement also gave Steve options to buy stock at preferred prices.

Steve and Harriet signed the papers that gave the Burnham Falls Shellac Company in a daze of relief. It was six months since Joe had died.

Afterwards they learned that Amtec had no intention of converting the shellac factory to making compounds of Steve's formula—that would be done in two of their plants out West where they could be produced by processes and equipment already familiar to operating personnel. A man from Amtec's Cleveland plant came to take over Steve's job of factory manager. They began to manufacture shellac under the Amtec label, but with the resources of the Amtec distribution system, they could sell shellac profitably all over the eastern and southern states at prices far below those Joe had reached. Steve walked out of the shellac factory for the last time wondering why Amtec had bothered with that humble building and its humble operation. His contract with Amtec was two weeks old, and he was to report to the research division in New York.

It was when Steve asked about the future of the shellac factory that he learned the value of what he had sold.

On the strength of Steve's formula, along with the results of research done in their own laboratories, Amtec had been given a grant from the government to build a new research centre. It was to be located in Burnham Falls, on the land that had gone with the sale of the factory. Close to it, also on the land that Steve had sold, they would build the housing for the families of their scientists. They had been looking for a location for their centre when Steve and Burnham Falls presented themselves.

If he felt he had made a bad bargain, Steve never spoke to Clif of it. In fact, Clif or Burnham Falls saw very little of Steve during the eighteen months following the sale of the factory. He spent a good part of his time out West, in Culver City and Tulsa. It was understood that he would not be back permanently to Burnham Falls until the Laboratories were finished.

There was plenty to keep Burnham Falls talking during those months—and the townspeople as a whole seemed to have

46

mixed feelings about Amtec. The factory was doing well, some new equipment had been brought in and more men taken on; the output was bigger and there was more activity on the railway siding. No one liked the new Amtec label that replaced the old one Joe Carpenter had used. The Laboratories and the two hundred houses seemed, to the startled eyes of the town, to go up overnight; the size of the project and the need for speed put it beyond the range of any local contractor, and not much local labour was employed. Barnham Falls enjoyed, however, the extra business that having construction teams camped on their doorstep for eighteen months brought.

During this time Clif watched Harriet's loneliness deepen. When he had questioned her about joining Steve out West for a visit, she had shaken her head. On a kind of rebound from Joe's loose spending, she seemed bent on a course of austerity that would quickly get them out of debt. Seeing the emptiness of those months, Clif wondered if it wasn't too high a price to pay. He would have liked to urge her, against all prudence, to take herself to New York and buy some clothes, and from there fly out to Steve. And then sometimes, as he listened to Harriet talk of the need of economy until they had some money put aside, he wondered if she wasn't talking to disguise her uneasiness because Steve hadn't asked her to come—was it in fact, the talk of a woman afraid to acknowledge that her husband had become used to her existing in the background.

But from to-day on, Clif thought, Burnham Falls would start to enter completely into the climate of thought and activity that having a big corporation in their midst must bring. They would soon have a new plant where components of defence weapons were made. They would have a working population that was not native to Burnham Falls or the surrounding countryside, who would occupy houses in yet another development which Clif knew meant only rows of similar boxes, however the Chairman of the Board of Amtec chose to call them.

In the long shadows of the afternoon, two boats were putting out on the lake from Downside, the figures of the men in them black and wooden against the water. Clif screwed the top back on the empty flask.

47

Neither Laura Peters nor Sally Redmond had driven directly to their various destinations when the lunch was over; each of them had been sitting beside her husband, each commenting from her different viewpoint on what she had seen in the last few hours, while they had passed through the centre of town; then the turn-off to Amtec Park had come into view and neither had been able to resist the sudden impulse to go and look again at the new house that waited for them.

On the way up the hill they passed construction trucks and teams still getting the black top on the roads, still land-scaping the new gardens, cutting drainage channels. The blank curtainless windows of the new houses stared out at them; the place was raw and unfinished and waiting. Both of the women fell silent as the cars bumped over the ruts; the world of the corporation, and of Amtec fell away from them.

Sally and Tom Redmond found their house by reading the numbers along the street where each house was almost a duplicate of the one beside it; they went inside exuberantly, like children, and Sally ran from room to room, dizzy with the space and light and shining freshness. They laughed and stood in each other's arms, telling each other the good and wonderful things that could happen to them.

The house built for Laura and Ed Peters stood off by itself on the knoll of Amtec Park. It had been designed especially for them, and it was surrounded by newly-sodded turf and trees, just as it had looked in the rendering made by New York's most fashionable architect. It was low, and set back to the hill, with glass walls facing south. But both Laura and Ed entered it with a certain caution. Each of them once before had entered a new home with the person to whom they were married; this time they were knowledgeable, and they did not feel invincible.

Harriet Dexter did not have a new house to return to but she had caught the mood of optimism, and she looked hopefully, and with fresh eyes at the Carpenter place when it came into view. Steve was beside her, and this was the end of his eighteen months of journeyings; the damaging years of doubt and worry were over. There might be peace now, and time for them to know each other again. There could be a chance that it might again be as it had once been in California.

And then, as if his thoughts had somehow crossed hers, he spoke.

He said, " Ed Peters told me to-day that there's a possibility Mal Hamilton may come here to do some consultant work for Amtec."

The words touched her coldly, and the hope of peace was gone.

CHAPTER FOUR

Afterwards, Harriet had often wondered why she had let herself be so completely Joe's daughter. She had been all that he had wanted her to be, and that, it seemed, was not what she had wanted herself. But she could find no satisfactory substitute, no real purpose for rebellion, and so had gone along with Joe, being the kind of girl and woman he had meant her to be. She remembered very early that she had learned not to cry for what she wanted, or for hurt or distress, because tears upset Joe, and caused him to draw back a little from her. And since she had committed herself to Joe, she was committed all the way. She learned to endure the coldness of those mornings on the lake, and not to shudder when she baited a hook, she learned to be silent about Joe's cooking at the lodge, and gratefully returned to Nell's in town. She practised swimming, until her stroke was powerful and swift, and learned to shoot with fair accuracy, gritting her teeth and following the men through the woods, and hating it when they sighted game and the crash of the shots through the still air, and the bloodied skin of the animal. She was rarely free to join the Saturday crowd at Carter's ice-cream parlour, or watch the school football games from the sidelines. She was popular enough, or would have been, she thought, if Joe hadn't wanted so much of her time, and she hadn't given it. Joe was busy doing the job he believed that Claudia would have done in bringing up Harriet and Josh, and he interpreted that as meaning that he must spend all of his life away from the factory with them. If Harriet reluctantly acquiesced, it was because she sensed his desperate loneliness, the kind of awful responsibility he felt

49

for his children, his urgent need to keep everything on the surface calm, happy and unified—and to believe that what he saw on the surface was real. And because, in the final reckoning, Harriet loved Joe—and needed him more than the crowd at Carter's—she agreed to be the image of what Joe thought a well-brought-up girl should be.

He had entered her for Vassar, and while she was not a brilliant student, she tried harder than she might have done to bring her grades up to a good level because he wanted to be proud of her in everything. If Harriet got to Vassar, and Josh got to Harvard and both acquitted themselves well, there was little more Joe was going to ask from life.

Joe recognised some limits on what he knew was right for Harriet, and he listened to what Dorothy, Clif's wife, had to say about clothes. Then he would take Harriet to New York, and he would buy expensive clothes for her, with nothing about them to suggest their cost, except the quality of the material, and their cut . . . skirts and sweaters of fine wool, a small string of pearls, a cashmere coat. Harriet knew that from age twelve, she was already in a Vassar uniform, simple and good, with no frills. Even her party clothes would never be looked at twice. She bought one party dress for herself in Burnham Flats, cheap, slightly flashy, and she wore it, in defiance of Joe, until she grew out of it; she had the idea that it was the only dress she owned that made her as much like the other girls at school as she wanted—she liked the way it fitted tightly to the waist, and made her immature bosom look important. With it she wore very high-heeled shoes, and Joe told her that she'd break her neck with them.

Between herself and her brother Josh there was no strain, and no lack of communication. Over the years, they entered into a largely unspoken agreement to do as little as possible to disturb their father. For Josh this was not difficult, for he had all Joe's love of doing things with his hands, all his skill with a rod and a gun and a horse; but he seemed better able than Harriet to get a few of his own wishes across to Joe, so that he tended to do things in his own fashion, and in his own time. It was even he who told Joe that Harriet had better stay off the horses, because she didn't care for them, and Joe had accepted the idea without protest. Sometimes Harriet thought that Josh was the nicest person she would ever know in all her life. He was not quite two years older than she.

50

For Harriet the years seemed slow, for she was in a hurry to catch up with Josh—and in the nature of things she never quite did catch up. Josh had won a freedom and independence for himself that she guessed would never be hers. He began the practice of going off on week-ends camping trips with his friends, leaving Harriet to go alone with Joe to the cabin. Joe cheered on these evidences of maturity in Josh, and at the same time clung closer to Harriet. He was not quite blind, however, to the longing looks she gave to Josh and his friends as they started off, and he interpreted them as meaning that Harriet herself wanted to see something outside of Burnham Falls. His solution was to take her to New York about once a month. They always stayed overnight at one of the fashionable hotels, went to a Broadway show, and a good restaurant afterwards, and ordered dishes that had never been heard of in Burnham Falls.

What he didn't know was that Harriet, who had lived mainly with masculine companionship since she was a baby, who had learned to make her way around a big hotel, and tip bell-boys without embarrassment, who had learned not to obtrude a feminine personality too strongly into a party of men at the lodge, was still painfully shy with boys of her own age. There had not been enough sessions at Carter's for her to learn the give and take of their talk, to hit back with the kind of remark that passed for wit among teen-agers. Her voice was quiet and low, and among her giggling friends, she seemed out of place, just a fraction behind the meaning of those whispered comments, not quite quick enough to laugh, a little too ready to be talked down.

Josh was still her closest companion; perhaps because he guessed her loneliness he was willing to listen more attentively to all her ramblings of what was going to happen after she left Burnham Falls. The summer before he left for Harvard he spent whatever time he could with Harriet, sensing that the break that would come when he left would be a complete break for them—that he could not return to their childhood brother and sister relationship. It must change, it could not be the same. He felt he had to give her what help he could in holding off his father, because for the first time Josh had learned the full weight of Joe's possessiveness. It was the summer of 1940 and, after Dunkirk, Josh had played with the thought of going to England to join the Royal Air Force. Joe had simply, and without discussion, refused his consent. After that, Harriet and Josh were aware

51

of a kind of irritability and impatience in Joe's attitude towards the war in Europe.

So Harriet and Josh talked of it among themselves, and in September Josh went to Harvard.

Harriet was sixteen that year, and now the mistake Joe had made was beginning to show up clearly. Although she went to Burnham Falls High School, she did not belong there. For her there were none of the simple pleasures Joe remembered and idealised from his own boyhood; nor was she able to flaunt her possessions, and assume a role of leadership because of Joe's position in Burnham Falls. When Joe began to talk of his plans to send her to Vassar he finished any hope she had of merging with the crowd at school.

It was Clif Burrell who finally saw what Joe had never seen. He told Joe that Harriet couldn't go on trying to live half-way between the rather shabby humdrum of the Barnham Falls High School and the world that Joe was throwing about her—the Rolls, the fishing lodge, the large house and the trips to New York. She would have to go where cashmere sweaters were commonplace rather than the exception. Joe listened to Clif, as he had done many times before, and Harriet became a weekly boarder at the Troughton School for Girls outside Poughkeepsie. Joe approved of it because it was near Vassar.

Troughton helped Harriet, but not quite in the way Joe and Clif had imagined it would. Fewer daughters of solid, well-to-do families were enrolled at Troughton than Joe would have liked; instead there was more than a sprinkling of the children of theatrical parents—because Troughton was not too far from New York, and because it was more convenient than having them live at home. There were some exaggerations in dress and speech and manners that Harriet could recognise as pure Broadway; there were also the two daughters of John McGuire, whose novels appeared regularly on the best-seller lists, and whose faintly scandalous love affairs were openly discussed by his children. Harriet lived vicariously the lives of the famous and well-known parents, and forgot to wonder what kind of impression she was making. The result was that she became popular among the girls because of her willingness to listen sympathetically. With this came confidence, and a poise, of a kind. She learned to speak up for what she wanted, and expect to have as good a chance as anyone else of getting it.

52

She looked eagerly to see if Josh approved the change when he came back to Burnham Falls for the summer vacation in 1941, but Josh had become a man very quickly, and she was still only seventeen years old; he was still Josh, gentle, even-tempered, but strangely preoccupied. He spent a month of the summer on a canoeing trip in Canada, and Harriet was left alone with Joe again. While Josh was away she went to spend ten days with Norah and Mary McGuire, who were living with a housekeeper in their New York apartment while their father was in Spain pursuing a story and his latest mistress. At dinner one night Norah suddenly produced vintage champagne from her father's store, and it was the first time Harriet had ever drunk more than a few sedate sips. They each drank more than they knew, and the next morning Harriet woke to a painful headache and nausea, and was rather surprised to find that, contrary to Joe's warnings, it was not the end of the world.

When she returned to Burnham Falls, Josh had come back and Mal Hamilton was working at the fishing cabin.

Mal Hamilton was the local success story—or he would be when he had time to prove what was already more than potential. He was more of a success story because people remembered that the odds couldn't have been stronger against him. Charlie Hamilton, his father, had been the town drunk, a bullying, loud-talking Scotsman who had landed in Burnham Falls for no reason that anyone could ever discover. All that was known of him was that he had crossed over from Canada as a young man, and had started to walk to New York. At Burnham Falls he had stopped to earn some money by doing odd jobs, and he had stayed there—firstly because he had no pressing reason for moving on, and secondly because he had got Rose Tyler pregnant, and rather indifferently decided to marry her. Rose's father, Nat, hadn't worked since the depression, but he owned the run-down old farmhouse where he lived, and twelve rocky acres that were choked with timber. Charlie moved in with Rose and Nat, and two children were born, Malcolm, and a girl, Mary, who died of typhoid when she was five years old. The family subsisted on relief, and the few dollars Charlie earned when he was sober.

Mal Hamilton had fought everything there was to fight—poverty, ignorance, indifference, and the prejudice of Burnham Falls, which believed that nothing good could come of the

53

Tyler stock. There was even a certain unwillingness on the part of Mal's teachers to put him at the head of his class for he was an ugly, tattered boy, with his father's red hair, often dirty, and without any manners to speak of. But no one could keep Mal Hamilton down, and his brilliance was too obvious to be subdued or extinguished. There was nothing of the reticent scholar about Mal—he was loud and pushing, and he paraded his achievements with a brash cockiness before Burnham Falls' startled eyes. He worked before school and after school at whatever jobs he could get, and people paid the extra cents he asked per hour because his work was better and more thoroughly done than any other boy's. The money he earned went to buy books, and he kept it out of his father's reach by opening an account at the Burnham Falls First National Bank. He waited in the bank all of one hot summer's day, his dusty, bare feet marking the polished floor, until the manager, George Keston, finally consented to see him. Mal told George Keston that his father would try to take the money away from him, and he also told him how he intended to use it. George was so impressed that he sought out Charlie Hamilton and threatened him with action by every public authority he could name if he touched Mal's money, and Charlie was frightened enough to do nothing more than mutter sullenly. From that day George Keston was Mal's unofficial champion, excusing the boy's brusqueness and aggressiveness on the score of his upbringing, and the temperament of a genius he believed he had discovered. He even went through all the forgotten text books, biographies, and encyclopædias on his shelves to see what might be of use to Mal, and urged his friends to do the same. Very few people in Burnham Falls bought books, so Mal's haul wasn't great. Privately he considered them out-of-date, but he said nothing because he recognised George Keston as a powerful ally.

Mal Hamilton seemed to have a way of compelling attention from people ; perhaps it was that his ugly, gaunt face became almost a symbol of conscience to them, as his near-illiterate mother and grandmother were permanent reminders that all was not perfect in Burnham Falls. Perhaps the town could have forgotten about Charlie and Rose, and the arthritic old Nat—but Mal didn't let them forget. He was everywhere, mowing lawns, painting basements, serving in Crosby's market, greasing cars at Morton's Garage. Whenever people cleared out their cellars and attics, they gave more than

54

they intended of the contents to Mal, and he took them, without pride and without shame—clothes, bottles, scrap metal, used lumber. He was often given meals in the kitchens of Burnham Falls, and he accepted them too, with a muttered word of thanks. But, by this time he was an object of town pride rather than pity, for he began to record some of the highest marks in the state at his Regional Examinations, and it became almost a duty for the people of Burnham Falls to do what they could for him. When he graduated from high school he was class valedictorian, with his raw, bony wrists shooting beyond frayed cuffs, and George Keston looked on with approval, and thought that Charlie and Rose Hamilton had no business to be there in the gathering. Mal had the choice of three scholarships to different colleges. He drew out some money from George's bank, bought himself a suit of clothes, a cheap suitcase, and left Burnham Falls.

The town hardly saw him for the four years he was at college, though George Keston had letters from him occasionally, and he reported that even though Mal was working to feed and clothe himself at college, he was still managing to put some money in the bank. The money came back to Burnham Falls, as if he had not yet learned to trust it in any other place. They heard that he spent one summer lumbering in Oregon, and another on a ranch in Colorado; and they also heard that he continued to top his classes in science and mathematics. Burnham Falls saw him once when he came back to attend his grandfather's funeral; he had grown taller, and the harsh lines of his face hadn't softened, though he now wore clothes that fitted him well enough. His body was tough and hard, and his speech as spare as ever. Everyone wondered why he had come back, for there had been no love between grandfather and grandson. Then they learned that it was not Rose, but Mal who had inherited the crumbling old house, and the twelve acres. Mal left Burnham Falls again, and Charlie and Rose stayed on at the house.

He went through college, stayed on an extra year and got his Master's degree. Charlie began to talk, half-bragging, half-complaining that his son had no use for anything more than book-learning, and it was time he earned some money, and began to support his folks. When Rose died, Mal did not, this time, come back to Burnham Falls for her funeral.

"I don't blame him," was all George Keston said.

55

He went to work for a chemical firm—a fairly routine job that did not pay well, but gave him time to himself. Two years later he had his Doctorate in Physics, and when George Keston got his letter, he talked of it around the town with as much satisfaction as if Mal had been his own son. Charlie Hamilton heard the news from the girl who served in the diner at the station, and he went out and got drunk. They found him lying unconscious at the back of the war memorial, and a few days later he died in the county hospital of pneumonia.

George Keston wired Mal, and he replied that he was coming back immediately. It was the summer of 1941.

Burnham Falls saw little change in Mal Hamilton, except, if anything he was harder and tougher—but he was tougher with himself than anyone else. He was still sparing of speech, and his hands still bore the scars from the lumber camp. There was still not enough time for Mal Hamilton to do all that had to be done. They learned that he had thrown up his job, and had been hired at a much larger salary to run the West Coast branch of an experimental chemical company. The job didn't start until September. He told George Keston he'd spend the rest of the summer in Burnham Falls.

If Burnham Falls believed that the aggressive, hard-bargaining boy was for ever buried in the Doctor of Physics, it was mistaken. Mal got a loan from the First National, and George Keston personally guaranteed it. With the money he borrowed he started to patch up and paint the Tyler house; he put in new kitchen fittings, built new closets and a bathroom, added a deep screen porch off the living-room; he mended broken floor-boards and stairs, and painted the rooms in soft greys and white, and the kitchen was yellow, so that it sparkled when the morning sun came in. He added shutters to soften the blind, staring windows. It had been a solid house, built to last, and it came to life under his hands. Its great beauty was a fieldstone fireplace which filled one whole wall of the living-room and which leaked badly. He called in Stan Cooper, the Burnham Falls mason, to fix it. He carted away the accumulation of cans and junk from the yard, cleared the riot of honeysuckle and blackberry, and laid a lawn ready to be seeded in the fall. The ever-greens were trimmed and clipped, and a neat white post and picket fence put in place. Then he cleared a broad path through the wood to where his twelve acres touched on a

56

small lake; here he built a diving-pontoon hard by a big, flat-topped rock that jutted into the water. As a child, Mal had swum here, solitary, on summer evenings; most people had forgotten that it existed. Now it was remembered as an asset that went with the Tyler house.

During the summer Mal came into town every few days in an old truck he had bought to pick up more lumber and paint. People knew he meant to sell the house when it was finished, and they were curious about its progress—but more curious about Mal himself. Matrons who had been pleased to have young Mal Hamilton come to take away the rubbish from their cellars, now stopped him in Main Street and asked him to dinner. He always refused, and did not trouble to explain why. He was still the Mal Hamilton they remembered —curt, almost rude, with no time to waste. Especially grieved over his refusal to socialise was George Keston, who felt he had a legitimate claim on Mal, and would have liked to take him about the town, to boast of his achievements. The most Mal would do was share a cup of coffee with him in the diner—which was hardly the place for the President of the First National. Burnham Falls expected more from a Ph.D. than the thin, tall figure in the faded denim and spotted paint cap; it was disappointed.

George Keston shook his head, and again made excuses. " I guess he's just worked too hard all his life to know how to stop. It isn't human the way Mal Hamilton works."

This last was a reference to the fact that Mal, with the Tyler house almost finished, had taken work as Stan Cooper's labourer. His loan was running out, and mason's fees were high, so he hauled stone and cement for Stan in payment for the repairs to the fireplace and chimney. His hands grew rougher, and he never learned to wear gloves. He worked off his debt to Stan, and as the last closet at the Tyler house had been painted and papered, he stayed on as a mason's labourer, earning four dollars an hour. Burnham Falls was shocked, but it knew that for Mal Hamilton, the opinion of the town did not exist. He merely put up the FOR SALE notice outside the house, and went on taking orders from Stan Cooper.

He was hauling stone from the edge of the lake at Downside for a new terrace and steps to replace the old wooden ones at Joe Carpenter's cabin, when Harriet first saw him.

Harriet Carpenter and Mal Hamilton were a world apart—
57

and more. He was ten years older than Harriet, and the years had been full of the kind of struggle and discipline she could only guess at. He let a stone drop dully into place on the pile, and looked up and saw her.

"Hello," she said. "I'm Harriet."

Without knowing quite why, she held her hand out to him formally. He wiped the whitish dust off his own before taking it. She was aware of the softness of her flesh grasped within that roughness.

"Hello, Harriet."

With neat, economical movements he felt in his pocket for a pack of cigarettes, and held it towards her. She had started to smoke that summer, although Joe disapproved, and she took one now, happy that Mal Hamilton, who had time to spare for no one in Burnham Falls, should want to spend some with her. They found seats on two of the biggest stones, and faced each other.

Mal squinted at her as he inhaled. "You've just been in New York? . . . Like it there?"

She nodded eagerly. "I enjoy it . . . especially this time. I've been staying with John McGuire's daughters."

But Mal, who had read only the classics required to pass his English exams, had never heard of John McGuire. He was totally ignorant of the world of best-sellers and literary fashions, and he had not read a piece of fiction since leaving college, nor even a book review. It was the first time Harriet began to comprehend the narrowness of Mal's life—in which, as far as she could judge, there had been only work. He did not seem to mind, or even to be aware of what he had missed. She learned that he had been living in New York for two years, and had never visited a gallery.

He shrugged. "There's no one going to pay me right now for knowing whether or not there's a Leonardo hanging in the Metropolitan."

"Don't you want to know yourself?"

"That's a kind of a damn-fool question to ask, Harriet. The only thing I want right now is money, and if you think I've spent most of my life to this point reading books for the love of them, then you're mistaken. They have to pay off. Later on there'll be time for the galleries and the best-sellers . . . if I find I need them."

Then he finished his cigarette and went back to work, and that was all their first meeting amounted to. But he seemed to welcome her when she appeared at the cabin the next

58

time, and the next time after that. She wondered a little at the ease of their contact when Mal Hamilton so ruthlessly held off every other encroachment on his privacy and time. He had so often been represented to her as a person of iron discipline and control, self-sufficient and aloof, that she had no way of knowing the unspeakable loneliness of the man, the bonds of patience and restraint that had bound him for so long, and which found some relief at the sight of the girl, slim and russet-haired, with skin tinted olive above her brown sweater, standing in the dappled sunlight, holding out her hand gravely. She was almost a woman, but she had not learned the tricks of a woman, which he mistrusted and feared. There was a childish awkwardness about her still, an eagerness, a questioning that he had wanted to satisfy. The women Mal Hamilton had known had meant less than nothing to him; he had needed only the feel of their warm, female bodies, and had been bored with the necessity of feeding them, and listening to their talk beforehand. Around the universities he had seen girls like Harriet, but he had never exchanged even a word with them—because they were expensive, and because they were always protected and cherished by someone like Joe Carpenter. But Harriet had looked at him confidently and undemandingly; she was a woman, and a child—pulling uncertainly on her cigarette— and on her, trustingly, he had suddenly unburdened some of the loneliness, the explosive ambitions and hopes that had been pent up inside him since the years when he had collected discards from Joe Carpenter's back door. For the first time in his life he discovered that one of the luxuries of women was that they could sometimes be talked to.

There were many calls on Stan Cooper about that time, and he worked only intermittently on the Carpenter lodge, so that Mal's work there also was sporadic. He may or may not have known that Harriet drove every day to the lodge on the chance that he might be there, and they might share a cigarette and ten minutes' talk.

During those weeks of August, she seemed to reach out urgently for womanhood—because Mal had, in some fashion, evoked it in her. He made no overtures to her, never came closer to her physically than the moment when he held out the cigarette pack. But he made no concessions to her age when he talked of the things he had done, and the things that had been done to him. She knew that she was hearing

59

what no one had ever heard from Mal's lips. She saw the rawness of the boy who had learned early in Burnham Falls that he had to be tough and insensitive to survive, and she saw the ways in which the town had taught him this. The world outside the town had never been harder than the town itself, and she began, guiltily, to understand the cruelty and meanness around her. Mal had no pity for himself, and no pity for anyone else, he said. He would never come back to Burnham Falls again because, when he had sold the house, he would have taken everything it could give him. She thought about this, and realised the justice of it. Mal taught her far more than the McGuire girls did.

Joe noticed their friendship with some disquiet, knowing well enough Mal's reputation for aloofness and brusqueness. And yet there was nothing to object to in Mal's attitude to Harriet, and Joe remembered that when news of Mal had filtered back to Burnham Falls, he had held him up as an example to Josh and Harriet of what determination could accomplish. He almost believed that Burnham Falls was responsible for Mal's progress. Mal did not trouble to contradict him.

Harriet had hoped that Josh also could be Mal's friend, but there was no contact between the two. If Josh attempted to join them by the lake shore, or even, hesitantly, to load a wheel-barrow with stone, Mal's cold gaze would be on him critically, and Josh would grow clumsy and tongue-tied. After a while he left them alone, and Harriet, trying to reach back for the friendship with Josh which she had loved, was rebuffed. Josh was preoccupied and uncommunicative.

Labour Day passed, and Josh prepared to go back to Harvard, and Harriet to Troughton. Mal's house had not been sold, and the town was saying that he had priced it too high. Harriet was already restless at the thought of Troughton, and strangely, this time she knew she would miss Mal more than Josh. Mal was preparing himself to move on to his job on the West Coast, and as yet Harriet had not dared to ask him if he would write to her. She was afraid that by mentioning it, she might jolt their relationship back to what it superficially was—that of a schoolgirl and a grown man.

Then, the week-end before he was due to go to Harvard, Josh suddenly announced that he was going to New York. Joe had been counting on his company at the lodge that week-end, and he was annoyed.

60

"If you're going to see a girl," he shouted at Josh, "what's wrong with telling me about it?"

Josh remained silent, and he took the Friday night express. On Saturday night when he came back to Burnham Falls he was wearing an Air Force uniform, and he had a twenty-four hour pass. His company was starting for Texas the next day.

Harriet and Joe were both at the lodge. They heard no sound of a car, because Josh had hitch-hiked from New York, and had been dropped on the road at the Downside turn-off. He opened the door gently, and stood blinking in the light.

"Hello, Dad. . . . Harriet."

The newspaper was frozen in Joe's hands. He sat staring at his son, and after a long interval found words.

"Josh . . . what have you done?" His tone was quiet and cold.

Josh dropped his bag noisily on the floor, and pulled off his cap. He looked away from his father, towards Harriet.

"Get me something to eat, will you, Harriet? I'm hungry." Then he turned back to Joe. "I'm sorry to give you a shock like this, Dad. But I had to do it . . . whether you agreed or not. It's my decision. I hope you'll come to understand it."

In reply, Joe dropped his newspaper and got to his feet. "I don't understand it, Josh . . . I don't think I ever will." He turned his back on Josh, and they watched him in silence as he walked to the open door on to the terrace, down the unfinished steps, and along the path to the lake. There was a faint moon, and for a time they could see the outline of his figure.

"Go after him, Josh!" Harriet urged. "Talk to him . . . explain things."

He moved wearily towards the kitchen. "I'm tired of explaining to Dad, Harriet. If he doesn't know I'm grown up, talking won't make him see it now." Then he shrugged. "Come on!" he said. "What about some food, huh?"

She questioned him rapidly while she fixed bacon and eggs and coffee, but his replies were monosyllabic. He wrote down for her his serial number, and the post he was going to in Texas.

"You'll see, Josh—he'll write. As soon as he gets over this . . . shock . . . he'll write. It's just that he was all so tied up in you going to Harvard . . . he'll get over it . . ."

61

"I don't care if he writes or not. I don't need to be forgiven like a bad child who's run away from home."

"Oh, Josh . . . he'll see that! Later on he'll see it!" Then she gave a little exclamation as he wiped his mouth in the napkin, and the chair scraped on the floor as he rose. "Josh!—where are you going?"

"Back to New York," he said.

"You're not going!—oh, give him till the morning, at least."

He leaned across the table. "Harriet, it's time you and I stopped doing all the giving in this family. It's time we stopped spoiling and protecting our father." He walked back to where his bag and cap were. She ran towards him.

"How will you get back? You've missed the last train."

"The same way I came—hitch-hike."

"Wait for me, Josh. I'll walk a bit with you." She gestured towards her slippers and dressing-gown. "Just let me slip on a skirt and sweater." She looked at him appealingly. "Wait, please, Josh, wait!"

"O.K."

She dressed with feverish, clumsy-fingered haste, listening for sounds of movement in the next room. She was afraid, as she thrust her feet into shoes, and jerked at the zipper of her skirt, that Josh would not wait. When she came out, the room was empty, and Josh's bag was gone. She looked towards the open door to the terrace, and the lake, glimmering dully through the trees.

"Josh? Are you there?"

There was no reply, but she fancied she saw something moving along the path to the lake. She picked her way among the stones still lying about on the terrace, and started for the lake. Under the trees it was quiet and dark, with only the lightest breeze moving through the upper branches. "Josh?" she called softly. "Josh?"

But at the edge of the lake, where the trees broke, she saw only her father. He was standing on the jetty, where the boat was tied up, smoking a cigarette. Josh had not come to say good-bye. She turned and hurried back, past the lodge to the road.

"Josh! Are you there? Wait for me! Josh!"

There was no sound at all in the darkness of the road ahead. She broke into a run.

In the two miles of road that twisted among the trees Harriet several times thought she heard Josh's footsteps, but

62

she called loudly, and there was no reply. A stitch in her side forced her to drop into a walk. It was hard to say how much of a start he had, but the knowledge that it was only a few minutes, and that he was burdened by the bag, kept her hurrying. But Josh was an athlete, and walking was nothing to him. At each bend in the road, where the moonlight touched it, she expected to see him; when she came to the place where the white guard rails separated the road from the sheer drop to the lake, she at last caught a glimpse of him.

"Josh! It's me, Harriet! Wait!" He didn't turn; he didn't appear to hear her. She started to run again, and the pain gripped her sharply as she struggled for breath.

About two hundred yards from where the Downside road touched the main road, she saw the headlights of a car approaching. Josh, she knew, was already standing there. The headlights flashed quickly among the trees, slowed, and stopped. After a second she caught the sound of a door slamming, and then she saw the onward rush of the lights. She did not go back to the cabin. Instead, she went on to the main road, walked along it for half a mile, and then turned off on the dirt road that wound and twisted the three miles to Mal Hamilton's house.

She went in past the newly-painted white fence, limping slightly because her heel hurt from a blister; the house was totally in darkness. A little sob escaped her, because it hadn't occurred to her that Mal might not be there. Naïvely, she had never thought that he would do anything with his evenings but spend them at home. Then she saw the glow of a cigarette on the dark porch.

"Mal!"

She heard a muttered word, and saw the rapid movement of the cigarette; then the screen door swung open.

"It's me, Mal! . . . Harriet!"

He peered down at her intently. "You little fool—you crazy little fool! What are you doing here?"

"Josh has gone, Mal! He's joined the Air Force, and he's gone! He's quarrelled with Dad."

He took her by the arm, and drew her gently inside the porch. There was no light, but she could distinguish the form of a camp bed against the wall. He led her to it, and motioned her to sit. He sat beside her, and handed her a cigarette. Jerkily, she told him what had happened.

63

He was silent for some moments, then he said, "So you walked here . . . why, Harriet?"

Her voice broke, and the tears, which she had been holding back since the car door had slammed on the highway, started down her cheeks.

"Mal Hamilton! . . . Who's being a fool now? Is everyone going to treat me as a child for ever? Why do you *think* I came?"

Suddenly she tossed the cigarette down, drew nearer to him, and put her hands on his shoulders, gripping them tightly. "Why do you think I came?" she repeated urgently, close to his ear.

She had wanted to feel his arms about her, and now they were stronger, more expressive than she had imagined. All the loneliness and hunger she had glimpsed in Mal Hamilton was here, in the grip of his arms, in the rough, caressing movement of his hand over her hair. He kissed her only once, hard, and passionately, and she responded knowingly to it. Then he drew back a little from her.

"Harriet . . . I've had women before. And if I need to, I can go into town right now and find one. It doesn't have to be you. I don't have to use you."

"I want to, Mal. I want you."

He pushed her dishevelled hair back from her face. "It can't be me, Harriet. I can't let myself be the man you choose to prove that you also can quarrel with your father. In any other way, I'd want it to be me, but not this way."

He gently disengaged her hands, and stood up.

"Come inside. I'll get you some coffee." He did not wait for her reply, but went to a door at the end of the porch, which opened on to the kitchen. The light streamed out, and fell across Harriet's face. He did not look back. She sat there, her head bent into her hands, quivering and bewildered. The feel of his arms and his kiss had been real enough— but so had his rejection of her. He had stripped her morally of every argument, and left her pain and humiliation. Perhaps this was the final and most valuable thing that Mal Hamilton had to teach her.

Her voice reached her. "Come inside, Harriet. If anyone passes on the road, they can see you in the light."

She stood up and went to the screen door, pressing her face against it. "Are you afraid someone will see me?"

He shrugged. "It's your concern, not mine. Burnham Falls

64

doesn't expect any better from me. You have to live here.
. . . Suit yourself."

She stepped into the bare kitchen, bright with new paint.
The naked electric light bulb shone harshly on the shiny walls,
and on Mal's face, gaunt and austere. His lips came together
in a hard line.

"You don't care at all about Josh going, do you?" she said.
He poured the coffee into two mugs. "Why should I?
It happens to everyone, and it's time it happened to the
Carpenter family. Your father can't go on tying you and
Josh to him with golden string for the rest of your lives.
If Josh wanted to go into the Air Force—then he's done the
only thing." For the first time Harriet heard some warmth
in his voice when he had spoken Josh's name.

She nodded dumbly, and took the mug from him. It was
hot, and she sipped it carefully, looking round her to avoid
his eyes. There were no cooking utensils visible except
the coffee-pot; the kitchen hardly looked as if it was used
at all. Beyond the kitchen was the empty dining-room. The
walls and ceilings and floors had an untouched look of newness
about them. She saw the reason for the camp bed on the
porch. He had not used any of these rooms, leaving their
clean freshness for whoever would buy the house. Then
it occurred to her that perhaps he had bad enough memories
of the house not to want to use it. But she knew that if
that was the reason, Mal would never tell her. Mal gave
very little away—least of all himself.

She finished her coffee, and he washed the mugs, and put
them away, with his clean, economical movements.

"Come on. I'll drive you back."

He switched out the light, and she followed him meekly.
The old truck he drove refused the starter a few times,
then roared into shuddering life. Harriet clung to the door as
they bounced over the five miles to Downside.

At the place where the main Downside road forked with
the road to the lodge, he stopped the truck.

"You'd better walk the rest of the way, Harriet. Then
it's up to you whether you tell your father where you've
been. For my part, I don't care—I don't owe Joe Carpenter
anything, and he can think what he damn' well likes. What
you decide for yourself—that's what's important. Good-
bye, Harriet."

She hesitated. "Good . . . good-bye, Mal." Then, with her

C.W.   65   C hand on the door handle, she suddenly leaned over and kissed him. " Forgive me, Mal."

The truck rattled off down the road, and she turned back to the cabin. From far away she could see all the lights were on, and the door was wide open. Her father stood there, waiting.

" Is that you, Harriet? Where in heaven's name have you been? I didn't want to rouse the countryside, or I would have called the police. I saw the lights on the road. . . ."

She stood squarely in the light, and faced him. All of Mal's anger and harshness suddenly filled her.

" It doesn't matter where I've been. Josh has gone, and you let him go. I won't forgive you for that."

No more words passed between Harriet and Joe on the subject of Josh. She packed and left for Troughton two days later, without seeing Mal again. At Troughton she found a letter waiting from Josh, no more than a few lines, telling her about the dust of Texas, and nothing at all about what it felt like to be living service life. He was well, and he wanted to borrow twenty dollars from her. She sent off the money, and wrote an elaborately casual letter to Joe, giving him the news of Josh, but omitting the mention of the money. When Joe wrote back, he talked of everything else but Josh. Harriet would be coming home only one week-end of each month this year, and Joe was lonely. He told her so.

When she returned to Burnham Falls for the first week-end, the fall colours were in full flood. She wrote to Josh about them, because the letters from Texas were homesick for the northern coolness and softness. Then she took the long walk over the dirt roads to Mal's house. The FOR SALE notice was gone, and a strange car stood in the driveway. There were venetian blinds on the front windows. She felt foolish standing in the road staring at a stranger's house, so she cut through the woods at the side, and went round to Mal's lake. It was still and cold ; she wondered what he thought of California, and if anything could be more beautiful than this little lake.

She mentioned Mal to Clif Burrell, and he needed no urging to talk about the sale of the house. " He held out for the price he wanted, and he got it. George Keston told me he paid back the loan, and made a couple of thousand dollars

66

out of it. That's not bad when you remember what the old Tyler place was like,"

When she went back to Troughton, there was a box of preserved fruits from California waiting. Mal's name was on the package, but there was no return address. She took the gesture as final, and accepted it—and could even recognise the wisdom in it, for all the hurt it contained.

Through the months of fall and early winter, Joe never inquired about Josh, or spoke his name. Harriet could never discover how much attention he paid to the war news from Europe, for people, knowing how he felt about Josh, forbore to mention it in his presence. Only Clif Burrell dared, with impunity, to talk to Harriet about Josh, ignoring completely Joe's angry silence. She told him what details she had learned of Josh's training—there were rumours, she said, that he would go out to the Pacific as soon as the training was completed. In reply to this hint of trouble, Joe would talk loudly of the Japanese assurances of non-aggression.

The Sunday the news of Pearl Harbour came, he was on the phone to Troughton almost immediately.

"Harriet," he said, "I'm going to Texas to see Josh."

She gripped the receiver, and a cold sweat broke on her body. She felt for a second as if she were frozen, but she managed to say, "Yes . . . yes, Dad." And then she added quickly, "Shouldn't you call and check if he's still there, first. He may have been moved out. I don't suppose they'll keep them long . . . now."

"Don't be silly, Harriet. Josh isn't a general. I can't just pick up a phone and expect to speak to him. I'll send him a wire, and take the first plane I can get. What's his serial number? . . ."

Harriet did no more to dissuade him, and prayed a little that he would be in time. Two days later she had another call from Joe from Texas.

"It wasn't any use, Harriet." His voice sounded tired, with a thin, nervous edge that bespoke fear and dismay. "They've pulled out. His unit's not at the camp any more, and of course they won't tell me where he's gone. I can't do anything now but go home and wait. They said he got my wire—or at least it isn't here, so they presume he got it. All hell's loose here, and I'm just a stupid, doting father, getting in everybody's way. I'm flying back in the morning."

"Yes, Dad."

67

He held the phone for some moments in silence. She waited, sensing the struggle and the loneliness. Then he said suddenly, "I'm sorry, Harriet—I'm sorry about Josh." She listened to that dead, far-away click as he hung up.

There were weeks to wait before Josh's letter finally reached them, the weeks that were the bewilderment of a country unexpectedly at war. There was the momentary hesitation while people drew breath, and tried to make plans. Some girls left Troughton because their fathers had gone into the forces, and the school could no longer be paid for, some left because they were almost old enough to join up themselves, and they went home to battle the question with their families. Troughton, for some reason vaguely allied to the war, tightened up discipline, and imposed its own rationing. All the students took courses in first aid; everyone was still shocked about that first defeat. Uniformed men, who had been a rare sight, became more common. And then the first heavily censored letter came from Josh to Joe. He was in the Pacific, and he had been in combat. Harriet was so frightened she didn't speak of it in Troughton, and when the McGuire girls talked about Josh, she pretended he was stationed thousands of miles from the fighting. She had a curious belief that if she didn't talk about Josh he might somehow be unnoticed, and come through.

Joe was in every civilian volunteer organisation in the Burnham Falls district, and was called to serve on the Draft Board. He raised money for war bonds and the Red Cross; he did not miss Harriet so much now because he was seldom home. With men leaving the factory for the services, he had to make up the back-log of work; government contracts kept the plant moving at capacity. He wrote to Josh three times a week, and he did not complain that everyone was overworked at home. "The Carpenter place" became the headquarters of the Red Cross for the district, and Joe cleared the big rooms on the ground floor of inessential furniture; he moved into two small rooms in the old wing.

Harriet finished at Troughton in June, and wanted to go to live with the McGuires for the summer, to work for the Red Cross in New York. She had just turned eighteen.

"There's plenty of work to do here," Joe said, "if you really mean you want to work. It's less glamorous—but it's work."

So she went back to Burnham Falls to work for the Red Cross—work that was dull and routine, and had no compensations except the knowledge that it was useful. Occasion-

68

ally she thought of Mal, but the image was fading and blurred.

She remembered how the summer came suddenly to life the first week-end that Clif brought Stephen Dexter to the lodge. Steve was the son of one of Clif's oldest friends, who had gone through Harvard Law School with him. He had just received his Doctorate from M.I.T., having been held back by the Draft Board to complete his course. He was now doing his officer's Basic Training at Kempton. He was twenty-seven, grey-eyed, and dark-haired, with a lean, intelligent face, and clever, well-shaped hands. Harriet was not the only one who thought him extraordinarily good looking. He hated the sterile, mindless grind of the Army, and he was childishly grateful for a break from camp and a bed on one of the sofas at the lodge. Before dawn he was out on the lake, but he didn't bother to fish. When he came to stay overnight on a twenty-four hour pass two weeks later, Harriet went with him to the lake in the first light. She listened to Steve talk, and she was in love.

After that the days of the summer dissolved into the endless countless hours of waiting to hear from Steve. She was afraid to leave home in case he should telephone; whenever he had only a few hours' pass she would borrow Clif's car and drive over to Kempton—Joe was using only one car, and stringently observing the gasoline rationing. Her meetings with Steve were a seesaw between pleasure in his company, and fear that he found her dull, or adolescent. He was quietly-spoken, and efficient—awesomely efficient, Harriet thought—and he smoked too many cigarettes. He was bored with his training routine, and frustrated by the thought of the years ahead.

" It isn't as if they'll put a guy like me in to fight, Harriet," he said once, leaning back in Clif's car, smoking, with his eyes half-closed. " God knows, I don't want to get killed any more than the other guy. But they'll stick me in some pokey lab somewhere and forget about me. I'll spend the war checking the work six other guys have checked, and when it's all over I'll have nothing but some lousy years and an ulcer to show for it."

But most of the time he left the Army behind him when he left Kempton; and then he was amusing, and gay in a quiet fashion, singing snatches of ribald songs that made her laugh, and trying to learn to cook at the lodge, and succeeding pretty well.

69

"I'm a poor man," he used to say with mock seriousness. "Isn't it the American tradition that every poor boy on his way to wealth and fame has to know how to darn his own socks and cook? The trouble is that my socks are always too far gone before I notice they have a hole at all."

A few hours after he put it on his uniform was usually crumpled and unmilitary-looking; his salute was sloppy. The Army hadn't done much to straighten the slight hunch of his shoulders.

One Friday he phoned her from Kempton. "I've got a week-end pass. Do you want to pick me up and we'll go to New York?"

When she went to meet him outside the camp she was conscious of herself for the first time as an adult; she was conscious of Steve's presence as a man, of the glances of other women, of the excitement and urgency of the atmosphere about her. She belonged completely with all the other women who were meeting men in uniform, but she was special because she was meeting Steve.

He came forward and kissed her without hesitation, a warm kiss that gave her a badge of belonging to him before all these people. "My God, Harriet, you look wonderful— you look shining, and young—and beautiful. I'm going to have to take you away from all these guys who'd kick my teeth in for the chance of talking to you."

Later in New York they danced in a place where the bill was outrageous, and the champagne and food was poor. To Harriet it was better than she had ever tasted.

"Harriet, I should be asking you if you'll sleep with me— and all I can think of saying is 'Can you marry me in a week's time? Or sooner?' The course is almost over, and we'll be pulling out."

She would have gone to bed with him, but he seemed to have forgotten that he had asked her to, because he was talking too much about their getting married.

They were married one week later at the Carpenter house —with the big bare rooms hastily cleared of the Red Cross activities. Joe was torn between pleasure that Harriet was marrying exactly the kind of person he wanted her to marry, and disappointment that she was marrying at all—and putting aside Vassar. Steve's father, a gentle scholarly lawyer— a widower—came down from New England; he looked like Steve, and Harriet felt it would be easy to love him. The rooms were thronged with Army personnel from Kempton;

70

Harriet found out, and was rather surprised by the knowledge, that in spite of his contempt for the Army, Steve was popular with his fellow trainees. He was a second lieutenant, and graduated near the bottom of his class. It was the first time Harriet learned that with Steve, what he did not like barely existed for him.

They had a one-night honeymoon in New York, during which Harriet discovered that Steve was passionate and tender by turns, and that she had no need of her vague fears because she responded to him as if the act of love with him was something for which she had been waiting all her life. He had a way of making her feel young and yet mature ; that her body was beautiful and desirable, and still a familiar, beloved thing. As she lay naked drinking her coffee in bed the next morning, with Steve smoking beside her, she felt confident and successful. She laughed suddenly, with happiness and pride.

Steve was sent with his unit to Camp Roberts in California. Here he waited " doing nothing," he wrote Harriet, for a month, and then was posted to the Signal Corps, and sent to work on an experimental project at U.C.L.A. " The work is strictly security," his letter ran, " but I can tell you that the campus of the University of California at Los Angeles is huge and sprawling, like all this city. You should see it."

Joe was aghast when Harriet began to plan to go to Los Angeles. " You don't know what it's like! There's a housing shortage, no one can get an apartment in L.A. with all the factories on full shifts. You'll be miserable out there, and probably stuck in some hole twenty miles from U.C.L.A. Can't you wait here?" he pleaded. " Will it do Steve any good to see you lonely and uncomfortable out there? . . ."

" That's just the point," she said. " I'm married to Steve, and I want to stay married to him. I want to go to bed with him, and I want to be on the spot so that he won't go to bed with anyone else. This is my personal bit of the war . . . and it won't surprise Steve a bit when I go out to him. I think he has a right to expect it. I have to let him know that I mean to hold on to him. The only way I can tell him that is to show that I don't mind living in a hole twenty miles away from U.C.L.A."

And so she had gone, and she had known from Steve immediately that she had been right to go. His face wore that tight look—the look of boredom and frustration that had been on it the first time she had seen him.

71

He had managed to get her a reservation in a run-down hotel, and he lay in her arms thankfully, relaxing at last. "Oh, God, it's good to have you back, Harriet. They've done exactly what I thought they would—and I'm stuck! Maybe you can save my reason while I sit this out. . . ."

He had gone to work under the vague name of Chemical Warfare, and he could not talk about what the project was. "The application is impossibly remote," he said, "and I doubt that anyone will ever use one particle of what we're doing. We're working along with civilians . . . but at least they can go home every night. There are only six of us there, and none of us has any talent for the attractive notice of the brass. They will probably discover us in the files several years after the war is over."

He was billeted in temporary Army barracks on the campus, and he had been promoted to first lieutenant.

Harriet took a job on the assembly line at Lockheed Aircraft, and rented a room in the house of a woman who worked close to her on the line. Her name was Mary Edwardes and her husband worked the midnight shift at Lockheed. They were making a lot of money out of the war. They sold Harriet their second car because the gas rationing had grown tight. She applied for her own ration card, and the car meant freedom for herself and Steve from the stifling, hot little bedroom, and the aimless walking on the campus at U.C.L.A. Steve was free at nights, and a part of each week-end. It would have been good if they had not lived with the knowledge that they had a long time to wait—and that any day they might wake up and find that Steve was "on orders" overseas. So they lived each day with the knowledge that they were the lucky ones—fantastically lucky. They didn't dare to talk about their luck, in case it should vanish.

After four months the lab group was joined by a research group. The new unit was under the command of Mal Hamilton. He held the rank of major.

Harriet told Steve all that she knew about Mal—except what had happened the night Josh had left. Steve seemed suddenly to have come to life in the few days he had been working with the unit.

"The man's a genius, Harriet! . . . Or else he just has sheer ability to spot where people are going off wrong. This project's a big thing. I don't suppose we'll ever be told the whole implication of it, but our part is quite big enough." He stretched luxuriously. "It feels good to be doing some-

72

thing that counts, instead of sitting on my backside, and sulking over a no-account little job. . . . Makes me feel better about the guys that are taking it for me out there. . . ."

Hariet gripped him suddenly. "You don't want to go, Steve? You're not going to apply for overseas duty? . . ."

"I'm not a hero, Harriet. I go when they send me, not before." Then he smiled. "Besides . . . who in his right mind would want to leave behind a creature like you?" Then he caught her shoulder, and pulled her towards him on the bed.

Harriet was frightened by the idea of contacting Mal, but the decision was made by Mal himself, who called her at the Edwardes house.

"Why have you been hiding yourself?" he said, and she thought that his voice sounded more relaxed and good-humoured than she remembered it. "Steve has only just gotten around to telling me. Have you turned stuffy, Harriet?"

She laughed. "Well, Steve is a lieutenant, remember . . . and you're his C.O. How was he to know that you ever remembered Harriet Carpenter from Burnham Falls?"

His tone changed a little. "Listen, Harriet—I usually pay quite a lot of attention to what Lieutenant Dexter says, and I count myself lucky to have him here in the unit. You don't pick up M.I.T. graduates on the street, and this is a brilliant guy."

"That makes two of you," Harriet said.

"What?"

"Never mind. I was just mumbling."

"Well—all right. We'll all meet for dinner, shall we? That's settled!" He hung up briskly.

She waited alone for Steve and Mal in a bar on Wilshire. It was dark, and she couldn't see Mal very well, but his manner told her that a great deal had happened to him in eighteen months apart from the gold leaf on his shoulder tab. He still had that thin, almost gaunt appearance but it went well with his uniform. He raised his glass to Harriet gravely. "I'm glad you got married, Harriet—and that you're here. I was afraid Burnham Falls might take hold by the hair, and not let you go."

"The war does a lot of things, Mal. . . ."

He shrugged. "To all of us. I was dating a girl who lived in San Francisco when war broke out. We got married on December eight, before I joined up."

73

Harriet's eyebrows shot up. "Married?—Where is she now?"

"San Francisco. We're separated—we're getting a divorce."

"Oh . . . I'm sorry."

He took a sip of the martini. "There was hardly time for it to be a tragedy—we were only together seven months. We just mistook the excitement of war for something of lasting excitement about each other."

He fumbled in his wallet and produced a snapshot. Harriet bent to examine it beside the shaded table-lamp. She saw a beautiful girl, tall, with black hair whipped by the wind.

"Mal! . . . She's absolutely lovely!"

He nodded. "That's what I thought."

Steve moved close to Harriet to look at the snapshot. "She sure is! . . . This her car?"

Mal made a slight motion with his hand. "I was crazy enough about her to give her a foreign sports job for a wedding present. She liked to drive very fast, and I thought that all beautiful women should have cars like that. It was the first time in my life I'd ever earned a decent salary, and I gave it all to her. She had the car about six weeks—smashed it up on the Coast Highway, and nearly killed herself."

Harriet said nothing. She was grateful that the dimness of the bar hid her expression somewhat. Vaguely she had begun to comprehend what the change was in Mal, what only eighteen months had done to him. She sensed that with leaving Burnham Falls, with selling the house and putting away every association with the town, he had suddenly opened up to live the kind of life he had denied himself through all the years of school and college and the years after. With money in his pocket, for the first time he had been free of the necessity to hoard it. He had gone out to grab at life, to buy what he had only been able to look at before. Up till then he had closed his mind to people and emotions, and he was unskilled in judging them. The strange friendship between herself and Mal that summer had been the beginning of relaxation in him, of giving way at last to his wants and desires. From that friendship with a schoolgirl he had gone seeking something fuller, overeager now that the bonds of austerity and discipline had gone. He had found a beautiful girl and married her, and had given her a car as a silly plaything, because for him it was a symbol of what had been unattainable, and what he could now suddenly afford to buy and to give away. She looked

74

closely at Mal, and she could sense no bitterness in him, or in his words. He had accepted what happened as a bad bargain, shrugged his shoulders, and walked away. But he had not closed up again. He was open and expectant in a way he had never been in Burnham Falls. His face, no longer so tight and concentrated, was much more attractive than it had been. He looked as if his problems no longer rode about on his shoulders.

He raised his glass. " So that's my small history—too bad it didn't turn out like yours, but I'm not grieving. Drink up, Harriet—Steve—we have a lot of time to make up."

The months went by, and a year was gone, and Harriet began to think that perhaps the war would pass over Steve and even pass over Josh, who had survived in the Pacific so long, and, now that the defeats were being wiped out, would surely live through until the end came. She never thought of it as victory, because she knew there would be no triumph in her when it was finished, only a deep thankfulness if Steve and Josh were still alive. In this thought she also included Mal.

Because their research unit was small, it had been possible for a friendship to grow between Steve and Mal in spite of their difference in rank. The men in the unit talked to one another as scientists, not as soldiers, and since none of them were regulars, there was no one to uphold, or even remember, the formalities of rank. Neither Steve nor Mal ever spoke of their work, even when, as it sometimes happened, there was a rush to get through some phase, and they worked at the lab round the clock, and Harriet would see neither of them, except for a quick meal, for three or four weeks. Then at other times the work load was lighter, and there would be a whole week-end free; they would pool their gas ration and drive into the desert, looking at the mountains, snow-capped and remote, and feeling the rough, dry wind on their faces. In these moments when Steve was away from the lab, and momentarily putting aside the problems waiting for an answer, he would begin to talk about after the war. He wanted to stay in California.

" What do you think?" he asked Mal. They sat over beers in Palm Springs. " I've got a few ideas in plastics I'd like to develop, and I think I could attract some capital into them. This is a pretty good place to start, isn't it?"

Mal shrugged. " The best place will always be where you

prove those ideas. When you prove them, there'll be plenty of people with money to invest."

" Well . . . what are you going to do?"

" Take a job for a few years and save some money. Then I think I'll go out on my own. There ought to be enough people with problems who'll hire me without having to pay me a salary."

" You and I might . . ." Steve's voice trailed off. He looked down at his beer quickly.

" Might get together?" Mal finished. " We might do that, Steve. It could be worth a good try. . . ."

They said no more about it, but it was there, at the back of their minds whenever anyone mentioned the future. But mostly no one talked about the future.

During that year Mal had two promotions and became a full colonel. Steve moved up to the rank of captain. Joe wrote about the boom of business at the factory, still working at full capacity on war contracts, and he told them the news from Burnham Falls.

Then Josh wrote that he was engaged to an Australian Army nurse. The snapshot he sent showed a sweet-faced girl with delicate features, and pale hair. Harriet wondered how Burnham Falls would look in the eyes of an Australian; she smiled to herself when she thought that it was just possible that this Army nurse would be the first Australian ever to come to Burnham Falls.

Then after Christmas 1944 the Allied Armies started the break-through that led right into Germany. By May the war was over in Europe, and Harriet began to feel frightened. All the attention now focussed on the Pacific, and the outcome of the war there was inevitable; but Josh had had more than three years of fighting, and she wondered if he could last the time. Along with that, from Mal's frequent trips to Washington, and to another place he didn't name, she sensed that the work in the lab was reaching some kind of conclusion. Before Japan could be beaten there still seemed plenty of time for Steve to be sent overseas, and to be killed.

It happened as she imagined it might; Steve got his orders and was gone within twenty-four hours. It was A.P.O. San Francisco. Mal took her to dinner the night after he left, and tried to reassure her.

" I'm sorry, Harriet—I was told to send a man for a particular purpose, and Steve was the obvious one. I can't

76

talk about it—you know that. But I can tell you he isn't going to be involved in fighting. That's all I can say. For you, it's a matter of waiting."

She nodded to him, dumbly and gratefully, gathering up that precious crumb of comfort. She believed him, and was thankful for his presence, and his calmness. When he drove her home afterwards, she sat with her hands folded in her lap, silently, remembering how Mal had driven her back to the lodge that night when she had walked to his house; to-night was a little like that time. She felt complete trust in Mal; Steve was going to be all right. It was, after all, only a matter of waiting, and the waiting would be over soon. A feeling of peace descended on her.

Having settled the matter of Steve's return, and living contentedly with the thought, the telegram was a worse shock than it might have been. The military transport plane carrying Steve had run into enemy fighters and had been shot down, and no survivors had been located. The telegram was waiting for her at the Edwardes house when she got back from Lockheed, and so was Mal. It was he who told her before she ripped the envelope open.

He held her for hours afterwards like a child, until at last the pills he gave her took effect, and she could sleep. And it was he who telephoned Joe in Burnham Falls, and Steve's father.

The next months were a time of grieving, cold, and steady and unrelieved, a time of frightening loneliness, a corroding time when Harriet felt as if some inner part of her were being rubbed and worn away until her sensibilities were thin and quivering. She had loved Steve—yes, but what she had accepted before, and taken for granted, she now wanted back with a desperate hunger. With Steve's love she had become a woman, and as a woman she needed him with her. It seemed impossible to her that she must grow reconciled to the fact that the waiting time was now endless. She wanted love, but she was not prepared to admit that her lover could not be Steve.

Mal was a part of those months, though distant and shadowy because her thoughts were not with him, nor was she noticing him very much. But it seemed that always when she had reached a point when exhaustion and sleeplessness had made her numb and uncaring, Mal would appear at the Edwardes house, and take her out to dinner, driving perhaps in the Hollywood hills, or to Malibu. He ignored her disinterest and silence, talking about nothing in particular, forcing her to make some replies to his questions. He ordered martinis for her until the hard knot in her stomach eased a little, until her words came more quickly and did not have to be dragged from her. Sometimes she was aware that she was on the verge of drunkenness, but it, in its turn, brought her a deadening kind of sleep, and she was grateful. He never took her to the officers' mess, or mentioned the work in the lab. Without fully realising it, she started to count on him to be with her. One day three months after the telegram, she found herself telephoning him to see if he could get away from the lab early enough to go to the beach at Santa Monica. It had been the first voluntary motion she had made towards living in that time.

So when the second telegram came it was almost a reflex action to call Mal at the lab. It was nearly midnight, and he had been there since nine that morning. "I'll meet you outside at the parking lot," Harriet said, and hung up.

She was sitting, immobile and shrunken in the front seat of the car. As he approached she looked at him with dull eyes, and slid over to the passenger seat.

"You drive," she said. Her tone was a hoarse whisper.

"Harriet, what is it?"

She faced him fully then. "It's Josh this time, Mal. I've had a wire from Dad. He was shot down."

He put out a hand to touch her, but she shrank back. "No . . ." Then she shook her head wildly. "I don't think I can take it a second time, Mal. I'm afraid . . . of what I'll do when I start to believe it's true."

He pressed the starter, and backed out of the lot. The brick buildings swept by them with a rush of air, and then he was out in the dark Los Angeles streets. He drove then for hours, the long flat roads to the desert. The September air was cool on their faces, and the wind whipped Harriet's hair into her eyes, stinging and blinding her. She did nothing to hold it back, just sat there with tense, folded hands. In the faint starlight they could see the dim outlines of the mass of the two mountains, San Jacinto and San Bernardino, towering back off the pass. The desert wind was cold now, the empty spaces silent and black, broken abruptly by the lights of the all-night diners, and the neon signs of the motels. They swept through Palm Springs. Harriet saw none of it; she was aware of nothing until Mal abruptly

78

drew to the side of the road and switched off the engine. Then he turned to her, and put both his hands on hers as they lay in her lap.

"Harriet . . . I'm afraid for you when I see your hands folded . . . like this. You do it each time—the night Josh went away, the time the news came about Steve. Why can't you cry instead of folding your hands, and shutting your grief up between them."

She looked down at them, slowly spread her fingers apart. "How else shall I contain it, Mal? I have to live with it, and Joe taught me not to cry."

He lifted her hands and held them within his own. "You have to learn to cry, Harriet. You have to learn to trust someone well enough to trust them with your grief. You have to move close to someone . . . to share your pain like a human, not nurse it in misery, dumbly, like an animal."

She caught back her breath in a long sigh.

"Do you trust me, Harriet?"

She nodded. "Yes . . . yes, completely."

He got out of the car, and went around to her side. She felt his arms about her body, and the surprising strength and ease as he lifted her, and carried her across the sand.

The stars were clear, and infinitely far away; a cold wind drove across the desert, and moaned low in the cactus and sage brush. His hands upon her firm and skilful, and he talked softly, close to her ear. It was a fearful wonder to feel the pain as he entered her, and she shouted aloud with it, but her shout was almost one of fierce gratitude and joy. In the movements of her body, responding to his, she rode out the demons of grief and loneliness, using their passion to express and exorcise all the protest, the resentment. She heard her own voice crying out in the silence, crying Mal's name, and Steve's and Josh's; but the pain in her was now a physical one, one that Mal was imposing on her, and she braced her hand and shoulders back in the sand, and thrust herself at him, claiming him, drawing him to her again and again, calling out to him for it not to stop. And as they moved together in a wild, rocking motion, she suddenly felt the tears on her face, and the unearthly peace in her mind and body as release came.

They drove back to Los Angeles on the long, flat roads, through the quiet hours of the dawn and sunrise, seeing the first flush on the peaks. Their journey was as silent as the

79

outward one had been; they were both weary, but they sat close together, and Harriet's hand lay limp and still on Mal's leg. The city had begun to stir for the day when they entered it. Mal pulled in at a drive-in, and after they had ordered breakfast, and while Harriet was combing her haid and putting on lipstick, he walked to the next corner and bought a paper. He hurried back to the car and she could tell that his thoughts were not with her, but concentrated wholly on what was in the paper.

He opened the door and slid in beside her. "They've dropped an atom bomb on Japan—Hiroshima," he said.

It was all there; they read it in silence, appalled and stunned by the sum of its meaning. Gradually its implications began to dawn on Harriet, the probability of a Japanese surrender, and the end of the war. The thought of Josh was bitter now.

She turned to him suddenly. "Mal . . . did you and Steve have anything to do with this?"

He shook his head. "Not directly." He tapped the paper. "This must have been the most closely guarded secret of the war. But we were working on instruments that rode in the plane with it . . . but, of course, we didn't know what they'd be used for. I guess Steve would have worked on it if he'd made it out to Tinian."

She folded over the paper and laid it on her lap. "The war will probably end soon, won't it," she said quietly.

"I suppose so."

They waited in silence until their breakfast came. When the girl had clipped the trays on, and handed them their coffee, Mal took the paper from Harriet and handed it to her. "Here—have you seen this."

The girl glanced at the headlines. "Oh . . . that bomb, you mean. Yes, we heard it on the radio. That sure was a big one. Thanks."

She walked away from them slowly, reading.

Mal called her from his office that night. She stood in the Edwardes' hall to take the call, and she listened to Mal's voice; in the kitchen the Edwardes were having a rumbling, continuous argument about what they were going to do now that the war was going to end, and they'd be laid off at Lockheed.

"Are you all right, Harriet?" Mal said. "Will you be able to sleep? Shall I come over?"

"No . . . I'm all right, Mal. I feel sleepy, and I know I'll be all right."

There was a long pause, and then she heard the crackle of paper close to the phone, and then the click of a cigarette lighter. "Harriet?"

"Yes?"

"When . . . when you have time to sort things out a little . . . will you think about marrying me?"

She cradled the phone close to her, closing her eyes for a second, and feeling her weariness, but also a quiet peace. "I love you, Mal. Good night."

"Good night."

They never saw each other after that morning in the drive-in. Harriet went on the night shift after that, and two mornings later, when she got back to the Edwardes', Mary met her at the door.

"It's another of those telegrams, Harriet." She twisted her hands nervously. "I'm late now for my shift, but I had to wait . . . I didn't think there was anyone else close to you, but I thought I'd wait. . . ."

Harriet ripped it open. It was from the Army Department, and it informed her that Captain Stephen Dexter was alive. He was being flown into a hospital in San Francisco. When she got the story from him afterwards she learned that he and two other men had survived when the plane went down, and had reached a small island in a rubber dinghy. They had been fed and nursed by the natives there, and had waited until a naval patrol had sighted their signals. The area had been clear of Japanese, and so they had known it was only a matter of waiting.

Harriet just had time to telephone Mal before her plane left for San Francisco. As they talked her flight number was announced, and she hung up. Walking towards the plane on the tarmac, she realised that she couldn't recall a single word of what they had said to each other.

CHAPTER FIVE

Laura Peters drove back to New York on the afternoon the Laboratories opened in a sober mood. Until this day she had only half-believed that the move to Burnham Falls was final and inevitable, even though in the last year she and

81

Ed had planned every detail of their house, had become members of the River Bend Club, and she had bought a whole new wardrobe of country clothes for this altered existence.

It had seemed an enjoyable pastime—from their Park Avenue apartment—to plan a country house. The trouble was that she hadn't really been able to believe in it until she and Ed had walked to-day through the empty rooms, and knew that within a week they would be living in them. The panic had come down on her then abruptly, and this time she wasn't able to shake it off. It wasn't any use pretending that Burnham Falls was the periphery of New York; it was irreconcilably remote from what Laura thought of as New York—the tight little area a dozen blocks wide stretching diagonally across Manhattan from the East Seventies to Times Square.

It had been Larry, her first husband, who had made her conscious of the brittle, glittering world that he loved, and who had made her feel that success on its terms was the only thing that could matter. He had loved her also, but he had loved her as a part of the world he sought—a fellow-seeker of the limelight, a companion on a voyage. Larry might not ever become a great writer, but he already had a Pulitzer Prize to prove how well he understood his world.

She had met him four months after she had arrived from Los Angeles, time enough to have used up the little store of money she had, and to have called three times at every agent's office on her list. In Los Angeles she had done the usual extra's work at the studios, and had played three small roles in Little Theatre. They had brought no movie contracts, not even a screen test. She moved on to New York because every casting agent in Hollywood had had her on his books since she was eight years old; she was now nineteen and she had been around Los Angeles too long for anyone to discover her. But in New York, as on the Coast, it was not nearly enough to be merely pretty.

So she worked nights as a waitress at Auguste's, a small French restaurant on West 47th Street which catered to the theatrical profession—not the big time stuff, such as producers and directors. Auguste's was for the unglamorous workers in the theatre—the wardrobe mistresses, the stage hands, the electricians. In those days Larry had been an assistant stage manager.

82

He watched her for many nights before he actually spoke to her. He was a plain, unremarkable man, short and heavyset, in his late thirties. He was working with Arthur Grimsby's hit musical *Golden Opportunity,* and he told her right away that he was going to write plays; it took a little more time to learn that he was already successful as a short story writer —*Cosmopolitan,* the *New Yorker, The Atlantic.* As a staff writer for *Stars and Stripes* in the Pacific, he had been able to keep on writing and selling fiction, as well as doing his routine work, all through the war. Now, in 1946, he should have been ready to make a career of it—except that he was hungry for the theatre, not the printed page. He had finished, he told her, four plays, but none of them was yet the one he wanted to show to a Broadway producer. He had had one play produced in summer stock just before the war.

She looked at him with respect; she had never known a writer before, at least not one who made any money from it.

He began to wait for her every night after he had eaten at Auguste's. They would ride together in the subway to her hotel off Broadway in the West Nineties; then he walked ten blocks south to his own third-floor walk-up. He wrote until seven or eight o'clock in the morning, and slept until it was time to go to the theatre. There was a business-like determination about Larry; he wasted little time on dreaming.

It puzzled Laura that he had never expected her to do more than kiss him; he had been in and around the theatre long enough to know what were accepted as the rules. He was neither naïve nor unsure of himself. Since the time when she had played as an extra in an early Shirley Temple movie which had given her mother the idea that she was destined to become a star, Laura had more or less understood that beauty was an item for barter; when she was sixteen the knowledge was no longer vague, but certain and defined.

On Sundays, when the theatre and Auguste's were closed, they walked in the Park for a few hours, and then Larry took her back to his apartment and cooked an elaborate meal for her on a tiny stove and a hot-plate. He was a good cook, quick and neat, and he learned early that she was useless in the kitchen.

The New York summer moved into its full stride; the sidewalks and buildings enclosed an endless, almost terrifying heat. Larry's apartment was stifling, but not so bad as Laura's, which was next to the roof. It was too hot to walk for long in the Park on Sundays, and Laura spent most of the day lounging in the big chair in Larry's room. The blinds were drawn against the glare outside. After Larry had prepared the meal, he handed her the Sunday papers, and he himself went to the typewriter. He sat at his work table for hours at a stretch, the sweat running off his face, and his white T-shirt clinging to his body.

She thought about him a great deal as she lay there, somnolent in the heat. The principal feeling she had for him was gratitude, because he had saved her from the aching loneliness of New York. He seemed as humble and dependable as a dog, giving, and asking for nothing.

One day, a day in August when the heat lay upon the city like a blanket, she spoke her thoughts.

"Larry . . . Larry, why don't you want to make love to me?"

He didn't seem surprised, but he took his time about answering. He took off his glasses, and leaned back in the chair.

"Because I'm in love with you, Laura, and I'm patient."

"I don't understand . . ." His manner disturbed her; she wished she had not asked the question.

"I don't want an affair with you, Laura. I want you to love me."

He turned back to the typewriter, but the keys didn't start tapping.

She moved very softly, easing herself out of the broken-springed chair, laying the papers gently on the floor. She unbuttoned her blouse, and drew it off, and then let her skirt drop. Noiselessly she slipped out of her sandals, and took off her bra and briefs. Then she went across to him. He started a little at her touch, and she bent and put her lips against his.

"Larry . . ." she said quietly, "until I love you, will you take me as I am?"

His hand came up, and he touched her breasts wonderingly; then he put both arms about her, and pressed his face against her firm belly.

"God, you're so beautiful, Laura!"

He was a good lover, as he was good at most things.

She kept trying for a part, because something about the
84

theatre was eating into her now—in spite of the shoddy teachers her mother had sent her to, and the ideas she had formed in the studios that acting was a mechanical thing. She read *Variety*, and followed Larry's tips about who was casting. The job at Auguste's left her days free to sit about in agents' offices, but it gave her little time for sleep. She grew thinner.

By dint of nailing Arthur Grimsby down for three minutes, Larry managed to get her in to read for a seven-line part in a play Grimsby was producing. She knew he consented only because Larry was a valued employee, whose efficiency Grimsby respected. She tried the part and made a miserable hash of it. Larry was seated in the darkened theatre, a few rows behind Grimsby. Afterwards he took her to Gallagher's and ordered roast beef and cheesecake for her, and made her eat it.

"You've got to be taught, Laura," he said. "God!—it was terrible what you did on that stage. You don't know how to speak—you don't even know how to walk. You looked like an awkward kid, and you were meant to be a sexy bundle making a play for a man."

Larry had been promoted to stage manager for the show Laura had read for, a play called *One by One,* by a young Pacific veteran. Larry was going to Boston for rehearsals and the try-out.

"If only Marshall can get the point across, we'll have a smash hit . . . and I'll have a steady job for two years."

"Don't you mind working on another man's play?"

He shrugged. "I've got something of my own to say, and I'll say it . . . all in good season. There's room for a lot of people in the theatre."

So he went to Boston, and Laura missed him acutely. She grew despondent, even though she had a note from him every day.

Then he called from Boston. "Laura, we're in! It's a hit! The critics are crazy about it!"

"Well . . . that's wonderful!" she managed to say. "I mean . . . really wonderful!" She felt a sudden pang of envy for the success that abruptly belonged to a young, unknown man.

He said, "It'll run two years . . . at least."

She laughed faintly; she was feeling very tired. "Larry . . . you sound as if it was *your* play."

"Baby, I don't care whose play it is just so long as it
85

gives me two seasons of steady work. With luck I won't have to go on the road for two season, and I'll have a play ready for Broadway at the end of that time, or I'll bust!"

On Broadway, *One by One* was a smash hit. Larry gloated over the reviews as if they had been written about his own play.

"This is money in the bank," he said to Laura, pointing to *The Times*. "Now we can get married."

She stiffened. "Who said anything about getting married."

He reached out and took her face between his two hands. "Baby . . . because I need you here with me all the time, not just on Sundays. And you . . . I think you need me, too. You need someone to take care of you, and there's no reason why it shouldn't be me."

She frowned, and a little tremor went through her body. She was at a moment of committing her future to Larry— and then she laughed wryly inside herself because her present was such a poor thing. She didn't know whether she had any great faith in Larry's ability to bring off successfully the play he was writing—or whether he had a great dream of the theatre and would indulge it at the cost of ignoring his talent in another direction. Larry could be making a mistake, and perhaps she was about to join him in it. But if not Larry—then what? Or whom? She didn't love Larry but outside this beat-up apartment on the West Side there was the world of strangers, the vague promises of help and there was the loneliness of this great, crushing, brutal city. And there was the deepening conviction that she couldn't make it by herself.

"Yes, Larry . . . we'll get married."

He did all that his promise to take care of her implied. He asked Grimsby for a raise, and got it because *One by One* was a success, and Larry had helped to make it so. They got the marriage licence immediately, and Larry made Laura quit her job at Auguste's. She was married in a beige suit which Larry had chosen and paid for, and for the first time she saw what an expensive garment could do for her. Larry judged fabric, style and colour with an expert, professional eye.

"From now on," he said, "you'll have to be properly dressed. A face like yours doesn't need decking out to distract attention from it—everything has to be plain and good."

"What's wrong with the clothes I have now?"

86

" They're terrible—just terrible," he said. " They look like ice-cream sundaes."

" And who'll pay for all this?" she demanded sullenly.

" I will, of course. We'll economise by staying on in my apartment, but I don't want you to put your foot outside the door unless you look as an actress should look."

She shrugged irritably. " All right, Svengali. But I don't know what you expect me to turn into."

" Now shut up, and pay attention, Laura," he said amiably. " You want to be an actress? Right! Then we'll manufacture an actress if we haven't got a born one. You'll have to forget all the junk you learned in Hollywood."

He enrolled her with Goodman for dramatic lessons, and with Joe Aaronson for voice training—both of them the best, he said. He also sent her to a ballet teacher for deportment. She was abruptly plunged into a schedule of practice and classes that seemed much more exhausting than the work at Auguste's.

She was learning to wear clothes, and to choose them with an accurate image of how she wanted to look firmly in her mind. Larry persuaded her to let her hair grow, and sent her to a good hairdresser who coloured it to a dark honey which brought out warm tones in her skin, in place of the white, chalky look it had had. Over the months she saw a new shell being laid over the old one, and what she saw pleased her; but underneath she felt that she was still the ill-trained, messy blonde who had come from Los Angeles. She was afraid it still showed through.

Larry's routine had not altered with marriage. He still ate every night at Auguste's, still worked until seven or eight o'clock every morning.

She usually fell asleep on their wall-bed while Larry worked; she fell asleep with a book in her hands. When she wasn't practising, or learning a part, Larry made her read. She read plays, novels, biographies and poetry that came from the bulging, untidy shelves that filled one wall of their room. Larry expected her to be literate by his own standards.

" For God's sake!" she protested wearily. " What are you trying to do with me? Look, my father hacked a cab all his life, and my mother waited table at the hamburger place on Vine and Hollywood. I never even *heard* of these people," she pointed at the titles, " before I came here."

" In the theatre you can be anyone or anything—just so

87

long as you can convince other people. What you started with doesn't matter. And what's in those books is part of your stock-in-trade."

She was only half-satisfied, but she did what he told her, because she didn't know what else to believe. Their lives were dedicated and hard-working. After a year of it, Laura began to wonder if it was to any purpose. *One by One* settled down for its second season on Broadway.

Then, just after the New Year, Larry told her that he was planning to invest some money in the summer theatre at Hyde Park on the condition that she was taken on in the company. She heard the news with an overwhelming relief and an obedient gratitude to Larry; the thought of the summer gave some purpose and direction to her studies, and she worked harder than before.

In the spring the bookings for *One by One* began to fall off, and no one thought it could last through another summer. By May the closing notices were up. Larry announced that his play was ready to show to Grimsby.

Until then, he had refused to let Laura read it. She took the copy he gave her now, and knew that she was afraid to start. The fact that Larry considered this play, his fifth, worthy of presenting to a Broadway producer was a final step; if he was mistaken about the play, then he was also mistaken in his whole idea of the theatre. Their future lay in this thin typescript in her hands. She was too frightened to be able to read it with detachment. Some of it barely seemed to make sense to her, and she knew it was because panic was blinding her to whatever meaning it possessed. Finally, she confessed it to Larry.

He shrugged. " You're too close to it, Baby. Just put it out of your head until Grimsby can get around to reading it."

Laura had to leave for Hyde Park before Grimsby read it. Now that *One by One* had closed, Larry was working full time writing another play, and trying to sell his latest short story to tide him over the summer. Laura was scheduled for small parts in five productions at Hyde Park, and on the strength of Larry's investment, she was given the plum of playing Alexander in *The Little Foxes*; the starring roles would be played by the famous husband-and-wife team of Vera Terraine and John Langston. They had been starring on Broadway and all over the States since the twenties, and in certain plays their names meant a sold-out house. Laura

88

grew afraid even at the thought of appearing on the same stage with them.

" Play it for all it's worth," was all Larry said, " and don't let Vera bitch you up."

She went to Hyde Park alone, though Larry promised to come up for each dress rehearsal and opening. She missed him in many strange ways ; after eighteen months with Goodman and Aaronson she was no longer raw and did not completely lack confidence, but she missed Larry's comforting solidarity, the strength and sureness which his knowledge of the theatre always transmitted to her. It was something of a disappointment when he came for the first opening to find him preoccupied. Grimsby had read the play, and was showing cautious excitement about it; the long negotiations were about to start. But Larry was pleased with her handling of the small part, and she lived through the rest of the week with mixed feelings of pleasure and hope.

When he came to Hyde Park for the next show, Larry told her that Grimsby had said he definitely wanted to produce the play in the fall or winter. Part of the terms Larry was fighting for was to get the leading feminine role for Laura. Grimsby was unbudging in his refusal, even though Larry pointed out that if he got stars for the two male leads the woman's part was written so that it could be carried by the two strong male roles. Laura was beautiful, and sufficiently trained, he said.

Grimsby didn't want her, and said so flatly, and he might never have changed his mind if it hadn't been for the notices of the Hyde Park revival of The Little Foxes. Vera Terraine and John Langston guaranteed it some notice in the Press, and they gave their usual polished performances. Perhaps it was Laura's freshness that accounted for the interest in her, or perhaps it was that Larry's near-desperation at the deadlock in the talks with Grimsby somehow sparked her to a tremendous effort. She played without self-consciousness, determined to get notice and praise from the critics for Larry to carry back to Grimsby. She got what she wanted, and at the end of the week, Grimsby came to Hyde Park to see her. He agreed, even then reluctantly, to sign her for the part.

She went through the rest of the summer in a daze, aware, now that the big part was over, of a new humility, a frightened knowledge of how close she had been to missing her chance.

89

She snatched greedily at all the experience those weeks could give her, not even minding the chores of scenery painting, and the mending the wardrobe mistress passed out. She was wrapped up in the thought of Larry's play, and it was a shock to have suddenly the invitation to play again the part of Alexandra when Vera Terraine and John Langston did a four-week revival of *The Little Foxes* on Broadway in September.

It was the tourist season, and the audience for those four weeks were out-of-towners, drawn by the familiarity of the play and the fame of Terraine and Langston. Here, on her own stamping-ground, Vera Terraine did not permit Laura to gather more than the usual two-line mention from the critics, but what was said was good, and her one Broadway appearance permitted Grimsby to give her star billing when Larry's play opened in late November.

The playbills read:

ROD CHANDLER AND MARCUS NORTH
and introducing LAURA CARROLL
in
" THE LEAVEN "
a play by
LAWRENCE WARDE

Laura had never been so frightened in her life. The weeks of rehearsal before the try-out in Philadelphia were a nightmare, but no one except Larry knew it. She was helped by Rod Chandler and Marcus North, who both had excellent roles, and didn't mind helping her to look good—because they could afford to. Their task was made easy by the way Larry had written her part; it was Laura herself, with very few differences. The play did not depend upon Laura; all she had to do was to turn in a competent, professional job.

From the Philadelphia try-out, and the Broadway opening, Chandler and North got rave notices; Laura emerged very creditably. She was praised for her graceful performance, and her sense of timing. Two of the critics mentioned her excellent delivery, her clear, low-pitched voice that carried to every seat in the house. . . " It was a pleasure to welcome Miss Carroll to Broadway. She will decorate it for many seasons to come."

But the excitement of the reviews was for Lawrence Warde.

90

He would be, they predicted, one of America's major dramatists.

Laura and Larry came home to the third floor walk-up after Arthur Grimsby's party, clutching their bundle of newspapers; they stood in the centre of the room and hugged each other in relief and tired ecstacy. After the nervous glitter of the opening and the party, this shabby, frayed room seemed warm and comforting. They knew, of course, that it was part of a world that they were leaving, and, just for that moment, they could almost regret it.

II

The Leaven ran on Broadway for two seasons. A month before it closed, Larry asked Laura for a divorce.

It might have been easier for Laura to understand if she had suspected what was going to happen. There might have been some steps she could have taken, even futile ones to make at least a gesture of fighting to keep Larry. But when he told her, she knew at once that it was too late to do anything. She had lived with him complacently, and she had lost him before she knew it.

The Leaven had been sold to the movies, but there was no way, this time, that Larry could secure for Laura her original role. The part was earmarked for a star already under contract to the film company, and it was being altered and built up to conform with the public idea of the kind of woman she was. Afterwards, when Larry recalled this, he reminded Laura that she had blamed him for her failure to get the movie role.

The Leaven was produced successfully in London. Larry had gone over for the opening. The two weeks he had planned to stay stretched into nearly two months. He wrote her that he was working on parts of the first draft of his new play with the producer. Laura was rehearsing a television show and she barely had time to notice his absence.

He came back and finished the new play. It was then she found out that it contained no part for her.

"Laura, be reasonable," he said. "I can't write with only one person in mind all the time. There'll be other parts offered to you when *The Leaven* ends . . . any producer who didn't use you would be losing a lot of publicity."

91

The second play opened a couple of months before *The Leaven* closed. It was a better play than *The Leaven*, and the critics' notices sold the house out for months ahead. Larry had his name on two theatres on Broadway. He went to London almost immediately to prepare for the opening there. When he came back he asked her for a divorce.

"Why?" She stared at him, helpless and shocked.

"There's someone else I want to marry."

"Who?" She cast around wildly in her mind seeking the woman, and knew at once that it was no one in New York.

"Her name is Mary Blair. She's Harvey Cantrill's secretary."

It took her a second to remember that Cantrill was his London producer. "That's why you stayed . . ." she said.

He shrugged. "Why not? Did you notice I wasn't here?"

He was about to turn away. Suddenly her sense of outrage crumbled; she was left only bewilderment. The controlled voice that was one of her chief assets on the stage, wavered and broke. "Larry . . . Larry, why? You loved me once . . . I *know* you loved me."

He came back and faced her. "Yes . . . that's true. I did. I loved you very much, Laura. But I was mistaken."

"How? What do you mean?"

He gestured, groping for words. "I had an ideal . . . an image, if you like. I saw you as a raw material which had the potential of perfection. I wanted to mould you. . . . I wrote you into *The Leaven* as the woman I thought you would become. I made a stupid mistake."

She burst out hotly, "Well, is it *my* fault that I turned out to be me instead of some crazy dream you had."

"No," he said slowly, "it's not your fault, Laura. I handed you over to teachers and I saw them shape your body and your voice and your face. You were an apt pupil, and you learned well. I thought that I could teach you the other things . . . wit, wisdom, kindliness. I thought that you would love me. That was pretty stupid. I should be writer enough to know that love doesn't come because you wish it would."

"I haven't cheated on you," she raged. "You know there hasn't been anyone else, even though there've been chances . . . and you were always working and never came to the theatre. . . ."

92

" Just not cheating isn't enough, Laura. A marriage needs something a little more active than that." He flung out his hands quickly. " Well, it was my fault, I suppose. I taught you all the external tricks of the theatre, and how to be a success—and then I stood by and watched you become absorbed by hairdressers and dressmakers and photographers and all the other paraphernalia of being a star. I started it, and I didn't know how to stop it."

" The trouble with you, Larry, is that you really didn't want anything at all for me—you didn't want my success, and you didn't like it. You just wanted me at home sitting at your feet."

" You're probably right," he said. " That's why I'm marrying Mary Blair."

When the divorce went through she had her settlement from Larry, which was a generous one, and which he gave ungrudgingly. There were also the two mink coats, and the jewellery he had given her. What he couldn't give her was a conviction of her own talent—her ability to go on without him.

She felt a pang of envy and regret when she read that the second play had been awarded the New York Critics Award and then the Pulitzer Prize. But the bleakest day was the one when she saw Larry and a woman she knew must be Mary Blair at lunch at Sardi's. Mary Blair was almost plain, with her brown hair dragged back too severely from her thin face ; she would not have attracted attention anywhere. She was totally absorbed in Larry, and as they left the restaurant he linked his arm confidingly in hers. Laura felt a sense of desolation as she watched them.

III

Almost the last thing Larry had said to her was " Wear the right clothes . . . and choose your parts carefully."

She had reason to think about this often. In the two years after the divorce she had appeared in two plays on Broadway that had flopped, and another that had tried-out in Washington, and had never come into New York. It was easier to pick the clothes than the parts, and after two flops the parts weren't offered by the top producers any more. She sat in her apartment and waited for the telephone to ring—

93

after starring on Broadway it was no longer possible to call hopefully at producers' offices; the phone rang less and less frequently.

There was work for her to do, however. Television was booming, and the medium was an insatiable maw for performers and writers. She appeared in the afternoon matinée shows, and the night-time half-hour dramas, and her agent Al Roberts would call all the newspaper television critics in the hope that they would catch the show, and give Laura a mention. Sometimes her picture appeared on the television page of the evening papers. The shows were shot from vast bare studios, and from draughty legit theatres that had fallen to the new popularity of television. Half a dozen times she flew out to Los Angeles to do a show that originated from the great new factories for television that the networks had built out there. It was work, but there was no magic in it. Her training still stayed with her, and she did a satisfactory, if not notable job.

She heard that Larry was having another play produced in the fall. By this time she was desperate enough to call him and ask if there was a part in it for her. He told her that there wasn't, and he made a fair pretence of being regretful over it.

It was after the talk with Larry that she decided to tell Al Roberts that she would take the job he had found for her, to do a series of filmed television commercials for the appliance division of Amtec. She had no illusions about what this meant—it meant that she would become a glamorised saleswoman of stoves, dishwashers and refrigerators, and that it was very likely the end of any hope of going back into the theatre. But it needed money to support an apartment in the East Fifties and the kind of life that went with it. The Amtec offer was very handsome, and it was a three-year exclusive contract. It was three years in which she could afford East Fiftieth Street and the mink coats.

With what was left of her time after Amtec had had its cut, she studied with Goodman. It was a gesture of desperation, as she felt herself slipping farther and farther away from the place she wanted to go. She knew that she was only buying herself the illusion of being an actress, and that in the public's mind she was now firmly identified with refrigerators, but she told herself that Amtec paid her well enough to be able to afford the indulgence. And she bought and read many of the books and plays that had

94

been on Larry's shelves, and which she had not had time to read before the divorce.

And in the meantime her name became famous across America for the way she would walk across a model kitchen and flick the control of a stove or washing-machine. The Amtec dealers loved her, and Amtec began to plan a whole magazine advertising campaign featuring her.

Goodman was studying the double-page spread in *Life* when she walked into the studio one day. He favoured her with his most concentrated stare. "I suppose this pays very well," he said, tapping her brightly-coloured photo.

"Yes," she answered defensively, "but I don't get it for nothing—it's a full-time job."

"Is it?" he said thoughtfully, "is it, now?" Then he put aside the magazine. "Well—shall we get down to some work?"

Laura met Ed Peters several times during her first year of working for Amtec, but she had heard him spoken of often enough to give her some idea of his strength in the corporation. Everyone knew Ed Peters, and some feared him. He was an executive vice-president in charge of the appliance division of Amtec. Amtec had no natural heirs to the positions of President of the Corporation, or Chairman of the Board, and there were already some who backed Ed Peters for one or both of those jobs when the time came. He was then forty-six years old.

He had not seemed a man to fear on the occasions when she had met him—usually at the dealers' conventions. He was pleasant to look at without being strictly handsome, his crew-cut hair streaked with grey. He had charming, quiet manners which bore the stamp of Princeton. There was nothing about him that suggested the toughness of the men who had pioneered Amtec in the field of electronics in its early days. Rather there was a suggestion of subtlety, of an ability to manœuvre and deal. Without being told Laura guessed that Ed Peters' training was legal; there was the feel of a lawyer about him.

She had her first real contact with him a little more than a year after she had joined Amtec. It came about because Al Roberts had an offer from Jerome Perkins for Laura to appear in a Broadway production—not a starring role, but a meaty supporting part that could bring her a lot of attention.

95

Amtec hardly bothered to discuss the situation. It merely reminded her of her signature on a three-year exclusive contract, and said it had no plans to release her, and that she could not be spared to meet the demands of eight shows a week on Broadway, as well as their own schedule for her. She had no choice but to turn down Jerome Perkins' offer.

It was then that Ed Peters called her and asked her to dine with him.

She began the evening in a mood of sick disappointment, and a kind of impotent rebellion which included Ed Peters and his invitation—but which she had not had the courage to refuse. He was an easy and skilful talker, and she wavered under the spell of his words. Mollified she heard him say how valuable she was to Amtec, how famous she had become as a result of their advertising, how many choice parts would be waiting for her at the end of the contract—and the implication was that when this contract was finished they would draw another one which would permit her more freedom. In the meantime she had security, and the leisure to study with Goodman. He made Amtec seem something that was no less than paternal, encircling arms about her. She listened, and believed him.

In the next six months he asked her occasionally to have dinner with him; sometimes they went to the theatre together. He was charming, but he held himself close, and gave nothing of himself. He asked nothing of Laura either, and he seemed for ever lost behind the upward-curling smoke of his cigarette. He seemed to take pleasure in her appearance, but he looked at her only as he might have looked at the portrait of a beautiful woman, not the reality. He told her very little about himself, but he seemed to take it for granted that she would question others about him.

By letting her questions, apparently casual, drop at the right moment, she began to piece together a picture of Ed Peters' career.

She was told that he had started in his father's law firm in Philadelphia—a firm that handled only corporation law. The firm was conservative and prosperous, and it was in keeping that Ed should, at this stage, marry a Philadelphia girl who had money to go with her beauty. Her name was Joan Stratton. They had two daughters, Elizabeth and Clare.

It was Ed Peters himself who told her that he had moved to the Justice Department in Washington after three years of fighting an anti-trust suit brought against M. M. & S.

at the end of which the corporation had entered a consent decree, and had got off with a minimum payment. It was a triumph for a young lawyer, and when the Justice Department had made their offer, his father had been strongly in favour of him taking it for a few years for the experience it would give him in corporate practice, and the contacts he would develop within the various government departments. He had been caught in Washington when the war broke out, and the Justice Department refused to release him for active service.

During the next years he had helped prepare and write many of the contracts the Government had given to industry which sent the vast flow of material overseas. He learned the workings of the giant corporations that held defence contracts, he learned to know the men who controlled them, and those who were their brains and minds.

His social activities in Washington were directed towards a better acquaintance with the heads of corporations who were in and out of the city constantly on defence business. Most of those who would talk to Laura about Ed Peters said it was during the war that he and his wife had grown apart; that she had become bored with the endless entertaining of people who would never be friends of hers, and were not meant to be.

A year after the war ended Ed's father died, and Ed had decided not to go back into the Philadelphian firm, but to accept an offer from Amtec to come to them as Assistant Corporate Counsel. During the war the Government had chosen to ignore the monopolies that had grown up, but now they were starting once again to prepare anti-trust suits. There was one pending against Amtec.

He did not stay long in the legal division of the corporation. Amtec had branched out into manufacturing appliances, and he had persuaded E. J. Harrison, who was then President of Amtec, to let him switch to the appliances division, which was a wholly-owned subsidiary of Amtec. He had gone on writing the contracts with suppliers, procuring the raw materials, using his contacts in the Defence Department when he wanted to sell to the military, learning every aspect of sales and advertising with an eagerness and absorption that drove every other consideration from his life: At the right moment he had pointed up the weakness of the man who headed the company, and he had become president in his place. After the years of scarcity during the war, the public was on a buying spree, absorbing product more quickly than the manufacturers could make it. Ed's division showed an upward spiral of profit that never slowed. He became something for E. J. Harrison to boast of as his discovery. At forty-three he had moved back into the parent company of Amtec as one of the executive vice-presidents, with the new President of the Appliance Division, and all the heads of departments reporting to him. He had moved up very quickly, and along the way he had made enemies.

For these, then, there was some satisfaction when the news broke that his wife, Joan, had left him. After a Reno divorce, in which Ed won custody of his two daughters, Joan had immediately married a foreign correspondent of one of the New York papers. They had met in Washington during the war.

This much information about Ed Peters Laura gathered over the months. She still knew very little about the man himself. As an actress she appreciated the degree of control he exercised, and was sometimes dismayed by it. She understood him well enough, however, to know that they had entered another phase in their relationship the first time that he asked her to come to his apartment to have dinner with his daughters.

The younger one, Clare, was fair and docile, and she presented no problems to Ed Peters; he could manage her with ease, and she accepted this as an evidence of love. Elizabeth, at thirteen, was in open rebellion against her father, and expressed it in being everything he most disliked. In the process of her combat with him, she seemed to be slowly destroying herself. Laura felt a touch of pity as she was introduced to the overweight, pimply girl, whose lank hair and untidy clothes expressed a profound contempt for her father's love of order. She had cold blue eyes that examined Laura carefully.

"You're beautiful, aren't you," she stated as she dropped Laura's hand. "My father doesn't like ugly women."

And then, unexpectedly, she added, "If you like you can put your coat in my room."

Ed made no motion to stop them, and Laura followed Elizabeth to a room littered with clothes, records and school books. The girl sat on the rumpled bed while Laura ran a comb through her hair at the mirror.

"This place is a mess, isn't it? My father is always on to me about it—but the servants don't give a damn, and I don't

98

see why I should fuss over it just because he puts his head in here once a month."

"Perhaps you'd be more comfortable if it were tidy," Laura said gently. She was covertly studying the photo of a dark-haired woman which stood on the dressing-table. Elizabeth noticed her.

"That's my mother. She's beautiful too." She got up from the bed slowly. "She has a wonderful time—they live in Paris, and my mother goes with Doug all over Europe whenever he has to cover a story. She writes to me every week, and when I'm eighteen I'm going over to spend a summer with her." Suddenly she pointed. "And that," she said, indicating a framed picture turned to the wall, "is my great-grandmother. My father makes me hang it there. She lives on a farm in Pennsylvania. We have to go and spend every Christmas with her."

Ed began to call Laura more frequently, and often they dined with Elizabeth and Clare before they went to the theatre. Elizabeth, garrulous in Laura's presence, was almost always silent with her father. She began to invent excuses to get Laura into her room, and her talk was alternatively friendly and hostile. Gradually her craving for companionship drew her closer, and haltingly she asked Laura about getting her hair permed, and about the colours she should wear. Before Laura's visits she made an effort to tidy her room. She admired Laura's carefully tended hands, and after a while she stopped biting her nails.

Clare was pretty and smiling, and she showed a dutiful deference to Laura. For her part, Laura thought her a dull child—except for the expensive clothes, Clare might have been herself at nine years old.

"You have a knack with Elizabeth," Ed said one evening as they left the apartment. "She tries to improve her appearance when you're around, and she's stopped gorging herself on candy."

She knew, once he had said that, that he intended to ask her to marry him. But characteristically he took his own time about it.

She also knew that if she did not want to marry Ed she had to withdraw now, because he would not forgive a refusal. She hesitated, and put off thinking about it, but it remained there, at the back of her mind, a wavering question mark.

99

She found herself agreeing, though she knew what it implied, when Ed asked her to be his hostess at a dinner-party he was giving for some of the officers of Amtec. E. J. Harrison and his wife would be there. When Laura heard this she knew that the matter between herself and Ed was settled. She was irresistibly drawn towards the promise of security.

E. J.'s long conversation with her that evening, and his string of compliments, was tacit acknowledgment of her acceptance into the corporation world. She and Ed were married quietly a month after the dinner-party, and Ed took her immediately down to Pennsylvania to meet his grandmother.

The farm was a colonial house that was one of the show places of the county, and on the piano in the drawing-room stood signed photographs of senators, ambassadors, and one of Calvin Coolidge who had visited there during his term of office. The house had been much used for entertaining during Ed's father's time. Among the beautiful furniture that bore the patina of age, Laura felt raw and new, and she understood even less why Ed had wanted to marry her. It was his grandmother, an imposing woman past eighty, who gave her a reason.

"Joan was sloppy and emotional," she said, "—bad for Ed, and bad for his children. No discipline." She tapped the arm of her chair thoughtfully. "We have always prized discipline and thoroughness in this family."

They did not stay long in Pennsylvania because Ed was wanted back in New York. At the apartment Clare greeted them with a dutiful kiss for both, and Elizabeth with a rather gauche enthusiasm. Laura hung her clothes in the closets of Ed's bedroom—which Ed had told her she could decorate to suit herself—and wondered what was going to happen next. Her contract with Amtec had four months to run.

She finished out her contract, and went on to fund-raising committees of two charities in which Amtec was interested. She called Al Roberts to ask him if there was anything coming up on Broadway for her. She could picture him, leaning back in his chair, feet on the desk, while he laughed into the telephone.

"What do you want to keep in this rat race for?" he said. "You're in clover."

"Yes, I know—but keep looking for me, will you?"

Six months after they were married, Ed was told confidentially by E. J. that the board had selected him for the

100

job of president of the new laboratories which they had started to build at Burnham Falls, New York.

Laura was aghast. "You mean we've got to leave New York?"

Ed shrugged. "What else?" He turned to her with some irritation. "Don't you understand what this means? I'm no scientist, and I don't want to be pulled away from the centre of things here. At the same time the Board knows what a son-of-a-bitch job they've handed me. If you let a bunch of scientists loose by themselves up there, they'll play with their test tubes all day, and maybe in fifty years come up with one or two scientific curiosities. We have defence contracts to meet certain specifications, and it's my job to see that they're met, and on time. I'm to be the pressure man, and the contact man with Washington. I'm also expected to keep a finger in the new plant when they get it ready. I'm supposed to keep the lab men happy, and the military happy and Congress happy, and at the same time keep prodding to get a commercial product out of whatever the lab boys dream up for the missiles. It's a job they've handed to a lawyer, because they can't trust it to a scientist. It's a son-of-a-bitch job, and if I can make it work, I'm right in line for being President of Amtec."

Laura said hesitantly, "I asked Al Roberts to find me something on Broadway. What happens if he does?"

"Then you'll have to turn it down," he said. "You haven't time for two jobs."

CHAPTER SIX

"You'll have to have it without ice," Tom said as he handed the Scotch to Sally, "the way you were brought up to drink it by that good Irishman, Mike Brennan."

Sally smiled, and took the glass. "You should have heard the storm when Uncle Oliver came over and found Dad had Scotch in the house, instead of Irish whiskey—he ranted for ten minutes about giving profits to those bloody Imperialist English."

She rotated the liquid in the glass a little, and surveyed it with mock thoughtfulness. Then she leaned back in her chair with a small, contented sigh. "I feel wonderfully immoral being in a motel with you, Tom. It's the best thing in

101

the world for a married woman not to feel respectable with her husband for a while. It keeps a marriage from being dull."

Tom pulled the two pillows up against the headboard of one of the beds, and settled himself against them. "Dear, sweet bride," he said, shaking his head, " if you're worried about having a dull marriage after only a few months, then we're both in trouble. And as for not feeling like a respectable married woman, let me tell you that every room in this place has been solidly occupied by Amtec ever since the Laboratories got going—there's not been a woman here who wasn't respectably married to the man whose room she was in. There's one thing to be said for Amtec—it'll keep you on the straight and narrow through sheer lack of opportunity."

"There are other motels up the road . . ." Sally said sweetly.

" And Big Brother is watching you," Tom answered.

" You're the second person to-day who's said that to me. I met a local lawyer at the lunch—an old man who's lived here all his life, and who took a pretty dim view of Amtec and Amtec Park. I suppose," she added slowly, " it can be a bit hard to take something like this suddenly planked down in your front yard."

" The town needed it," Tom said. " They all admit that much, even if they all don't like it."

" Yes . . . I suppose so." She twirled her glass again, slowly. " Do you think Amtec is going to like it? . . . I mean in the end? Is it going to be a success?"

" With the millions of dollars they've poured into this place, it has to be a success. That glass factory up on the hill is going to produce results, or they'll just keep on buying more and bigger scientists until it does. And the dead wood will go quicker than you can look. That's why they've got a man like Peters riding herd on us all. From a scientist's point of view, he's strictly a know-nothing . . . but he does know what Amtec wants out of this place."

" It doesn't sound exactly . . . comfortable."

He shrugged. " Corporations aren't meant to be comfortable —but if you're a scientist you go with them, because they're the only ones with enough money to do research. That's the idea in getting all their research people together here— better communications, and quicker results."

" It must be hard for the people who came from Tulsa and Culver City to settle in . . . at least the ones from New York can run back and see the old haunts."

102

Tom shrugged. "Homesickness is about the least of their problems. The three factions seem to be staying in cliques —with the two Western ones united in their deep suspicion of the smart-aleck Easterners. Everyone'll shake down after a while, I guess. We'll have to."

Then he put his glass down on the bedside table, and punched the pillows into a more comfortable shape; there was a touch of irritability in his movement. "Hell, Sal, we've had Amtec all day. Let's kid ourselves that we left it outside the door, shall we? What have you been doing all week? . . . God, I've missed you, Sal!"

For four weeks since the Laboratories had started to function Tom had lived in the motel, going back to the apartment in New York on week-ends. He detested being separated from Sally, but since they had to start payments on the house and the new furniture, they had neither been able to afford to lose her four weeks' salary, or what it would have cost to have her stay in the motel with him. He had tried not to think too much about Sally in these weeks, because the thought of her distracted and disturbed him; but now she was close beside him, and she was staying the whole night with him, and he could let himself feast on the sight of her, the long, lovely legs slung carelessly over the side of the armchair, the skirt hitched up past the knees, the blouse pulled tightly across her full, provocative breasts. Sally's face was not beautiful, but she had a joyful, yet sensuous grace in her perfect body that endlessly fascinated him. It was an outworn, standing joke with him that she could have made the chorus line at the Latin Quarter at any time she had wanted to quit Columbia. They had been married only a few months after she had graduated with honours in English Lit. Tom was very proud of Sally.

A teasing smile started slowly on her lips. "Well—I like that! '—What have you been doing all week?' Let me tell you, Tom Redmond . . . I quit my job last Friday, my husband was home all week-end, and was no help at all—and ever since then I've been packing books, and wrapping things up in newspaper ready for the boxes, and then not being able to remember what's inside." She extended her arms in a long stretch which made him want to go over to her. "It was like leaving off work to carry bricks."

'Sal—has it been rotten for you? I should have come down . . ."

"Fool! As if I can't wrap a few plates without breaking
103

up." She smiled fully at him. "I'll tell you what I *did* do, though. Before I wrapped the plates I decided to ask Marge and Dick over for supper, and then Pat came, and she brought that artist boy-friend of hers, Sam—you remember him, don't you? We stuffed ourselves on spaghetti, and we had two bottles of wine, and they felt sorry for me because that would be my last non-Company party, and I told them I was sorry for *them* because they weren't moving to Burnham Falls."

He was suddenly contrite, as he looked at her gay, laughing face. "Sal, you're sure you don't mind—this place—well, it's all right, but there won't be Marge and Pat, and all the rest of them."

"And do Marge and Pat and whoever the rest of them are make up a life? . . . There are always people, Tom—plenty of people. That's one of my problems. I've always got too many people in my life. I want more time for you . . . just quiet time with you. And I want some time to myself to get on with the novel. What better place than Burnham Falls for that?"

He looked down at his drink, savouring the pleasure that her words had given him. Sally was so popular—he still remembered the crowd that had always followed her at Columbia, perhaps drawn, as he was, by her warmth and friendliness, by her joy in whatever came her way. It made him feel exclusive and special that she wanted to spend time alone with him. And yet he felt guilty about it, as if he were depriving others of what was rare and precious.

"You think you'll be able to write here, Sal? . . . I mean, it won't be too dull?".

"Of course not! It's exactly what I need. I need to stop talking for a while, and start thinking."

She continued slowly, frowning a little. "You know, Tom, I'm learning a lot about the physical side of writing that I didn't know before. This week has been the first time that I've had whole days in which to do nothing but write . . . and when there's no deadline pressing on you, it's the hardest thing in the world to keep yourself sitting at the typewriter. You just look around the room and you can see a thousand other things that need doing. I guess I'll just have to face up to the fact that writing a book is a lot more than just making notes on it."

"You will, Sal," he said. "You've got a lot of guts."

She shrugged. "Perhaps I've only got the guts and the
104

will-power for the short things—the things that show results quickly. I've always been Sally-who-gets-things-done . . . but quickly. This could take me years, Tom—and I've only just started to realise it. It frightens me a bit."

" It wouldn't be worth doing if it didn't frighten you."

She put down her glass, stood up and came towards him. It was a slow, tentative movement, and she sought for words. " You know," she said, " there are times now when I can't remember or imagine what it was like before I had you, and times when I think that I don't deserve what I've got . . ."

" Hush, Sal . . . hush!"

She knelt beside the bed, and put her head in his lap; at once his hand reached out and began to caress the dark curling hair. Her voice was muffled when she spoke again.

" Darling, there's so much and I don't know how to say it. I love you, and we're going to have wonderful, beautiful children together . . . and there's that gorgeous new house waiting for us. You're ambitious, and I know that what you achieve is as much for me as for yourself. And still you're generous enough to want me to write because it's what I want. Dear God . . . I don't know how to say thank you."

His caressing motion grew stronger, rougher. " Sal, you know you're talking nonsense? Writing or not, I want a happy woman with me. You'll do whatever you think you have to do."

" I want to do what's right for you," she cried. " I mean . . . in everything. If the book gets in the way—if it gets between you and me, or something you want, then there'll be no book. I promise you that nothing is more important than you, Tom."

Looking down he saw that her eyes were filled with tears. " Sal, you're a crazy thing." He went over. " Come here . . . come here."

Within his arms he could feel her shaking a little, but when he kissed her, the shaking was stilled. Then he could feel the voluptuous splendour of her body as it moved against his. The response to each other was instantaneous—it had always been that way, right from the beginning. Without hesitation, and without clumsy speed he reached for the zipper at the back of her dress.

She lay very still, in the deeper stillness of the room, and
105

listened to the far-away swish of automobiles passing on the road outside. As the headlights swept the front of the motel, a repeated pattern of light fell across the venetian blinds. The early spring dusk had come, and had strengthened to darkness. She had no idea how long she had slept—it could have been minutes or hours. Beside her, Tom was also still, his breathing heavy and regular. As they had slept, their naked bodies had stayed close to each other, as if, even with their passion exhausted and consummated, they still could not bear the wrench of a physical parting. They lay so close, their bodies curled into each other with the grace and ease of animals, that there was room to spare in the bed. Sally pulled the blanket a little closer about Tom's shoulder, her eyes wide open in the friendly darkness; she savoured the sound of his breathing, the sense of peace and love and confidence. She felt that she should pray, or do something like it, because there had to be some way, some positive action, by which she could express this happiness.

She knew only the habit she had been taught all her life. . . . " Holy Mother—thank you." Whenever there had been joy or grief in the Brennan family, they had always prayed together, her father mostly out of respect for her mother's piety, the children because they did as they were told. She remembered all the events of the family history that had been marked off by those rosaries—the wedding anniversaries, the First Communion, the graduations. Sally also remembered the time her father had refused to pray with her, or to talk to her. That had been the time when Johnny Ryan had asked her to marry him, and she had said no. Her mother had come into her room and said quietly, " We'll just kneel and say a few decades, Sal . . . you must give your father time to get over his anger. He had his heart set on it you know."

She did know, and she wondered sometimes how she had had the courage to turn down Johnny, how she had been so very sure, even then, that there had to be someone like Tom for her, that there had to be more than the admiration and liking Johnny Ryan could attract from almost everyone he knew. Of course Mike had had his heart set on it; the marriage would have made him proud, would have been firmly along the lines of the tradition of the Irish in America. This was something her father cherished even more than the material benefits the marriage of his daughter to Johnny Ryan would have brought.

106

Mike had lived all his life under the influence of his older brother, Oliver, who had received a prison term, and almost a death sentence for his part in the Easter Rising of 1916. This gave him a special, honoured place in the eyes of his countrymen, and in Mike he inspired awe and profound respect. When he was released from prison he published the verses, written in the Gaelic, he had composed there. Then he became for Mike the embodiment of the shining, romantic qualities of the soldier-poet, a boy's hero who was appropriately worshipped. Oliver stayed behind when his parents and Mike emigrated to America. He stayed behind and spent his life in service to the Government of De Valera, and to the hope of the reunification of Ireland. For a time he had been Minister without portfolio, had been a prime mover in the drive to get tourist trade to Ireland, and he had continued to write and publish poetry. Two volumes of his poems had been translated and published in New York. It was the idealised image of his brother which Mike had striven to live up to all his life, an image which had also, in a sense, shaped the lives of Mike's children.

The Brennans had settled in Brooklyn, and Mike had been apprenticed to the printing trade. His unfulfilled need to follow Oliver's example had led him naturally towards the Democratic Party, and his trade had been useful to them. He not only printed for them, but gradually learned the whole business of party propaganda, and since the Democratic sweep of the thirties he had held full-time jobs for the Party. He knew he was a faithful, but only a small cog in the wheel; but it was the best he could do for Oliver. His greatest pride was still in his brother's achievements.

If Sally had married Johnny Ryan the marriage would have been something Mike could have offered to Oliver. Johnny's father was high in the list of City officials, a man who had made money before being invited into the administration and so could afford to play the political game with some dignity; Johnny himself was a famous quarter-back on the Notre-Dame team. In Mike's eyes, there could have been no better marriage for Sally.

The Brennans lived in a Brooklyn apartment that was too crowded by the six children that had been born to Eileen and Mike; they were a boisterous, talkative, sentimental family—ambitious, and a little more hard-working than most of their neighbours. Four of the children went to college—not glamorously or easily, but by scholarships, by working

107

during the vacations, and by reason of the unnatural frugality Mike and Eileen practised.

Mike had genuinely grieved when Sally had turned down Johnny Ryan, and he had looked with suspicious, unfavourable eyes on Tom Redmond. He had been hardly reconciled to the thought of Sally marrying Tom by the time of the wedding, the time that Tom's people had come up from Houston, and the time that Oliver had made his first visit to the United States.

Tom's father was a judge of the Texas Supreme Court, a scholarly man whose Southern accent had been clipped only a little by his attendance at a Northern college.

Beside Johnny Ryan, Tom seemed a nonentity—his first-class honours in physics from Georgia Tech seemed pallid beside the fame of Johnny Ryan, his humble job in Amtec was nothing to what Johnny, propelled by his father, might attain. . . . Congress, the Senate, the State Governorship. Tom had been recruited for Amtec straight off the campus of Georgia Tech, and had been doing post-graduate work, his course paid for by Amtec, at Columbia, when he had met Sally. The fact that Tom had already got his Ph.D. meant almost nothing to Mike.

She knew afterwards that the memorable thing about her wedding for Mike had been Oliver's presence at it. He was certainly enough to overshadow any bride. He was in New York on the first stage of a lecture tour through the States, and his business was to drum up publicity for the Irish tourist trade. He looked as an Irish poet and revolutionary hero should have looked—tall and bony, with careless, beautiful tweeds; Sally privately considered him a superb showman, and she loved him because he understood within minutes how it was between her and Tom.

Sally had moved into Tom's apartment down in the village —the one-room apartment that had a view of the Hudson. She had taken a job, with the New York Public Library, a temporary one because they already knew that in the spring Tom would be moved to Burnham Falls. Sometimes on Sundays Sally would go over to Brooklyn to meet her father and go with him to the midday Mass, and Tom would be waiting for them outside the church when it was over; they would walk back to the Brennan apartment for Sunday dinner. Seeing the happiness in Sally's face, Mike came to give an unwilling kind of respect to Tom. When she talked of writing, he listened approvingly, thinking of Oliver; Tom's pride in Sally was obvious.

In the kitchen, her mother, basting the roast, said thoughtfully to Sally, " You've got the right man, Sal. There can't be two peacocks in the one family—and he'll let you strut and show off to your heart's content."

Sally protested. " I don't want to show off—I want to write!"

Eileen gave her a long look. " And what else is writing, may I ask?"

In the darkness of the motel room, Sally heard those words again, and her arms tightened a little about Tom. She had got the right man—sane, and wise and calm. She felt a small, loving world of security close about her, and she lay and thought about the empty house that stood waiting for them.

CHAPTER SEVEN

On Main Street the darkness of the spring evening was cold. The budding elms thrust gaunt branches towards a cold, brilliant sky. The warmth of the day had gone completely with the sun. The street was almost deserted; those who lingered there looked as if they had no particular reason for hurrying home. It was the dinner hour, close to seven o'clock; most of the stores were closed, the single lights in their windows seemed blank and stark. The wind whipped in coldly from the lake.

Behind the cosmetic counter of Carter's drug store, Jeannie Talbot shifted from one foot to the other, her eyes on the wall clock with the ancient spotted face that was so incongruous beside all the recently installed modern fittings. Then she turned aside, picked up her duster, and once more wiped over the already spotless surface of the counter. She looked with pride at the display of bottles and jars, tinted the delicate pastel shades that were the trade marks of the manufacturers, at the gleaming gold lipstick cases and compacts. She enjoyed the world of fantasy that surrounded cosmetics, which was probably why she was an able saleswoman of them. Every afternoon she came here from school to preside over this counter during the busy hours,

109

to make patient, helpful suggestions while her own class-mates took an agonising length of time to choose a shade of lipstick, or, when an older woman was her customer, to slip into the sales talk she had memorised from the advertisements. She had learned tact and persuasion ; when she held a jar of cream in her hand and told them what it promised, they looked at her own glowing, youthful skin and they believed her. On her advice Wally Carter had even taken to stocking two of the more expensive brands, and they were now selling at least as well as the others. Jeannie had reminded him that with the new families coming into Amtec Park he had got to start thinking about a different class of customer, and that he'd better make up his mind to stock a few of the famous makes of perfume. Wally grumbled, but he did what she said.

Jeannie now laid aside the duster ; she had five minutes still to go. She made one last notation in her order book, and closed it with a little snap. Technically it was Wally who still gave the actual orders to the salemen, but a number of them were now calling in the hours Jeannie was in the store whenever they had a new product to introduce ; she liked the small sense of importance this gave her.

When the clock pointed to seven, Jeannie went in past the dispensing rooms, to the room at the back. She took her coat and scarf off the hanger and put them on. " Good night, Mr. Carter," she said as she passed the dispensing bench again.

" Good night, Jeannie. Take care. . . ."

There was only one customer in the store—a man she had never seen—sitting at the soda counter sipping his coffee as if he didn't want to go out again into the cold. She nodded a good night to Benny, the counter man.

" 'Night, Jeannie." He paused a second in refilling the coffee urn to watch her go.

Outside, she instinctively pulled her coat closer against the cold. As she stepped out into the street, Jerry Keston turned from the display of men's clothing he had been studying in the next-door window.

" Hi, Jeannie."

" Hi." They fell into step together naturally. " Why didn't you come inside? It's cold out here."

He shrugged and grinned. " What would I do? Buy a lipstick?"

Two or three times a week she found him waiting outside

110

Carter's when she was finished. They always walked together back to her house near the shellac plant. They were in the same class at the Burnham Falls High School, and would be graduating together in June.

To-night they walked for some way in companionable silence, halting at the traffic light, listening to the crash of gears as Abel Morris' jeep changed down on the hill. They were opposite the dignified, two-story building of the First National Bank as they crossed.

"Dad must have gone home," Jerry said. "His light was on when I passed."

Jeannie glanced back at the unlighted bank windows. "I wonder what it feels like to be alone in the bank—shut up with all that money. Kind of scary, I'd think."

"Well, I'll soon know, won't I?" he replied. "I've got to start in to work there right after graduation."

"What about the camping trip? . . . Won't he let you? . . ."

Jerry gave an exaggerated sigh. "Not a hope. He says I've got to get a full summer in the bank under my belt before I start college. He's all up in the air about the Amtec Laboratories getting started and all the new people coming in . . . says he heard rumours that the Carlisle bank is opening up here, and he wants as much new business as he can get settled with First National before that happens. I'm supposed to learn all about it in a couple of months. . . ." His tone was a dull, resentful acceptance of the fact. At the moment he could see nothing ahead but the four years of college, with each vacation spent under the eye of his father at the bank. He had an air of masculine grievance about him that was very appealing. Jeannie slipped her hand through his arm, and squeezed it gently.

"Never mind—you'll have some time off. There's lots to do."

"You bet!" he said, suddenly regaining enthusiasm. "I made him promise that I could have the car whenever I wanted it this summer . . . and he's just about promised that he'll let me have my own when I go to college if I stick it out at the bank. We'll be able to take trips to New York, Jeannie—see the sights. You'll like that, won't you?"

"Oh . . . sure!" she said, a trifle uncertainly. "You mean Times Square, and all that sort of thing."

"What's wrong with Times Square? It's sure a change from Main Street! Look, Jeannie, I'll take you to some
111

ritzy restaurants . . . I'll be earning pretty good money. . . ."

The thought of the long car rides on the summer evenings was beguiling, but she didn't know if she quite liked the idea of the expensive restaurants. She didn't have the right clothes. But Jerry sounded happier now, and that was good. She tightened her hold on his arm a little; they were deep within the shadows of the tree-lined street that led down to the shellac plant. The houses had started to straggle out, with gaps between them. The railroad track came close to the road here. They passed two more houses and reached the edge of the vacant land that spread down the hill from the new laboratories. The small lake glinted dully under the stars. A few hundred yards farther on was the newly painted shellac factory, and a little beyond that was the small white frame house where the Talbots lived. The road curved here, and the Laboratories came into view.

"Gee!" Jeannie said. "They've got it lit up! I've never noticed that before!"

"To-night's the first night. I don't suppose they wanted to do it before the official opening. They're going to light it up every night. Awful waste of electricity!"

Jeannie halted to stand and stare at it. The glass building was lighted from inside—a long, glowing bar of light in the surrounding darkness, a steely, cold light, impersonal and aloof. At first it attracted her, made her think of the shining clean jars and bottles she handled at Carter's.

"It's . . . it's just like those photos in magazines," she breathed, suddenly in awe of the place.

"Dad says they're going to light the fountains too, when they get them in place." They stood together in the deserted road, staring upwards. "Dad knows every single thing that happens in that place almost before they know it themselves. I think he dreams about Amtec at night."

Then the lights of an oncoming car swept across them, and the spell was broken. They started walking again.

"Dad told me to-day that that character he's always talking about—that Mal Hamilton—is coming back to Burnham Falls to do some work for Amtec. Gee, you'd think it was Dad's long-lost brother the way he talked about it."

Jeannie nodded. The story of Mal Hamilton's career in Burnham Falls was familiar to her, although he was gone from the place before she had been born. There had been something about Mal that stuck in people's minds, and it was true that George Keston had never let anyone about

112

him forget. Jerry had been brought up on the saga of Mal Hamilton—how he had fought prejudice and poverty, and got to college without help from anyone. He had heard it all so often that he thoroughly disliked the sound of the other's name. Every time his father uttered it, it was a reproach for Jerry's own comfortable living, the ease with which things came to him. He moved his shoulders irritably, as if shrugging off the thought, and he suddenly spoke out his discontent.

"I tell you, Jeannie, I'd like to get out of this place!"

"Why . . . Jerry, what do you mean?"

"Well, hell! The way Dad's planning it, I'll be here in Burnham Falls for the rest of my life. That sounds great, doesn't it? When I go into the Army I might be lucky enough to be sent as far as New Jersey, and that'll be that! I mean I don't want to come home from college and settle down to exactly the same sort of life Dad has had. . . ."

Jeannie broke in. "Now you listen to me, Jerry Keston!" She pulled on his arm roughly, urgently. "You're a fool to talk like this! You've got to have an education before you can go anywhere or do anything. Maybe when you've finished with the Army you'll be glad to come back here— maybe you won't. You can't blame your father for hoping. . ."

"Well, don't *you* want to go?" he demanded.

"Away from Burnham Falls? Not very much—and not for good. I like it here. It's comfortable."

"You're not kidding, Jeannie?"

She glanced sideways at him; he was tall, but so was she, and their gaze was almost level. "Of course I'm not kidding! I'm going to learn shorthand and typing over at Elmbury this summer, and Mr. Dexter said he thinks he can get me a job with Amtec in the fall."

"Well, don't you want to try a slice of life somewhere else?"

"Where? . . . New York, for instance? You can keep that! I'd have a routine little job like millions of other girls, for which I'd have to dress like a fashion model every day—and pay those sky-high rents for some pokey little apartment. Do you think I haven't thought about it? In my book, Burnham Falls has got enough of what I want."

"Gee, Jeannie, a smart, pretty girl like you is wasted in a . . ."

"Maybe I'm smart enough to know what I want." Her
113

voice had an edge to it, a coldness; she was defending something she loved, and she was too young not to feel ruffled by Jerry's accusation that she was dull and unadventurous, that she was too conventional to make use of her own talents. Whatever she dreamed of in her idle moments, dreams that took her far from Burnham Flats, she recognised them as such.

She was looking straight ahead, turning an angry profile to Jerry. Her hand dropped away from his arm. Then she felt his gentle touch on her shoulder as he swung her to face him.

"Jeannie, I'm sorry . . . honestly, I'm sorry. I didn't mean to upset you. It's nice to know you like being here, and you don't want to rush off and be a film star, or Miss America . . . and all that junk. It's going to make a whole lot of difference to me having you around."

She stretched up and put her arms about his neck. Their kiss was a mutual clinging together in the face of an uncertain future. They were young, and their bodies needed the comfort and security of each other; they kissed with a desperate, lonely kind of passion, a kiss that started as a gesture of affection, and then as it lengthened, grew to a full and complete enjoyment of the act itself. In the shadow of the trees, they clung to each other very tightly, shaken a little with the urgency and tumult of youth.

Jeannie flung open the door, and a rush of cold air swept into the kitchen. Her mother was frying something in a spluttering pan at the stove, a long fork in one hand, and a pot holder in the other. Chrissie was sitting in a faded flannel nightgown at the table, her golden head bent over a picture book.

Jeannie closed the door quickly. "Hi, Mom!" She stooped and gave her sister a quick hug and dropped a kiss on her rounded, silken cheek. "How's my pink baby rabbit?" she said. Then she called in a louder voice to the front room. "Hi, Dad! I'm home!"

She was shining and flushed, and transformed into sheer beauty. Her mother glanced back over her shoulder.

"Hallo, dear. Take your things off now—we're just ready to sit down."

114

II

George Keston had flicked off the light switch and was fumbling for the right key on his ring when he saw Jeannie Talbot and Jerry standing at the traffic light opposite the bank. He waited where he was in the darkness until they had moved off; he had a rather embarrassed relationship with his son, and he had never learned to treat lightly the fact that all teen-agers had romances before they left school. Rather than meet them, and hear himself make foolish conversation with Jeannie, he waited until they had crossed the road and passed out of sight.

He knew it was not Jerry's fault but they were so inarticulate with each other; it was supposed to be the father who was mature and experienced enough to make the overtures. But in his case the overtures, fumbling and uncertain, had never worked. He was too old to be Jerry's father. He had not married till he was past forty, and Jerry had come late in the marriage and had been his only child. He was aware of his failure, and the thought depressed him.

It was not that Jerry showed any lack in his development. He was everything a man could have wanted in a son—intelligent, quick and courteous, and the captain of the football team—the ideal of the American boy. And he was tall and good looking, with blond, sun-streaked hair, and a tan that did not fade even in winter. His body was tough and co-ordinated. George Keston wondered how he and his frail wife had come to have such a child. At times he felt humble before Jerry.

All of Burnham Falls knew that Jerry had been dating Jeannie Talbot steadily for a year. It was natural that they should have chosen each other; it seemed to George that they were so outstandingly superior to the other young people about them. Jeannie was a superb physical specimen; you did not expect a girl like that to have brains—and yet she did. If you got tired of looking at Jeannie, George Keston thought it would be nice to talk to her.

But he worried a little about Jerry's friendship with Jeannie. It was possible that when he was through college he might marry her—he didn't even permit himself to think that it might happen before then. The objections George had to Jeannie were hardly real, tangible ones. Her background and family,

115

of course, wouldn't exactly help Jerry, but there were no reasons except snobbish ones why they should hinder him, either. Ted Talbot was one of Burnham Falls' most respected men—not for what he had accomplished in life, but purely as a human being. He was a good man, kind and generous with what little he had, and his wife and children were decent and hard-working and clean—and no one could say less than that of them. It was Jeannie herself who bothered George. She didn't look as if she came from a family like the Talbots—she looked ripe and easy, a voluptuous blonde with curving hips and breasts, and a sensuous sway in her walk. It was not what she did that so much worried him, it was that she was a person who would always attract talk and notice to her, in the way most women did not.

George knew he could not tell Jerry not to date Jeannie just because she was pretty, and because she attracted men. If Jerry could get a girl like that, he was entitled to her. There were no other reasonable objections to her—she had never dated anyone before Jerry, and she had never been seen in a parked car during the high school dances. People spoke of her as "a nice girl." George knew he was being unfair to her, but she had a healthy, abundant sensuality that would have made any man uneasy.

But there was nothing he was going to do about it. He wanted to keep his son; he wanted Jerry to succeed to his position at First National, he wanted him to have the safe, tidy life that he, George, had always had in Burnham Falls. Perhaps Jeannie Talbot would be the instrument for keeping him here; if she could do that, George would never question anything else about her.

He pulled the door behind him, and double locked it. He felt cold as he backed the car out of the lot and drove along Main Street. He was getting old, he thought—or was it just that it had been a crowded day? The big white banner flapping in the wind reminded him that it had been crowded with many unusual happenings. It would be a long time before Burnham Falls forgot the day that Amtec came to town.

116

BOOK TWO

CHAPTER ONE

Burnham Falls grew accustomed to having the Laboratories and Amtec Park in its midst, in just the way it had grown used to the construction camp, the itinerant workers, and the new name on the shellac factory. It had its big row over the site of the new school, and that was settled, not to everyone's satisfaction, but at least settled. Things started to cost a little more in Burnham Falls because there was a bigger demand for services and goods; at the same time more money flowed into the town. As in a marriage the first enchantment fell away, and Amtec and Burnham Falls settled to finding a working relationship with each other; there were compromises each way. Neither side was wholly winning.

Harriet had been very much involved in the external hustle of that first year of Amtec; she was conscious of being expected to stand on both sides of the line in every dispute that came up. She had been part of the school problem, the water supply problem, the road construction problem—these were the every-day things of her life. And at the back of that, in the quiet place that no external thing seemed to touch, she was waiting for Mal Hamilton to return to Burnham Falls. She was waiting for the day, and dreading it. Steve mentioned him from time to time—there was one delay after another in reaching the phase of the work on which he would be needed as consultant; then Steve didn't mention him any more, and Harriet began to believe that the idea of bringing him to Burnham Falls had been shelved. She didn't want to ask about it; it seemed better not to know.

And Laura Peters was waiting for something else; she was waiting for the day when she would cease to feel a resentment against the routine of life in Burnham Falls. She was waiting for the sense of panic to pass, the sense that she was wasting time. She did what she had to as the wife of the President of Amtec Laboratories, but no more. Her thoughts and interests still turned to New York. As she waited out the days in Burnham Falls she felt as if she were on a long, enforced convalescence there, and that soon someone would

117

come and tell her she could return. She was still hoping for Al Roberts to find her a part in a Broadway production.

Jeannie Talbot finished her business course at Elmbury, but she did not take the job with Amtec which Steve offered to arrange for her. Instead she went full time into Wally Carter's drug store, and she worked for a salary and commission. This was done in spite of the objections of her father, who thought that she was too clever to lose herself behind a drug store counter. But Jeannie had her own plans, and she listened with only half an ear. During the first year that Jerry was away at college, she spent most of her evenings studying book-keeping. Selma began to urge her to have more dates with other boys and she sometimes thought privately that four years was too long for Jeannie to wait for Jerry. George Keston was happy that she seemed content to wait. And as for Jeannie herself, she kept her plan in mind, and said nothing much to anyone.

And the first year in Burnham Falls went by Sally Redmond almost unnoticed, because she was happy.

II

The 4.25 express from New York to Derwent made a stop at Burnham Falls, and it was the only train of the afternoon worth catching. As the platform gates crashed open, Harriet quickened her pace towards them; there was already a crowd waiting to board the train, and as always the old hands who had found their way in by one of the open gates farther along the concourse would already be seated. She walked down the ramp quickly, following the crowd. Her nostrils contracted a little at the acrid, bitter smell that always met one at this point; she associated the smell with a sense of regret, the knowledge that it was the end of a New York visit. In the old days she had preferred driving back to Burnham Falls rather than taking the train—the act of leaving the city was more drawn out, less final and complete.

Harriet stepped into the third coach, and as she struggled with the heavy door and two dress boxes, she heard Laura Peters' voice behind her.

"Harriet! Here, let me. I'm not so loaded." An immaculately gloved hand reached past her and pushed open the door.

For a second Laura's perfume shut away all other smells.

It was the middle of June, and the temperature stood near ninety, yet she looked cool and unweary, as if it were the beginning of the day rather than the end.

"Oh! Thank you!" Harriet passed through the door, and waited for Laura to follow. They had ridden together on the 4.25 a number of times; Laura seemed to welcome Harriet's company. They talked of nothing in particular, idle women's talk of shopping and fashions, books, the theatre—but never, Harriet had noticed, about Burnham Falls. Harriet had learned to let Laura choose what she would talk about; it was one of the small courtesies paid to the president's wife.

She waited now for Laura to select the seat. There were only two other people in the coach.

Laura frowned. "The air-conditioning doesn't seem to be working. Let's go on to the next one—in any case, this isn't a smoker." She strode down the long aisle, and opened the farther door before Harriet could reach it. Harriet saw that she also was carrying a dress box, but it didn't seem to hamper her movements at all.

"You've been shopping too," Harriet said, rather pointlessly.

"Yes—and had my hair done," Laura answered. It was already well known in Burnham Falls that Laura went to New York every week just to have her hair done—in any case, the fact spoke for itself. Harriet nodded in approval as she studied the back of the other's head.

Laura glanced over her shoulder. "I picked up a dress from Bergdorf's that was being altered—I don't let them send things any more. If there's something wrong it's such a nuisance bringing it back."

Harriet understood why Laura's tone sounded aggrieved; it was the difference between the box travelling sixty miles and six city blocks. It epitomised the petty annoyances and frustrations a woman like Laura would find in country living. "I've discovered," Laura said, in a rare moment of bluntness, "that you can have everything in Burnham Falls that you have in New York—but it's just a little more difficult." Then she checked herself. "Of course, there are compensations . . ." she added quickly.

The next coach was the club car; it was already more than half full. Harriet still followed Laura, hoping she would quickly choose her seat and sit down; she could feel the weariness of the city pavements in her whole body, the

119

struggle against the heat, the determination to get through a whole day's shopping before train time. She felt ragged at the edges, her nerves too tight, and craving relief. She wished now that Laura would decide on the club car; it would be wonderful to sit and sip a long drink gently. Harriet half-opened her mouth to suggest it, and then, with great deliberation, made herself remain silent. It was hard to keep remembering that she could no longer do exactly what she wanted in matters like these.

Laura stopped in front of one of the tables, and put her box on the floor. Harriet sighed with relief. For a second she hardly felt the hand that reached out and took her arm, giving it a little, urgent shake.

"Harriet!"

She knew the voice; she believed she had forgotten it, but it was there, as familiar as a part of her everyday life, belonging to her, and well-remembered. She turned slowly, reluctantly.

"Mal . . ."

He got to his feet. She hadn't forgotten, either, how tall he was—as tall as Steve. She looked up into his face, that ugly-attractive face, too harsh and closed still, the blue eyes alert and shrewd; she looked at him, and all her careful preparations for this moment were suddenly vanished.

"I . . ." she began helplessly. "They told me you were coming, Mal. It's good to see you."

Her voice was all right, she decided—but toneless, too dead. He would know what was wrong with her, of course, and perhaps he would think her unsophisticated because she couldn't play this scene better. But why did it have to be here, unexpectedly, in the midst of strangers? In all the months of picturing how their first meeting would be, she had never seen it quite as bad as this. She was completely off-balance, stupid with weariness and, now, this terrible sense of panic. It was thirteen years since she had laid eyes on Mal Hamilton, and now they stood next to each other, like every-day commuters, on the 4.25 from Grand Central.

"It's been a long time." Hearing his ordinary, conventional words, she knew that he had been shocked also, and the tight evenness of his face was disturbed.

"Sit down, Harriet!" he said suddenly. "For God's sake,, sit down!" She experienced the intense familiarity of him again—here was his old, peremptory impatience, his refusal to stay long in the mould of convention. They were not

120

strangers, and never would be. He lifted his hat and brief-case from the seat beside him. "Here! Sit Down!"

She could have smiled at him then—Mal, who hadn't changed very much. But she shook her head. "I'm sorry, I can't . . . I'm with someone."

"Oh, to hell with that! You can see her some other time. Tell her you met an old friend."

"It isn't quite as easy as that, Mal. She's Laura Peters—married to Steve's boss."

He looked at her closely. "Does it matter?"

She nodded. "Yes, it does. I'm sorry, Mal—but it does." She gestured clumsily, impeded by the boxes. "You know these things well enough, Mal. It *does* matter."

He shrugged. "All right, then. I'll join you. She can't object to that, since I suppose I'm working for Amtec too."

Harriet ran her tongue over the dry lips. Suddenly the air-conditioning seemed too chill; the weariness was in her bones and she felt that she couldn't continue this fight with herself for the next hour and twenty minutes until the train pulled into Burnham Falls. "I wish you wouldn't do that," she said quietly. "As you said, it's been a long time. . . . I need a breathing space to get used to it."

"You've had all the time you'll ever have to get used to it," he said roughly. "I'm here, Harriet—and that's all there is to it." He jerked his head towards the end of the car, where Laura had seated herself and was looking at them. "Mrs. Peters seems to be waiting. . . ."

Harriet was afraid that her uneasiness was too visible as she introduced Mal to Laura, but he took over for her, and covered her silence with his own talk. He put Laura's box and Harriet's two on the rack, along with his hat and brief-case, settled himself in the seat between them, and ordered drinks. The pause gave Harriet a chance; she took several deep breaths, and felt the tightness in her throat relax some-what. It was almost like a return to life after it had stopped momentarily. She hoped that her face and voice were more normal now, that Laura would put her silence down to fatigue.

But she saw then she almost need not have worried. The drinks arived, and the event hardly interrupted the talk between Laura and Mal. She realised that this did not seem strange to Laura; she was accustomed to taking the full attention of most men she encountered, but it went further than that, for Laura was plainly interested in what Mal was saying, and in him as a person.

121

" . . . and this is the first time," Mal was saying, "that I've been to Burnham Falls since before the war.'" He added, smiling a little, " Now I'm working as a very expensive consultant for your husband's company, Mrs. Peters."

" And are you worth it?" Laura said.

" I make them believe I am.".

She laughed, throwing back her head a little in that strangely graceful way she had. " Well—good for you! They'll always pay for what they believe."

Harriet cleared her throat then, and said quickly, " I think a lot of people believe what you say, Mal. I've been reading about you over the years . . . *Fortune* and *Time* . . ."

He looked pleased. " I have a good public relations man."

Laura leaned across to look at Harriet. " Have you two known each other long?"

Mal spoke for her. " The last summer I was in Burnham Falls Harriet was still in high school, and I was feeling the weight of my Ph.D. Then Steve and I were in the same outfit during the war . . . we were doing research in a lab at U.C.L.A. Harriet came out to be with Steve, and she had a job at Lockheed . . ."

The talk went on, but for Harriet it had stopped at " a job at Lockheed." He had said it, had spoken of it, naturally and calmly. They had not looked at each other's face since that morning they had sat outside the drive-in, and read in the newspaper about Hiroshima ; she had been afraid to bring that memory out clearly, but he had done it for her. By preference he had told her that it was with him too. What kind of a memory it was for him, tender or bitter, she could not tell. She began to pay strict attention to him then, to search for indications of what the years between had been to him.

Superficially she knew what they had been. Mal had been very successful in what he had chosen to do, which was, in effect, to play a lone hand and steer clear of complete commitment to any one company. The early years must have been hard ones, Harriet thought . . . the waiting to be called in as consultant on technical problems and turning down the offers to remain permanently with the company, maintaining an office and staff in the hope that they would be needed, keeping the contacts open with the experts in the different fields while still not able to bring work to them. But he had held out somehow, and it had paid off. His main office was

122

still in Los Angeles, but there was now a small New York office. He had kept his success on his own terms. Within certain loose limits, he was free to do as he wanted—which was why he talked to Laura as if she was a woman first, and not only the wife of the president of an Amtec subsidiary.

"Exactly what is a consultant supposed to do?" Laura had taken a cigarette from the case Mal offered to her and Harriet, and she was bent a little towards him now as he lighted it.

"Well—he never knows until he gets to see the problem. Mostly what I do is look over the project, think of all the companies and individuals who've done work along those lines, and go and buy some information from them—for which I charge firms like Amtec twice as much."

"You're much too honest," Laura said.

He shook his head. "The funny thing is that the more I disclose of my methods of gathering information, the less I'm believed. No one thinks for a moment that I'm telling the truth. No single man could possibly have time or opportunity to go deep into all the projects I'm asked to look over. My main concern is to know who *does* know."

"Have you done work for Amtec before?"

"Yes—in Culver City and Tulsa—some in New York. I've been working with them on and off for years."

"What do you do when it's ' off '?"

"When no one wants to pay for my services I take myself off to South America, or Europe or Africa . . . or try to persuade someone that they need me to work there. I once spent four months in Venezuela getting paid barely more than my keep in a second-rate hotel. But I thought it was worth it. . . ."

"Are you married, Mr. Hamilton? What does your wife think of all this?"

"I'm not married."

He was not exactly as he had been thirteen years ago. A few more of the sharp edges had worn away ; he kept his direct, no-nonsense manner, but he was more subtle with it. It was the relaxation of a man who has been successful, who can now afford not to hit so hard to make his point. He was used to women—the way he talked to Laura told Harriet that. She did not cherish any foolish thought that he had remained faithful to the memory of what they had been and said to each other thirteen years ago. He could never have known, as she had not, that one day they would sit

123

together in the 4.25 for Burnham Falls, and even if he had known, it would have been no reason for a man like Mal to keep aloof from other women. He had been a lot of places in the world, and he carried the aura and tang of it; he was attractive—she knew now that he was very attractive to women. His gaunt, rugged face was the stamp of the life he led. He was not cast of the mould of the conventional world, and you knew, just by looking at him, that if the conventional world had not given him success, he would have found his own form of it in Brazil or the Belgian Congo, or the middle of Australia. It was this quality in his face and speech and movements that made Laura fix her eyes on him in absorbed attention, that made Harriet recall vividly that incredible car drive into the desert, the manner of his taking her. There was no fumbling with Mal —he was sure, and quick, and needle-sharp.

He glanced at Harriet. "Europe gave me some of that culture you were always urging on me." Then he turned to explain to Laura. "Harriet used to worry because back before the war I never took my nose out of a lab long enough to read a book or look at a piece of sculpture. Later I took time . . . for that and a lot of other things I hadn't been able to afford before. But I found the farther from civilisation the statues and paintings, the more primitive, the better I like them. I'm really not much for standing in a gallery in Florence "

He continued to talk, keeping Laura's attention away from Harriet. They had a second drink, and outside the windows the city had given way to the long spread of the suburbs and the commuter towns. Harriet registered the normal things of this trip—the supermarkets, the cluster of stores about each station, the flow of traffic on the highways, the early-evening exodus, the cars in long lines in the shimmering heat. This was normal, but Mal's presence here was not. Hungrily, carefully, she took in each detail of him—his clothes were expensive, and not too new; he wore them with ease. The scuffed brief-case on the rack above was made of coach hide. It pleased her that he had learned to carry material success well, but not too obviously. It hardly seemed possible that this was Charlie Hamilton's son, this assured man holding with such ease the interest of a beautiful, restless woman. Mal must know that the eyes of every man in the coach had rested on Laura with approval and admiration; and he also knew that so far she had not looked away from him.

Outside the windows there was open grazing to be seen now, and some orchards. They were coming close to Burnham Falls.

That Harriet thought was what thirteen years had done with Mal. And herself—what had he seen when he had looked up at her coming along the coach? A hot, rather crumpled woman, with a nose shiny from the heat, a dispirited housewife, energy drained from her walk on the burning pavements, carrying the awkward dress boxes and her gloves clutched in a ball in her hand. But it was worse than that—he had witnessed her fumble this situation when she should have been ready for it, seen the way she had left him to carry a conversation with Laura while she sat here in stupid silence, twisting her glass slowly, and watching the moisture condense in damp rings on the table. He must have known, in that very first minute, what thirteen years had done to her. She felt the tight ache in her throat again, a sense of failure and disappointment in herself.

Far up ahead she heard the whistle blow as the diesel approached the level-crossing on the outskirts of Burnham Falls.

They got off the train together, Mal now carrying the suitcase he had left in the rack at the end of the coach. Mal said nothing as they walked along the platform. Harriet was trying to see it with his eyes, and yet she knew there would not be too much changed in this part of town, and in any case, Mal had seen too much change, had been part of too much change himself, to feel any surprise in it. Here were the lake, and the courthouse, the old churches and the new one, the old stores with the new fronts, and the new neon signs. The big changes in Burnham Falls were not immediately obvious. Then she wondered painfully if he had not got his first intimation of change when he had looked at her.

"Where are you staying, Mr. Hamilton?" Laura asked. "Could I give you a lift?"

"Thank you—but I'm picking up a rental car from Morton's. I'll be staying at a motel over on Route 40. I'm only here for three nights this trip."

They were standing by the parking lot, where Laura's

125

Thunderbird seemed to dominate all the other cars. Laura turned to Harriet. " No need to take a taxi . . . I'll drop you by your house."

" Oh . . . please don't bother. It's out of your way."

" No bother at all," Laura said, and her tone settled the matter. " It'll only take a few minutes."

Harriet got herself into the front seat with Laura, but she seemed to herself to be hardly part of the scene. The usual things went on, Laura settling herself at the driver's seat, Mal stowing the boxes in the back. She heard her own voice telling Mal to come over to the house, and thinking that he probably wouldn't. Then Laura raised her gloved hand in a brief salute, and they were out of the parking lot. Harriet glanced behind her as they started along Main Street, and Mal was still standing there, astride the suitcase, his hat pushed a little to the back of his head, staring after them. She felt a great sense of loneliness.

When the Thunderbird had finally disappeared, Mal picked up his suitcase, and started to cross the road. It was about ten degrees cooler here than in New York. There was activity around the station—the arrival of cars to pick up passengers from the 4.25, the efforts of the owners of the two taxi services to fill up their cabs before sending them out. The school summer vacation had started, and the street was crowded with young people—girls in shorts swinging their pony-tails as they walked, boys in T-shirts. Carter's drug store was remodelled, Mal noticed. He glanced inside, thinking about buying some cigarettes, and maybe finding someone he recognised ; the soda fountain was lined with teen-agers. He walked on. He knew none of the faces of the people he passed—the young matrons in sleeveless cotton dresses, the men with sports shirts out over their pants. He passed the courthouse, and then suddenly he turned and retraced his steps. He walked until he was back past the station again. At the traffic light, new since his time, he crossed the road. The Burnham Falls First National Bank looked as always, the ivy-covered grey stone suitably conservative among all the new shop fronts.

It was after banking hours, and he rapped on the glass doors, where the shades were pulled half-way down. It was possible there was no one there. He waited a while, and then rapped again. He saw feet and trousers on the other side of the glass, and then the blind was raised. A tall young man,

126

dark haired and good looking, mouthed to him that the place was closed. Then, when he saw that Mal wasn't going to go away, and perhaps reassured by his appearance, he opened the door a little way.

" Is George Keston here?" Mal said. " My name's Hamilton —Mal Hamilton. I just got into town."

The young man hesitated, then his eyes widened with a kind of recognition. " Mr. Hamilton? . . . Why, yes—I guess he'll see you." He stepped back from the door and opened it wide.

Afterwards George Keston told everyone he met that he had been the first person Mal Hamilton came to see when he came back to Burnham Falls. It gave George a lot of satisfaction to say that.

CHAPTER TWO

Sally wiped the back of her hand across her brow, and noticed then that the perspiration had run off her hands a little, and had smudged the ink on the paper. It was a day at the end of June, and the whole valley lay in a humid bath of heat and moisture. There had been a lot of rain early in the month, and the valley was green and pleasant; under the trees the shadows were deep and cool-looking, like the still green water in the shallows of the lakes. But they were deceptive; there was no relief from the heat in the whole valley, except in the air-conditioned super-market, and the few stores in the town that were struggling to compete with it—only those and the soft, muted laboratories and offices, where no human discomforts could be permitted to disturb the efficient progress of the work.

She took her eyes reluctantly away from the scene before her—the gentle trees, the green lawns, the gay, pretty houses of Amtec Park—and tried to concentrate on the paper on the desk before her. The heat seemed to form a kind of mist between her and the smudged paper, something she wanted to push away physically. It would have been quicker— and neater—of course to use the typewriter, but when the words came slowly, grudgingly, like this, she felt a greater sense of movement and progress if she wrote in longhand; it was a closer, more real contact with the elusive thoughts, and with the words by which she tried to express them. She

127

sighed, wrote down half a sentence, then struck it out. It was a struggle to put an idea on paper, and to develop it— or not even to develop, just to get it down, crudely and nakedly, and when it was down it usually proved not to have been worth the struggle. A heaviness and lassitude possessed her whole body, and she wasn't making much of a fight against it. Suddenly, in a rage of frustration, she crumpled the paper, with its dull, useless words, into a ball in her hands, and tossed it into the waste basket.

The heaviness and lassitude came from being pregnant— because not even the fierce heat of the New York summers had ever affected her this way. At the end of March, she had known she was pregnant. At first she had felt satisfaction —a kind of earthly joy in her achievement, and the achieve- ment it would be to bring the child to full term and bear it triumphantly. In her happiness, she had to keep reminding herself that this event was not unique, it was happening every day everywhere in the world. Already, even in those early weeks she associated herself intimately and personally with the foetus in her womb; it had never been for her a mindless nothing, but already a personality to feel and communicate with. The shock came when she discovered that she was not going to carry the child with great ease. She almost didn't believe the exhausting sickness, the after- noons spent lying on the bed. It enraged her to find that her healthy, strong body had betrayed her in the one function she had counted on it to perform with no trouble. She even found it difficult to remember what it had been like before —Sally Redmond at Columbia who had excelled in physical training, who swam a controlled, swift Australian crawl, who danced tirelessly half the night—what had happened to her? She wondered fretfully why this child, conceived in love, eagerly desired, should be so difficult to carry; she had always believed that when her time came to have children, it would be done with no more fuss than a cat having kittens. It seemed a denial of the child to be ill because of it. She had so much wanted these months to be happy, peaceful ones, so that the child would be strong and beautiful. She knew now she must love the child much more because it was not an easy one.

She tried to let no one except the doctor see that the pregnancy bothered her too much—not even Tom. She was vaguely ashamed of her weakness in a sphere where most women fuctioned superbly. So many of the young wives

128

who had come to Amtec Park were pregnant—nonchalantly, confidently pregnant with their first, second or third child. Two houses along the street was Andrea Dawkins, whose slight, childishly immature body made Sally feel like an Amazon, and who was matter-of-factly pregnant for the fourth time, and not in the least troubled by it. Idly Sally wondered if life in a corporation was the ideal climate for breeding—the deep implications of security were there, the sense that life would flow on evenly and prosperously for ever, managed and guided by a paternal, solicitous company. Almost like the advertisements in *Fortune*, Sally thought. The group medical insurance had a maternity clause, so that a child coming into the world didn't appear to cost money. The philosophy of fear was discouraged. Growing families meant each man had a bigger stake in keeping his job. Who would want to leave the charming, bright houses of Amtec Park, who would want to take his family away from the nursery crèche, or the beautiful modern school they were building in this lovely valley. It was very serene and peaceful, and in serenity and peace, women bred children. And why not? Sally asked herself.

She collected her small bundle of papers, and took them with her into the kitchen. The kitchen, with its yellow Formica counters, was her favourite room in the house. It was everything that Amtec had promised—well equipped, well planned, solidly built, and for Sally, after the dark, cramped kitchen of the Brooklyn apartment house, and the tiny cupboard that had served as a kitchen in Greenwich Village, this room was still almost a bright unbelievable dream. She took active, positive pleasure in the dishwasher, the size of the refrigerator, the garbage disposal, the special shelf for the mixer, the toaster and the juicer. She liked the cheerfulness of this room—and she liked the colour of the oranges on the yellow table.

She got herself a glass of iced tea, and took it to the counter that ran along under the big window. While she sipped it, she fingered through the pages she had brought with her, stopping to read a paragraph, a sentence here and there. What she had written wasn't, in places, as bad as she had imagined—here and there a word or phrase lifted it momentarily to a different level, a little foreign, uneven light was shed on the otherwise tranquil flow of the sentences. Yet those brief touches of originality or unusual value made the rest of it noticeably ordinary; it would almost have been better if they hadn't been there at all—and yet for the sake of them she had to keep on with it. She shuffled the pages, counting them like a miser, feeling the sweat break again on her hands as she made a final count, and realised how few they were. Was this the total result of more than a year's work? She felt guilty and panic-stricken. In a year of nothing more to do than cook and clean a house that practically cleaned itself, she had only a few chapters to show. Where had the time gone? What had she done with it? Fearfully she touched the pages.

Her mind slipped back through the last year. Moving in here hadn't been difficult—this house with its shining new paint and empty closets, had just been waiting for someone to start living in it. They had unpacked their bags, settled their brand-new furniture, and that should have been the end of the interruptions. But other things had crept in —things she had never reckoned with in the picture of living in Burnham Falls, certain things and practices she had been unable to stand out against. There was the matter of the sewing . . . all the wives of the young members of Amtec had been proud of the economies they had effected in moving . . . making their own curtains and drapes had been one of them. Tom had privately told Sally that in his opinion they weren't economies at all, but even he had kept quiet when Julia Anderson had insisted on lending Sally her sewing-machine, and Sally, unfamiliar with the whole process, had had to buy a book on sewing, and learn how to do it. After two months, she had hung new drapes at every window in the house, but she didn't even admit to Tom that she could have bought nicer ready-made ones for about the same money. One of the by-products was that Sally got a reputation among the company wives for being energetic and capable, and suddenly she found herself on the committee that was being formed to raise funds for an enlargement to the Burnham Falls library.

Then there had been the cooking. Sally had been a good enough cook of the simple, no-nonsense kind of dishes that her mother had put on the table. When she and Tom had been to their first two dinner and supper parties in Amtec Park, she knew she would have to change that. First of all, in Burnham Falls there were none of the bake shops that seemed to be round every corner in New York, with the cheese cake and strawberry pies waiting in their refrigerated cases; so Sally bought the ready-mix cake packets in the supermarket,

130

but these didn't quite satisfy her, and she began to hunt through the recipe books and to spend whole afternoons making cakes and biscuits that Tom ate almost in a sitting. It seemed to Sally just like going back to learn to boil water again as she strove to reproduce the look of the coloured pictures of the salads and dishes and pies that she found in the recipe books. Tom protested about the fuss and bother when she tried out the dishes first on him, but when it came their turn to give a supper party, he glowed with pride at the praise for the food and the table decoration. Sally was even proud of herself, but at the back of her mind there was a little lingering regret for the days of the cheerful, spontaneous wine and bread and spaghetti served on cracked plates to their friends sitting round on the floor.

Was that where the time had gone, she wondered? Had she given it to sewing and cooking and proving to herself and Tom and everyone around them what a successful wife she was being? And a lot of it had been unnecessary because she knew quite well that Tom loved her too much for her to have to prove anything to him; if the drapes had been failures and the cakes had never risen he wouldn't have thought it any fault of hers. And if it was writing she chose, instead of cooking and sewing, he would approve of that also. But along with this went the knowledge that she did Tom's standing with Amtec more good when she got on the library committee, than when she sat stewing over a few tatty sheets of paper that in three years might be a novel, or might end in the waste basket.

She looked up from the paper, and noticed that Marcia Webster had gone out into the garden and was coiling up the hose. That meant it was getting late, because every evening Marcia coiled up the hose and put it out of the way before David, her husband, drove the car past the side of the house to the garage. So few of the men ever walked the half-mile or so to the Laboratories. Sally moved back from the window, and instinctively, in a defensive gesture, she took the papers and slipped them into a drawer. Marcia had already strolled over to have coffee and cake with her twice this week, and might do so again if she saw Sally sitting idly by the window. So far the same defensive instinct had stopped Sally from letting anyone but Tom know about the novel. What you announced you were going to do, you had to prove . . . at least, if you were Sally Redmond you had to. And she was not quite that certain of herself.

131

Suddenly, as she closed the drawer, she was conscious of a kind of helpless rage inside her, a feeling as strong and violent as the passions that took hold of her father from time to time and turned him briefly into an unreasonable tyrant. It was a rage against the pretty tidiness of this room, against the three cakes and the biscuits she had baked that morning in expectation of guests over the week-end, against the library, committee, and the Thursday Club, and the gardening club someone two streets away was organising; it was a rage against these time-takers, against these sappers of the energy she needed to get a few ideas on paper, even, for a moment, against the baby that made her ill and dulled her wits. Damn them! . . . She had to save something for herself out of all this. Angrily she took the pages out of the drawer again, and went back to the desk in the living-room.

She was still sitting there, covering sheets with her untidy, rapid script, when Tom arrived home.

He came over and dropped a kiss on the back of her neck. She looked up at him, a little dazed, for the moment hardly seeing him through the crowd of ideas that had suddenly pushed themselves upon her. She was flushed and hot, a little triumphant.

" I didn't hear the car," she said.

" Too busy, by the looks of it. Had a good day?"

" A-ha," she nodded. " So-so . . . I should be asking you that question."

" Well, we didn't make a major break-through, if that's what you mean. Nothing much happened . . . at least not around where I was." He tossed his jacket on to a chair, and threw himself full-length on to the sofa.

" What a dull job!" Sally wrinkled her nose. " Do you mean no one discovered how to go round Mars backwards to-day?"

" No, and if they did, it would probably be in another department, and I'd read about it in the paper. . . . What's for dinner?"

" Something from *Ladies Home Journal.*"

He made a feint of throwing a cushion at her. " What— ice cubes sprinkled with parsley?"

" I thought we'd splurge . . . it's lobster tails. Darned expensive!"

" Good! Let's go eat now, shall we?"

132

"What's the hurry?"

"Well—Alan Taylor suggested we go bowling with them. Two other couples are driving over to Middleton to that big new bowling alley."

A little quiver of annoyance went through Sally, but she kept her voice even. "Oh, Tom—it's so hot!"

"Well, it'll be air-conditioned there. Much cooler than here!"

Sally turned the pen slowly in her fingers. Her left hand was still resting on the desk, touching the little bundle of papers; they felt warm and familiar under her hand, like a friend that had been long absent. There hadn't been nearly enough time to get down all the things that had seemed so suddenly released by the rage that had swept through her; for an hour afterwards she had experienced a marvellous sharpening and clarifying of her thoughts, a new twist and motivation that had made this dull chapter abruptly spring to life. She knew, in her present mood, she could have written with ease for another four hours, and some of this feeling might be captured.

"Do we have to go, Tom? Couldn't we make it some other night?"

He shifted a little on the sofa. "Well . . . I more or less accepted . . . found myself saying we hadn't planned to do anything else, and Taylor's sort of counting on me to make up a team."

As Sally said nothing, he added, with a kind of urgency: "Couldn't you come, Sal? He particularly asked for you to come . . . and he *is* the head of my department."

She laid down the pen. "O.K.—we'll go! Let's go and eat the lobster." She rose briskly. "And maybe you'd better pour me a good big Scotch."

II

Milly's Squires' face had taken on some animation; the tilt of her eyebrows was questioning and curious. She stood with her hand on the door knob, staring into the half-dark room, where the venetians had been drawn against the late after-noon sun. Clif Burrell looked up from the paper he had been staring at, but not reading.

"Well, Milly—what is it?"

133

" Mr. Hamilton to see you, Mr. Burrell."

" Hamilton?" Clif's eyelids flickered rapidly as he considered the name. " Mal Hamilton?"

" Yes." Milly was excited. The lustre of Mal Hamilton's scientific genius might have dimmed a little for Burnham Falls since the Laboratories had set up in their midst, but Mal was still a sort of legend, and Milly had gazed at him wide-eyed.

" Oh, fine! Ask him to come in, Milly."

About to turn, she paused. " If you don't mind, Mr. Burrell, I'll finish copying out those references in the morning. I should get home to Mother right away. She's had a couple of bad nights this week, and she's not feeling well. I don't like the way she looks at all."

" Of course, Milly. Run along now—and give your mother my regards." He didn't look at her directly. They both knew that copying up the references from the books he had borrowed from the courthouse library was just a convenient fiction of work to be got through. There was very little work now in Clif's office, and most days Milly sat steadily reading a paper-back propped up against the typewriter. Clif knew that if Milly had had more energy or ambition she would have found another job.

" Thank you, Mr. Burrell. Good night!"

" Good night, Milly."

In the outer room Clif could hear Milly's demure voice. He got to his feet expectantly. Even against the high door frame Mal looked tall. Clif went towards him with outstretched hand.

" Well, Mal! George Keston told me you were back! How are you? Nice of you to drop by."

Mal put his hat on a side table covered with irregular stacks of books, few of them law books. He gripped Clif's hand warmly. " Well—I didn't just ' drop by,' Mr. Burrell. I was invited to dinner with the Dexters to-night, and Steve said I might call here and pick you up, since you were going there also. I hope it's not too early . . . I got through at the Laboratories sooner than I thought."

Clif smiled. " Not a bit. I'm very glad you came. I didn't expect to have a chance to see you so soon. George Keston's been talking about the possibility of you coming for more than a year. We'd just about given you up."

Mal took the chair Clif indicated, a high, wheel-backed chair polished and lustrous from long use. He took his time

134

looking about the room, the untidy room with its smell of old cigar smoke and the books piled on to shelves that covered the walls. There were wood ashes in the grate, and the room hadn't been painted for many years. Clif remained silent during the scrutiny.

Mal came back to him, not quite apologetically. "You don't mind my staring about, Mr. Burrell? I once looked into this room when I was a kid of about twelve, and there were more books here than I had ever seen in a house before. I promised myself that by the time I was twenty I'd have read just as many—and more. Of course I hadn't . . . but twenty seemed a long way off then. I wouldn't like to look now and find how few I've managed to read in all the years since then. . . ."

Clif waved his hand. "Nobody reads all they intend to. Those books . . . haven't read all of them myself, and forgotten most of what was in the rest. It's sad what happens to knowledge . . . but sadder still to think that a boy like you actually *wanted* my books, and I was just blind enough not to know it. Towns like Burnham Falls don't often get boys like young Mal Hamilton, and they should recognise and nurture them. And I'm as guilty as the next. . . ."

Mal half-smiled and shrugged. "Burnham Falls doesn't owe me a thing, Mr. Burrell—nor I it. I got help here . . not more or less than I would have got elsewhere. I pushed and elbowed my way along with about all the grace of a young hog rooting for food. People didn't like me . . . and looking back, I don't see why they should have."

Clif leaned back in his chair, grinning a little in appreciation. "Here I've been thinking that you'd be sleek and fat, and full of smooth speeches on how the poor-but-honest boy made good. Steve's shown me some press clippings about you from time to time . . . you have an impressive record of success."

He shrugged again. "No more so than Steve. Mine came earlier, and it's a different kind. But look at Steve himself . . . good position with a big company who can afford to give him whatever he wants for research. He came in on the top with Amtec, and that's a damn' good place to be."

"Do you really believe that?" Clif said gravely.

"Sure I believe it! It's not for me—that kind of job never was for me. But if that's what you want, then it's one of the best!"

"I've sometimes wondered . . ." Clif said. "Steve never

135

talks about his work—security reasons, as well as his own natural reticence—but I've wondered if the Amtec deal was what he really wanted."

"How can he have anything different?" Mal asked calmly. "What other place is there for him?—or any other scientist? In one way or another he'll work either for a Foundation, a corporation or the military. Steve was one of the few who managed to make a discovery in a home lab, and he made it just in time, before his money ran out. He knows, as well as anyone else, that he couldn't have made any development of it without Amtec, or someone like them. The day of the basement chemist is gone, Mr. Burrell. It takes thousands of men, and millions of dollars to put one of those babies up in the sky. There's no such thing as an individual act in science any more."

"You work alone . . ."

Mal shook his head. "I don't research alone, Mr. Burrell. I just advise on one tiny aspect of the whole, and there are enough companies concerned with that aspect to keep me busy. I'm not a research scientist . . . that's for guys like Steve."

"He's good?" It was not precisely a question.

Mal nodded slowly. "Amtec is lucky to have him."

"Ah . . ." Clif took his own time to think about what Mal had said. He rummaged at length in the deep bottom drawer of his desk to find a fresh box of cigars. The good mellow aroma drifted softly through the room, the fresh scent momentarily overpowering the residue of the thousands of cigars that had been smoked there. He proffered the box to Mal.

"Do you use these?"

Mal shook his head, at the same time bringing out his cigarettes. "No—I've always thought it was a habit that belonged to more reflective men than myself. I seem to have been for ever up and on the run."

"You were a young man in a hurry . . . you seem to have proved it was worth while."

Mal did not reply as Clif went through the business of getting the cigar lighted. The old man broke the match between his fingers, and dropped it into the waste basket.

"We've plenty of time," he said, getting to his feet. "How about taking a drink out on to the side porch? Generally catch a breeze there this time of day."

136

Mal got to his feet. "Leave your jacket there," Clif continued. "You'll be more comfortable without it."

He led the way along a passage covered with worn carpet which connected his professional rooms with the rest of the house. From the main hall with the stair well, Mal could see open double doors that gave a glimpse of an old-fashioned dining-room and living-room on each side. Like Clif's office, they were in half-darkness, but they looked lifeless and unused. A middle-aged woman came through the swing-door at the end of the hall. She looked expectantly at them.

"Oh . . . Mrs. Martin! Could we have ice and some glasses on the side porch, please? And the decanters . . ."

"Yes—right away, Mr. Burrell."

When she had disappeared, Clif turned to Mal, and said softly, "It's all right to sit outside drinking when I have company. When I'm drinking alone, she gets upset if it isn't done inside." He motioned Mal to follow him.

They settled themselves in the shabby, deep cane chairs, turned a little to give a view on to Main Street. Between them and the street were four tall maples, shading the lawn which was Ted Talbot's pride. Clif had been right—here a slight breeze stirred now, and rustled the leaves of the maples. Mrs. Martin came and placed the tray on the table between them. It was a massive silver tray, heavy with engraving and scrolled edges; the glasses and decanters were fine engraved crystal, sparkling in the afternoon sun. She bustled over setting them out, with the air of a woman who was glad to have the excuse of using them.

"Thank you, Mrs. Martin," Clif said in his deep, rumbling voice. She lingered a little, eyeing Mal with interest, but finally they heard the flat slap as the screen door closed behind her.

"New in the town since your time," Clif said. "She's been here almost since Dorothy died. Lives with her husband over on Becket Street. She'd like to polish me up—same as she does these glasses, but I'm set in my bad habits, and she knows it. Nice woman, though—pretty harmless, as housekeepers go."

"Lot of new things and people since my time," Mal said. He vaguely saluted Clif before he drank. He sipped, and let the whisky lie on his tongue. "Say—this is good stuff!"

"Twelve years old," Cliff said. "I figure if I'm going to

137

rot my guts with liquor, it might as well be a good one. I might last longer to drink more of it that way."

He continued, waving his glass in the direction of the street. "Yes, a lot of new things and faces, Mal. What do you think of it all?"

"It's damn' good," Mal said firmly. "Best thing that could have happened! I tell you, Mr. Burrell, this town owes a debt to Steve Dexter for bringing Amtec here. I hope they know it."

"They know it," Clif said dryly. "And they tell him so—and expect him to make excuses when something comes up they don't like. He does his best—I think he really suffers if he thinks the town is being hurt in any way. But Steve was never a joiner . . . he's lived too long in his laboratory to feel very much at home in crowds. Oh, they've roped him into all the appropriate boards and committees, but he isn't really with it at all. Burnham Falls can't turn him into another Joe Carpenter."

"And just as well, too," Mal said bluntly. "Joe Carpenter was a short-sighted old sentimentalist who was always trying to turn the clock back."

"Joe had his points . . . he wasn't altogether wrong."

Mal laid down his glass. "I took a drive round town early this morning before I went up to the Laboratories. This is a different town, and that's because of Steve and not Joe."

"Different . . ." Clif said mildly. "But is it better?"

"Certainly it's better! I took a good look at it all . . . all those houses in Amtec Park, and the new development for people who'll be coming in to work at the plant when it's ready. That plant's going to be a big one, Mr. Burrell . . . it'll take care of every man who wants to work in Burnham Falls, and it'll bring business into this town like it's never had before. Don't tell me the town hasn't felt the benefit from that trailer camp for the construction crews?"

"Oh, yes—it's felt it all right. I can't deny that. But some of the crews are hardly worthy additions to Burnham Falls. Some of them are kind of rough. There's fights outside the bars just about every Saturday night."

"But their money looks good, doesn't it?"

"Yes, their money looks good," Clif said stonily.

Mal raised his hand and pointed at Clif. "That con-

138

solidated school they're building—isn't that a better thing for the town?"

"I couldn't say, Mal. We need a bigger school because we have many more children."

Yes but this school is going to have the things that the old Burnham Falls High never had—big and well-equipped labs, better library, better gym and lecture halls. Steve told me all about it. By anyone's standards, this is going to be a fine school."

"If it gets the right teachers . . ."

"Teachers or not, Mr. Burrell—all I know is that if there had been a school like this in Burnham Falls when I was growing up, I'd have had to do a lot less rooting and elbowing to get where I wanted to go. This school is a recognition of the kids like Mal Hamilton you were talking about. If it needs Amtec and higher taxes to bring it about, then for God's sake let's have them!"

Clif nodded slowly. "I guess I'm older and more out of touch than I think."

They sat in silence for some time, each having enjoyed the ruffled feeling of the other, the sense of an argument swiftly pursued. Clif knew that he must necessarily be cast in the role of defender of things past. But Mal was the man of science, the man of new things, the new age. They had to argue—it was expected of them. But not argue so strongly as to spoil this evening hour, with the breeze growing cooler as they sat there, and the shade deepening under the trees.

Clif reached over for the decanter, and pushed it towards Mal. "Here, fill it up this time. Women are always so parsimonious when they pour liquor."

CHAPTER THREE

Jeannie wore nothing under her blouse but a bra, and Jerry had reached around and unhooked it; he unbuttoned the blouse and slipped the bra down. Her breasts were round and mature, but still the high, firm breasts of a young girl. He cupped one in each hand gently. Then abruptly, with a kind of desperation, his grip tightened.

"Please, Jeannie . . . take off your things. I can't stand this!"

Now he put his head between her breasts, and his lips tugged urgently. "Please, Jeannie."

The weight of his body had pushed her sideways on the car seat, so that he was almost lying on top of her; he put one arm under her back, and pulled her closer in to him, pressing her as tightly against him as he could. He could smell a clean soap smell from her, the fragrant warmth of her skin. Then he felt her hands, her strong hands, pushing against his shoulders; her body had stiffened to loosen his grasp.

"We mustn't do this, Jerry! It's crazy . . . please don't ask me to!"

"I can't help it, Jeannie . . . please . . . please!"

"No . . . we mustn't!"

Roughly he pulled her back to him. "Why not? Don't you want it? Don't you feel like I do?"

There was a short pause. Her voice was muffled when she spoke. 'Yes, I want it, Jerry. But I'm afraid. I don't want to have a baby!"

"You don't have to worry—I'll be careful. I promise you you don't have to worry."

"No!" she whispered. "No! . . . Sometimes there's an accident. It isn't worth the risk . . . and all the worry."

His hold on her slackened, and he moved back from her a little. "Well, damn you! Why did you let me touch you in the first place?"

She let out a low cry of protest. "Jerry, that isn't fair! You know it isn't! I wanted to be here. I . . .I like you to touch me like that. But I can't let you go all the way. And you know why!"

His words choked a little with scorn and frustration. "You girls . . . you're all the same! You let a guy kiss you, and lead him on, and then when it gets to the big question, you chicken out. You're all cheats . . . all of you!"

In her turn, she grew angry. "What else do you expect? What other way is there to be? I'm human, like you . . . but I'm the one that'll have to take the consequences if there's a baby. What's a girl supposed to do? Never have a date because she knows that pretty soon she's got to tell the boy that she won't——? A girl has to do that, or shut herself up at home all the time."

"You're so calm about it," he said bitterly. "You've got all the answers, haven't you? If you really loved me, you wouldn't keep on saying no all the time."

140

"But I *do* love you, Jerry!" Her voice broke in a desperate little sob. "I do really love you!"

He moved away from her, back to the driver's side of the seat, saying nothing. The blood seemed to be smashing in his temples, and he gripped the seat with both hands to stop them trembling. He slid down in the seat, resting his neck against it and staring straight up into the dark canopy of the trees above him. The sweat had broken all over him now; he could feel his hands clammy against the seat, and his shirt was sticking to his back. Beside him, Jeannie had not moved.

He had parked the car by the side of the dirt road that led down to the Carpenter fishing cabin. At the end of the road were the group of fishing cabins and the lake, but the trees were too dense for them to catch even a glint of the starlight on the water. Around them was all the unbroken silence of the Downside estate; there was not enough wind to raise a ripple on the lake. Jerry's keen, listening ears could not even hear the lap of the water against the rocks, or the gentle scrape of the row boats against the old wooden pier. The fishing cabins were empty and shuttered.

He knew he had no business to be parked along this road, which was the right-of-way to the cabins. Technically, anything off this road belonged to Downside, and he was trespassing. But the Downside road was almost always deserted at night, and he had had an excuse ready if he had met a car coming from the seminary. None of the high school kids ever came here to park with their dates; with all the privacy of the place, the feeling that they were on the only road that led to the seminary had a strangely inhibiting effect. Most of them had forgotten about the dirt road that led to the cabins.

Jerry liked it here because it was one of the few places he felt like driving to with Jeannie. She was different from other girls, he thought, in a special way. It had never occurred to him to take her to the places that the kids parked their cars around Burnham Falls—the spots on the lake where the trees made friendly shadow, and where theirs could be one of six or seven cars with silent, amorous couples in it. Jeannie just wasn't the sort of girl you took to places like that—he couldn't quite explain why he felt this way about her, but at the back of his mind he always carried the remark he had heard Vanesco, the town's barber, make one

141

day as he watched Jeannie walk by the shop—"Girl who looks like that got to be twice as careful as others because every old hen in the town'd be cackling about her. . . ." Jerry didn't want anyone cackling about Jeannie because of him.

The thought brought him back to what she had just said. In the warm darkness he was acutely conscious of her sitting there, the whole length of the long seat between them. Jeannie knew all about the "old hens" of the town, about the talk that could circulate so quickly about a blonde with a voluptuous figure. Jeannie wasn't any fool, and when she had made her angry protest he had known in his heart that it was valid. But validity or reasonableness had little to do with how he felt when he could touch Jeannie, and kiss her soft, warm mouth, feel the response of her body within his arms, hear the shaken, urgent whisperings in his ear.

He glanced across at her. In the faint light he could see her staring straight ahead, as still and motionless as the air about them. He had pushed her blouse back off her shoulders, and she sat there with her arms by her sides, almost naked to the waist. He was aware of the simple dignity and pride in her bearing. Having repulsed him, she did not hasten to gather her clothes about her with expressions of outraged modesty. Jeannie knew she was as much responsible as he for the fact that she sat here half-naked beside him, and there were no bitter, prim recriminations. Jeannie didn't whine. She was honest and fair . . . much more fair than he had been.

At last he spoke, swallowing to get rid of the dryness in his throat.

"Jeannie, let's get married."

Slowly she turned her head. The light was too faint to let him see her expression. She didn't answer.

"Did you hear what I said?" he demanded impatiently. "I want to get married."

"I heard you," she answered. "But I don't think you know what you're saying."

"Sure I know—I just said, 'Let's get married.' "

Her voice was soft—the soft, gentle tone that he loved to hear. "That's sweet of you, Jerry . . . honestly, that's sweet. But we're just a couple of kids. We can't get married."

"We're both eighteen . . ."

"Yes," she interrupted, "and you've only finished one year of college. What happens to that, Jerry?"

142

"We'll manage. We'll get married, and I'll get a job in the evenings, and there's the bank during the summers. We could get an apartment near the campus. Thousands of freshmen get married, Jeannie . . . there's nothing strange about that."

"Hush, Jerry—there's no use talking like that. I wouldn't marry you now, and put a millstone round your neck. Getting through college isn't a cinch. Even if I supported myself while you got through it still wouldn't be college the way your father wants it for you—the way a boy should have it."

"What's my father got to do with this? . . ."

"Quite a lot," she said, "and I don't want to spoil things for you. Your father meant you to enjoy college, and then come back and help run this town. He meant you to look around before you decided to get married. A boy of eighteen who gets married starts to be an old man."

"That's just a lot of talk, Jeannie. You're just saying these things. I want to hear about your side of it. I want to hear what you want to do, not what you think I ought to do."

"Me?" He heard her faint sigh. "I'd like nothing more than to marry you, Jerry. I've never loved anyone else but you, and I don't think I could. I'd like to marry you and settle down here in Burnham Falls. . . ."

"Then why don't you?"

"Not now—it's too soon! I don't want to be known as the girl who grabbed Jerry Keston before he had a chance to get out of this town and see what other girls looked like —college graduates—girls from different kinds of family. I'm afraid to do that, because maybe in a few years you might start to believe that was what happened. I couldn't bear it if you thought you'd been trapped."

"For God's sake, Jeannie, this is just a lot of bull! Girls don't talk like that! If they want to get married, they *get* married!"

"Now you just listen to me!" she said firmly. "I know what I'm talking about. If we get married it'll be in three or four years' time, when you've had a good look around at what college girls have to offer and when you've decided that Burnham Falls isn't such a bad place."

"And what will you do?"

"I'll stay here and work," she said calmly, "and wait for you to come back. If you come back I'll know it's because you want to."

143

He turned to her, bewildered and a little outraged. "I never heard a girl talk like you, Jeannie. They just think about getting married and . . . everything."

She turned to him fiercely. "You don't suppose I *don't* think about getting married? I never wanted anything so much in my whole life as to marry you, Jerry. But when we get married—if we get married—I want this town to think that you're as lucky to get me as I am to get you."

"I don't know . . ."

"Wait," she said. "Let me finish! There's a lot of things you don't know—you and this town. That new plant's going to mean another five or six hundred families moving in . . . and all the activity that's going to bring. By the time you've finished college, Jerry, this won't be a sleepy little town any more . . . but almost no one's recognised this. Look . . . my own father! He thought he could get along nicely with his beaten-up equipment and his old jeep, and that outfit from Elmbury walked in and took the business from under his nose. If he'd had any real guts, he'd have mortgaged everything and raised some money to give them a bit of competition. But that's my dad—and I don't suppose I really want him to change. But it doesn't mean I have to be exactly like him."

"Jeannie! What's all this about?"

"I've been doing pretty well at Carter's—and Wally's raising my salary to get me to stay. Since the families moved into Amtec Park I've been selling much more of the expensive brands, and Wally knows if the women come to me to buy Elizabeth Arden, they'll stop and buy their drugs from him. And I think this is just the beginning, Jerry. . . . Burnham Falls isn't only a summer town any more, and we've got to remember that. Perhaps if I do well there's a possibility of branching out . . . maybe into a place of my own, to sell lingerie and sweaters, stockings, robes. There's a lot of business in that kind of thing . . . simple, not too expensive. I'll bet if I could save half the money, The First National would give me a loan on the rest. Your father would think it was good business, Jerry."

He was silent. For more than three minutes he said nothing at all; he had turned away from her and was staring down the road towards the lake, which he couldn't see. Some of her enthusiasm had fallen away from her in this time, and she seemed suddenly much more aware of her surroundings.

144

She slipped her bra back on her shoulders and hooked it, and pulled her blouse closed. The silence continued.

"What's the matter, Jerry? Do you think I'm crazy?"

"No—not crazy. Too darned smart, if anything. You'll be a bustling career woman making this town sit up and take notice by the time I've finished college. And by the time I've done my stint in the Army, you'll probably be running for Mayor. I just never figured you for that kind of girl at all."

"I'm not trying to bust into your world, Jerry. All I want to do is sell a few face creams and lipsticks. Is that so bad? Or would you rather I made it my ambition to get to be Mr. Ed Peters' private secretary? What I'm trying to say is that there are plenty of simple, unspectacular ways to do well without ever going five miles outside Burnham Falls. There's too much work to do right here—and this town could be for you, if you'd see it that way. We need some honest men to help run things—or else we can sit back and let Amtec run the whole show. After all, why don't we? Just turn over the schools, the churches, the town hall. I'm sure they'd do the job well, and as honestly as most—and it would be much less trouble for us. Only it wouldn't be Burnham Falls any more, would it?

"I mean," she continued quickly, "I mean, your father knows there's a job to be done in more than banking. But maybe you think it's more glamorous to be a teller in a Wall Street bank."

"How do you know what I think?" he said sullenly. "You've hardly let me open my mouth!"

"Well, then—say it!"

"I don't know where to start—or how!" He turned to her in a half-pleading gesture. "I don't know what's come over you. I think you're warm and sweet, and I want to kiss you . . . and I've been thinking that was what you wanted too. And then suddenly—crash! I start getting a spiel like a Chamber of Commerce clerk. It doesn't sound like you at all."

"What does it sound—mean and greedy?"

He shrugged. "One of the things I like about your father, Jeannie, is that he's so—well, relaxed about life. He doesn't let it fret him. I've always thought of you that way."

"Jerry, I love and respect my dad. And I don't want him to be any different from the way he is. But if I feel like

145

using my energies in a different way from his, is that so wrong?" She attempted a short, shaky laugh. "I'm a big, healthy girl . . . and I can get around to lots of things as well as raising kids and reading cook books. I somehow think I can do them all, if I'm given the chance."

"And what am I supposed to do—stand and cheer on the sidelines?"

Her voice grew curt. "If that's the way you feel about it, we'd better not discuss it any further."

"You bet we won't discuss it," he snapped. "But you'd better start to do some thinking. I'm asking you to marry me, and just leave me to handle my dad and all the rest of the details. Otherwise we can forget about the whole thing. If you think I'm going to stand around and watch while you turn into Miss Superwoman of Burnham Falls, you're pretty much mistaken."

"Oh—you're just jealous, like all men, when a woman has an ounce of brains and chooses not to let them rot. I think you *like* lazy women—they make you feel good!"

"Perhaps I do! At least they're *women*!"

Abruptly he leaned forward and jabbed the starter, and the car came to life. Then he filled and backed with sharp, aggressive movements slamming on the brakes at the last possible moment. Jeannie was thrown wildly against the door. She straightened in the seat, and gripped the edge of the window to steady herself. The big headlights of the car stabbed the darkness ahead; behind them was a cloud of dust. They bumped and jolted along the washed-out ruts of the dirt road, going too fast for the narrow twists and bends in it. Jeannie was troubled by the violence of Jerry's anger—he was usually so easy-going and amenable to what she said. If she had dared, she would have asked him to slow down —she would have put her hand across and touched him, and he would have yielded. But she could not. The headlights reflected the crazy rhythm of the car, flashing to the sky, and down again as they hit the bumps, striking the dark mass of the woods as they rounded the bends.

With a last final lurch they emerged from the dirt road to the pavement. Jerry turned back towards Burnham Falls. With the good surface under him, he increased the speed. Jeannie clung more tightly, and her mouth went a little dry with fear. Jerry had never driven like this before—she felt she knew nothing at all of the person who sat tensely at the wheel. It was as if she drove with a stranger. She crouched in

146

the corner, small and lonely and afraid. They were coming to the spot where the road ran along the shore of the lake, the place where it dropped sharply to the rocks and water below. She saw the white guard rails suddenly race towards them with a sickening speed; she closed her eyes, and clamped her lips down tight to keep from screaming.

But there was no impact, and no sound of splintering wood. The even pace of the car continued, following the turns of the winding road. Some of normalcy returned to Jerry at last; gradually the speed fell off. At the junction of the Downside road and the highway, he stopped dead before turning. Jeannie opened her eyes again.

CHAPTER FOUR

Laura slammed the front door behind her with unnecessary force. She pulled off her hat with a gesture that was both impatient and irritable.

"Gracie! . . . Gracie!" She walked quickly through the entrance foyer to the bedroom wing of the house. Behind her she could hear the kitchen door swinging open and the quick steps of the maid. But Laura did not stop or look around; she continued straight on to her bedroom, where she dropped her handbag, gloves and hat on to a chair.

"You called, Mrs. Peters?"

Laura didn't look at her; she went into the dressing-room. Gracie automatically picked up the things she had left on the chair, and followed her. Their eyes met for a second in the mirror before Gracie slid open a section of the wardrobe and began to put the things away.

"Empty the handbag first!" Laura said. She unzipped her dress and stepped out of it. Gracie picked it up and hung it in silence. As Laura pulled her slip over her head she said, "Mix me a martini, Gracie. Double . . . well chilled. And leave the ice and tray ready for Mr. Peters when he comes in."

"Yes, ma'am." Laura went into the bathroom and shut the door.

Inside she put both hands on the edge of the basin, and her head dropped forward limply; her eyes closed. Relax, she told herself . . . relax. The porcelain of the basin was cool beneath her hands. She reached forward and turned on

147

the cold tap, and put her wrists under it. She soaked a cloth in cold water, and held it up to her temples and forehead. When at last she let herself look in the mirror, the tension creases between her eyebrows had loosened a trifle. " Careful . . . careful," she whispered softly. " You'll give yourself lines, and in a couple of years . . ."

She turned on the shower. The tepid water didn't seem to refresh her. She would have liked to soak in the tub for twenty minutes, but there wasn't time for that. She put her arms high above her head, and tried to stretch the tension out of her body, as she had been taught to, but now it didn't seem to do very much for her—not as in the old days when she had been working with Goodman, or rehearsing for *The Leaven,* and Larry had made her go through all her exercises faithfully so that she would relax before she slept. Perhaps the difference lay in the work she had been doing then and now—the difference in being tired because Goodman worked her too hard, and because she had barely been able to control her boredom at a P.T.A. meeting.

She stepped out of the shower, and dried herself carefully, even in her haste still going through all the motions that were a part of the ritual—massaging lotion into her legs, arms and shoulders, with an extra amount on the elbows and heels, dusting herself lavishly with powder. She resented this need for haste, and the fact that it was necessary to bathe and change here instead of in a hotel in New York before their dinner engagement. It was impossible to retain the look of untouched freshness she demanded of herself after a sixty-mile drive. But Ed had refused, rather shortly, to leave the Laboratories any earlier, and had pointedly reminded her of her own meeting that afternoon. So now she was rushed and nervous, irritated by the circumstances that seemed to conspire to make her appear not at her best. The careful examination she gave her reflection in the mirror that covered one wall of the bathroom was not narcissistic, but deeply critical—the slightest sign of extra flesh or sagging muscle meant that she had to give a little longer each day to exercise, and to start leaving the butter off her breakfast toast. There were no signs—not yet ; but you had to keep watching, just as you kept watching for the lines between the eyebrows.

She left the towels on the floor, and went through into the dressing-room. From one of the drawers she took out a fine, lacy elastic foundation garment, that zipped up the front,

148

and covered her from breast to thighs. It had been made especially for her, had cost $150, and she had five more in the drawer. They had been designed so that, on television, her gowns would fit without a wrinkle. She put on stockings, and slipped on light evening sandals, put her robe on, but did not fasten it. It was then she walked over to the dressing-table, and took the first sip of the martini Gracie had left on a silver tray.

The chill of the liquid had clouded the glass; she twisted the cool stem a little, and some spilled and trickled down over her fingers. She put them to her tongue and licked them; they tasted of the talcum. She quickly took another sip, a long one. She liked the raw, sharp taste against her tongue, and the way it burned in her throat. There wasn't anything quite like a martini—at first it repelled, sent a shudder through your whole body, then you felt the glow spread through you, the slight blurring of the edge of fatigue, a little click that abruptly lifted you from the mood that had been, into a state far more meaningful and sharp. It had a way of shifting the focus. She drank half of it almost in a gulp.

Now she sat idly and thought—when she didn't have time for thought. She thought of the day past, but by now some of the irritation had gone . . . and the evening before her seemed as it ought to be, as it had always been before Burn-ham Falls. She shrugged, and tried to put aside what she had done that day, because it had nothing to do with the evening. She had no intention of walking into the Oak Room to meet Phil Conrad trailing the aura of a suburban housewife. Let him think that she spent her days reading Proust and O'Neill, and that she had never heard of the P.T.A.

The day had begun when she had looked up from the newspaper at the breakfast table and seen Selma Talbot getting out of her husband's jeep at the side gate down on the road. The woman walked up the path to the side door, wear-ing her washed-out cotton dress; she was big-breasted and full-hipped, and her face had the worn look of a woman for whom life has not been easy. But there was something rather splendid about her at the same time—perhaps in that free, swinging walk, Laura thought, or the way she held her head, with its coil of faded gold hair. Selma came to do the heavy cleaning three days a week. Laura rarely saw her. She was part of the background, an adjunct to Gracie and

149

the cook. But this morning the sight of her vaguely disturbed Laura ; she didn't know why anyone like Selma Talbot, who scrubbed floors and did the ironing, should look so untroubled and serene. It was while she watched Selma walk up that path that the phone rang with the start of the day's irritations.

The phone call was from Harriet Dexter, warning her that she would be facing some ruffled feelings at that afternoon's meeting. The new consolidated school building had been started in Burnham Falls, but it would take a further year to complete, and already some of the planning seemed out of date. The administration problems were already there. The first major clash on curricula and the use of space designed into the building was shaping up between Susan Hill, the present principal of the elementary school, and Marion Jennings, who was a noted educator, and the wife of Lionel Jennings, one of the top men at the Laboratories. She had been on the faculty at U.C.L.A., and it was known that when the new school was ready Susan Hill would be asked to retire, and Marion Jennings would take over as principal. The trouble lay in the fact that Miss Hill had been born in Burnham Falls and had taught school there for almost forty years ; she was solidly backed by the older members of the community, who saw the new school merely as a piece of extravagant modern pampering of the children, and as a steep climb in their tax bills. Burnham Falls would back Susan Hill all the way—in spite of her non-progressive ideas, she was a good teacher, with a natural gift for training children. On the other hand, Marion Jennings had written two books on education that were widely used in the West—on any count, Burnham Falls was extraordinarily lucky to have her to take over the new consolidated school. Clearly the job of principal was beyond the administrative experience or capacities of Susan Hill.

Laura listened to all this with a growing feeling of dismay. She had, rather unwillingly, accepted election to the school board, because she had recognised it as a gesture to her position as Ed's wife. What she didn't know until afterwards was that Harriet Dexter had stepped down to allow her to take that place. As a member of the school-board, she had also to be active in P.T.A.—the fact that Ed had two daughters made her, technically, a parent. She had dutifully listened to Marion Jennings' advice on how to proceed, but she learned more from Harriet. None of this eased her

150

sense of bewilderment and frustration as she took her place for the meetings; she was a childless woman helping to make decisions that would affect other women's children—and the only role she understood or was fit for was to stand behind the footlights in a theatre, or to talk into a television camera. It seemed daily to grow more impossible to traverse the distance between Burnham Falls and Broadway.

At the end of her conversation with Harriet, she asked her to lunch. It was not a day to be alone.

But the worst thing had been picking up the new copy of *Life* and seeing the two-page spread on Larry—pictures of Larry working in his apartment in New York, and dining with a group of people at Chambord. His wife, Mary, was beside him in the group, not looking at all changed from the time Laura had seen her, wearing the quiet dress, and the too-severe hair style. Then there were pictures of them together in London and Paris, where his new play had been produced even before its Broadway opening—and the pictures of the villa in Italy they had rented for the summer. The story was titled "International Playwright." Larry wrote the kind of plays that transposed with ease across the Atlantic. Of Mary there was the brief remark that, although she appeared to remain in the background, Larry referred to her constantly, and refused to travel unless she was with him. It was simply stated that she was his second wife. There was no indication of the identity of Larry's first wife.

Because of the article she drank two martinis at lunchtime, and forced one on Harriet, who didn't want it. It wasn't a good start for a P.T.A. meeting. She was vaguely ashamed because she gargled to take away the smell of the alcohol before she set out with Harriet. On the way to the meeting she drove the Thunderbird wildly, and a little dangerously. She felt that she should apologise to Harriet about the driving, but she didn't.

Through the long drawn-out meeting she endured a splitting headache, and when she asked Harriet for aspirin, she was grateful because Harriet didn't look either sympathetic or reproachful. She knew she wasn't being effective as the bridge between the new people of Amtec and the town—not what she thought everyone had expected her to be. She made little or no impression on the meeting, merely nodding in agreement with the speaker from time to time, and drawing elaborate doodles on the pad on which she was supposed to make notes.

151

But she forgot a little about Larry and the meeting as she sat before the mirror now with the martini glass between her fingers. There was the evening to think about, the return to the familiar things—the walk through the crowded room in a dress that made every man look at her in a way that every woman envied, the talk of show business, the big names and the big salaries. She belonged there, and even after a year of Burnham Falls, she still believed that she would find her way back. Then she looked at the clock and realised that if they were to be on time for the appointment with E. J. Harrison and Phil Conrad they would have to be on the road in thirty minutes from now. It was suddenly painful to remember when the Oak Room and the Plaza had been only five blocks away.

With a return of her nervous haste she jerked open the drawers and started taking out the cosmetic bottles. And then she looked up to the mirror and saw Elizabeth standing in the doorway.

"Hallo," the girl said hesitantly.

Laura forced a smile. "Hi," she said brightly. "Come in."

After the move to Burnham Falls. Elizabeth had seemed to enjoy the novelty of country living, but now that the second long summer vacation had come round, time hung heavily. She did not make friends; she was weary and bored, yawning through the hot days, lying under the trees, her book beside her unread, wandering restlessly through the house, sitting hypnotised for whole afternoons before the television set. She was like a fractious young girl, breaking and destroying her playthings and yet unable to replace them with anything better. She stood now and stared at her stepmother with a listless, mournful gaze.

As always, she made Laura feel uncomfortable. Laura dipped into the foundation cream and began applying it quickly and skilfully about her eyes. "It was a terrible afternoon," she said, grasping for something to say to Elizabeth. "The trouble is, I just shouldn't be on any school-boards or committees. . . ."

The girl shrugged, cutting her short. "Oh, well . . . you don't have to do much. They have to ask you on because of Daddy, but you needn't really *do* anything."

For a fraction of the second Laura's fingers stopped, then she quickly reached for the powder. "No . . . I suppose
152

you're right." She gave a shaky little laugh. "No one expects me to *do* anything."

Elizabeth had come closer to the dressing-table. Her lumpy, awkward body seemed to fill all the space in the mirror; she crowded on Laura overpoweringly. She was untidy, and her hair was pulled back lankly into an elastic band.

Laura shifted her stool a trifle; immediately Elizabeth moved back.

"Did you enjoy going to the Dexters' yesterday?" Laura asked. "The boys are nice, aren't they? Tim and . . . what's the older one's name?"

"Gene," Elizabeth supplied.

"Oh, yes—Gene. I suppose his name is Eugene. They say he's very clever. Harriet told me he gets excellent grades in school. But it's Tim, the young one, who takes after Steve. He's mad on physics and chemistry . . . but not Gene. Did you like Gene?"

Elizabeth shrugged again. "I suppose so . . . I didn't see much of him. Or either of them. They're both too young to interest me much. They belong in Clare's group. Tim spent *hours* showing her that electronic junk he has in his room, and Gene stood in the doorway and watched, and neither of them knew that that little fool didn't understand a word of what Tim was saying. They can only see that silly baby face . . ."

"And what did you do?" Laura said, more gently.

"Me? . . . Oh, I talked to Mrs. Dexter mostly. She's nice, isn't she, Laura? I mean, sort of . . . comfortable . . ."

"Yes." Laura nodded to her in the mirror. "Yes, she is."

"And there's this old woman who works for them . . . Nell. She's been with them since Mrs. Dexter was a little girl. She told me that her nephew is married to Selma— you know, who works here. And her grand-niece is that marvellous-looking girl who sells the cosmetics in Carter's. You remember her, Laura? The one who sold you perfume when you went in there to buy soap.'"

Laura smiled a little at the recollection. She picked up the hand-mirror, and began darkening and shaping her eyebrows. Elizabeth leaned in closer again. "I want to see how you do your eyes again. I practised, like you told me, but it didn't come out right. . . ." She put her face very near Laura's, and Laura moved away from her slightly, pretending that she needed to get nearer to the light.

153

"What else did you do at the Dexters'?" Laura said quickly. She hated anything to break the concentration she gave to the art of making-up; especially she didn't want it to-night, when it mattered more than it had done for some time.

"Well, I helped Mrs. Dexter do some gardening, and then we swept out the floor of that old Rolls they have." Her face took on some animation. "That's a wonderful car! And do you know, she let me drive it!"

Laura glanced at her. "She let you drive it?"

"Well, just to the gate, and back. But I told her I'd never been in a car before that had that old-fashioned gear shift on the floor, and so she explained to me how it worked, and then she let me have a go with it. Gee, that's a marvellous-looking car—all that polished wood, and everything!"

Elizabeth picked up the eye shadow stick. "You use this kind of silvery stuff at night?"

"Yes, it seems to spark up my eyes a little."

Next Elizabeth took up the foundation cream, opened and smelled it, and then laid it down, leaving the lid off. Laura hated having any of her cosmetics left exposed to dust.

"Is Daddy going to have a swimming-pool put in this summer?" Elizabeth asked. It was said without the faintest enthusiasm.

"Wouldn't you like that? Don't you think you'd like to be able to swim whenever you wanted?"

"There are plenty of lakes around here to swim in." Then she added swiftly, "No one else has a swimming-pool in this town."

"Don't you want a pool?" It had never occurred to Laura that such a thing might be unwelcome. Remembering her own childhood of wanting and envying those who had what she wanted, she was utterly bewildered. "Wouldn't it be nice for . . . your friends?"

Elizabeth shrugged again, indifferently acquiescing. "Pools are so chi-chi—I'll bet we have those horrible tables and umbrellas around it."

"I'll let you pick whatever you want," Laura promised. "What about that?"

"It doesn't matter that much," Elizabeth said. She had lost interest. For a minute she reflectively bit on a hangnail. Then she said abruptly, "The Dexters have a nice house, don't they?"

154

"Do you like it?"

"I've always liked it—kind of big and roomy. Mrs. Dexter told me those big trees have been there more than two hundred years."

Laura had finished at the dressing-table, and she got up and took from the wardrobe a dress of dull olive-green jersey, muted and soft, that clung to her figure like wax. As she zipped it up, she said to Elizabeth, "Your grandmother's place in Pennsylvania is old, too."

"Oh, Grandmother's! That's only a show-place." She plumped herself down on the dressing-stool. "I wish we lived in a place like the Dexters'."

"Why, don't you like this house?" Laura was turned away from her, searching for the copper-beaded handbag that went with the dress.

"Oh, it's all right, I suppose. But you can't *go* anywhere in this house. All this glass—you stand inside the front door, and you can see from end to end of it. And all those crazy pictures Daddy's hung on the walls! It looks like a museum!"

"Those pictures are worth a great deal of money," Laura said mildly. "Their price is going up all the time—as you'll know when you inherit them. They're a good investment. And this house . . . well, you read what they said about it in the *New York Times*."

"Oh, yes, I know. A show-place—just a different kind from Grandmother's."

"It isn't so bad," Laura said, turning back to the girl. "It could be . . . Elizabeth! . . . *Put that down! Not* martinis! Not yet!"

The girl returned the glass angrily to the tray, spilling most of what was left.

"Oh, damn you! I was only having a *sip*! What do you think I am—a kid, or something?" Her face had flushed an ugly red; she looked big and clumsy, and wretched, twisting one hand nervously in the other. She moved jerkily past Laura to the door, then paused.

"Well, it won't be long before I'm eighteen, and then I can go and live with my mother in Paris! I won't be shut up any more in this stupid one-horse town!"

On her way out she banged her elbow against the door jamb. Laura listened to her heavy footsteps along the passage, and the slam of her bedroom door. Half a minute later came the blaring sound of a rock-and-roll record,

155

with the volume turned up high. The noise seemed to vibrate through the house. Laura found herself clenching her hands.

Then, through the sound of the record she heard the too-sharp braking of Ed's car in the driveway, but his quick light footsteps in the foyer made hardly any sound.

"For God's sake, what's that row!" He came through the bedroom, and paused as he caught sight of Laura standing in the dressing-room.

"Well, hell, can't you *do* something about it? Make her turn it off! And get me a drink, will you? We're going to be late!"

II

The glass had been well chilled before the martini was poured, and even the stem felt cool to her touch; she gripped it in a nervous, tight enjoyment, and let the sounds of the voices flow over her, the excited, brittle voices that always had an unceasing urgency in them. She listened to the dull crack of ice against glass, saw the studied motions of women smoking cigarettes in holders, the flash of jewellery, real and fake, noticed the alert scanning by those already seated of each new group that entered the dining-room, the readiness to claim acquaintances, the extravagance of the greetings—all the familiar tricks and gambits to gain a few seconds of attention, to be for a moment the focal point. Then at last she leaned back and relaxed her grip of the thin stem; it was good to feel at home again.

She drew a cigarette from her case, and immediately Phil Conrad, seated beside her, proffered his lighter.

"Laura, it's wonderful to see you looking so well," he said smoothly. "But I'm glad country life hasn't changed you into an outdoor-girl type . . . you know, suntan, and close-cropped hair." He looked across the table to include E. J. Harrison, and Ed, sitting opposite. "You know, there's nothing I admire so much as a really well-turned-out woman, and in my book, Laura has always taken the prize."

She drew on her cigarette, and wondered if the remark had offended Bette Harrison, who was corseted just a little too tightly into her five-hundred-dollar dress. Bette Harrison was almost thirty years younger than E. J., and his third wife; recently she had started to put on flesh, and her once

156

doll-like features had begun to coarsen a little. It did Ed no good to have Bette ruffled by compliments paid to his wife. But to-night, Phil Conrad could say anything he wanted, and they would all take it without a murmur—because to-night Amtec was trying to buy Phil Conrad, and he hadn't yet said " yes."

Laura gestured to deprecate his last words. " What did you expect me to do? . . . Change my name to Maggie and use a perfume that smelled like hay? I'm hardly that good an actress."

E. J. patted her hand approvingly. " You're a very fine actress, my dear—as Amtec has reason to be grateful for."

" Amtec?" Phil said. " What does——?" Then he recovered himself quickly. " Oh, yes . . . the commercials. You know, Laura, I caught one or two of those . . and you managed to stand beside a kitchen stove and still look beautiful. Quite a feat."

E. J. kept hold of her hand. " Laura did very well for Amtec with those commercials . . . we don't forget that." He leaned closer and gave her hand a squeeze. Later, after he had drunk a good deal more, when dinner was over and they were leaving, he would take the opportunity to kiss her, not affectionately or in camaraderie, but holding her too purposefully and too close. Ed would pretend not to notice. And because he was Ed's boss, she would let him kiss her in that way.

" And speaking of commercials . . ." Phil went on, " I hope this deal doesn't mean I'm supposed to stand in front of the camera and sell corporate goodwill." He said it with a trace of a laugh, but at the same time he nodded almost imperceptibly across at Martin Ewen, who was meant to take over from this point.

Laura sat back, and let them talk. She had nothing to add to this part of the evening; her role was to sit and to look decorative, a strong and tangible link between Amtec and the world of show business, the world of Philip Conrad.

At the moment, Conrad was riding the top of his world, which was why Amtec wanted him. He had three successful shows currently running on Broadway, and in the past few years he had turned two of his previous hit plays into movies, and both of them had made big slices of money at the box office. He was a star-maker for the Broadway stage. He was forty-four years old, and some people said his fall would be as swift as his climb, that he had had luck, not taste or talent. But for the moment he had the name and the prestige, and Amtec wanted to buy them.

They were trying to persuade him to lend the Conrad name, the Conrad touch, and the Conrad stars to a proposed series of dramas for television—which Amtec would sponsor for corporate advertising and prestige. They would be ninety-minute specials, produced with the kind of budget and stars that Conrad would demand, and Amtec would be glad to pay for. Overtures had first been made to Conrad two months ago; he had listened, with no very great show of interest, and had, as yet, neither said yes nor no. And there would not be a definite answer until the price had gone higher, and he was given stock options in Amtec.

To-night's meeting was only one in a series of equally inconclusive ones. It was understood that no real terms would be discussed at this table; in any case, it was not the function of the Chairman of the Board and a president of one of the Amtec subsidiaries to make Conrad an offer. They were simply here to let him know that the interest in the project went to the highest level of Amtec, and that they had a proper respect for Conrad's status. Conrad was not going to be bought by money only; he demanded courting and wooing.

So they sat around the table, smiling and genial, with only the vaguest references to the purpose that had brought them all together . . . E. J. Harrison and Bette, Martin Ewen, Conrad's business manager, Conrad, E., and Laura. Conrad had been divorced two years ago, and had not remarried. He had been invited to bring a companion, but had brought Ewen instead.

Ed Peters was there only because of Laura. In striving to create a balance between the business and æsthetic overtures of this meeting, E. J. had found an answer in Laura She had been a Broadway star, her name was well known in show business, for years she had had a slight acquaintance with Conrad, and a year ago she had persuaded Ed to invest rather heavily in one of Conrad's productions. This last fact wouldn't have especially endeared her to Conrad, because his productions were usually over-subscribed, but *The Lark at Morning* was the work of an unknown English writer, and Conrad had had difficulty raising the money for it, and even casting it. *The Lark at Morning* had opened to rave reviews last January, and had already returned the money to the
158

backers. Conrad was said to have a special affection for the play, and it extended to the people who had helped bring it to Broadway. E. J. had wanted Laura and Ed at this dinner as proof that Amtec was not controlled only by people who dealt in figures and machines. As further proof he had brought Ed's collection of modern art into the conversation. When Conrad had expressed polite interest in it, Laura had seen E. J. glance meaningfully at her, and she knew that she was to press Conrad to visit them —to see the pictures, the new research centre, and the Pirello statues.

But for the most part Laura sat and listened passively to the conversation. She was not hungry, and hardly touched the lobster she had asked for. E. J. had ordered a lovely hock, dry and light, but the martinis had blurred the taste for her; even the smell of it was lost a little. She regretted that; Larry had taught her some of his own appreciation of fine wines. She was aware—in the way that a woman always senses it—that Phil Conrad kept looking towards her with more than ordinary interest; she did nothing about it, and did not try to draw his attention back to herself when he looked away. But he kept coming back, and she was warmed and reassured by it. She felt languid, where before she had been tense; it was a soothing dream-like sensation. She liked the knowledge that she was making no special effort to please, and still was pleasing. The dinner came to an end with nothing concrete having been said by Conrad or E. J. The negotiations were still in existence, neither forward nor back, it seemed. They all smiled genially at each other, and nothing much was said. Laura sensed that the wooing of Phil Conrad could take a long time.

Bette Harrison led the way out of the room, and Laura felt as a beautiful woman feels when she is forced to stand back and allow another woman to precede her.

CHAPTER FIVE

A kind of hush had now settled on the Carpenter place, the hush that replaces the bustle of preparation; now it was the time of waiting. The summer night was warm; the breeze was barely strong enough to stir the leaves of the oaks, and it carried with it the scents of the countryside

159

in summer—a dusty scent because there had been too little rain, and the scent of the roses that bloomed on the creeper below the bedroom window. From where she sat at the dressing-table Harriet could smell the roses, even above the perfume she wore; she was dressed, and had finished her make-up and her hair. The room was tidy and waiting for the women who would stand and talk here during the evening, while others bent towards the mirror to apply powder and lipstick. There was nothing more to do but go and re-inspect all the things that had been ready before she came upstairs to change.

She walked downstairs slowly, but Steve heard her step, and he came out of the small room at the back of the house where he kept his books and papers. As she reached the bottom of the stairs he gave a little admiring whistle.

"Excuse me, ma'am—are you doing anything to-night? Could I have the pleasure of your company?" Then he added, "Wonderful—what's it called? Whipped chocolate mocha?"

She smoothed the folds of the skirt; it was a dark coffee colour with large black spots raised on it. "*I* think it's nice," she said. "It's almost too nice to associate with anything so political as this evening's gathering."

"But Phil Conrad . . ." Steve was grinning. "He's used to looking at the best and so "—he gestured towards her—" we have the best!"

Harriet wrinkled her nose. "What I don't like is the idea of it's being a kind of Command Performance." She assumed an exaggerated imitation of Laura's voice. "*Harriet . . . we would like to bring Phil Conrad over to your house, and perhaps you would ask a few people to meet him.*" She gave an elegant snort. "And then told me exactly *whom* we should ask!" She sighed. "It seems to me that ever since we had the house redecorated, Laura thinks it's a quaint idea to invite her guests to come and see over the Dexters' charming old relic of a house."

"Oh, hell!" Steve shrugged. "It's either here or the country club. The choice is obvious."

"I get your point," Harriet agreed. "But I still think this is a rather dull gathering to ask the distinguished and debonair Phil Conrad to. At least, I assume he's debonair—aren't all men of the theatre supposed to be?"

"No—some of them are merely fat. But I hear Phil
160

Conrad is all the things he's supposed to be." He leaned against the door jamb, hands in pockets. "Perhaps this evening will be a pleasant change for him—perhaps that's why Ed Peters planned it. After all, you can alway count on Ed not leaving much to chance."

"Well . . . the guest list was heavily stacked on the intellectual side . . . the Jenningses, the Armstrongs. . . . No one who's merely administrative gets a look in."

"My dear girl," Steve said mildly, "these are scientists, not intellectuals. You must learn to distinguish. None of us has opened a book that departs from our speciality for years. Perhaps Amtec wants to give Conrad the impression that a Nobel Prize is dangling over one of our heads, and that he'd be proud to be associated with the company. In any case, for whatever reason, Amtec is putting a good deal of trust in you to-night . . . trusting you to arrange a gathering that might be small town, but isn't suburban, and to show Conrad that earnest men of science have beautiful wives."

She smiled at him. "Sometimes, when you remember, you can say the nicest things."

Abruptly the half-mocking look left his own face. He came towards her, and placed a kiss lightly on her lips. "I'll remember too seldom, Harriet, it's because I'm a fool who doesn't deserve you . . . and because I've grown used to trusting you, and knowing that you're here. A bad habit, and I wonder why I haven't lost you because of it long before this." His grip tightened a little. "Stay with me?"

She nodded. "Yes." She drew back a little, before he could kiss her again. "I . . . I just want to check things once more before people start arriving."

He released her reluctantly, and she was gone from him at the same instant. He turned and followed her towards the dining-room.

He said then, with a touch of irritation, "Wouldn't it have been less fuss to have the whole thing catered? You and Nell have been on the go since six this morning. . . ."

"That would have been a mistake—Laura stressed that Phil Conrad was just coming for a quiet country week-end, and I took the hint that I was to make this party look as impromptu as was compatible with giving them something decent to eat." She gave a little sigh. "Always so much more trouble to be casually informal, than to hire the whole works and be done with it. If I had my way there'd be three white-coated gentlemen doing the whole thing, instead of Nell and Selma rushing frantically in the kitchen and me trying to stay calm out here."

She was a little ahead of him, as she opened back the double doors into the dining-room.

" But it does look nice, doesn't it?"

The scent of the roses met them first—golden and red garden roses, fat and sensuous, in white Minton bowls. The long table was laid with the fine cloth, china and silver which Harriet had inherited from Claudia; the centre of it bare and waiting for the buffet dishes from the kitchen. This room, with the rest of the house, had been repainted in the spring, and for here Harriet had chosen dull gold curtains that were left open now to admit whatever breeze would enter. The simple spoke-backed chairs stood against the walls, their shapes reflected in the richly-waxed floor. It was a handsome room, with the tall windows facing the view of the town and the lake—not an overformal room, but not lax or indulgent.

" Yes—it is nice," Steve said.

It was more than nice, Harriet thought. It looked as good now as ever it had done in Joe's heyday—better perhaps, because the house had mellowed, the floors and furniture had acquired a deeper patina from age and constant waxing, and in spite of the redecorating, it still retained its look of usage. A new heating system had been installed, an extra bathroom carved out of the over-generous master bedroom, a big pantry downstairs turned into a cloakroom. There was a dishwater in the kitchen, and a new washer and dryer in the basement. Outside the house glistened with fresh white paint, and in two seasons of regular attendance Ted Talbot had brought the lawn back to something approaching the state Joe had liked to see it in. Yes, the house looked fine, Harriet thought, but restoring it had cost every penny of Steve's salary—and they were still paying on the mortgage Joe had left to them. The savings account at the First National didn't look one bit better than it had at the moment Steve had gone to work for Amtec. There had been no choice— Amtec expected Steve to represent them adequately, and they had complied. If they went into debt to do it, then they were no different from every other family in the same circumstances. Harriet had vague hopes that some day, perhaps after Gene and Tim were through college, it might be possible to put some money aside each year. But the time was

162

not now. Once again she smoothed the folds of her skirt, remembering how she had skimped and saved the first eighteen months after Steve had joined Amtec in order to pay off their debts—and Steve, busy on the West Coast, and in England, had almost forgotten her existence—which was what mostly happened to the martyrs of the world, she thought, and quite often they deserved it. She remembered how she had gone to the Amtec opening here in Burnham Falls in a shabby, out-of-date suit; then in time she had learned that she helped neither Steve nor herself by these obvious kinds of economies, and she had had to learn to spend without feeling guilty. There wasn't much place in Amtec for the existence of good old-fashioned Yankee thrift, because, after all, it was a form of mistrust of the pension plans and the sickness and accident benefits. All that mattered was to keep your job, and there would be no other problems. You had only to place your trust in unlimited productivity and prosperity of the whole country, and Amtec's place in it—and then you rode all the way with Amtec. That was the doctrine, and she and Steve had adhered to it when they redecorated the house, and bought the new furnishings. It looked now as Joe Carpenter would have been proud to see it look, but it was a little spoiled for them because it had been done more for other people than themselves. She looked at the room now and thought that it belonged more to Phil Conrad than to her, Harriet. She felt a little bit cheated.

"You'll have that dress worn out if you don't stop rubbing it," Steve said gently beside her.

She almost started at the sound of his voice, and realised that she had been staring unseeingly at the empty room. "Oh! . . ." Then she smiled. "I wasn't rubbing—I was stroking. I'm enjoying wearing it."

"You should," he said. "You look very lovely."

She turned plucking at his sleeve. "Come on . . . I haven't any more time to stand admiring. I'll send Selma in with the ice. It's almost time for people to start arriving."

"How did it go to-day at the cabin?" he said, as she started towards the kitchen. He sounded as if he had grabbed at the question unthinkingly, looking for something that would pull her back to him.

She stopped and turned round again. "Oh . . . fine—I suppose. Jeff Anderson delivered the new fridge, which immediately made everything else in the kitchen look a hundred years old—and I had him check over all the cords and

163

light sockets. The place looks O.K. . . . all rather faded and shabby, though. The sofas are a bit rattly, and the beds not as soft as I seem to remember them. If it's a rustic fishing cabin Phil Conrad wants, then he's certainly got it.

"Oh, to hell with Phil Conrad! The Peterses are damn' lucky to have the place to offer him. That's one of the best fishing lakes in the whole district. What more does he want beside a lake stuffed with fish, and a cabin with electricity, running water and a clean bed? That's doing it in style."

"Apparently that's how they plan to do it," Harriet said dryly. "At least judging from the kind of canned and frozen stuff Laura sent over to stock the larder—Nova Scotia salmon, caviare, smoked oysters—a case of liquor—canned ham and Swedish meat balls. Elizabeth brought it all over, and explained to me earnestly that Laura and Ed would bring the *real* food with them to-morrow morning when they went there with Mr. Conrad. Somehow I've never imagined Laura slaving over the stove—except in those commercials— but this is one time she'll *have* to play the rustic gal or the whole effect will be spoiled. It would hardly do if they brought the cook with them."

"I thought they were supposed to live off the fish they caught!" Steve said. He jerked at his tie, meaning to straighten it, but instead he pulled it more out of place. Harriet stood half-turned ready to go. He said, "You don't sound too friendly towards Laura."

"I'm not," Harriet said shortly. "Not after she sent Elizabeth on her errands because she was spending the day in New York."

"Did Elizabeth go with you to the cabin?"

"Yes—she spent the whole day with us. I think she enjoyed it—she scrubbed the kitchen floor, and helped me sweep the bedrooms and dust. Quite a change for Ed Peters' daughter. Gene and Tim were with us—they swept up outside, after a fashion, and had one of their raging quarrels. Gene took off into the woods. By the way . . . there's a couple of planks missing from the jetty. I hope Mr. Conrad doesn't fall through."

Steve shrugged. "Couldn't happen to a nicer guy."

She took a step away and then looked back. "Oh! . . . And I broke the sacred guest list. After all, this *is* our house and our fishing cabin. I asked Clif to come along. I thought Phil Conrad should meet at least one person who was here

164

before Amtec . . . sort of prehistoric, you know. One of the natives."

"Well, I asked another native . . . I forgot to tell you."

"Who?"

"Mal Hamilton . . . he turned up to-day with a new set of drawings for us to look at. He's on his way up North, and I persuaded him to take a room at the motel, and to come along here. I thought he might liven things up—a little less like one of the faculty."

"Yes," she smiled weakly. "Yes . . . fine. Good idea." She fingered her skirt again. "I'll tell Selma to bring in the ice."

The tap of her heels on the polished wood sounded unnaturally loud as she walked down the hall.

The kitchen door was behind the stairs, and she paused there, listening. For a second she thought Steve was about to follow her, but he moved instead into the living-room, and she could hear the clink of glasses and bottles on the table where the drinks were set out. He was whistling again— the thin, tuneless whistle that meant he was preoccupied. It had a lonely sound, that whistle. He should not have been there alone, rearranging glasses that did not need it; he should have been part of the nervous, last-minute flurry before the party, part of the noise and voices here on the other side of the door—Gene's and Tim's voices, and Nell's deeper tones cutting across them, and a gentler response from Selma. Harriet knew it was her fault that he was out there alone—she had rebuffed him, and he had retreated. With her hand on the door, ready to push it open, she paused.

"Oh, Mal . . . Mal . . . What am I doing?"

For three weeks, since that day on the train, he had scarcely been absent from her thoughts—the feeling of him being there was like a haunting little obbligato that accompanied her every waking moment, but which grew even more real as she slept. In every humdrum circumstance of her day, in every part of the town life, she was picturing Mal; she searched for his face among the shoppers on Main Street, and watched for the familiar red hair and gaunt face among the crowds. She kept waiting to hear his voice, the shock and surprise of it as it had happened on the train—waiting for a random mention of his name. It was a madness she had carried with her for three weeks, and she couldn't put it away.

Twice Steve had brought him to the house for dinner

165

—that first time he had come with Clif, but the second time Steve hadn't even called to warn her. They had arrived together in Steve's car from the Laboratories, and the first warning she had had was the sound of their voices in the hall. They had sat on the porch and had a drink together, and she had joined them and once again had been unnaturally silent; but when she had gone to wash before dinner she had seen that her face was flushed and excited, like a school-girl's, and her hand went immediately to the perfume on the dressing-table, and she was dabbing it on before she realised the implication of her action. Guiltily she had put it down, and gone quickly to help Nell serve the meal. Then several times during the evening she had caught herself staring at Mal without restraint or caution, and she felt wretched because Steve might have seen it too.

She was even jealous of Gene and Tim because they took to Mal immediately, and monopolised his attention through the meal. She was shamed by the feeling, but her shame did not lessen it.

After those first few moments in the train they had never spoken together alone for a single minute—but from her need grew the game of searching for him, and waiting for him.

She knew now, as she stood with her hand on the kitchen door, that, consciously or unconsciously, she had been waiting all day to hear that he would be coming to-night. No one had been certain that he would be in Burnham Falls to-day because his schedule was irregular and unpredictable. All she knew was that Mal had promised Steve some drawings by the end of the week, and there was a good chance that if he was in Burnham Falls to-day, he might also be in their house this evening. Ever since Steve had come home, she had been wanting to ask, and had not been able to; with every passing moment her sense of disappointment had grown deeper, and she had had the feeling of a child about to cry—unreasonably and bitterly. It didn't do any good either, to tell herself that she was behaving like a fool.

And then Steve had said he was coming, and she felt weak with relief and pleasure.

She looked down at her dress, and the new shoes, that were frivolous and flattering. The dress and the shoes and the hair style from one of the exclusive New York hairdressers —after which she had inwardly apologised to Laura—were not so much for Phil Conrad's party, as for the unvoiced hope that perhaps Mal would see her wearing them. As

166

stupid and shaming as it was, she had to admit it. And to-night she had looked more attractive than she had done in a long time, and Steve had been aware of it, and had reached out to her. She had rebuffed him, and he was alone now.

"Why . . . you're about to make a fool of yourself over Mal Hamilton," she said silently. As she mouthed the words, a terrible awareness of her situation came to her. Once before, on the night that Josh had left Burnham Falls, she had thrown herself into Mal's arms—and in the next room she could hear the voices of her children, reminding her that it had all happened a very long time ago.

She raised her head, and pushed open the door.

Jeannie Talbot was standing by the kitchen table when she went in, wrapped in one of Nell's big white aprons. She was stooped over the chopping-board, chopping parsley with nice precision, and listening to something Tim was saying.

"Jeannie! I didn't expect to see you here!"

She looked up. "Oh, hi, Mrs. Dexter—I didn't think you'd mind. I thought I'd come along and give Mom and Aunt Nell a hand with the washing up." Then she smiled. "That wasn't the real reason—I haven't been here since it was redecorated and I wanted to look at it. It's beautiful, isn't it?"

Harriet returned her smile. She always felt unaccountably drawn towards Jeannie; there was a rich warmth about her that somehow made the women about her seem meagre and pale—all women except her own mother. In the past year she had matured rapidly; she looked slender because she was tall, but Harriet noted the full breasts and the hips that curved voluptuously. She was unaffectedly sensuous, in a way that Harriet thought many men would find irresistible.

"Glad to have you, Jeannie—any time." Then she added, "But what about Jerry? . . . I thought he monopolised any spare time you had."

She shrugged. "He's pretty busy himself—Mr. Keston thinks it's good for his soul—or something—to work late at the bank a few nights a week. Then . . . Jerry and I don't exactly see eye to eye about a few things, and so he's been giving me the aloof treatment lately." Then she smiled and inclined her head towards the boy beside her. "But I haven't been lonely—Tim has been entertaining me nicely."

Tim flushed a little, and was unable to keep the grin of pleasure off his face. "Stop teasing, Jeannie," he said. He

167

turned to his mother. "You look real pretty, Mom." And then he rushed on. "How do I look?"

He straightened himself for Harriet's inspection. He was wearing his best grey flannel suit, and a dark blue tie. His hair was carefully slicked back.

"Aw—listen to little Lord Fauntleroy, will you?" Gene looked at his younger brother scornfully, and then turned back to a tray of canapés, from which he selected one, inspected it, and then returned it in favour of another one.

Harriet gave a little squawk. "Gene! . . . *Don't* do that. Eat one, if you like, but don't *paw* them all. They'll all look so grubby!"

"Aw—well, I'm hungry."

Nell looked round from the sink. "You're always hungry! There just isn't any filling your stomach these days. If you must eat, take it from the stuff that isn't set out. And get yourself upstairs and washed and changed into something decent. You're not fit to be seen."

He flushed and looked across at his mother. "Do I have to, Mom?" he demanded.

She nodded. "Yes—a clean shirt, at least. You don't have to put on a tie. You should have done it long ago . . . hurry now."

"Aw . . . who the hell's going to see me!" He shuffled unwillingly towards the door, his shoulders hunched and his head bent slightly forward over his tall body, in a way that was exactly Steve's. He took a handful of nuts as he went by the bowl, spilled some, and muttered in disgust as he bent to pick them up again. Harriet suddenly noticed that his jeans, which had been too long for him three months ago, were showing a long stretch of ankle. His face was still dark and flushed, and she wanted to put her arms about him and cradle his head, but Gene was too old for that . . . at least he was too old when he was watched by Tim and Jeannie. He fumbled awkwardly with the nuts as he put them back. She gave him a quick smile as he moved towards the door, but his eyes were lowered again, and he didn't see it, and so he went, uncomforted and uncheered. Now she associated his loneliness with Steve's, and she felt she had failed both of them.

Empty-handed, she stood staring at the activity around her, the final bustle in the kitchen, as if she was not part of it.

She came suddenly out of her trance to see Jeannie, knife poised in her hand, looking curiously at her.

168

"I think I heard a car outside, Mrs. Dexter."

"A car?" She blinked. "Oh . . . yes!" She started to leave. "Selma, bring the ice out right away, please."

She went into the hall with a welcoming smile already fixed on her face.

II

Harriet paused in the door of the living-room for a moment before she went back to the kitchen to tell Selma to start more coffee going. She narrowed her eyes a little as she watched the group, wondering if the evening had gone as well as it seemed, or if perhaps she had passed through it in a kind of bright daze that did not permit the overtones to penetrate. Looking at it as detachedly as she could, it seemed, on the surface, well enough.

A group this size fitted comfortably into the big living-room—they sat about in the deep chairs and the two long sofas, and there was little movement among them, except the raising and lowering of the coffee cups and the brandy glasses, or when they broke into laughter. They were absorbed in the woman at the piano. Harriet wondered how she could have known Maggie Jeffries for more than a year, and not suspected her comic gift of mimicry. She sat now at the piano, improvising mostly—or so it seemed—her glass of Scotch within reach. The only person who appeared not to be enjoying the show was her husband, Harlan. It had started because Maggie had drunk more whisky than usual, and had sprouted courage to ignore Harlan's black looks when she started tinkering at the piano. Harlan was the youngest director at the Laboratories, and Harriet had never heard him utter a word that had not seemed rehearsed and considered. Maggie escaped his influence only with the Scotch, suddenly revealing a small genius of the intimate, cabaret style singing. Her voice was quite bad, but oddly fascinating. Only Harlan's nervous glances at Ed Peters marred the group's concentration on her.

But for once, Ed Peters looked relaxed, though Laura, sitting on the sofa opposite him, was not. She seemed to Harriet a trifle thinner but that only accentuated the lovely hollows under the high cheek-bones. She was more beautiful. Her long white hands, scarlet-tipped, fidgeted with an unlit cigarette, and presently Phil Conrad, sitting beside her,

169

noticed it, and leaned towards her to light it. He immediately turned back to watch Maggie. It was then that Harriet realised that Laura herself was not paying attention.

Across the room, Steve noticed her standing by the door, and gave her a little smile and a nod that indicated satisfaction, even pleasure. She thought that Steve had changed in a year, since he was now aware of things that had before never concerned him. He had counted and measured the successes and failures of this evening just as carefully as she. But so had she changed, and everyone else in Burnham Falls . . . and then her gaze moved to Clif, sitting opposite Laura. She knew he had deliberately seated himself there, claiming that it was a legitimate pleasure at his age to stare at beautiful women without giving offence; even Ed Peters had smiled when he had said this. Clif had not changed, Harriet thought —or perhaps his change had been to stand even firmer in the customs and ways that had been Burnham Falls before Amtec came. He had cast himself in a role of unnatural rigidity, and this was his change.

Her gaze moved on . . . Marion Jennings, probably even more brilliant than her husband, who was one of Amtec's best men . . . she was waiting to get her hands on Burnham Falls High School to prove what she could accomplish with her theories on education . . . placid, content Ginny Armstrong, sitting beside Harry, amused, but darting glances now and then towards Ed Peters, and wondering how Maggie could have the gall to shed her inhibitions before not only Ed Peters, but before a Broadway producer. To-morrow, Harriet thought, Amtec Park would buzz with the news that Maggie Jeffries had let go at the Dexter party. The strange thing was that Phil Conrad, instead of backing away defensively from an amateur, seemed to be enjoying himself. Everyone in the room, including Ed, was taking his cue from Conrad's face. So long as it was relaxed and even faintly amused, the party was a success. It had taken Harriet some time to grow used to the idea that social success for Steve was almost as important to his future with Amtec as what he produced in his laboratory. Steve himself had learned reluctantly, but finally.

Her survey was finished, and she was satisfied, and her eyes returned to the empty chair where Mal had been sitting. He had been gone now for more than twenty minutes—she knew it had been that long because she had been uneasily conscious of his absence. She knew also that going for more

170

coffee was merely an excuse to seek Mal. For the last ten minutes she had struggled with the desire, and now she could not help herself. She was going because, while he was in her house, she could not bear the thought of being out of range of his voice, of not being a part of whatever concerned or interested him. She had to know what he was doing, what he was thinking and saying. She had to get herself noticed by him. It occurred to her, as she left the living-room, that she was no more sophisticated than Gene and Tim in the way she competed for his attention. Her cheeks burned a little at the thought of it, but still she didn't go back to the living-room.

She pushed open the kitchen door, and found him there, as she had expected. A sudden hush greeted her entrance, and they all looked towards her expectantly.

" Oh . . . I . . ." She ran her tongue quickly over her dry lips, suddenly out of countenance in her own kitchen. Mal was leaning back against the sink, with a coffee cup in his hand. He greeted her with a quick smile, but she still had the uncomfortable feeling that until she had opened the door, he had forgotten her existence. Nell was putting plates away in a high cupboard, Selma preparing another tray with the coffee things. Gene sat at the table, eating a wedge of cake; Tim was behind him, and had obviously been engrossed in what Mal was saying. Jeannie, still wrapped in the white apron, stood by the stove, also eating cake. The kitchen was spotless and swept, the dishes all put away. On the table was the package of left-overs she had told Nell to wrap for Selma. Nell had the kettle on, the waiting teapot beside it. Now, with the work done, this was the start of their own party. Harriet had the distinct impression that she was an unwelcome interruption.

" I think we'll be ready for another round of coffee in a few minutes, Nell."

" It's just started perking," Nell said, glancing at the coffee-maker. She closed the cupboard, and climbed down off the stool. " And how's the company out there?" she said irreverently. " Getting drunk and spilling liquor on your dad's good tapestry chairs?"

Harriet sighed. " Not enough to notice."

" I'll notice all right when it comes time to clean up," Nell answered. She cut herself a wedge of cake, and took a fork out of the drawer. She glanced at Gene. " Another piece?"

171

" Yeh." He held out his plate.

Harriet looked from Gene to Tim. " You should both be in bed," she said weakly. She was conscious that Mal was watching her, and she felt awkward in the role of mother to these two grown children. The gap between herself now and as he had known her in Los Angeles was ruthlessly and effectively bridged in the persons of Gene and Tim.

" Mom . . . not just now," Tim said. " Mal was just telling us . . ."

She had the courage to look at him fully for the first time. Out here the light was bright and unshaded, not like the flattering dimness of the living-room. Half-defensively she had so far avoided turning full-face towards him, aware of the slight sag of weariness about her mouth and eyes. But she couldn't go on playing a game of pretence ; she lifted her face towards the light.

" You sneaked away," she said to him. " What was the matter? . . . Dull party."

" No . . . not at all." He put down his cup on the sink, and instantly Jeannie moved to refill it from the battered old percolator in which they had brewed coffee for themselves. There was something conspiratorial in her quick movement, implying that if the rhythm was broken, he would escape them and go back to the group in the other room. It was then Harriet noticed he had been using one of the ordinary kitchen cups. He looked so comfortable, so much a part of things, and absurdly she was the outsider.

" You forget," he continued, " that I have a split personality about Burnham Falls these days. There's just as much of the old I want to see as the new."

Nell looked pleased, and tried to hide it. " Go on now —you never had much use for Nell Talbot in the old days. Could never get a word out of you. . . ."

Mal laughed. " Because I was scared stiff of you—for all the hand-outs you gave me from the ice box. I remember I'd just eat and run. . . ."

Harriet listened, but did not hear the banter that passed. They were all getting in the way, she thought. There was never a moment for her to face Mal without people in between. She felt cut off from him, lost. And then she wondered if he wanted it to be this way. Each time she encountered him, there seemed to be an audience about him, jostling each other for his attention. He seemed to do very little to achieve it, but it was there—and she must remain

172

one of the crowd. And it was even worse now, because she was on the fringe of the crowd. She looked despairingly at her children, and knew there was no way to break through. She sought for something to say, but there was so little time. Selma was preparing to take the fresh coffee into the living-room, and she would have to go too. A sense of dismay crowded on her. She looked from Jeannie's bright, expectant face to the eager faces of Gene and Tim, and then to Nell's habitually disapproving expression unsuccessfully struggling against her pleasure in Mal's presence in her kitchen. This was where the real party was going on, Harriet thought—it was here, not in the front room, with the brandy glasses and Maggie at the piano. Here, they were settling down to enjoy themselves in a way that wasn't possible in the other room. They seemed so free, and strangely young—even Nell, who was old.

Selma straightened her apron, and patted the black dress over her full hips. She picked up the tray. " Shall I take it in now, Mrs. Dexter?"

" Yes, Selma . . . please," she said reluctantly.

There was no further excuse to linger, and Mal did not even appear to notice that she was going. Almost before she left the kitchen the easy fellowship had settled in again and her coming had left hardly a mark.

It occurred to her as she returned to the living-room, that of all the guests there that night, only Mal was in a position to dare to leave the group in the living-room and go on his own way.

She wished it weren't moonlight, because it made everything so stupidly unreal, and gave her sleepless fantasies a value they would never have had in the broad light of day. The whole room was moon-touched, distorted. She saw the shapes of the furniture, her slip lying over a chair, Steve's shoes on the floor beside the closet but this was not the old-fashioned, familiar room that Joe and Claudia had inhabited; it seemed like a stage set, and she was a waxen dummy, and the man beside her in the big bed a stranger. She knew she was like this because only this way could she consciously permit the thought of Mal to intrude here. But he was an intrusion, a guilty one.

Finally, because the thoughts would not go away, she knew she must take them elsewhere. She sat up and slid one leg down to the floor. The old bed squeaked a little, and

173

she heard a check in the even rhythm of Steve's breathing.

"Whereya going?" he mumbled.

"Can't sleep . . . going down for some milk."

She didn't look back at him, but reached for her dressing-gown from the chair beside the bed. Before she touched it she heard Steve's movement behind her, and felt his hand on her thigh. Then his other hand grasped her waist, and he pulled her back gently. She lay sideways across the bed, and he pushed himself over next to her.

"Don't hurry away . . . not yet." He nuzzled his face into her neck while his hands urged away her nightgown. He had such sure hands, always, Harriet thought. For a second her body stiffened as she felt his hands—an instant's fierce rejection because Steve was not the man she wanted to possess her. But his hands were skilful, and her guilt was an insistent, aching thing that had to make atonement. She gave herself completely to his hands, and the pressure of his lips against her breasts. Then she turned wildly and pressed herself against him, her legs cradling him, urging him.

She spoke his name aloud, to make his presence more real, to wipe out the other name. "Steve . . ."

When he slept again, she went down to the kitchen. There were no traces of the party left; all was in order, and silent. She put the old coffee-pot on the stove, heaped fresh coffee into it, and went and sat at the table waiting for it to perk. Her body was slack and weary; she had spent herself with Steve, and had found no release, though she believed he had not known it. Her head slumped forward a little over the table. She was afraid to look up because when she looked up again she knew she would see the image of Mal leaning against the sink, gesturing slightly with the hand that held the cup, and around him again would be the circle of interested, admiring faces.

"Oh, God," she whispered, "how long do I have to live like this?" As she got up she seemed to stumble a little.

The pre-dawn greyness was finished, and full daylight was breaking now. She poured the coffee into an old mug that Gene had used as a baby, and carried it with her. She opened the front door wide to admit the dawn breeze; the screen door needed oiling. She closed it gently behind her. She settled herself in one of the chairs on the porch, and watched the light reaching into the valley, watched it start to colour

174

the grey of the lake. The houses of Burnham Falls began to lift up out of their anonymous mass; she could name almost everyone who slept under the placid old roofs, she knew most of their histories, as they knew hers. A diesel hooted in the morning stillness, and a freight train rattled over the level-crossing.

CHAPTER SIX

Sally Redmond also heard the hoot of the diesel echo through the valley. She liked the sound; it had grown to be a familiar thing in the time she had lived here. She looked towards Tom's hunched figure in the other bed, and smiled a little to see how tightly his eyes were closed in sleep, as if he concentrated on even that with the intensity he gave to everything else in his life. But now he also looked young, and surprisingly vulnerable. Or was it, she thought, just the indulgent fantasy of every pregnant woman to see in every man the image of her unborn child.

Through the half-closed venetian blind the light was growing stronger. In a few minutes the sun would be up. She loved these early silent hours before the valley began to stir. She liked to sit by the kitchen window with a cup of tea in her hand—the hang-over from the Irish household she had grown up in—and gaze over the roofs of the houses on the slope of the hill below her, and across to the Laboratories on the hill. Tom called it her day-dreaming time, and it was true that, with no cars on the highway and none climbing the road to the Laboratories, with the early sun so bright on the glass and aluminium, the building could almost have been the shining castle of her childhood story books.

She eased herself out of bed carefully, and slipped into her robe. In the kitchen were the stacked cups and plates from last night, when the Johnsons had dropped over, and they had talked until after midnight. Sally ignored them now, and put water on the stove for tea. She was in her bare feet; the floor felt deliciously cool, and to-day would be another hot one in the valley. It was Saturday, and Tom would have two days at home. She hunched a little over the stove as she waited for the kettle to come to the boil, and acknowledged it was strange that she still thought of week-ends in the

175

nature of holidays, when they had long ago ceased to be precisely that. The week-ends were busier than the other days, but it was a business they called leisure.

She took her tea to the stool by the window, curling her toes sensuously around the chromium rungs. She was thinking now about the party that had gone on last night at the Dexters', over on the other side of town. Through various sources the news that Phil Conrad would spend the week-end in Burnham Falls had leaked out. It was known in Amtec Park exactly which of the top echelon had been invited to meet him, and there was speculation about the feelings of those who had been left out. In Sally's mind there was something tremendously important about that invitation—an acknowledgment by Amtec of the possession of qualities that were a little more than those strictly required by one's job. To be invited to meet Phil Conrad you had to have a little glamour, or detachment, or at least the ability not to show how impressed you were. Phil Conrad was used to the company of urbane, sophisticated people and it wouldn't have done to expose him to the risk of boredom by company chatter. Sally, married to a junior member of one of the research teams and still years away from any of the protocol problems that last night's party represented, still knew exactly what the situation had been. She guessed readily enough why Harriet Dexter's house had been chosen. While she had never been in it, had never spoken to Harriet Dexter, she knew a lot about that house. It had a dignity and permanence about it that bore no relation whatever to the newness of Amtec Park, and which Laura Peters' house, with its expensive landscaping, could not achieve. It had something to do with those huge oak trees on the lawn, and the grey slate roof on the old wing. They said the house was stuffed with silver that Harriet's father had collected, and had some fine antique furniture. In a sense it was a more modest equivalent of the modern art Ed Peters owned . It was not surprising the choice had fallen on the Dexter house. Sally's mind went again to those executives who had not been invited . . . mentally she ran down the list . . . the Sommerses, the Harveys, the Triffs, the Sewells. In each case she could almost guess the reason why, and it had something to do with the wives—one too voluble about the welfare work she did, one too absorbed in her children, one fat and physically unattractive. A little flush mounted in her cheeks as she thought of it, and she sipped at her tea quickly. They expected a lot of you—to have all the virtues of a wife and mother, and to know when to hide them, to read the right books and keep your figure. If you had a college degree to be careful not to snub the woman who didn't—who might also be the wife of the president. There were pitfalls, and you had to be aware of them. She thought of the women at that party, and had a good idea of what it had been like, because by now she had observed each of them often enough in public to know what kind of women they were. At the moment they represented the women Ed Peters thought of as suitable to entertain Phil Conrad.

Her mind slipped ahead of her into the years when Tom would no longer be a junior member of anyone's team—when Tom would head his own team, and eventually reach the position of Director. Between then and now she had to be a dozen kinds of women all at once, and offend no one in the process. She had to help Tom, without seeming to do so. And in the end, if they were lucky, they would end up living in one of the best houses in Amtec Park—or its equivalent somewhere else in the country—and they would be the sort of people invited to parties to meet Phil Conrad's sort of person. If the time in between it seemed a little bit bleak in prospect, she knew it only required enough guts and enthusiasm to turn it into something much better. After all, she reasoned, Tom was committed to this kind of life, and she with him—and she would be a fool to find anything wrong with it. It was only a small voice that told her anything could be wrong, and that was easily ignored.

The sound of a car starting up somewhere on the lower road at Amtec Park brought an awareness of time passing —and the utilising of time was part of the plan that would take herself and Tom where they wanted to go. She moved quickly, and reached for her shopping-pad from the drawer close by her hand. Then her glance fell on the yellow pages of the typescript lying face-downwards with only its edges showing beyond the table mats that were piled on top. Slowly she drew it out, thinking how forlorn and unesteemed it looked stuffed in there out of sight. As she straightened the pages and slipped them back into the clip, she began to count back the days since she had worked on it, and felt a little sick to realise that they amounted to over three weeks. Her eyes slipped down the pages, and here and there she saw the beginnings of an idea that could have been good, if worked over and properly developed. She knew quite

177

well what she had on paper was only a draft of a novel, and even that still incomplete. There would have to be three or four times this amount of work before it could be near a state worth submitting to a publisher. She wondered if it could be worth it for just the few gleams of talent she saw in these pages, and then she thought of her father, and Oliver, who would have said it was. Oliver had preached to her that talent could tolerate no interference, that he himself would never be more than a second-rate poet because he gave part of his mind to politics. Angrily and guiltily now she tried to reject the idea, to argue that life had to be led on an ordinary level, that talent couldn't demand the sacrifice of other people to it . . . in this case Tom and her child.

Her hands clasped her body, protectively hugging her burden. In these last few weeks she had been carrying the child more easily, and there had been fewer hours spent lying on the bed lost in a daze of sickness and fatigue. She began to believe at last that her child could be borne splendidly to the joyful climax she wanted. So she had been happy and content in these weeks, placidly waiting her time, enjoying the society of the other pregnant wives in a way she had always thought she would despise. She had not begrudged the hours spent over the coffee cups, not at all; she had seemed to be building a peaceful climate of approval and acceptance for herself and her child. The urge now was to seek the shelter of other women's company and esteem, rather than the frightening state of loneliness that working on the novel would bring. And so the novel had been laid aside, not even looked at, for almost a month. Reason told her that neglect might cause it to slip away entirely. But she clasped her arms about her body more tightly, and thought only of her baby and Tom.

She still had not told anyone, apart from Tom, that she was trying to complete a book. It was a defensive measure, meant to guard her from ridicule if she were never able to finish it, or finished, to find a publisher for it. To announce that she was writing a novel would be to hurl a challenge at the non-creativity of other women, to project herself into the dangerous world of the individual who was trying to express something in a single voice, apart from the group, the world where failure would not be honest failure, but the just reward of pride and over-confidence. She shivered a little as she thought of what such a failure could do to Tom's position. To be laughed at would be worse for him than anything else. Only spectacular success would compensate for the seeming insult she would offer to the various clubs and committees she belonged to when she had to give the reason why she couldn't devote much time to them. And spectacular success, she reminded herself, very seldom came to first novels—or even fifth novels. She could see a way out only when the baby was born, and she would have the excuse of staying home with it. She looked at the untidy pages in her hand, and wondered if the novel would wait for that—or would it have slipped beyond her when she sought it again.

She heard the splash of running water in the bathroom, and stuffed the manuscript back into the drawer. Tom had not asked about the book for some time now—she wanted to believe that he had done it because he didn't want to make her unhappy by admitting that it made no progress. But at the back of her mind was the vague fear that he, too, cared a little less about it—that her own indifference had killed some of his interest. She didn't want to think that there was anything in their lives they had once considered important and to which they were now indifferent. She turned and put a bright smile on her face as he entered the kitchen.

He was barefoot, looking sleepy in his rumpled pyjamas and his uncombed hair standing up straight. When he kissed her lightly, his mouth smelled of toothpaste.

"What's this idea of getting up at the crack of dawn? . . . It's Saturday." He moved slowly to the faucet and filled the coffee-maker, his movements heavy as if he had not yet properly come awake.

She slipped back on to the stool, preparing to enjoy these next minutes with him. She loved the closeness between them at these times, the sense that they were truly alone, with the world beyond the green summer garden closed out.

Explanation was not really needed—he made a joke of this habit of hers. "I just like to be up early—before everything starts moving. I like this time—the promise of a warm, fine day before it actually happens."

"You sit here brooding over your world?" he said teasingly.

"Is it such a bad one?" she answered, too sharply. She wanted no criticism from Tom now of the place they were in, or anything about them. She could not have him question

179

what she had already settled in her own mind. "What's wrong with it?"

He opened his eyes wider, surprised. "Why—nothing. Nothing at all. What did I say was wrong with it?"

She didn't answer him, but slid off the stool and got some clean cups and saucers. It was disturbing to find her sense of peace and enjoyment gone just with those few words; she was annoyed with him for taking it away, but she couldn't let her annoyance grow, because that was worse.

"How are things at the Laboratories?" she said as she set out the milk and sugar. It was a stupid question, but it was better than the silence.

He accepted the remark for what it was, a peace offering. "O.K. . . . Armstrong and Taylor are going down to Canaveral next week to watch the tests of some new fuel."

"Why doesn't Dr. Dexter ever go down? . . ."

He shrugged. "That's a little beyond my level, Sal. I don't know why the brass make these decisions. Perhaps Dexter can't be spared. It isn't always the most important guy who gets sent out. Peters will probably go down because he has some buddies there . . . and leave the technical talking to Armstrong and Taylor."

"How long before you go?"

He grinned. "When I'm not so wet behind the ears." Then he grew serious. "But Taylor handed me a nice project to get on with while he's away. I meant to tell you about it last night before the Johnsons came. It's one of the side issues of a job we're working on, and he thinks there's enough stuff to develop into a paper. Not conclusive, but a lead for anyone who's working in that direction. We won't be pursuing it any further, but it could be a nice little prestige bit . . . the first thing I get my name on."

Her face lit up. "Oh, Tom! . . . *your* name."

"Well, Taylor's name has to go on it too, since he's Head of Department. But this side issue was a bit of my own thinking, and he says I should get credit."

"Oh, Tom, that's wonderful. That's really wonderful."

"Hey . . . calm down! It's nothing very important, and won't even cast a ripple in scientific circles. But Amtec is anxious to publish as much as possible from the Laboratories, and Taylor wants me to work on getting the paper into shape, and see if it makes up into something worth putting out

180

under his name. When I've got all the data sorted out, of course, it may not look as good as it does now. . . ."

" But it's a start, Tom. It shows what Taylor thinks of you."

" Don't get too misty-eyed about it, Sal. He thinks only as much of me as the amount of work he can squeeze out of me. Don't forget he gets credit for results he can get out of his department. So we don't talk about this until it's a certainty . . . till it's actually in print."

" I won't . . . I promise. Oh, but, Tom . . . it *is* wonderful. I'm proud of you!" The disturbing questions were gone now, vanished. There wasn't any reason to doubt that Tom could last the years that separated him from Taylor's position, or from being the sort of person who was invited to meet Phil Conrad.

She put her arms about his neck. " I'm proud of you," she said again.

He moved in closer to her, feeling her swollen belly and her full breasts through the long nylon robe. It seemed that he held a richness within his arms. " And I love you," he answered her.

He untied the ribbon at the neck of the robe, and brushed it and the nightgown back off her shoulders. Her breasts were much fuller now, and the nipples had turned a brownish colour; he bent down and bit them gently between his teeth. She put her head back a little and laughed with pleasure, as if she already felt her child there.

" Come back to bed, Sal."

They left the kettle steaming on the stove. The only other sound then was the padding of their bare feet on the floor.

II

The phone rang early that Saturday morning in the Talbot house. Selma heard it as she poked the sizzling bacon, and prepared to drain the fat off. Ted rose from the table, pausing to move Chrissie's milk nearer to her hand, but before he was half-way across the room, the ringing stopped.

Jeannie called from the next room. " It's all right, Dad. I've got it."

Selma laid aside the bacon for Jeannie, and cracked an

181

egg into the fat. As soon as it was done, she laid it on a hot plate and set it before Ted. She also put the fresh coffee on the table, and wiped Chrissie's mouth which was smeared with soggy cereal. Jeannie came into the kitchen before she was finished. In spite of the fact that they had both been at the Dexters' until after one o'clock that morning, Jeannie's face was not even slightly shadowed with fatigue. She wore her usual clean shirt-maker dress, stockings and freshly polished shoes. Selma had often wondered if some of Jeannie's success behind Carter's cosmetics counter wasn't due to the fact that she gave the impression of having dressed with as much care to go there as to a business appointment in New York. She made people think that Burnham Falls wasn't really a small town. This morning she looked as if someone had just handed her a present.

" That was Jerry," she announced.

Both Selma and Ted looked at her quickly, questioning. She didn't immediately satisfy their curiosity. " Sit down, Mom," she said. " I'll fix my own egg." Then as she cracked her egg, she looked back at her mother. " Will I fix one for you?" She motioned towards her mother's plate. " You've only got toast there."

Selma shrugged slightly as she poured her coffee. " I don't feel hungry."

" Oh, come on!" Jeannie said. " One egg and a little bacon won't hurt you. You never eat a proper breakfast. . . ."

She took Selma's silence for acquiescence, and cracked the second egg. Behind her back, Selma permitted herself a smile; she found Jeannie's maternal attitude amusing, but never said so. Jeannie scooped out the eggs, and carried both plates over to the table.

As she sat down she said, " You got a job on this morning, Dad?"

He nodded, wiping up the egg yolk with a piece of toast. " Yeh—a little job to finish up at Downside." He looked at his younger daughter. " Want to come, Chrissie? Want to come to Downside with Dad?"

Chrissie put down her spoon, and wiped her own mouth before her mother could reach out. " Yes—will Brother Matthew be there?"

" I expect so. Only you're not to ask for candy this time. Wait till he gives them to you."

Jeannie said, " You can drop me in town on your way through, Dad. I'd like to unpack some stock before we
182

get too busy. Last Saturday we were so busy I didn't have time to turn around. People were waiting to be served, and I had about fifty different shades of lipstick out at once. . . ."

Selma couldn't wait any longer. "Are you seeing Jerry this evening?" she asked.

Jeannie put a piece of toast in her mouth. "No—this evening he has to go with his people over to visit at Elmbury. But he's asked me to drive to New York with him to-morrow. There's a show he wants to see at the Coliseum. We'll be having dinner in town."

"Didn't think you were so friendly with Jerry these days," Selma said. "Not from what you said to Mrs. Dexter last night."

Jeannie smiled, and it was the slightly smug smile of someone who has bided her time well. "Oh . . . well, I didn't think he'd come around so quickly. I was pretty cool with him last time he called, and then he came into the drug store one day last week, and I kept right on being busy. You know how he hates to come into the store . . . he thinks I shouldn't be there. . . ."

"An' he's right," Ted said. "You *shouldn't* be there . . . smart girl like you with a full training course at business school should be doing something better than serving behind a counter. Any fool can do that . . . but then I've given up trying to make you see sense. You're just like all the kids these days. . ."

"Oh, Dad, don't start *that* again. I've explained to you before that it isn't just like standing behind *anyone's* counter. The way Wally's paying me now, it's as if I owned a little piece of that business. After all, I built up that side of it, and Wally knows it. Do you think I could make this kind of money typing in the pool at Amtec?"

"Money isn't everything," Ted said with unusual severity. "I want my girl doing something better than standing behind a counter—and I paid for you to learn something better."

Jeannie laid down her fork. "Dad, don't you see? Some day it's possible I might own my own business. And what's a typing job compared to that!"

Ted shook his head in bewilderment at such overriding ambition. "Some day I want to see you happily married. And if it's Jerry you've set your heart on, then let me tell you this isn't the way to get him."

"If he really loves me," Jeannie said, looking down at her plate, "he'll have me as I am . . . not some silly bitch giving
183

herself airs because she has a nice genteel job working for Amtec instead of behind a counter. Since when has honest hard work been such a new thing in this family?"

Selma was suddenly conscious that Ted looked old as he argued hopelessly with Jeannie, and that both faces were crossed with unaccustomed tension. She was conscious too of Ted's hands, horny and calloused, with the dirt from his gardening jobs grained deeply into the cracks, and under the nails.

CHAPTER SEVEN

Mal knew when he woke in the motel that it was late. Almost before he had opened his eyes he was aware of the sounds of the traffic on the highway, the intensified, busy sounds of a Saturday morning in the summer, the family cars converging on the super-market down the highway, and the cars of the men who were leaving their families behind and going fishing, the second-hand cars of the teen-agers who would drive all day just for the pleasure of it, and for the sense of escape. Mal heard the sounds, and opened his eyes wide; the sun was beating on the closed blinds. Through the long years of travelling from place to place he had developed the habit of recalling at the instant he woke, exactly where he was, and why. This morning, as usual, he knew—Burnham Falls on a Saturday morning, and last night he had spent with Harriet and Steve at the Carpenter house.

It was something else to remember that by this time he had intended to be well on the way to Toronto. He looked at his watch, and somehow he didn't care that he wasn't going to reach Toronto to-day, and perhaps not even to-morrow. His client wasn't expecting him there until Monday, and now Mal played with the idea of spending another night in Burnham Falls, driving back to New York late Sunday, and taking a plane to Toronto. He enjoyed driving long distances by himself; it provided a kind of longed-for solitude on which nothing and no one could intrude. That was the reason why he had driven to Burnham Falls the day before, with the intention of heading straight on for Canada. But it was just as easy to give up the thought of pushing on for the North; it was a deep satisfaction for him to reflect that he could lie here and make up his mind which of two places

184

he would be in, and no telephone would ring to command him to do otherwise, and there was no one who would reproach him for whatever way his whim went. He valued intensely the thought of such freedom; he was rarely lonely.

After he was showered and shaved he drove slowly by the supermarket, noting the big parking lot that was filled with cars, and then the outskirts of Burnham Falls straggled towards him. Here, also, the streets were lined with cars —narrow streets that had never been intended for this volume of traffic, and which could only be improved by slicing into the front lawns and the two graveyards, and as far back as the very steps of the courthouse and the churches. Watching people desperately hunting for a parking place, he knew why the supermarket down the highway was flourishing. He cruised around until another car pulled out and then he backed in swiftly, and deposited his nickel in the parking meter. The diner was just across the road, and for all the warmth of the morning, he found he was hungry. As he crossed the road, he kept looking about in half-expectation of seeing some of the faces from the Dexter party last night, but then he realised that the women, efficient housewives all of them, would have done their week-end shopping the day before, and the men would be doing whatever it was that executives did on a Saturday morning.

He ordered a stack of wheatcakes and sausages, and coffee. The girl brought his coffee at once, and as he started to drink it, he looked up and saw George Keston passing. George was with his son Jerry—George in his business suit, and Jerry wearing the tie and plain white shirt that looked so oddly out of place in the middle of the casual dress all about him. Mal leaned forward and rapped on the window. George's face broke into a smile when he recognised him, but he shook his head and gestured helplessly when Mal beckoned him inside. Then abruptly his reluctance vanished, and he turned back and went to the door of the diner. Mal rose to greet him.

" Hallo, there, Mal," he said. " Glad to see you. You remember Jerry, don't you?"

" Sure. How are you, Jerry?" Mal in turn shook the young man's hand. " Have a cup of coffee with me." He gestured towards the booth.

" Haven't time, Mal. Saturday's busy with us—and I've just spent nearly an hour over at John Martin's office—he's

185

the insurance man. He had a mutual client of ours there who enjoys telling her bank manager when and where she'll see him, and she's rich enough to be able to do it." He smiled a little feebly as he spoke. "But there are other things I'd rather do on a hot morning."

"Well, take a spell. The bank will wait another ten minutes."

"I suppose it will—at that." He plumped down heavily in the booth, and Jerry slid himself in silently and neatly. For his size he was well co-ordinated, his movements smooth and graceful. Then Mal remembered that George had boasted that his son was an athlete. The young man regarded him unsmilingly and with frank curiosity. Mal sensed that he disliked and resented him, and he couldn't think why.

"How's business, George?" he said as the extra cups of coffee were brought.

"Fine—just fine. The town's booming. Amtec has brought a lot of money in here, and they encourage their folks to spend it right here in town. All this construction's damn' good for business."

"But what about when they finish the plant and the housing development. The men are itinerant. . . ."

"Yes, but there'll be the wages from the new plant, and about three hundred-odd new families moving in to man the plant. These defence contracts—they're good business, you know."

Mal nodded. "I have good reason to know. They've kept me busy long enough." He sipped his coffee. "And the town likes it? Place looks overcrowded to me."

George shrugged. "What can they do about it? It's money in their pockets. All those automobiles out there . . ." he gestured towards Main Street—"represent a family buying something. It's change all right, but who wants to stand in the way of progress?" He glanced quickly at his watch as he spoke.

Mal turned to Jerry. "And what do you think of it? Are you going to stay here?"

Jerry's face was blank, but Mal noticed that his shoulders tightened slightly, and he seemed reluctant to answer. "I have three more years in college, and then the draft taps me. When that's done will be plenty of time to decide."

George spoke quickly. His tone was aggressive, and Mal guessed that he and Jerry had argued this point many times. "Perry's draft is deferred until he finishes college. Five

186

years from now you won't know this town—the highway will be through, and the new plant settled in. I've got definite information that the Carnegie Bank will locate here during the next two years, and I'm going to need every trained young fellow I can get my hands on. Jerry doesn't know what he's passing up if he doesn't come back here. This place has got a lot to offer. . . ."

Jerry suddenly rose, his face hostile and set. " I'm sorry, Dad, I'll have to get along. There's a pile of work over there, and you *did* say you expected me to go to the Mellons' to-night. I'll have to be through by six. . . ." He nodded to Mal. " S'long, Mr. Hamilton. It was nice to see you again." Somehow he made the words sound insulting, though his tone was smooth. " It's kind of a real big thing with my Dad to have you back in town. He's always telling me how you made your own way, and how well you've done. Of course, *you* left Burnham Falls . . ." He saluted him vaguely. " Good-bye, Mr. Hamilton."

The insult was open and intended when he paid for his own coffee on the way out.

After George Keston left him Mal went across to Carter's to get some cigarettes. The cool breath of the air-conditioning met him as he entered, and he grinned a little as he noticed the streamlined fixtures, the recessed lighting, the clean, antiseptic look of the rubber-tiled floor that was shiny with wax. He faintly regretted the marble-topped tables they had once had in the fountain section, but he admitted that Wally Carter could fit more customers into the booths and the chromium stools along the counter. It was efficient, but not homely any more. As he paid for his cigarettes he wondered why he should even faintly regret the old Carter's, since ease and efficiency of operation were his gods, and beside that, in the old days he had never had time or money to spend in Carter's, and it shouldn't matter a damn to him what it looked like now.

As he turned to the door he saw Jeannie at the long cosmetics counter on the far side of the store. She was looking at him expectantly, and half-smiling; she was wearing a pale pink shirt-maker dress that looked as if it was just fresh from the iron. There was nothing about her to suggest how late she had stayed at the Carpenter house the night before.

" Hello, Mr. Hamilton!"

" Hi, there, Jeannie." She was displaying a box of soap to

187

a customer, and two more were waiting. A couple of high school girls with tanned legs in Bermuda shorts were bending to examine the display in the showcase counter. Jeannie gave him another quick smile and turned to wrap the soap and ring up the sale on the cash register.

"You're busy, Jeannie," he commented purposelessly as he swung open the door to leave.

"I need six hands!" Then she laughed. "But I like it that way."

All her customers turned to look at Mal as he left the store. Outside the heat was waiting, the heat and the Saturday morning noise was stronger. Even the breeze blowing in from Lake Burnham didn't help much.

He bought a bag of apples at a shop on Main Street whose interior was dim, and which had half-heartedly tried to convert into a small supermarket, or "superette," as it said on the window outside. It was run by people whose name Mal didn't recognise, and it wasn't doing much business. The fruit was good, but the prices were high. He put the bag on the seat beside him, and he munched an apple slowly as he drove through the town. He cruised aimlessly for a while, turning off Main sharply on Chester to go past the new school. It was almost finished, and was almost indistinguishable from a thousand other schools across the country. It stood about half-way between the town and Amtec Park, with open playing fields on both sides of it. It was big and clean-looking, and dull—and he knew its laboratories would have all the equipment he had once dreamed of using in the old school building on Dunbar Street.

He continued on past Amtec Park, and the Laboratories, past the Talbot house, slowing down as he reached the shellac factory and the half-finished plant. Next to it was the trailer camp for the construction workers, who worked on the plant and on the housing development on the other side of town. It was an ugly, cluttered sprawl that he had seen many times from the windows of the Laboratories; washing was strung on lines between the trailers, and all the grass had vanished. It was a dust patch, which in bad weather turned to mud. It had the disreputable, cynical air of an impermanent shanty-town, a grouping of people and belongings that cared nothing for Burnham Falls, and owed nothing to it. It stood there in blatant, uncaring contrast to the clean lines and mown lawns of the Laboratories on the hill above it. The manage-

188

ment of Amtec had complained to the construction bosses, who did nothing about it, and over the months it had grown worse as the litter of cans and boxes, old paraffin stoves and junk collected about each trailer. Amtec had called a crash programme to get the plant completed and into production; the workers were on overtime and their pockets were stuffed with dollars. They drank good whisky, and cooked prime steaks on their makeshift barbecue pits. They didn't give a damn about what Amtec thought.

After the trailer camp, Mal picked up speed again. Three miles farther on, just past the old White farm, he saw the road he had been seeking, and he turned into it. It was an old road, not much used even when the White farm had been functioning, and now almost abandoned. It was unpaved, and deeply rutted; ice, and the rushing water from summer storms had gouged deep holes in it. He imagined that the only ones who used it now were the fishermen who fished the waters of the small lake it skirted on one side. Pitching and bouncing, Mal followed it for three more miles as it skirted the back of the golf course. It came out on the Farmington road just a little above the entrance to the country club. Before he reached the last bend that led on to the highway, Mal pulled into the side and stopped.

He took the apples and his rolled-up jacket from the car, locked it, and started off through the woods. The land was level and a bit swampy at first, and then it rose steeply, displaying great falls of lichened rock that were almost lost in the deep green shadow of the crowding trees. The earth was carpeted with dry, dead leaves, and the birds seemed strangely noisy in the quiet. The sounds of the cars on the highway below had diminished to a gentle swish.

In his wallet somewhere was a guest card for the club, but he didn't intend to use it, and it gave him a somewhat childish pleasure to know that if he was seen he would look like any other cautious trespasser as he beat through the heavy brush and wood that fringed the golf course. In the brush the heat was humid and sticky, and the mosquitoes began to plague him. The traces of the old path he had followed as a boy were still there, overgrown in parts, with fallen trees crossing it, and the weedy, paper-like grey birches bent over parallel to the ground from the weight of the ice in the winter. Some of them had been torn out by the wind, and the earth clung about their dead roots. The path wound steadily up the side of the hill, slippery with dry, dead

189

leaves. In Mal's time as a child in Burnham Falls, this had been a favourite place for the kids to go in summer. At the top there was the great circle of granite boulders from which you could get a view over the whole town and down through the valley. It had been part of Joe Carpenter's land then, but Joe didn't mind them building a fire and cooking sausages there, as long as the fire was thoroughly out before they left. Also, they weren't allowed to shoot in his woods. Mostly these rules had been respected, and Joe left them pretty much alone. Mal knew from the look of the path that almost no one went there now.

He reached the top at last, put down his jacket and the apples, and stretched himself full length on the sloping granite, which was hot to his touch. The granite shapes were all about him, almost as tall as he remembered them. Below was the valley—the town, the lakes, the summer cottages, and all the new things that had come to the valley since. Directly below, close at hand, was the Carpenter place.

The heat hit up at him; he began to sweat, and even that felt good. He felt his body go limp, and after a while he slept.

When he opened his eyes again the sun had shifted, and he lay in shade. The afternoon shadows were fingering out across the valley; he rolled over and lay with his head pillowed in his arms. Presently he reached out and got an apple from the bag, and ate it greedily, and then he sat up and tossed the core high in the air, as far as he could, listening to the crash it made as it fell somewhere in the trees. Then he picked up his jacket and the apples, and started down the opposite side of the hill from the way he had come, down towards the Carpenter place.

He climbed the stone wall at the back of the house, noting how far the brush had encroached on the square that had been Joe Carpenter's lawn. The Rolls was in the garage, but there was no sign of Steve's car; he wondered what it was he missed, and then realised that so far he had heard no sound of voices in the quiet afternoon air. There was no sign of Gene or Tim about. The screen door cut off his view into the kitchen.

"Hallo!" he said. "Are you there, Nell?"

He heard the sound of a chair scrape on the floor. "Mal——? Is that you, Mal?"

It was Harriet's voice. She appeared at the screen door,
190

and swung it open. She stood there looking at him, her face shadowed with a kind of weariness he had never seen there before; she wore a simple blue cotton dress which brought out the warmth of her skin and hair. She had the look of being totally unprepared for him, and she didn't try to cover her expression.

"Mal . . . I was just thinking about you. I didn't hear the car . . ."

"I came over the hill. The car's back on the side road."

"You didn't go to Toronto?" she said as she stood back to let him pass into the kitchen.

"No." He offered no explanation. He stood quite still, looking about him, liking the order and serenity of the kitchen.

Harriet said. "Nell's resting. . . . I make her go and rest every afternoon."

He turned and looked at her. "It seemed quiet. . . . Aren't Gene and Tim about?"

"They're off somewhere with Willie Prescott. They *should* be at Arlene Sommers' birthday party, but they refused to go, and I couldn't make them." She put her hand to her face. "It's difficult sometimes . . . trying to tell Gene and Tim where they should have their friends. Steve is bound to see Art Sommers sometime on Monday at the Laboratories, and he's such a bad liar. . . ."

"Where's Steve now?"

"At the lab." Harriet moved to the sink, and filled the kettle. "I'm having some tea . . . would you like a cup? Or some coffee? I'll fix you a drink later and we'll take it on to the porch, but I want my tea first."

"Yes . . . yes, I'll have some tea." The novelty of the idea was attractive. Mal pulled out a chair and sat down. "Does Steve often work Saturdays?"

She nodded. "I think . . . most Saturdays. Sometimes Sunday, as well. Only he doesn't think of it as work. It's almost a recreation. You see, he's able to get into the laboratory on week-ends for a few hours without interruption. He has so little time for laboratory work during the week, and it's still the only thing that really interests him."

"Steve should be head of the Laboratories," Mal said carefully. "And he should be in the laboratory all the time. He's too good to waste on administration. He should have Ed Peters' position."

"Steve doesn't like administration . . . and Ed Peters'

191

job is nothing but that. You don't understand, Mal. Ed has been with Amtec a long time. He knows the company . . . he knows what it wants. Steve remembers only half the time that he works for Amtec."

Mal watched her spooning the tea into the pot. "Wouldn't you like to see Steve have that job?"

She poured the boiling water in carefully. "I wouldn't stand in the way of anything that Steve wanted. But life would be very different for all of us if Steve had Ed's position. The president is a sort of company . . . showpiece. He has to be in sight . . . and his family. Steve couldn't spend the week-ends at the Laboratories, and the boys couldn't *not* go to Arlene Sommers' birthday party."

Mal took the cup she passed to him, and watched her cut a chocolate frosted cake; he remembered now that it was the same cake Nell had been famous for in Burnham Falls before he went away.

"And what about you, Harriet?" he said, stirring the tea reflectively. "Aren't there any plans of yours it might get in the way of? You look as if you're still waiting . . . yes, waiting for something you've been expecting for a long time."

She didn't look at him. "What else can happen to me? What would I want to happen?"

"How should I know?" he said abruptly. "How should I know what a woman wants. I've never made much of a success of understanding women."

She faced him directly across the kitchen table, her expression alert now, and a little angry. "Is there ever so very much to understand, Mal? Or are you one more man who chooses to think like that because it's less trouble?"

He shrugged impatiently. "What are you talking about?" He began to regret questioning her, because the words had obviously dug deeply into her, and she was moved and disturbed. An ever-ready fear of involvement and responsibility stirred in him; ever since his marriage he had viewed women with delight, but with no desire to possess exclusively any one of them. Each of his affairs had ended with a certain amiability on both sides because it had always been understood that they would end; he was not looking for bitter memories. Now as he sat here he remembered that once he had asked Harriet to marry him. It was something he would not let himself remember too often. Harriet was the exception to all the other women—now, as she had been then. In his life he had asked only two women to marry him, and

192

Harriet had been one of them. He looked at her troubled face, and some of her own confusion reached out and touched him —he, Mal, who was never confused.

She replied slowly. "Women have less choice than you think, Mal. What plans could I have that aren't Steve's? . . . Most men are fighting for their lives in whatever they're doing, and a wife can only be either with him or against him. The role is still a passive one—unless a woman wants a kind of court jester, or a fool. Whatever Steve is, he's neither of those things. . . ."

"You're old-fashioned, Harriet. You're still Joe Carpenter's daughter, waiting for the orders, the commands. I wonder if you've done any single thing in your life that you really wanted to do . . . and not what you thought someone expected of you."

She smiled warily, mockingly. "If you're trying to get a rise out of me, Mal, you'd better forget it. You have your kind of life—and I have mine. Let's say we're both satisfied."

They were sitting on the porch, the tray with glasses, bottles and the ice bucket between them, when Steve drove up. They had been sitting there for nearly an hour, in a silence that was almost companionable, hearing from the back of the house the familiar kitchen noises as Nell prepared dinner. Harriet was at last at ease, glad that finally she and Mal had broken the polite spell that had lain over their meetings since he had come back to Burnham Falls. They had each edged a little into the territory of the other; they had looked at each other, and known that there was much more to say, and that perhaps they would choose never to say it. Harriet knew that she was not free of Mal, but she no longer felt humiliated and foolish in her bondage. She would no longer fight other people, including her own sons, for his attention. She had hit into Mal's tough, imperturbable façade and made a small dent. It was good to know she wasn't completely ineffectual.

Steve left the car in the driveway, and his worn, handsome face creased into a smile of pleasure as he saw Mal. He was wearing a crumpled sports shirt, open at the neck; as usual he was smoking. Harriet had a sudden vision of him as he would be at fifty—weary-eyed in his distinguished untidiness, and a power in Amtec. She felt as if she had never really looked at Steve until this moment, never known this man. In his fashion he was just as tough as Mal, but his endurance was greater, and of a different kind. She studied him with a respectful, thoughtful gaze as he came up the steps towards them.

II

It was a relief to Laura when Ed finally excused himself and left for Downside. The Cadillac started up the dirt road from the cabin, Ed looking neat and fresh even after the day's fishing with Phil Conrad, as if the wind and sun didn't touch him. Laura was glad he was gone because his presence put a restraint on the kind of theatre gossip she wanted to hear from Conrad. She collected a fresh tray of ice and hurried back to the sofa where Phil sat, conscious of a rare excitement within herself, a hopefulness . . . though she could not honestly have said what it was she hoped for.

" I didn't know Ed was interested in Catholic affairs . . ." Phil said with deliberate inquiry as she set the ice bucket down on the rickety table.

" He's not." She lit a cigarette, and paused to draw on it, knowing that this was one motion she performed with consummate grace, and that it had won the acclaim of an instant's study from Phil.

" You forget," she said, " that this is just about a company town. Ed has to be all things to all men—just now he's gone along to talk to Monseigneur Gregory, drink some of his good Scotch, and on leaving present him with a cheque from Amtec for the Diocesan Charity Fund. In a sense, Downside isn't local—being a seminary—but it's part of the whole picture here in Burnham Falls. Similarly, all the other denominations will get cheques, and Ed will either present them in person or send a letter, according to their importance. . . ."

Conrad reached out and poured his own drink. " Somehow, Laura, I never fit you into a place like this—doing this kind of a . . . job."

She looked at him cautiously, afraid to commit herself to a reply. " Oh . . .?"

His mouth suddenly split in a wide grin, an unusually relaxed expression for Phil Conrad. " I suppose you know what I almost said? I almost said 'this kind of a *role.*'"

194

Now she smiled too, a little secretively, as if they were conspirators against the rest of Burnham Falls.

"I know . . . I know. Most of the time it feels like a role, and the time I spend in New York is where the role ends and the living begins."

"Poor foolish Laura . . ." he said softly. "That's always been your trouble. You never knew when the role ended and real life began."

She drew back a little. "Are you sure you know what you're talking about?"

"Sure I know. It stuck out a mile to anyone who knew you and Larry at that time. You went on playing the role Larry wrote for you, and the fact was that Larry, like most writers, outgrew that set of characters."

Her hand hesitated just a second as she reached for her glass. "You didn't know Larry well enough to be able to know something like that. It isn't true . . . it's just something you wanted to get off your chest to whatever actress it seemed to fit." She tried to frame the accusation lightly, but even in her own ears her voice sounded oddly high and excited.

"You forget that Larry and I are fairly simpatico . . . nothing intense, but we're always glad to have lunch together whenever we run into each other around town. Some day I hope he'll give me one of his plays to do."

She ignored his last words. She leaned towards him almost hungrily, and she spoke without prudence or caution.

"Then if you know him so well, tell me something."

He drew on his cigarette. "If I can."

"Tell me why Mary Blair? . . . Why *that* woman? She's plain and thin, and quiet as a mouse. Larry liked *beautiful* women."

"Maybe 'still as a mouse' would be a better description of her, Laura; there's a difference. I don't know what Mary Blair's got. She doesn't attract me, and yet I find her oddly relaxing. And Larry depends on her—he depends on her every second of his day. And she's always with him, always there."

"Oh, well . . . if *that's* what she is. A mother . . . a nurse-maid. . . ."

He gestured to silence her. "Hey, wait a minute! Maybe Larry was smart enough to know that. He doesn't have a great talent, but he has a quite definite talent. And he

195

husbands it. He pampers it, Laura, and looks after it. And the woman he's married to must do the same."

He went on, talking slowly now, as if recollecting. "You know . . . marriage to a beautiful woman is almost a career in itself. In this country beauty commands such a reward just for existing. Larry needed some homage himself. People went to the theatre to see his plays, but in restaurants heads turned to look at you, Laura. You've got to be a certain kind of man to be successfully married to a beautiful woman. It's a game, and a gamble. Larry wasn't that kind of man."

"He grew tired of me. That was all," she said.

"He grew tired of the competition. Now some men would find the competition a challenge. . . ."

All of Laura's senses sharpened then. For the first time in over a year she felt more than superficially desirable, she felt something more than the chardboard figure on the magazine spreads and the TV screen. Something in her came to life as it had never done before—even for Larry. She knew the feeling now of having to woo a man with something more than just her beauty.

It was almost dark when Ed returned from Downside. The headlights flashed across the front of the cabin, and he was puzzled that there were no lights in the windows. He was hungry and tired, a condition he wouldn't expose to Laura or Phil Conrad, and he was more than a little irritated to find no sign of a meal being prepared. Laura and Phil were still sitting on the sofa facing the window, apparently watching the last of the light vanish on the lake. But as always, Ed's discipline was intact, and now he brought a smile to his face as they turned casually to greet him— as if his return were of no importance to them.

III

"Hi, Jeannie!"

Jeannie stopped and looked around as she heard her name. It was after nine-thirty, and she was on her way out of Carter's. Only one booth along the wall was occupied, and the woman who had called was sitting there smiling at her moistly. Seated opposite her in the booth were two men.

Quickly Jeannie searched her memory for the woman's name. "Oh . . . hi, Mrs. . . . Mrs. Reitch. How are you?"

196

She was a construction worker's wife who frequently appeared in Carter's in the middle of the afternoon to eat an ice-cream soda and a pastry, and almost always stopped by Jeannie's counter to make a purchase. She spent her husband's money wildly on anything that caught her fancy, and she seemed pleased when she won a few minutes' notice and conversation with Jeannie or Ben, the counter man. She was childless, and desperately bored with Burnham Falls. She was handsome, in a big-boned fashion. She laughed now, showing her gums.

"None of this Mrs. Reitch stuff, Jeannie," she said. "My name's Val. And this is my husband, Carl . . . and Tony Patrino, who works with him."

"Hi," Carl Reitch said, staring at her but not moving. Tony Patrino half got to his feet. "Nice to know you."

Val Reitch patted the empty seat beside her. "You finished now, Jeannie? Come and take the weight of your feet. Have a sundae, or some coffee. . . ."

Jeannie hesitated a second before she accepted the suggestion, but she did accept it finally. "Thanks . . . I'll have a Coke." She knew she didn't particularly want to sit with Val and the two men, nor did she very much want to go home, either. After the argument at breakfast that morning there would be her father's hurt silence to face, and her mother's gentle attempts to heal the breach. Jeannie wasn't yet prepared to make humble approaches to her father, because she knew she couldn't go all the way in doing what he wanted her to do. Even to sit here with two workers from the construction camp was like a further act of defiance towards him. She looked at the roughened, calloused hands across the table from her, with the dirt rim under the nails, and she thought that she might have been looking at her father's own hands. At the same time she knew the difference, the difference between familiar and alien hands.

Carl Reitch had called for an order of Coke, and Ben brought it and set it down before her. She started to drink it quickly, aware of Ben's curious glance around the group, and aware now that Carl and the other man had been drinking. The smell of whisky reached her across the table. There was an awkward silence which Val finally brought to an end.

"You're workin' late, aren't you, Jeannie? Do you always have to stay this late?"

"Well . . . no. Not after seven. But we were busy this evening, and I just stayed on. Nothing else to do."

"I don't believe it." This came from Tony Patrino, who

197

leaned back in the booth and looked at her boldly. "I don't believe a girl like you hasn't got a date on a Saturday night. What's wrong with the guys in this town?" He was young, in his twenties, and darkly handsome, his head seemed to be set with surprising grace and delicacy on his powerful body. He wore a clean sports shirt, open at the neck, under a fawn linen jacket; she noticed the massive gold watch and band on his wrist. He had started to smile mockingly, and she was angry with herself because she felt the hot colour mount in her cheeks.

Val nudged her, laughingly. "Jeannie could have her pick, couldn't you, hon?" Then she looked across at her husband. "But she's got her head screwed on right . . . no wastin' time on construction workers for Jeannie. She's datin' steady with the bank president's son . . . a college boy, he is."

Carl laid down his cup. "And what's that supposed to mean?" he said to his wife. "I didn't see no college boys hanging around *you* in Meadville, Colorado. As I recall it a construction worker looked pretty good to you then, just so long as you got outa the place. . . ."

"Aw shut up!" she said, her good humour vanishing. "Listen, any time I want . . ."

Tony Patrino broke in. "Hell, this is Saturday night! You two going to spend the whole time fighting? Let's get the hell out of here and go get a steak at Barney's, and take in a movie at the drive-in. There's Jeannie here all on her lonesome, just pining for a steak and a movie. . . ."

Jeannie pushed the Coke away from her. She took her handbag and got to her feet. "Thanks . . . but they're expecting me at home."

"I'll drive you home."

"It's no distance. I always walk."

"What's the hurry?" Carl Reitch looked at her sulkily. "Don't you like the company?"

Jeannie looked down at him. "It isn't that at all. I told you they're expecting me at home."

"Oh, lay off her, Carl!" Val snapped. "If she wants to go, let her." She looked up at Jeannie with some hostility. "I'm sure we don't want to keep her if her folks don't know where she is."

Carl glared back at his wife. "What is she . . . a baby or something? Can't take care of herself?"

"Oh, forget it, Carl . . . and shut up!"

Tony Patrino said nothing.

198

Jeannie nodded to Val. " Thanks for the Coke, Mrs. Reitch. See you around."

Ben had gone to the back of the store, and there was momentarily no one at the counter as she left. As the door swung closed behind her she could hear Val Reitch's voice rising again and Carl's sullen interruption. And outside on the sidewalk, Main Street was dotted with the usual crowd of people who drifted into town on a warm Saturday evening, and across the road the early movie was breaking at the Astor. Suddenly Jeannie felt unutterably lonely. She wanted to feel Jerry's hand resting in hers, to have the familiar, comforting presence at her side. Behind her was the petty drunken quarrelling of the Reitch marriage, and ahead she faced a house where she was not at ease with her father She knew what he would think if he could have witnessed her encounter with the Reitches and Tony Patrino, and it almost seemed that Ted Talbot's violently prejudiced dislike of all the construction camp people was justified. She felt shamed in some way, because her father would have been shamed to see her there ; she felt also slightly soiled and dirtied because her dating with Jerry was a subject for Val Reitch's gossip. It was all right for Burnham Falls to speculate on whether she and Jerry would marry, but she suddenly found herself viewing the construction camp people with her father's eyes—as total outsiders, who would one day pack up and be gone, and leave nothing but the scarred ground where they had been. It took more than Val Reitch's paying for lipstick and perfume to give her the right to gossip in Burnham Falls. Jeannie began to think that she might almost be ready to apologise to her father when she got home.

She was within sight of the shellac factory when she sensed the car slowing behind her—not passing straight on with a swift stirring of the warm air as they always did. Nor did it turn, and go back towards the town. Puzzled, she turned to look at it, but she could see nothing beyond the powerful beam of the headlights, which outlined her fully, and seemed to pin her against the dark background of the trees.

IV

It was a little before eleven and Mal refused a lift from Steve back to where he had left his car. Instead he borrowed

199

a flashlight and started to walk. A dew had settled on the grass, but it was still warm, and a pale three-quarter moon was starting to swing up above the line of hills. He held the flashlight low by his side as he walked. Only two cars passed him, both of them coming from the country club, and he enjoyed the feeling of isolation and being alone in the darkness. After dinner Steve had brought out a fine brandy, and its mellowness was still with him.

It was farther to where the dirt road turned off than he remembered. When he came to it finally he had to walk with more care because the ruts were deep and filled with loose stones. The trees and brush closed in about the road now; only the faintest light from the moon filtered down through them. He had left his car pulled in so tight to the side of the road that he was almost upon it before he saw it.

He heard the first sound just as he pressed the starter, and he thought he was mistaken. Then, when the motor settled down, he heard it again.

"Wait . . . please wait!" It was a woman's voice, and it came from farther back on the road, away from the highway.

He gripped the flashlight, feeling its weight in his hand reassuringly. Then he opened the door cautiously.

"Hallo! . . . Hallo!" he called.

"Wait!" Now he knew the voice, and he switched on the flashlight. She was still some way from the car, limping, and without shoes. Her hair hung over her face wildly. He started to run towards her. She flinched in the strong beam of the flashlamp as he drew near, and for a second she strained to see past it, to identify him in the darkness. Then he stopped short, staring at her, and feeling a little sick as he looked.

Her shirtmaker dress had been ripped open down the front. Her bra hung about her waist, and her half-slip was bloodstained and torn. Her lips were bloody, and one eye was puffed and closed. There was blood on her bare breasts also. She was shivering.

Her lips were almost too swollen to let her speak.

"Please . . . will you get me to the hospital."

"Jeannie!"

She collapsed in a dead weight in his arms, and he didn't know whether she heard him speak her name before she lost

200

consciousness. He carried her to the car and laid her on the back seat.

V

Through the evening Laura felt as if she and Phil were conducting a private conversation in which Ed had no part. It was not that Ed was not talking—most of the talk came from him; there was a wordless communication between her and Phil, conveyed in the attitudes and opinions they had in common, the language of show business, the quick camaraderie from which Ed was excluded. With Phil as her audience Laura had sparked into life, and she enjoyed playing the two men against each other. She knew she had never been a witty woman, but this evening her comments almost had wit, a rather malicious wit that took Ed as its target. In this she was following Phil, who seemed to grow more charmingly evasive, more adroit as Ed's insistent probing skirted around the matter of whether or not Conrad would agree to do the television series for Amtec. It was the spectacle of elusive talent being pursued by the ponderous weight of corporate might and money. It was a teasing, deliberately provocative game in which Ed was more and more at a disadvantage. Never, it seemed to Laura, had she and Ed been farther from one another; her sympathies belonged on Phil's side of the game, and she did not care that Ed must see it. Towards midnight, as she rose and refilled the brandy glasses, Laura thought that for once she might see Ed's composure crack. He swallowed his brandy quickly, and there was a small sense of danger which she enjoyed. She had a feeling that the evening was approaching some kind of a crisis.

So it was almost an anti-climax when they heard the sounds of the car being driven at high speed on the dirt road. The crisis came from without, and it almost disappointed Laura.

Ed had risen and gone to open the door. Laura listened to the car door bang, and a few seconds later Steve Dexter appeared in the light from the doorway. He strode into the room without preliminaries, nodding briefly to Laura and to Phil. But he spoke to Ed.

"I'm glad you weren't in bed. There's trouble."

"Trouble?"

201

"Jeannie Talbot's been beaten up and raped on the back road down to the White farm. She says it was two men from the construction camp."

"Jesus!" The word ripped out of Ed. For a second his face registered his disgust, his unwillingness to admit this fresh problem, his annoyance. And then immediately all this was overcome. "Where is she?" His tone was thoughtful.

"At the Kempton General. I don't think she's in too bad shape, but there has to be evidence from the doctors . . . all that stuff. She says she was pulled into the car as she was walking home from Carter's. Then they drove to this back road . . ."

"Who found her?"

"Mal Hamilton . . . he'd been visiting at our house, and he'd left his car on the road all afternoon. He walked back to get it."

"How did you hear it?"

"The state troopers came to pick up Nell and take her to the hospital."

"And the girl's made an identification?"

"She knew the two men."

"Well, then!" Ed snapped his fingers. "Let's keep clear of this! The construction camp isn't Amtec's responsibility. Those men are hired by the contractors. Then main thing is not to imply any responsibility . . . let the lawyers fight over it later, if there is a fight, but don't make any move that looks like an admission."

"But——!"

Ed gestured to dismiss Steve's interruption. "Oh, come on, Steve!—this is old stuff with Amtec. We've had everything in our time—rapes and paternity suits and damage claims. We've learned to make the minimum gesture, and stay clear."

Steve's face tightened. "Ed, I didn't come here to listen to the past history of Amtec's lawsuits. I'm here to tell you exactly how Amtec has to stand in this business. You have a moral commitment here, if not a legal one—or you might as well forget all the public relations work Amtec has done in this town. You won't be able to buy public opinion back if you don't stand by Jeannie Talbot now. Ted Talbot's a poor man, and he hasn't much love for Amtec . . . but he and his family are some of the most respected people around here. And that includes Jeannie!"

"The men came from the construction camp," Ed repeated.

202

"Amtec brought them here. That's all Burnham Falls is going to think of. And it's Amtec who has to stay here after the contractors have packed up and gone. I'm telling you how you've got to play this thing, Ed. There's no other way if you mean to stay in Burnham Falls."

Irritably Ed went and got a cigarette from the box on the table. He seemed to have forgotten Laura, and even Phil Conrad. They all stood about, waiting for him to light the cigarette, waiting for him to speak—Steve with his tense, worried face, Laura looking weary, and Conrad with the air of someone who tried to efface himself from a family quarrel. Finally Ed turned back to Steve.

"O.K. . . . Do what you think best. Call in another doctor, if that's necessary. You can tell the Press you're authorised to make statements for Amtec. Only, for God's sake, don't get us in too deep."

"That wasn't what I meant. I think you should come, Ed. You'll have to find the right things to say to her parents. We should go to the hospital first, and then back to the construction camp. The troopers are there now."

Ed hesitated a moment longer, and then he went silently and got his jacket from the back of the chair. Holding it in his hand, he looked back at Steve.

"Are you sure you're not getting your concern for Amtec mixed up in your concern for the Talbots. She is the same one who was helping at your house last night, isn't she?"

Laura suddenly came alert. "That girl! That's Selma's daughter, the one who works in the drug store."

Steve nodded, but he looked at Ed. "I can't tell you, right now, where concern for one begins and the other ends. A town like Burnham Falls is too small to let them be entirely separate." He stopped talking abruptly, as if he were wearied and annoyed by the questioning. He watched Ed putting on his jacket, and filling his cigarette case. Then he said impatiently, "Let's go, Ed. The sooner we're at the hospital, the better."

Laura took a step forward. "Shall I come?"

Ed waved his hand in dismissal. "No—you won't be needed." He turned to Conrad. "I'm sorry this happened, Phil. It kind of messes up your week-end. But Laura will take care of you. I expect I'll be pretty tied up to-morrow. . . ."

Steve had the door open. He nodded curtly towards the others. "Good night."

203

Ed followed him quickly down the steps to the car.

When they were gone, Laura and Phil were alone together in a kind of communication that had strengthened vastly in the few hours that had lapsed since they had sat watching the light fade from the lake. The sense of crisis that had been building all evening had not been resolved, though; it had not disappeared in the kind of shock wave that had hit with the news of what had happened to Jeannie.

Laura sank down on the sofa before the empty fireplace. " Give me a cigarette, will you, Phil?"

He sat beside her as he lighted it, then flicked the match on to the hearth.

Laura gave a small shudder. " That poor girl! . . . She's so pretty—and young. Not even twenty yet, I guess. I bought some things from her once . . ."

She drew on her cigarette. " I wonder . . . everyone in this town goes to the Dexters when there's trouble. Steve—he's on the side of the town, *against* Amtec." Her eyes opened wider, and the cigarette was poised, forgotten, between her fingers. " He was telling Ed what to do!"

Then she added, " If the girl's right about those men being from the construction camp, there'll be hell to pay. And Ed will be in the middle of it. The poor kid . . . just imagine not even having the chance to give . . ."

With a sharp, decisive movement she flung the cigarette against the hearth with just the same gesture Phil had used. She turned to him, pressing her lips against his hard.

"Love me, Phil!" she said.

CHAPTER EIGHT

Sally Redmond was making breakfast that Sunday morning when Tom came and told her the news. He had driven down to the stationers to get a copy of the *New York Times*. Through the kitchen window Sally could see him as he walked across the lawn, and she knew that something had disturbed him. She had woken that morning with a pleasurable sense of anticipation and she wanted nothing to spoil the day. After breakfast Tom was driving her to ten o'clock Mass in Burnham Falls, and at noon they were going to the

204

lunch party Alan Taylor was giving the staff of his department at the country club. That afternoon was the play-off of the final round of the golf tournament for which Amtec had donated the purse. It was one of those social occasions where the invitation was almost a command; Sally knew it was important that nothing should spoil it.

She paused in her task of beating eggs as Tom came in. He had left the newspaper in the hall. " What's the matter?" she said at once.

Leaning against the sink, he told her what he had heard in the stationers about Jeannie Talbot. A slow anguish rose in her as she listened, a sick feeling of fear and pity. She sat down heavily on a chair, clutching her belly protectively, as if to guard the child.

" Oh, the poor kid," she said softly. " The poor kid." She felt immeasurably older than Jeannie, but now somehow sheltered and inexperienced by comparison. " She's so pretty, Tom—about the loveliest girl I've ever seen. And kind of . . . sweet, you know. I get all my things from her."

" I guess she doesn't look so good now," he said. " She got beaten up, they say."

A little moan escaped Sally. " Oh!" She ran her tongue across dry lips. " Have they got the men?"

Tom shook his head. " I don't know. Man in the store told me that the two guys have skipped. One of them's married, but he left his wife behind when he cleared off. They're supposed to have been drinking. . . ."

She suddenly started to shake. " Oh, it's terrible. . . ." She rocked herself to and fro, holding her stomach.

Tom held her, his hand stroking her hair. " Don't, honey . . . don't upset yourself, Hush, now. . . . It wouldn't have happened if she'd had a little more sense. She shouldn't have been on that road by herself at night."

Sally looked up quickly. " I'll bet she's been taking that walk all her life, and no one ever told her it wasn't safe. This is the country, Tom. These things aren't supposed to happen. Jeannie's house is only ten minutes from the middle of town . . . there's only that one empty stretch along the road." Her voice rose indignantly.

" Sal! Don't upset yourself—please don't!"

" And what's Amtec doing about it?" she demanded, ignoring him. " They're not going to have the tournament . . . are they?"

205

" Why wouldn't they?"

" Well . . . people ought to be out looking for those two men."

He shook his head. " Sal, be sensible. You can't turn the whole town into law enforcement officers just like that. They've probably gone across state lines now, and the police know how to handle this much better than a whole bunch of civilians fouling things up. There's not very much anyone can do. . . ." He stopped, awed and puzzled as he saw the tears start down her face. " Sal, baby, what is it? What's the matter."

" Tom—would you take me home for the day? Just for a few hours? Would you do that for me, Tom?"

He stroked her head again. " Why, Sal? Why do you want to go home?"

She shook her head, in a bewildered, uncertain fashion. " I . . . don't know. I just don't know. I suppose I want to get away from . . . all this. It's important, Tom." She took his arm urgently. " It's very important."

He hesitated, shifting his weight a little as he squatted, pondering what she had said. " Well . . . there's the lunch with the Taylors . . ."

" Tell them I'm sick!" she said promptly. " They know I'm pregnant. Or—tell them one of my family's sick. I've never pulled out of anything before—and Mrs. Taylor's always talking about one's duty to the family." She tightened the pressure on his arm a little to emphasise the point. " Please, Tom. It is important to me."

" O.K., Sal. If you want it." He kissed her gently on the forehead. " Hurry up, now. I'll call the Taylors, and we'll get on our way."

She looked up at him. " Thank you."

They hardly talked at all during the drive down to New York. Tom had the radio on, and they listened in silence to a Mozart piano concerto, and Aaron Copeland's " Rodeo." It was a bright, hot day, with the sky above them hard like blue enamel. The traffic streaming out of New York was very heavy, the triple lanes of crowded cars heading for lakes and golf courses and picnic grounds. Their side of the road was almost empty, and they drove swiftly and easily. It gave Sally a curious feeling to be going against the crowd, and part of it was her guilt over cancelling the lunch at the country club. On the other hand, the urge towards the familiar

206

pattern of the Sundays in Brooklyn was strong enough to almost stifle the guilt, or at least to keep it under. She knew Tom did not really understand her reaction to the story of Jeannie Talbot's rape, or why she was certain her horror and fear would be so much softened by contact with her family. He merely accepted her statement that it was so, and now they were driving on this empty side of the road away from the fresh green shade of their valley, towards an airless city apartment.

As they crossed Brooklyn Bridge and the Manhattan towers dropped behind them, Sally looked at her watch.

"We're just in time for High Mass at St. Paul's. Dad always goes to High Mass . . . I could meet him there."

As he pulled in at the kerb in front of the grey, tall church, he said to her, "Do you want me to come in with you, Sal? You look a bit peaky. . . ." She seemed pale and weary from the heat.

She shook her head. "I'm all right. Dad will be there— he always goes to the same seat. Besides, you'll take half an hour to find a parking place." She kissed him on the cheek, and got out of the car, a little awkwardly and heavily. Then she turned back to him and said, "Don't say anything about Jeannie Talbot to the family." He nodded in agreement, and thought as she walked across the pavement towards the steps, that her pregnancy was just beginning to show. Anxiously he watched her mount the steps, and told himself that he had been thoughtless not to have got out of the car and helped her. He thought of her as being vulnerable here in the city, as if she were menaced by the crowded buildings, and the hot pavement, and the noise, by the indifference of the people who stood waiting or gossiping outside the church. He watched her vanish into the dimness beyond the arched doorway. Then he remembered that she had left Burnham Falls to hurry back to the security of these surroundings.

After a ten-minute search he found a place to park. The Brennans' apartment was only three blocks from St. Paul's, and so the car could stay there all day. He walked slowly back towards the church. Most of the people who had stood outside were gone. Across the road from the church was a small, rather dark snack bar; he went in there and ordered coffee. The place wasn't air-conditioned, and the door stood wide open, catching the dust as well as the faint movement of air from the street. There were no other customers, and the counterman had taken apart the slicing machine to clean

207

it, and was listening to a sports forecaster on the tiny radio beside him. Above the monotonous radio voice, Tom could hear drifts of the organ music from the church; sometimes the sound of the traffic in between drowned it out. He had a second cup of coffee, smoked two cigarettes, and then found himself on the street again, crossing towards the church. The choir was singing now, the sound of the organ soft behind it.

Sally and he had been married in the sacristy of St. Paul's, and that was the only time he had ever been in a Catholic church. The doors stood wide open, and the Mass went on, seemingly oblivious of the traffic passing a few feet away. He walked up the steps hesitantly. The church was packed; all the seats were filled, and there was a crowd of people standing at the back. He mingled with them, sniffing the strange smell of incense, listening uncomprehendingly to the Latin of the hymns. It was a large church; the altar seemed a distant place, and the moving, robed figures on it incredibly remote. And yet all about him the people seemed to understand perfectly what was going on; they knelt and stood in unison without anyone telling them to, and they followed the service with the sureness of long custom.

He did not know how long he stood there, except that he came to like the feeling of being in this place. He was anonymous, but not quite alone. And somewhere in the crowd was Sally, and her father Mike, doing exactly what the people about him were doing. As the smooth, uninterrupted flow of the Mass continued, he vaguely began to comprehend why Sally, faced with her fear and horror in Burnham Falls, had turned back to an established rhythm and pattern of things and places she had known and dwelt with all her life. There was a sense of timeless continuity in this church, an acceptance of suffering and joy within the same frame of living. He found himself then thinking of Jeannie Talbot, and wishing she had the comfort of this moment.

When the service was over he went out quickly and stood waiting at the kerb, where he could scan the crowd coming down the steps. When he saw them, he came forward to greet Mike with his hand outstretched. The welcome on Mike's face was genuine; his worn face was brilliant with pride and pleasure as he held a hand protectively under Sally's elbow.

"It's great to see you, Tom! Why, it's like old times to have Sally beside me at Mass, and won't Eileen be surprised.

208

. . . Ah, you're a good lad, Tom, to bring her down. We miss her, you know. . . ."

Tom made the usual conversation with Mike as they walked the three blocks to the Brennan apartment. But he said nothing at all about having stood at the back of the church.

The day passed as all Sundays did in the Brennan apartment. Eileen had been to early Mass so that she could be ahead with the preparations for the large midday meal they always ate—whatever the temperature was outside. It varied little—roast lamb or roast beef, and a pie of whatever fruit was in season. Mike always got the whisky bottle out after Mass, and Eileen sipped a discreet glass, with a lot of soda, while she cooked. Sometimes they had a guest, but to-day there was only the family—the two unmarried boys, John and Peter, and Sally and Tom. When the Brennans got together, they liked to talk, mostly about themselves, and Sally's unexpected visit seemed to unleash a whole storm of family news and gossip. Tom said little, but frankly enjoyed listening. They seemed to stimulate each other to greater degrees of exaggeration; as the whisky was passed around, each incident was heightened and coloured, funnier or more pathetic than it had been in the original. Tom realised that each was vying for the centre of the limelight; they were like actors putting on a performance for each other. He listened, fascinated, and knew that Sally carried some of this heightened sense of living wherever she went, and that this, too, was one of the reasons why he loved her.

After lunch, John and Peter left; Mike sat with Tom in the living-room, smoking a pipe mostly in silence, while Sally helped Eileen with the dishes. When Sally came back he straightened in his chair, and the animation returned to his face.

"Well, darlin', how's the book going now? When am I going to get it into my hands to read? When will we be sending a copy to your Uncle Oliver?"

Sally made a face, and dropped heavily into an armchair.

"It's going very badly, Dad. I don't think it's ever going to be finished."

He looked at her gravely. "Sally, you don't mean that! With all the talent you have! . . . With all the great things you used to write at college!"

She sighed. "Dad, writing pieces at college is very different

209

from sitting down and thinking out a whole set of characters, and seeing them on their way through a story, and giving it direction and polish . . . and some meaning. Perhaps I was stupid to ever think I could do it. . . ."

He shook his head. " I'm sad to hear you say so. It used not to be this way with you. There was a time when you *knew* you could do this and just about anything else you wanted to do. You had the world by the tail . . . why are you willing to let it go?"

. She shook her head. " But I'm not Uncle Oliver. . . ."

Mike interrupted her. " You're right! You're *not* Oliver. You could be much better than Oliver if you don't waste your gifts." He threw out his hands, the pipe smoke swirling about him. " After all, Oliver writes Gaelic poetry that no one can read, but you—*you* have a great audience of people eager to read what's put before them." He thumped the crumpled Sunday papers by his side. " Look at that great wad of stuff to read . . . look at the paper-back racks in the drug store, look at the news-stands crammed with stuff. You know as well as I do that you have your place there, Sally."

" But I *don't* know. You make it all sound so easy. All I have to do is sit down and write. What about the thousand things that get in the way . . . I have a home to run . . . I'm going to have a baby."

" Don't let them get in your way," Mike said. " You had a thousand things to do at college, but you got through them."

" This is different, Dad. I'm living in a place where I'm expected to join in the things that the other wives are doing. I'm on the library committee, and I'm helping raise funds for a new parish auditorium, and we're organising a dramatic society. . . ."

" Nonsense!" he said. " Get out of these things if they stop you following your own bent. Your friends will respect you more for writing a book than raising a hundred dollars for the library."

" It doesn't work that way," Sally said heatedly, colouring and uncomfortable under the first criticism she had heard from her father for years. " It would be quite different if I were established . . . if I had some success to point to. I can't tell anyone in Burnham Falls that I'm trying to write a novel. If I didn't get it published, I'd be a laughing stock

210

. . . and that hurts Tom. You've got to remember Tom's position. . . ."

"Nothing will hurt Tom so much as an unhappy wife. If you start denying your talent before you even give it a chance, you've just shown it the door. Look at Oliver . . . when he wants to write he goes and writes. Nothing gets in the way."

"But Uncle Oliver is a *poet*—he's expected to do that!"

"And aren't you expected to use the talents God gave you—in the best way you can use them?" Again he thumped the papers. "There are thousands of people getting books published. Your name should be there among them. Just give up your afternoon tea parties, or whatever it is you women do, and sit down with a pen and paper and get on with it." He had leaned forward towards her to stress his words, and now he slumped back in the chair, as if he had reached a finality.

"Dad, if I could . . ." she began softly. The words were spoken tentatively, but there was already the sound of purpose in them.

After that Sally and Mike spent an hour talking about the book, talking around and through it, building pictures for each other of the time when it would be published, of what Oliver would say about it, of the chances of reaching the best-seller list, and the mass-circulation paper-backs. It was a happy world of fantasy in which Tom did not belong. He found himself quietly drinking tea with Eileen in the kitchen. But he did not in the least mind his exclusion because from Sally's face had vanished the look of fear and hurt that had so tormented him that morning.

II

There hadn't been a Sunday in Burnham Falls like this one for a long time. In a sense it reminded Clif a little of the Sunday of Pearl Harbour. He didn't go to church—he rarely went to church after Dorothy died—but he watched the usual crowds gathering to the three churches along Main Street and it seemed there was a tension in them, almost an excitement; they stayed much longer to talk after the services. Three times that morning cars belonging to the State Police passed along Main Street, and everyone stared

211

after them as if they expected to see Patrino and Reitch in the back seat. Mrs. Martin returned from church, and stood and talked to Clif for twenty minutes on the porch before going in to get lunch. The talk was all about Jeannie Talbot, of course, but it wasn't anything fresh, nothing he hadn't known by nine o'clock that morning. Clif endured it because he knew Mrs. Martin wouldn't do anything about lunch until she'd been through it all once again.

He had five phone calls that morning from people he hadn't seen for months, and who hadn't bothered to call him for much longer than that. None of them said so specifically, but it was obvious they were all hoping he had been in touch with Ted Talbot and might be prepared to gossip a little in exchange for their pleasantries.

Late in the afternoon he finally decided to call the Talbots. He had so far hesitated because he couldn't appear to be asking for legal business, and because he knew the invasion of privacy the Talbots would already have suffered that day. But Ted had worked for him for more than twenty years, and he had never asked for any kind of help. It occurred to Clif that he might not know how to ask for it now.

It was Selma who answered, and she told him Ted was at the hospital. Jeannie wasn't badly hurt, she said. There was a dull, frozen sound to her voice, as if she didn't fully realise the words she was saying, or know their meaning. To Clif it suggested that she was fighting hysteria.

"Ted knows he's only to ask me if he needs any help. You understand that, Mrs. Talbot?"

"Yes, Mr. Burrell," she said mechanically. "Thank you." And then hung up.

III

Phil Conrad didn't stay for the end of the golf tournament at the country club that Sunday afternoon. Ed Peters was to present the cup for Amtec when it was over, so he couldn't leave when his guest did. Laura drove him back to the house to pick up his bag and the car in which he had driven to Burnham Falls.

Conrad didn't give any reason or excuses for leaving early. But as he shook hands with Ed, he spoke the words Ed had been hoping to hear all through the week-end.

"It looks as if we'll only need one or two more meetings

212

with your people to iron out the last wrinkles, and then we"ll be set to sign the contract. We're thinking of the first show for November. . . ."

As soon as Conrad had driven away with Laura in the Cadillac, Ed went to the phone and called E. J. Harrison in New York. He knew that up to this point Conrad had given no definite commitment on the series of shows for Amtec, and he wanted E. J. to know that the decision had been reached during this week-end.

He listened to E. J.'s words of pleasure, but it was a distinct shock to suddenly hear the other's tone change as E. J. launched into a discussion of Jeannie Talbot's rape, and Amtec's implication in the affair. E. J. gave his advice crisply and with great sureness, and left Ed dumbly wondering how he had found out so quickly, and whom his informant had been. Ed had intended to send in a routine report, and to minimise its importance, but someone had reached E. J. before him. He came out of the phone booth, his face tight with fury. Who, he wondered, had slipped the word along the chain of command to get to E. J.? Sommers? . . . Harvey? . . . Taylor? . . . None of them would have dared to go directly over his head, but there were any number of ways of relaying the message with seeming innocence. At the eighteenth green he watched the faces of the men about him. Was it Sullivan or Andrews . . . or was it Dexter? Neither Steve nor Harriet Dexter had appeared to-day for the tournament.

Then one of Sullivan's assistant's sank his putt, and the applause of the crowd acknowledged him the winner. His face fixed in a congratulatory smile, Ed strode across the green to shake his hand.

Back at the house Laura mixed a martini for Phil before he left. Her movements were perfectly calm and steady, but she was battling with the knowledge that she would have to speak plainly to him, that she couldn't let him go without asking for some reassurance. Her tongue felt stiff and awkward, but she was frightened to trust to the only weapon she had ever needed to use on a man before. For Phil Conrad, beauty was not unique ; he was surrounded by beauty. She had to be more than that. For the first time in her life she had to hope and believe desperately that she was the particular kind of woman a man like Phil wanted. For the first time she came to hope that there was something

213

in her beyond beauty that a man would want. She was possessed by a sickening feeling of poverty.

"Phil, will I be seeing you—soon?"

He sipped his drink, and nodded, but it could have been just to approve its dryness and chill. "That's up to you, isn't it, Laura? I mean "—he paused to sip again—" you have to make the opportunities. We can hardly arrange a rendezvous in the woods at Burnham Falls, can we?"

It was cruel, she thought. And she wondered if he had done it deliberately because he had liked Larry, and had known that she had not even tried with Larry, and now it amused him to see her have to try so hard with him.

She took a deep breath. " I don't mind what I have to do," she said faintly.

And then later she stood in the driveway and watched him go, and she whispered after him, " I'll do anything at all —anything I have to do! Because if I don't have you—if I can't fill my nights and days with you—I think I'll die! Because there isn't anything else for me now."

She drank two more martinis before Ed came home, just sitting and staring at Phil's empty glass on the table before her.

IV

Tom and Sally waited until it was dark to drive back from Brooklyn to Burnham Falls. Tom let the top down on the car, and above them the stars were near and friendly. The warm evening air fanned around them gently as they drove. Sally sat close to Tom, sometimes touching his arm and knee with a soft gesture that was a vague indication of gratitude and pleasure. A few times she lighted a cigarette for him. Again their side of the highway was almost empty as the returning cars streamed back to the city. Sally no longer minded their apartness from the other people, the knowledge that they were going in a different direction.

V

Jeannie licked her dry lips, staring mindlessly into the darkness and stillness of the small room they had put her into at the Kempton General. The sedative they had given her hadn't

214

worked—probably because she had slept all through Sunday morning after the shot they'd given her earlier. In the afternoon her father and mother had come to see her, separately, because they had not wanted to bring Chrissie to the hospital. Jerry had not come. Her mother had said it was because the doctor had refused visitors—but Jeannie had only half-believed that.

The three-quarter moon had risen high, and was now on the wane. Vaguely she remembered the moon of last night. That was all that was safe to remember. The rest must be kept away until she was able to face it. One part of her mind had to remember because of the questions they asked; but the deeper part, the knowledge of injury and terror, must be kept down, away out of sight.

The night nurse looked in, and was aware of her wakefulness. "I'll get you something, Jeannie," she said softly. She spoke the words as if Jeannie were a child who needed comfort. She had been on duty last night when Jeannie had been admitted. Jeannie couldn't remember having seen her in Burnham Falls.

She returned soon with a mug of hot chocolate. "Sometimes something hot in the stomach's better than a pill," she said. Jeannie drank it through the glass straw, because her mouth was too swollen to shape to the rim of the mug. The nurse straightened the bedclothes and plumped the pillows; she didn't say anything again until she took the empty mug from Jeannie. "Yes—that'll be better. Sometimes you just need something for the stomach."

CHAPTER NINE

On Monday morning Sally saw Tom off to the Laboratories almost with a feeling of relief and impatience. When he was gone she washed the dishes quickly and left them to drain; then she made the bed and flicked a duster through the living-room. At the back of her mind she was aware of the report she had promised Father James at the parish church on the campaign for raising money for the auditorium, and she had also told Susan Watts that she would start phoning around to canvas support for the dramatic society. But now she did neither of these things. She went to the kitchen drawer and took out the manuscript. She carried it into

215

the living-room, and settled herself at the desk there, half-closing the venetian blind so that Marcia Webster would not see her from her own living-room, wave, and perhaps stroll over later for a cup of coffee, and to discuss the news about Jeannie Talbot. For the moment Sally wanted neither Jeannie, nor Burnham Falls, nor Amtec. By ten-thirty she had a page written. The phone rang three times that morning, and she didn't answer it.

I I

After lunch that Monday Clif Burrell walked slowly down Main Street to Vanesco's, the barber shop. One of the four chairs was vacant, and he went to it immediately, tossing his hat on to the bench that stretched along one wall. Rather wearily he acknowledged the small chorus of greetings; the heat and sun that bounced back off the concrete pavements seemed to grow worse each summer. And yet he could not give in to driving the car that short distance from his house.

"How are you, John?" he said, as Vanesco tucked the towels about his neck.

"Fine, Mr. Burrell. And yourself?"

"Great," Clif replied. He leaned far back in the chair. John went to work at once with the scissors; he had been cutting Clif's hair for more than fifteen years. He always started rapidly with the scissors before he started to talk.

"Well, Mr. Burrell—what do you make of this Jeannie Talbot business?"

In the mirror, Clif looked at him without pleasure. "What should I make of it? Damn' shame."

"That's what I said myself. I've known Jeannie since she was a little toddler waiting over on that bench while her dad got a trim—and that's exactly what I said myself when I heard it." He knew his mention of Jeannie Talbot had caught the attention of the whole room, and he raised his voice a little. "Though I think myself that Jeannie could've been a bit more careful. Since these construction crews moved in you never know who's about. . . .'"

"That ain't the way I heard it." The man who had spoken was seated in the chair nearest the window. Clif had seen him around but didn't know his name, and it irked him to think how Burnham Falls was slipping away from him. The

216

man twisted to face the room. Close to Clif's ear, John's scissors stopped their snipping motion.

"Seems she was real friendly with these two guys . . . she was drinking with them before it happened. The wife of one of the guys—you know, she was left behind at the camp—she's real sore at Jeannie. Says she egged them on . . . looks like Jeannie must've been all set for a little fun and it got kinda out of hand. . . ."

" Story I heard was that she was selling some face cream to Mrs. Reitch, and Patrino and Reitch were with her. Jeannie finished off work about then, and they all went out together. Heard it from Wally Carter. . . ."

John started vigorously with the scissors again as he observed Clif's frowning face in the mirror. "Did you know Jeannie, Mr. Burrell?" he said.

Clif nodded. Then he said, "Hurry it up, will you, John? I've got an appointment." He supposed that John knew almost as well as he did that there was no pressing appointment, but the lie didn't matter.

He spoke again, clearly, so that his voice carried through the room. "The law," he said, "has a wonderful way of clarifying these things. These two men, Patrino and Reitch, will be caught, and there will be a trial. *That* will be the time to make judgments."

"Hell, I wouldn't be in their shoes!" one of the men commented. "Way these things go, the jury's always got sympathy for the girl. It always comes out that none of it was *her* fault. She couldn't help wagging her fanny and being cute . . . and then when a guy reaches out for what's offered, she gets mad and acts all offended. Women is mostly cheats . . . and the juries'll go on letting 'em be. There wouldn't be half the rapes if women didn't act so damn' come-on."

In the chair next to Clif, Tom Burns, who ran the dry-cleaning store next door spoke. "Well . . . I dunno . . . when a girl's got a figure like Jeannie's, something's almost bound to happen to her. She's sure stacked." He met Clif's stare quite calmly because it had suddenly become permissible now in Burnham Falls to talk about Jeannie Talbot this way.

"I tell you it'll be some show when those guys come up for trial," John Vanesco said. "It'll blow the lid right off this town—the Talbots being church-going an' all that—and Amtec being sort of responsible for the construction

217

camp being here. I guess Mr. Ed Peters isn't too comfortable about the whole thing. Selma Talbot helps out at his house now and then. I hear he was at the hospital to see Jeannie right after it happened."

"Sure was queer how Mal Hamilton found her," Burns said. "I'd like to know what *he* was doin' on that road that time of night."

Clif struggled with the towels around his neck.

"That's O.K., John. I'm thin enough on top. Don't take it all." He climbed down from the chair stiffly, and reached into his pocket for money to pay John, at the same time shrugging off the other's efforts to brush his neck again. "See you again," he said.

There was silence while he settled his tie, and got his jacket and hat from the bench. But the talk started up again even before the door properly closed behind him.

When he walked out on to the street again, the heat seemed to hit him with physical force; after a few paces he was sweating, and he took out his handkerchief and carefully wiped his face. He recognised it as the gesture of an old man. He pushed his panama a little farther back on his head, and thought of going into Drake's Bar for a shot of whisky. He hesitated only because he had never, so far, taken to drinking in public at midday, obeying a loose kind of code that it was undignified to do so. Perhaps if he drank beer, people would know it was only because of the heat, and not the need for liquor. Then he shrugged away that idea, because he couldn't convince even himself with it. He was still thinking about the drink as he drew level with Drake's; he paused in a kind of shuffling hesitation before the door, and then, quite abruptly, he turned away. Inside he had seen a crowd of men, much like the one he had left at the barber shop—bigger than usual for this time of day —and he also recognised from their animation that the talk was hot and strong. He knew, without stepping inside that they were talking about Jeannie Talbot. Somehow, the sight of the place disgusted him for the first time. It was heavily shaded from the sun by awnings, and inside only two dimmed lights burned at the back of the bar. It was an atmosphere that invited comment more lurid and suggestive than at Vanesco''s. Jeannie's name would be common property for a time in this town, he thought, and people who had barely known her name would claim knowledge of her, if not friendship, and for a time around the bars it would be a sign of

218

sexual prowess to talk about her in a way that suggested intimacy. She had become everyone's possession, a girl whom women could either defend or draw away from, whom men could speak about with a knowing smile, and a broad innuendo.

He felt a little sick as he turned away, and absolutely powerless. He stared unseeingly into the blinding sun, and wondered what he ought to do.

It was a shock to feel the hand come down on his shoulder, to hear the voice so close to him.

"Hi, there, Mr. Burrell! How've you been? Haven't seen you about lately."

Clif faced the other man unwillingly, shrinking a little away from his touch, and not caring if it was noticed. "Oh—how are you, Benedict?" he said distantly.

"Can't complain—can't complain." The tone was too hearty, with an edge of triumph to it which Clif knew must mean that Benedict had something to tell him.

John Benedict had set up practice in Elmbury more than twenty years ago, and had developed a flourishing business on the basis of his homespun manner, and his occasional, deliberate bad grammar. He called himself a "people's lawyer"—and they believed him. Clif's Harvard Law School background had been the subject of many of Benedict's sly digs over the years, and it had been something of a trial for Clif when Benedict had established a branch office in Burnham Falls at the time that Amtec came into the town. It was run by a young man fresh from N.Y.U., and supervised at a distance by Benedict. He never came to Burnham Falls for minor business.

"Had an interesting client this morning, Clif." The use of his first name sounded like a deliberate insult, but Clif thought it probable that using people's first names had built up Benedict's business.

"Oh?" he said.

"Yes—Ted Talbot. You know—father of the girl that's had this trouble."

Clif took a deep breath; he had feared this from the moment he had seen Benedict, but he hadn't been quite prepared to accept that Ted had gone past him to seek help from the other lawyer. It was the worst he had feared, and it had happened. It was the first time that he knew completely and truly that he was finished in Burnham Falls.

"It's a nasty bit of trouble this girl's in . . ." Benedict said.

219

Clif thought it was typical of him that he had avoided using the word " rape " so far. It was part of his system of delicate vulgarisms, instead of straight words—almost like the way a mortician talked of the dead. Clif detested it.

" I thought it was the men who committed the rape that were in trouble," Clif observed.

" It's hard on the little girl, too," Benedict answered. " Of course, we don't do much criminal business, but Talbot asked me to find the right people to handle it when the men were caught and the trial date set. We have to see that justice is done by this poor little innocent girl," he added piously.

He was watching Clif's face closely, and now he thrust his hands in his pockets, and prepared to enjoy the rest of what he had to say. " Of course, Talbot would have gone to you, Clif, but I understand you're not handling cases any longer. . . ."

" I'm sure your firm will handle it to everyone's satisfaction," Clif replied stiffly.

Benedict beamed. " We'll do our best, Clif." Again he touched the other's arm with a gesture of intimacy. " But believe me, I'm looking forward to the day when I'll be able to put my feet up and forget about law. But I have to make a little something to put by first. It's different with you Harvard men. . . ."

On the way up Main Street towards his house Clif passed George Keston. Usually when they met they stopped to exchange a minute's talk, but to-day George kept right on walking.

" Hallo, Clif," he said, waving vaguely in his direction. He hurried straight by, and Clif pondered about him for a while, and wondered if he had only imagined that George looked embarrassed. By the time he had reached his front gate he had remembered that Jerry Keston was Jeannie's boy-friend.

He walked moodily indoors and went straight to the liquor cabinet. He poured himself a stiff shot of whisky, and drank it standing up. Then he poured another one, and drank it more slowly at his desk, thinking about what he had seen and heard downtown. It was like the buzzing of flies—distinct and unpleasant, not to be ignored. He thought that he should do something about it, but he didn't know what

220

to do that wouldn't make more fuss. Benedict had made it impossible for him to offer his help again to the Talbots and he was still enough hurt by Ted passing him over to make him unwilling to consider any way around that. He wondered what kind of fees Benedict would charge Ted, and he knew whatever they were, Ted could not afford them. He muttered angrily under his breath, and went and poured another drink. Milly Squires put her head in the room, and he told her curtly that he wasn't ready for her yet, and he saw her look disapprovingly at the bottle and the glass. By the time the third drink was finished, he had thought of something to do.

He went and got the clippers from the tool shed, and walked slowly around to the front lawn. The afternoon had grown hotter, even the faint breeze was gone now, and the air was still and dead, unmoving. He pricked his finger as he cut the first rose, and stood there sucking the little droplets of blood that oozed slowly, and wishing at the same time that he was inside in the shade. Then he bent and quickly stripped the bush—these were fat red blooms, whose scent hung heavy on the air. He thought of it as a dark scent, like their colour. Then he heard the telephone ring inside, and a minute later, Milly leaned out of her office window, and called to him.

" Mr. Burrell, it's for you."

He straightened slowly. He thought it was regrettable that Milly had no style in anything she did. " I imagined that, Milly," he said, " Who is it?"

" It's Mrs. Williams. She wants to talk to you about some changes in her will."

" Tell her I'll talk to her later. Tell her I'm not home."

Milly's eyes widened. " But, Mr. Burrell—she *knows* you're home. She said she saw you from the window."

He shook his head. " And she's going to die so soon she can't let me pick my roses in peace?'" He considered for a moment, and then he said, " Tell her to take her business to Benedict! Tell her I've retired!"

" But Mr. Burrell . . ."

He took no notice of Milly, but bent over the bushes again, thinking of Sarah Williams watching him from the window of her big white house across the street. It was the best thing that had happened that afternoon. After a time Milly decided that he had meant what he said, and she drew back. In spite of the heat, she slammed down the window. Clif

221

went on picking the roses unhurriedly until all the bushes were bare.

Clif hadn't been to the Kempton General Hospital for some years—it was where Dorothy had died after that last operation, and he didn't like the place. As he drove up he thought that it had changed more than just the extent of the fresh coat of paint, and then he realised that a big glass side porch had been added and there were convalescent patients out there, watching the arrival of cars with all the avid interest of people who are shut in. It occurred to him that wherever he went about the country these days there seemed to be people watching.

He was about to get out of the car when he saw Jerry Keston come down the front steps and walk towards the parking lot. Clif's car was the last in line, and Jerry didn't have to pass him to reach his own. His face was kept carefully turned away from the observers on the porch, but Clif was able to study it as the young man walked nearer. It was a dark and bitter look he wore, a look of humiliation. His head hung slightly forward, and he kept his eyes on the ground. When he backed the car out of line, he did it gently and quietly, as if he didn't want to attract attention.

When Jerry Keston was gone, Clif felt suddenly embarrassed by the size of the bunch of roses, and he saw it as a useless, flamboyant gesture that would deceive no one, least of all Jeannie. He thought of her lying in her bed, with her beaten, marked face, and he imagined what might have been said between her and Jerry, what had happened to cause Jerry to creep out of here like a sulky, frightened child. Clif knew he couldn't go and talk to Jeannie then—not take with him his silly bunch of roses and his old man's smell of whisky. Jeannie didn't need or want the comfort of an old man now.

So he just left the roses with a starched young girl at the reception desk, and asked her to see that Jeannie got them. She looked up briefly from her pad.

" Whom shall I say sent them? "

" It doesn't matter. No name."

When he left the Kempton General he drove to the Carpenter place. Harriet would be there, he thought. It would be cool, and there would be understanding in Harriet's calm face, and they wouldn't have to talk too much about Jeannie. He wouldn't even have a drink—he'd ask Harriet for some tea and she'd pour it for him from Claudia Carpenter's silver teapot. Harriet had the gift of making him feel important, even though he and she both knew he wasn't important any longer in Burnham Falls, or anywhere else.

III

By Thursday morning there was almost no food left in the refrigerator, and Sally decided reluctantly that she would have to beg a lift to the supermarket from Marcia Webster. Marcia was good-natured, and generally inclined to do what Sally suggested. Sally cut short the other's offer of coffee before they started, and hustled her towards the car. The pile of manuscript on the living-room desk had grown considerably in the last three days, and she was full of impatience with anything that took her away from it. On the way to the supermarket she was almost tempted to tell Marcia about the novel—in a way it would guarantee her from interruption in the future—and then decided against it. It would be better, in the end, to produce the finished book.

At the supermarket Sally rushed through the food-crammed aisles at a pace that bewildered Marcia, who liked a leisurely procession, and to deliberate each choice.

"What's the hurry?" she protested, as Sally started for the check-out counters.

"I've got a lot of things to do—letters to write," Sally said.

Marcia shrugged. "Well—from the way you've been pounding that typewriter in the last couple of days, I'd have thought you could have written to about forty cousins by this time." As she spoke she continued her slow study of the frozen food display.

Sally turned away to hide her flush of annoyance. She didn't offer any reply. She had forgotten how the constant tapping of the typewriter would reach across the pretty, trim garden between her house and Marcia's. No one in Amtec Park used the sleek little portables—which they all seemed to possess—for six hours a day, and if anyone did, it was noticeable. For an instant Sally wished herself back in the crowded apartment in New York, where, behind the closed front door, your world was your own, and no one knew or cared what you did—and where the rumble of the traffic in the street below would cover the sound of anything—weeping,

223

laughing, or even dying, if you wanted it that way. She compared it, in a moment's regret, with the house she had thought of as an intimate warm place of love for herself and Tom when they had first moved to Burnham Falls, and which now seemed to expand and open up to admit pressures and influences that made no recognition of their own special needs.

"Well, don't be in too much of a hurry," Marcia continued serenely, "that is, unless you want to be trapped at the counter with Madame Taylor."

Sally turned guiltily and looked down the aisle to where Alan Taylor's wife was waiting in line at the cash registers. Marcia's husband, Bill, also worked with Tom in Alan Taylor's department, and " Madame " Taylor was their private nickname for the boss's wife.

Marcia took three beef pies out of the freezer and laid them in her shopping-cart.

" I suppose you know," she said, " that Barbara Taylor was as mad as hell with you and Tom for ducking out on such short notice on Sunday. Her invitations are meant to be taken seriously, believe me!" She bobbed her head knowingly. "And it doesn't do Tom much good with Alan . . . or the company." Marcia deepened her voice then to an absurd imitation of Alan Taylor's. " ' The corporation expects dependability from its young men. . . .' "

Sally felt herself grow tense. " Did she really mind?"

Marcia shrugged. " I guess she did, Sal. You know how it is in the company . . . no one expects insubordination from the junior ranks."

Sally tried to steady a tremble in her voice. "Well . . . we telephoned and told her we wouldn't be there. I thought she'd hardly miss us in the crowd."

" Whether she missed you or not isn't the point, is it? You backed out of an invitation, and in the company book that means you're unco-operative. It doesn't go down too well."

" What can I do?" Sally said defensively. " I've already apologised."

" I guess you'll just have to wait until Madame Taylor decides to forgive you. The move has to come from her. I don't suppose . . ." She hesitated. " I don't suppose you've been invited to to-morrow's little gathering."

" What gathering. What are you talking about."

" Barbara Taylor asked all of the women who were at

224

the lunch on Sunday to meet Maurice Delbert's wife at a tea party at the club to-morrow."

" Maurice Delbert . . . You mean the Frenchman who's visiting——?"

Marcia nodded. " That's the one—Nobel Prize and all! He's very interested in something Alan's department is working on, and he and his wife are staying with the Taylors. I think the husbands are supposed to join us at the club for cocktails afterwards . . ."

She broke off. " Why, Sal—what's the matter. Are you sick?"

Sally shook her head wanly. " Thanks, Marcy, I'm all right. Just a bit tired. Not sleeping so well in the heat . . ."

The other nodded sympathetically, and Sally turned away from her, wheeling her basket round the corner of the aisle, out of sight of both Marcia and Barbara Taylor. She stood staring at a display of canned soup, trying to hold back the dismay and panic that flooded her. She didn't know quite how to face what had happened, or what Tom would think when he learned about it. Maurice Delbert was one of the most distinguished men ever to visit the Laboratories. Tom had spoken of him with admiration and awe, and had even told Sally, as if he were recounting a triumph, that he had glimpsed him in the corridor with Alan Taylor. Not only would Tom have given much to have been invited to cocktails with Delbert, but his very absence, when people of Bill Webster's position were invited, would be significant. It would place Tom below the line of people considered important or interested enough to meet Delbert.

In a daze Sally read the labels on the soup cans before her. . . . Tomato . . . Asparagus. She didn't really know what she was reading, but she reached up and took some cans indiscriminately, because she needed something to do.

And inside of her, beyond the noise of the supermarket and beyond the reality of the printed labels before her eyes, she was raging against the unfairness of the system, and raging against the stupidity of the blunder she had made.

" Tom . . . Tom!" she whispered miserably to herself. " I've done something wrong! I've hurt you. . . ."

It was almost noon when Sally got home. She ignored the manuscript on the living-room desk, and she spent the next hour on the telephone, canvassing support for the dramatic society, as she had promised Susan Watts she would do. Then

C.W. 225 H

she showered and dressed for a meeting of the library committee at two-thirty. She hadn't intended to go, but now she knew she must. Barbara Taylor was also on the committee. When they met, Sally would apologise with great humility for her absence on Sunday, tell some lies about her mother being ill, which she didn't want to do, and then she would offer to do some work for the Cancer Fund, in which Barbara Taylor was interested. Once before she had hinted that she would like Sally's help in raising money, and Sally had managed to ignore the hint. Now she would ignore it no longer. She would work for the Cancer Fund and everything else Barbara Taylor wanted her to work for, until the memory of last Sunday's mistake had been wiped out. But she had little hope that what she would promise Barbara Taylor this afternoon would bring an invitation for to-morrow.

Before she left for Betty Thompson's house, where the committee was meeting, she put away the manuscript, for she knew now that it wasn't just to Barbara Taylor, but to every other aspect of corporation life that she must devote her time and energies. She must never again neglect any of the things that were a part of the life of any woman who wanted to help her husband, who wanted to prove that she was capable of handling any of the social or civic duties the corporation gave to her. In the corporation not only the man, but the woman he had married, counted in unknowable, intangible ways; if she would fail Tom in this respect, it hardly mattered in what other ways she compensated. Last Sunday, on a sudden impulse, she had gone rushing headlong back to her family, escaping the atmosphere of the corporation and the town because they had seemed unsympathetic and even hostile. In doing this she had damaged Tom in the eyes of a man who could either push him forward or hold him back. The novel was part of the same pattern of impulse and indulgence of self, demanding time and loyalty that had nothing to do with Tom or the corporation. It was a luxury which they, she and Tom both, couldn't at the moment afford.

She was both angry and determined as she walked towards Betty Thompson's house on the other side of Amtec Park.

"Well, if it's an organiser they want," she told herself. "I'll be the best damned organiser they ever saw."

226

CHAPTER TEN

Jeannie grew tired and despairing of the trips to the police station to go through the photos of men arrested for other crimes in the neighbouring states, and perhaps among them to find and identify Patrino and Reitch. At first she looked at them impatiently, waiting to see the faces she knew, and then after a time it began to dawn in her that perhaps she was never going to see them. The conviction came slowly, unwillingly, but it grew steadily when she noticed that the sheriff didn't send the patrol car to pick her up any more, but just asked her to drop into the station, as if the matter had no great urgency. She knew from that that he didn't believe, either, that Patrino and Reitch would ever show on those files. One day he voiced his doubt. " There's a rape committed every thirty seconds in the United States, Jeannie," he said, and his tone carried a weary acceptance of the fact of crime. " Unless the guy concerned already had a criminal record, we don't have much hope of catching up with him. Those mug shots you look at—that's only the off-chance that either Patino or Reitch might have been using an alias. But I don't think so—I don't think so."

The town heard that Val Reitch had sold the house trailer, and left the construction camp. With Val's going, the case appeared to die—the fact that the police let her leave the district seemed to indicate that there was only a long chance of getting Patrino or Reitch, or if they did it would only be because they were arrested for some other crime. Jeannie and Burnham Falls read the signs that way, and even her father stopped calling daily into John Benedict's office and pressing for some action from his young assistant.

Jeannie's face healed, and the dentist put a cap on one of her teeth that had been chipped when she fell. That seemed all that could be done. That seemed to end the matter.

For Jeannie it wasn't ended because she didn't know how to take up her life again. Some kind of necessary vitality had been missing from her since that Sunday night; she seemed to have no will to do anything for longer than ten minutes at a time. She had not yet been back to her place behind the counter at Carter's; Wally had called her on the phone to tell her that he had hired young Judy Thomas to fill in until she wanted to come back.

227

"Just till you feel O.K. again, Jeannie. Just till then," he said, faintly apologetic.

The news didn't worry her, because it left her almost unmoved. She went back to practising her typing and shorthand in a kind of routine, mindless way that quite effectively shut out her thoughts. She didn't go anywhere, and she filled the rest of her days and evenings playing absentmindedly with Chrissie, or sitting vacantly in front of the television set. There was comfort of a kind in Chrissie's undemanding, babyish company. Only Chrissie did not know that she was waiting, or what she was waiting for.

But there was no phone call from Jerry; in the weeks that followed there was no sign from him, no message. The routine life of the town went on, carrying the Talbots with it, as it had always done.

II

Once, on one of his brief trips to Burnham Falls for Amtec, Mal Hamilton went to the Talbot house to see Jeannie. The visit was a mistake; he could see, even through Jeannie's listless, apathetic manner, that his presence embarrassed her. He had meant to reassure her, to offer some token of fellowship that might tell her that he regarded her like all other women, that he himself felt no embarrassment over the memory of that Saturday night. But she was too young to feel any fellowship with him, too absorbed in her own emotions. To her he was still a stranger. He smoked one cigarette, while Selma sat bolt upright, and Jeannie slouched on the sofa, and he tried desperately to make conversation with the two tight-lipped women. He stubbed out the cigarette, and rose to go with relief. Afterwards he drove straight to the Carpenter house, to Harriet.

He dropped into a chair on the veranda, declined the whisky Harriet offered him, and accepted tea from her instead.

"I thought it was the right thing to do," he said, telling her about his visit to Jeannie. "I knew we'd be bound to meet sometime, since I'm in Burnham Falls so often now, and I thought this was a better way than just running into her casually on the street. I wanted her to relax a little about it. You know what I mean? I wanted her to know that I thought she was a nice kid. . . ."

"She doesn't know you, Mal," Harriet said, stirring her

228

tea thoughtfully. "And I suppose she'd rather forget the way she met you. She's still in a kind of shock about it. I've dropped in to see her a couple of times, and she's just the same with me. Hardly talks . . . and doesn't seem to care whether I stay or go."

"I guess I should admit," Mal said, "that I really went there to straighten out her idea of *me*. I don't think she remembers much of what happened that night, after she called to me." He grinned, and shrugged. "Well . . . I don't suppose too many other men wouldn't want to revel a little in the role of playing rescuer to a beautiful young girl."

Their talk drifted from the subject of Jeannie. They said nothing of much consequence to each other, nothing that Nell could not have overheard, and he left very soon to drive back to New York.

But it was the first of the visits that he began to make whenever he was in Burnham Falls. Now he didn't wait for Steve's invitation; he would come always in the afternoon, when he was through with his business with Amtec and on the way back to New York. He never stayed more than half an hour, and sometimes he sat in the kitchen with Harriet and Nell, and other times he got no farther than the veranda. Nell liked to see him come; she set the tea tray as Claudia Carpenter had taught her, with the fine china and the lace-trimmed cloths. Harriet grew accustomed to seeing the delicate Minton in Mal's sinewy sun-burned hands in place of the whisky glass. He seemed to enjoy the ritual.

And when he left, he never spoke of coming again. His visits were always unannounced, and if Harriet were not there, he would drink a cup of tea with Nell, or with Gene and Tim when they were at home, and then go on his way. Harriet began to make reasons why she should always get back to the house in the late afternoons.

III

Within a week after Phil Conrad's visit to Burnham Falls, Laura had made arrangements to go back to dramatic lessons with Goodman. It was easier to do than she expected. She met Ed's objections with a bravado and coolness that her need for Phil gave to her, and with the security of the knowledge she had been slowly gaining since she came to Burnham Falls to back her up. She had come to know Ed's

229

fear that this marriage, also, might crash, and he feared what its failure would do to his standing in the corporation. He needed the glittering picture of a successful marriage to a glamorous woman behind him; he needed the respect and envy it aroused. He needed the image of his well-run home and expensively dressed wife in her white Thunderbird because it helped wipe out the memory of the woman who had walked away from marriage to him.

She had anounced her plans one night over dinner, when she knew that the presence of Elizabeth and Clare at the table would prevent an outburst from Ed. In the living-room, after Grace had served the coffee, he turned to her.

"Why are you taking lessons from Goodman again? You don't seriously suppose anyone will risk you in another play? You've been away from Broadway too long."

She put down her cup with a clatter. "I have my reasons —I'm not as dead on Broadway as you think."

"Then for God's sake don't get involved in any more flops."

"There won't be any more flops," she said. Then deliberately, triumphantly, she brought out her news. "Phil Conrad has asked me to read for a new television play he's putting in the Amtec series. It's called *The Other Kind*. He says he thinks I'm right for the leading role."

He gave her a long, careful look, wondering, she thought, if she were lying. He opened his mouth as if to speak, then closed it again. Laura knew why he held back his words. So she spoke for him.

"Amtec would like to see me in that role—on an Amtec show," she said. "It would be good for us—for both of us, Ed."

And so every Tuesday morning early she sped down the parkway in the Thunderbird towards New York. She drove too fast, she knew, and recklessly, and yet on Tuesday mornings she drove with a lightness and sureness that was never present at other times. On Tuesday night she saw Phil, and the awareness of it touched every action of the day.

The lessons with Goodman were her excuse for staying over-night in New York; it was very simple to tell Ed that she was too tired to drive back to Burnham Falls, and to witness him wanting to make an objection, and not daring to. She had a room permanently booked at the Plaza for Tuesday nights.

The day took on a familiar pattern. First she went to her

230

hairdressers, then an hour's shopping, a quick lunch, and then to Goodman's studio.

The first time the old man saw her he held out his hands to her in a sudden, unfamiliar gesture of warmth and admiration.

" Why, Laura—child, what's happened to you? You're beautiful!"

She felt herself blush. Over the years she had become accustomed to being told to her face that she was beautiful, but Goodman had never offered her the slightest tribute of that kind. He had regarded her as a working machine, nothing more personal than that. It was a very long time since she had taken such pleasure in a compliment.

He even took her hands in his. "What has happened to you?" he repeated. "I told myself that you'd fade away in the country—that you couldn't exist away from New York. But look at you!" He peered at her closely. "The marriage—it's a success, eh? Is that why you look as you do?"

It would have been easy to lie, but she didn't even try. She just looked at him, and, strangely, unbidden tears came to her eyes. But they were happy tears, and she smiled at him.

He shrugged. "Well, it's none of my business. But you are in love, and from this—maybe we can work. You've never been in love before. Perhaps that's why you weren't an actress."

It was wonderful to Laura to work with him again. All the old magic was there, the striving to reach out of herself to move him, the desire to win a word of praise from him. But added to it was the need now to express what was within herself, a choking, overwhelming emotion that demanded outlet and acknowledgment.

After three sessions Goodman said, "You are trying to say too much, Laura. This, like everything else, must be disciplined. But better too much than nothing."

Laura knew that there was too much within her now to confine successfully. She was not used to the feeling that possessed her, a kind of explosiveness and joy that was like nothing she had ever known. She was in love with Phil, and for the moment she wanted nothing more. She did not question the future beyond next Tuesday. From week to week she lived on memory and anticipation. In between was a haze.

231

where she wrapped herself in her own happiness and thrust aside every other consideration.

In the beginning it was a solid happiness. She was not sure of Phil, whether he really loved or wanted her, but she told herself that it was still early in the game, and she had her chance of winning. She thought she had a good chance. On Tuesday afternoons she would rush from Goodman's studio back to the Plaza, and there would be the telephone message from Phil, waiting for her like a piece of solid gold.

They met either in his hotel or hers. After his divorce he had moved into a hotel, and had so far not bothered to find himself an apartment. She would have liked it different; she would have liked the intimacy of an apartment and the feeling of a place that belonged to them more than a hotel suite belonged. But Phil was a man who disliked attachments to places or things. He had a gourmet's appreciation of good food, but he never wanted to prepare it himself, nor did he care who prepared it for him. He liked the impersonal quality of the room service because it made no demands on him.

"I've got too much on my mind to worry about who's going to wash my shirts or cook my meals," he said to Laura. "That's the business of laundries and restaurants."

She would indeed have liked it different, but she had no domestic skills herself, and so she could offer no reply. All she wanted and needed was to please him, and if it broke into the pleasure and exclusiveness of their evening to have waiters bring dinner in, then she didn't, at first, mind, because Phil himself did not. In the beginning she was more sure, more hopeful.

Because the first weeks were memorable—for both of them. She knew this, even if Phil never told her so in words. She would lie with her arms about him and feel his pleasure strongly, and know herself possessed by a man with desire and good reason. He was a skilful lover, practised, teaching a little and taking pleasure in her response. He did not know that her response was a new thing, something that only he made possible, and which only her need for him had brought out. It was in these first weeks she learned that before this she had never been very good in bed.

232

IV

It was Selma who brought Jeannie the news—Selma with her face sharpened by concern. It was Saturday morning, and she and Ted had been to the supermarket for the week's groceries. She dumped the last of the loaded boxes on the kitchen table, and started to unpack them briskly, making too much noise in the process.

Jeannie came in the kitchen doorway. She made a move forward to help her mother, and Selma, turning, wasn't able to avoid looking directly at her.

Instantly Jeannie tensed. "What's the matter?" she said. "Is there something wrong?"

Selma paused and licked her lips. "I heard something about Jerry—Mrs. Carter told me. I met her in the supermarket."

"What did you hear?" The words were rapped out fiercely.

"He's joined the Army. He's doing his hitch now instead of after college." She moved a little nearer Jeannie, as if pleading with her not to let the words hurt her. "He's—he's leaving on Monday."

"Monday——?" Jeannie's face had gone dead. The colour had drained from it quickly; it looked white and frozen. "Monday——!" She stood quite still for a moment, her brain locked in disbelief. Then quite suddenly she jerked her head back, struggling for some hope to lean against. "You're quite sure?" she said to Selma. "You're quite sure she said he'd definitely joined up? He isn't just *thinking* about it, is he? He's going on Monday—definitely?"

"That's what she said, Jeannie."

She turned and left the kitchen. Selma made a hesitant movement to follow her, then forced herself to stop. She went back and started to unpack the groceries; she felt and knew that she was useless at the moment. There was nothing for her to do except strain her ears for sounds from the other part of the house. Presently she heard the front door close gently, but when she looked cautiously from the window, Jeannie wasn't in the yard with Ted and Chrissie. She wasn't in the front garden either. Selma went back to the kitchen, and disregarding the groceries still strewn about, she lit one of her rare cigarettes. Then she noticed that her hands were trembling.

233

After a while Ted came in. He looked at his wife sitting slumped in the chair. "Have you told her?" he said.

She nodded. "Yes."

A rough sort of grunt in his throat was his only reply. He put on some coffee to heat, and in silence they sat together and drank it.

Jeannie went directly to the First National Bank. Not since that Saturday had she walked alone through town; she had dreaded the first time and had so far avoided it, but now she scarcely knew that she was threading her way through the Saturday morning summer crowd, and that some of them greeted her, and wanted to stop and talk, and some just stared. On the library steps there was the usual crowd of teen-agers, ones who had been a few grades lower than she at school. Almost every one of them stopped talking as she approached, and an unnatural quiet marked her passing. At once the voices sounded again, but the pitch was now a little more intense. She had broken into a hard perspiration by the time she swung open the doors of the First National.

Jerry wasn't at his usual teller's cage. He wasn't anywhere on the floor, and she couldn't see him at the back, either. A swift terror gripped her that he had already left Burnham Falls. For a moment she faced the closed door of George Keston's private office, and wondered what she would do. Then her eye fell on Tubby Beck, who cleaned the bank, and kept the heavy, old-fashioned writing-tables supplied with the deposit and withdrawal forms.

"Tubby!" She called him by the familiar name that everyone in Burnham Falls used; he was about her father's age.

"Hi, Jeannie! Glad to see you about." He seemed embarrassed.

"Where's Jerry?" she said. Her words came louder than she meant, and several people at the teller's cages looked around. Tubby glanced uncomfortably at George Keston's closed door.

"I dunno, Jeannie," he said.

"Well, did he come into the bank this morning?"

He shook his head. "Haven't seen him here. Guess he wouldn't be here, this bein' the last day. . . ." He stopped, and his jaw dropped a little. He shifted his feet uncertainly, and scratched his head.

"Thanks, Tubby. I'll try somewhere else.". She turned

234

on her heel, and went quickly, out into the noise of Main Street.

The Keston house was at the far end of Main Street, past all the shops and past the crowd of teen-agers on the library steps. Jeannie took no notice of them. There was nothing left of her any more that responded to the youth and curiosity in them; she forgot that most of them were only two years younger than she. She kept up her determined, quick walk until she was within sight of the Keston house, and then she faltered a little. It was big and prosperous, and its mown green lawns and shining paint were strangely unreal that morning, too calm and safe looking. In a fashion, the calmness and sobriety shook her own determination, but she couldn't allow herself to stop there, to admit fear and turn around. As she marched up the prim walk, she wondered how many people had noted her coming from porches and upstairs windows of the houses around. She had never before been conscious that there were unfriendly eyes to watch her in Burnham Falls.

Mrs. Keston opened the door. She was a thin, frail-looking woman, with soft, curly hair, and a delicate pink mouth. It rounded now a little in surprise as she saw Jeannie, and then straightened out quickly.

"Well, Jeannie . . ." she said quietly. "How are you?"

The Keston porch was deep, and the door recessed still farther, but even within its shadow, Jeannie felt that everyone in Burnham Falls must see the two of them now. The colour came to her face as it hadn't done during that long walk up Main Street. Jeannie had met Mrs. Keston only a few times before. Beside the other's graceful fragility she felt crude and overblown.

But she spoke firmly. "Mrs. Keston—could I come in?"

The other woman's eyes wandered to the houses opposite, and then she nodded. "Yes—come in."

As soon as the door was closed, Jeannie faced her again. "I'd like to see Jerry, please."

A look of hostility came at once into Grace Keston's face. It had been present, but controlled before; now it was open. "Jerry isn't here. What do you want him for?"

"When are you expecting him back?"

"Back?" Grace Keston's voice became acid. "How should I know when Jerry will be back? Jerry does what he likes."

"Well . . ." Jeannie said quietly, "I would like to wait. May I wait for him here, Mrs. Keston?"

235

"No!" The word came strong and loud from that small frame. "No—you can't wait! I don't want you here."

"I know you don't want me here." Jeannie's own voice was rising. "But I must see Jerry, and if I can't wait here, I'll wait outside. I don't think you'd like that—to have me wait outside on the pavement."

"He may be hours. He may not be back before to-night."

"I'll wait."

The other woman gestured angrily. "He doesn't want to see you. Don't you know that?"

"After these last weeks, I'd be a fool if I didn't know it."

"Then why do you persist? You're not Jerry's sort—you've proved that. Why can't you leave him alone. You have your own kind of friends."

Jeannie said slowly. "I had only one friend, and that was Jerry. I have to see him before he goes."

"You know he's going? . . . Well, all the town must know it now! He's going because of you, Jeannie, and I'll never forgive you for that."

"I'm not sending him away. I don't want him to go."

"It's a pity you didn't think of that before—of what you were doing to Jerry. He imagined he was in love with you, and you've made yourself and him the talk of the whole district. You played around with people like that Patrino and Reitch, and made a fool of Jerry."

"Jerry knows that isn't true! There's no truth in any of that talk!"

"You don't have to bother to lie to me. I know what sort of person you are—but Jerry's just got his eyes open. Of course, it's too late . . ." she added bitterly. "He's rushing off into the Army to get away from you—and everything else. He'll never finish college now. He says he will, but I know different. After he's been away two years, he'll never come back to Burnham Falls. It'll break his father's heart. I hope you know that—I just hope you know the damage you've done."

Jeannie stepped back from her in distaste.

"The damage was done to me, Mrs. Keston. Perhaps sometime you will remember that."

"I have no need to remember—except what concerns my son. You invited what happened to you, and you got what you deserved."

236

She turned to walk away, and then paused and glanced back, her eyes bright and harsh.

"Wait, if you must—but it won't do you any good. Jerry won't change, not now. You think all you need is your pretty face, but it doesn't look so pretty to Jerry now. You're going to need a lot more than that." She gazed at Jeannie solidly for a moment, then she added: "I don't think you've got it."

Jeannie waited alone in the Keston's living-room. Grace Keston hadn't indicated that that was where she was to wait; she had simply turned and left her, and her straight, thin back retreating down the hall had been indicative of all the contempt she had never openly expressed before. Uncertainly, Jeannie had wandered into the living-room, and taken a chair by the bay window which gave her a view of the street and the side entrance. The silence of the house was absolutely undisturbed. It could have been no more quiet if Grace Keston had not been there, but she was there, immovably hostile and accusing, and there was no escaping or ignoring her. Through the walls Jeannie could sense her, hating and fearful at the same time, hoping that Jerry would reject her, and yet afraid that he would not. Jeannie's hands, resting on the cool chintz slip-cover, began to sweat; she also was afraid.

It was more than three hours before Jerry came. Jeannie's eyes ached from staring at the street; the sun had moved around, and was now streaming directly through the window. Jeannie guessed that it would have been Grace Keston's habit to close the blinds at this time each day, but she made no appearance, as if Jeannie's presence held some kind of contagion; there was still no sound from the back of the house. Jeannie had grown numb and dazed by the time she saw Jerry walk quickly in from the street to the side door.

She hoped that Grace Keston would not be cruel enough to make her go and look for him in this strange house. She rose from her chair and walked half-way to the door. From the back of the house she heard voices, and then Jerry's footsteps in the hall. He came to the door of the living-room, and stood looking at her, as silent as his mother had been.

They faced each other, each inquiring of the other, and not knowing what kind of answer they wanted.

237

"I heard you were leaving on Monday," Jeannie said. "I had to see you . . ."

"Yes . . . I'm leaving."

"Why?"

He shrugged. "Why not? The Army will grab me as soon as I'm through college. I prefer to go now, and finish college later."

Abruptly she flung her arm out. "Oh, Jerry—don't play with me! I'm not a fool."

"I didn't think you were," he said slowly.

"Then don't treat me like one! Is it right what your mother says—that you're leaving because of me?"

"Is that what she says?" He shrugged again. "She ought to know that the Army takes a man some time or other. I might as well get it over with."

She gestured impatiently, wrinkling her brow. "I don't understand you! What—what is it you're supposed to be saying by all this? Jerry, please! Please just tell me what it all means, and I'll do anything for you. I'll do anything at all!"

He shook his head; a stubborn look of deliberate non-understanding came into his face. "You're making a big thing of this, Jeannie. There's nothing to it. I'm going into the Army. That's all."

"That can't be all!" she burst out. "There's much more—only you won't tell me any of it. Don't go away from me like this, Jerry, because I'll do anything you say, if only you won't go away from me! I'll marry you—right away!"

Again he shook his head. "I'm not asking you to marry me."

She acted as if he hadn't spoken. "We could get married right away. I could move around with you, Jerry. I'd get a job in whatever town was near your camp. If you didn't want it, we need never come back to Burnham Falls."

He leaned against the door jamb, staring up at the ceiling for a second, as if he were trying to collect his patience. "Jeannie—" he began, "let's stop all this. I'm not asking you to marry me. I don't *want* you to marry me."

"You don't want me to marry you. . . ." She repeated it, saying the words over again slowly. "You don't want me to marry you."

It was said in a husky whisper, which barely reached him across the room. Suddenly she sat down, placing herself on the edge of a chair and gazing down at the carpet. Her

238

hands were folded in her lap and her whole body assumed a frozen appearance, as if she were hardly breathing.

"Jeannie . . ." He took a tentative step towards her, then abruptly retreated, back to the dor.

She turned her head very slowly and looked at him. "Then you have never believed me—you have never believed me at all."

She took several deep breaths, long sounds that seemed to echo in the room. In her lap her hands clenched and unclenched, as if life and warmth were slowly returning. With it came her anger.

"You think what every dirty-minded gossip in this town thinks—you think it's possible that I might have gone willingly with Patrino and Reitch. Admit it, Jerry! That's what you think, isn't it? You've let yourself listen to the lies and the rumours, and now you believe them. You've got to run away from them—from me and from the town."

"It's got nothing at all to do with you. . . ."

She gestured irritably, contemptuously. "I told you not to treat me like a fool. I know why you're going. You're afraid to stay because something might overcome your better judgment, and you might actually marry me in a weak moment. You've got a banker's cool head, Jerry. You're afraid you'd be stuck with me . . . and there'd always be someone to rake up the old story, and make that dirty remark about Jerry Keston's wife. The town could forgive me for getting pregnant, but not for getting raped. Rape is too dirty, and too violent. You know all this, and you're getting out while there's still time."

"I'm not 'getting out'—as you put it. I've wanted you to marry me since we left school, and you've always told me to wait. I just got tired of waiting . . ."

She broke in, "That was my mistake—that was my big mistake! I won't make it again. I thought you loved me enough to make the waiting worth something. I even went on believing that even after the time you came to the hospital, and I guessed what people were saying about me. I believed it even through these weeks when you didn't call me, and I was nearly going crazy because I needed you so much. I knew you were upset—and worried—but I didn't doubt that you'd argue it out with yourself, finally, because I thought you've always known that I couldn't have gone with anyone but you."

Then her head jerked up harder as a new thought came

239

to her. "Or were you waiting for Patrino and Reitch to be arrested and go on trial—so that I could be publicly whitewashed?"

"Jeannie! That's not fair! That isn't true!"

"Isn't it?" Her anger and hurt was growing; she lashed out viciously. "I wonder if you decided to go into the Army when you began to realise that they might never be caught? I began to realise it, too, Jerry, and I have to live with it. But you don't. You're free to make that choice. And you've made it. . . ."

She stod up. "Well, that's it, isn't it? That's all there is. I came here prepared to plead with you, to convince you somehow that you mustn't leave here without me. Now it doesn't seem worth while even trying—I don't think I want to."

She was careful not to touch him as she passed him in the doorway. In the hall she stood back from him a little, and measured him up and down with her eyes.

"I intend to stick it out here, Jerry. I won't run away from Burnham Falls. If you come back, you'll never be quite free of me, because I intend to make a splash in this town. I'm going to run a business the way no one in this town ever ran one before. Everyone's going to know that I'm around. I'm not going to hide any more. I'm going to be all the things that I was meant to be—and when I get a husband, he's going to be the kind of man who'll *let* me be those things. Some day, when you're President of the First National, I'm going to walk into that bank and make a fat deposit, and you'll wish the floor would open up and swallow you. That's how it's going to be, Jerry."

"You little bitch!" was all he said.

She pulled the front door of the Kestons' house behind her with a resounding bang that echoed across the street. Her footsteps on the flagstone path were loud. She could have taken a short-cut to the Talbot house through a side street, but she walked straight along Main Street, and she greeted every familiar face in the Saturday crowd.

CHAPTER SEVEN

The empty streets of Elmbury looked desolate in the summer rain. It had rained on and off since morning; the gardens

240

were sodden and the flowers hung limp and heavy with the moisture. Monday was never a busy day in Elmbury, and the rain sweeping the deserted streets accentuated the fact. There were only two other cars moving on Chester Street besides Harriet's Rolls. She slumped a little wearily at the wheel as she waited for the light to change at the intersection; the lunch she had just had with Martha Torrens had been long and too full of talk. They had met to discuss plans for a joint meeting of the Elmbury and Burnham P.T.A. Laura Peters should have been with them, but that morning she had begged off on the excuse of a sudden, urgent trip to New York. It had become obvious to Harriet that Laura hated the chores thrust on her as Ed Peters' wife, and she knew that Laura was finding it more and more difficult to hide the fact from Burnham Falls as a whole. Frequently now she asked Harriet to take over for her, and it was an understood thing that she could not refuse, no more than Steve could refuse a request from Ed. So Harriet had sat through a heavy lunch with Martha, listening to the rain falling monotonously outside, and had stifled her yawns. Now as she waited for the light she yawned openly.

She took no particular notice of anything along Chester Street, but past the bus stop she became suddenly aware of the familiarity of a solitary figure standing there. She braked sharply and looked back over her shoulder. It was Jeannie Talbot, wearing a plastic raincoat, with a plastic rain bonnet tied over her hair. There was something strangely untypical about the hunch of her shoulders, and her stolid indifference to the rain. Harriet put the Rolls into reverse; Jeannie looked at her without animation when she stopped.

"Hello, Jeannie! Going back to Burnham Falls?" She leaned over and unlatched the door.

"Hello, Mrs. Dexter." Jeannie responded unsmilingly, and Harriet thought she moved towards the car with a certain reluctance. But she got in and pulled the door behind her. "Thanks," she said.

"Terrible day, isn't it?" Harriet remarked as the Rolls moved off along Chester Street. She sensed that Jeannie was in no mood for small talk, but she also guessed that if she didn't start some talk, Jeannie would let the drive back to Burnham Falls pass in silence. Harriet knew that the only bus of the afternoon wasn't due for more than an hour and a half, and Jeannie must have known it too. And yet she had stood in the rain with deliberate uncaring patience, and

241

had not even bothered to retreat to the shelter of the stationer's doorway directly behind her. Harriet was touched and dismayed by the stark unhidden loneliness in the girl's attitude. She wanted to reach over and grasp one of those limp hands lying in the other's lap, to offer comfort as she might have done to Tim and Gene. It was difficult to remember that Jeannie was no longer a schoolgirl—difficult until she glanced over and realised the maturity and sad poise of the face that was turned unseeingly on the wet road ahead. The expression was a withdrawn one, asking nothing, seeking nothing.

Jeannie didn't answer, and Harriet knew the remark had gone unheard—or Jeannie had treated it as it deserved.

She waited then, until they were clear of the town, on the new highway running straight and broad through the glistening wet fields of the dairy farms.

"Can you talk to me, Jeannie?" She said it diffidently, because it seemed such an enormous intrusion. "Is there some way I can help you?"

Only silence answered her. But she had seen Jeannie's lips quiver briefly before she regained a kind of savage control again.

Now Harriet did put out her hand and touched the girl, the lightest touch on the arm. "Can I help?" she repeated.

Jeannie looked at her. Some of the indifference was gone. She shrugged. "I don't know. Can anyone help me?"

"I don't know if anyone can help, Jeannie—but you can let me try." She pressed gently for the girl to talk. "You didn't want to get into the car?" she prompted.

Jeannie turned to her fully. "It wasn't that I didn't want to get into *your* car, Mrs. Dexter. It's just that . . . I didn't want to go back to Burnham Falls."

"Burnham Falls is where you belong," Harriet said. "It's always there to go back to. There are a lot of people in Burnham Falls who love you, Jeannie. Your father loves you . . . very much."

"Yes, he loves me," Jeannie answered with some heat. "But love isn't enough, Mrs. Dexter. It can't wrap a cloak round you and keep out the world. It can't stop you getting kicked and hurt. . . ."

Harriet checked the words she had been going to say, because Jeannie was speaking the truth, and all she had to offer were the same old platitudes—the same worn patterns by which she had cut out her life so long ago. It didn't

242

matter how much a father loved you, he couldn't change the world for you, as Jeannie had said. But she, Harriet, had refused to see that; she had meekly gone along with his wishes all her life because love seemed a convention, not a reality. Jeannie knew different. She loved her father fiercely, but also knew that he was powerless to help or change things. She was free for the rest of her life to love him without obligation or guilt. Suddenly Harriet envied her because she had the strength of this freedom.

"Jerry Keston left town this morning," Jeannie said. "I thought I couldn't live through a day like this, but here it all is, in its usual place, and everything seems normal and ordinary." She uttered a queer little sound that might have been meant for a laugh of bravado, but which came out wrong. "You know, I suppose half the town knows that Jerry's gone—and probably guesses why. And I thought I'd show just how little it bothered me, so I marched right into Carter's this morning, and expected to find my job waiting there for me. Wally told me that Judy Thomas had been filling in—just till I wanted to come back. Do you know what Wally said to me this morning, Mrs. Dexter?"

"No," Harriet answered. Her hands tightening a little on the wheel; she felt herself bracing inwardly.

"Well, he made me a nice gentle speech about not thinking it was quite the right time to come back . . . how he thought I would be happier somewhere else for the time being . . . how he didn't think I'd enjoy being there so much now since everyone knew Patrino and Reitch had been in that night, and that I'd talked with them in the booth. In a roundabout way he hinted that I'd be bothered by a lot of strangers who thought I was an easy pick-up. And, of course, since I was such a *nice* girl, and wouldn't want any of these things, that naturally I'd be happier somewhere else."

"Are you sure he really meant that, Jeannie?"

"I'll tell you what he meant! He meant that all the people at the construction camp are pretty sore about me, and that they would take their business to Bailey's if they saw me back behind the counter. And I've caused quite a bit of embarrassment and trouble for Amtec, too, and they'd rather not be reminded. Wally . . . he's not going to lose business for old time's sake, so out goes Jeannie!"

"I'm sorry . . ." Harriet mumbled inadequately.

"And you know—" Jeannie went on, "I thought there
243

weren't very many people in Burnham Falls who realised how much they depended on Amtec. But Wally knows it, and he knows how to play the game with them. He's smart."

" Not everyone is like Wally."

" All those who matter are! And the ones who aren't—well, they're not going to be running things in this town very long. I thought I was going to be one of the ones who ran things in the future, but Wally showed me different. It's like a politician who suddenly gets a scandal in the family. He's finished."

" You can't be finished here, Jeannie. There are other things to try—other people."

" Not the things or the people I want. Oh, yes, there are other things. But what kind? Wally told me about a job that was going in Elmbury—in Sandra's Terrace Shop. That's that dress shop on Chester Street that tries to be a bit Fifth Avenue. I didn't want to apply for it, but I didn't want to go home, either. So I caught the bus over, and went to see Mrs. Maybury, who owns it. Do you know the Terrace Shop? There are four assistants and Mrs. Maybury. She's very efficient and attractive, and as tough as an old copper kettle. There's only room for one person like that in a small town business. If you worked yourself to death there you'd never get a cent more than the salary she's offering. No chance of a partnership, or an interest . . ."

" Didn't she want to hire you?"

" Oh, sure she wanted to hire me! She got very persuasive once she recalled where she'd heard my name before. She had the very opposite idea from Wally—she could have used the publicity value of having me work in her store. I don't come from Elmbury, so there's no feeling against me there, and I suppose she figures there's a good number of women who'd come in just to get a good look at me. And she would have gotten the credit for helping out someone who was in trouble. Between her and Wally, I'm beginning to feel as if I'd just come out of jail."

" That won't last long. People forget—they find other things to talk about."

" Well, I'm not sticking around to see whether that's true or not. I'm leaving Burnham Falls—as soon as I can."

Harriet didn't say anything. If she spoke, she felt that for Ted and Selma's sake she should try to dissuade Jeannie from going. But in a sense she knew it was the only thing possible for a girl like this one beside her. Jeannie was not another

244

Harriet Carpenter, who had come back because she had not known what else to do. Jeannie was not patient and enduring; she had ambition and had to find a way for it to go. She would not wait meekly for people to forget, or allow herself to slip into the background so that their sense of security would not be disturbed. She had intended to be many things for and to the town, and the town would not let her. But inside, Harriet was crying a protest that Burnham Falls was losing Jeannie, when it had such need of people like her—people who had been part of the life of the town before Amtec came, who had known it before the strangers took over.

"I'm not going to stay around to be punished for Patrino and Reitch!" Jeannie cried suddenly. "Why should *I* be the scapegoat? Why should I have to be grateful to people like Wally Carter and Mrs. Maybury? Why do I have to stay in Burnham Falls to have that kind of treatment dished out to me—I can earn double for taking the same thing in New York!"

"Are you going to New York?"

Jeannie shrugged. "Where else is there? It's the first step, in any case. Dad and Mom won't mind so much because they think it's close—and I'll tell them I'll come home on week-ends. But I doubt that I will. Once you leave a small town, you shouldn't try to come back."

"It takes a lot of courage . . ." Harriet started to say.

"Not courage," Jeannie broke in. "It isn't courage when there isn't any alternative. What's there for me here? I can't ever take a job with Amtec, and I'll never get any support now to start my own business. Everything else is just second rate—filling in time until someone wants to marry me. I couldn't take that kind of a deal!"

Harriet strained to see ahead. A small wind had risen, and the rain was slanting against the windscreen. It was like the sad rain of autumn.

"So that's why I was standing at the bus stop—wishing the bus would never come, and I didn't have to go home and tell Dad and Mom."

Harriet had to slow down, because the rain was heavier, and the old-fashioned wipers cleared such a small part of the windscreen. Her body felt cold, and she didn't know whether it was the dampness of the air or the effect of what the girl beside her had said. There had been such dead, calm logic in what she said, and the truth had a sting in it.

Jeannie had looked at Burnham Falls, and found that it had nothing to give her now. It was what she, Harriet, should have done long ago, back before it was too late to do it.

Jeannie said slowly, and the words came from her painfully, " Jerry went away this morning, Mrs. Dexter. I wanted to stay in Burnham Falls and marry Jerry—because I loved him. Even with all that's happened I would have stayed if I'd known he loved me, and would come back. But he doesn't love me. I have nothing now—not Jerry—nor the town."

Harriet was aware that Jeannie's body was suddenly shaken with sobs. She hadn't expected her to cry. There was such a fatalistic toughness in her. And yet all women wept sometime, and Jeannie had the right to weep over a boy she had thought loved her, and a town where she thought she had her place. The sobs increased, hysterical little cries that Harriet guessed might have been her first tears since that Saturday night. Jeannie wasn't used to crying—in her, the act had no grace or appealing quality. She wept with a kind of wild violence that was protest and passion.

They were coming close to Burnham Falls, and Harriet knew that she couldn't just drive to the Talbot house and deposit Jeannie there with a pat of the hand and a few cheering words. Neither could she take her to her own house because Nell was there. So when they came to the Downside road, without a word to Jeannie she turned off the highway and headed for the lake and the fishing cabin.

The violence of Jeannie's sobs had subsided a little by the time they reached the cabin ; she seemed in a daze, giving a little hiccup as she tried to draw a long breath. She didn't question Harriet's taking her to the cabin—just following her obediently from the car, and waited in silence while she unlocked the door. Harriet took her raincoat from her, and steered her towards a sofa.

" Make yourself comfortable there. I won't be long."

In the kitchen she put on water to boil and poured a stiff shot of brandy into a glass. Jeannie looked at her with weary, tear-blurred eyes as she approached. She wiped a hand under her nose with an unconsciously childish gesture. Harriet fished in her handbag for a handkerchief and handed it to her. Then she held out the glass towards her.

Jeannie took it dubiously. " What's this?"

" Brandy."

246

"I haven't ever drunk brandy before." She looked down into the liquid and shivered slightly.

"Now's as good a time as any," Harriet said firmly. "Drink it—you're cold."

Jeannie took the first sip, and grimaced. Then she sipped again. Harriet left her to go and make the tea, and when she came back with the pot and two cups, and a blanket from one of the beds, Jeannie had almost finished the contents of the glass.

"Now I know what they mean by Dutch courage," she said.

"Slip your shoes off," Harriet said. "They're wet." She draped the blanket over Jeannie's legs, and then handed her a cup of tea. Jeannie carefully placed the glass on the floor. Harriet poured her own tea, and sat down opposite Jeannie.

Jeannie took a long drink of tea; she looked across the cup at Harriet. "Thanks, Mrs. Dexter. It was nice of you to know I couldn't have gone home then."

Harriet took a pack of cigarettes from her bag. She proffered it to Jeannie, but the other shook her head. "Isn't it time you called me Harriet? You're not a little girl any more."

Jeannie smiled wanly. "No, I'm not. I feel a hundred years old, which probably shows just how young I am. It's young, isn't it, to be so optimistic about everything—to be so sure. I was so sure of myself—and everything. Jerry and this town . . . I thought I had it all sewn up." She sighed. "There's a hell of a lot more to it than that."

She laid the teacup down beside the glass, and settled herself back against the cushions, slipping down farther under the blanket. Her face looked white and exhausted; her hair matted damply against her forehead.

"I won't be so sure again," she said, staring straight up at the ceiling. "You always have to make allowances for what you think can't happen."

She closed her eyes. Harriet leaned back in her chair, sipping her tea and watching the young, tense face opposite. A few times Jeannie's lips twitched, and her eyelids fluttered, but she didn't say anything. After a while the brandy began to take effect, and her breathing grew deeper and slower. The face softened and relaxed. When Harriet was sure she was asleep, she put down her own cup, and moved gently towards the door leading on to the terrace. The rain had

247

slackened to a fine, misting drizzle. She stepped outside and breathed in the dampness of the air under the dripping trees. The wind had died again.

The path to the lake was wet, and the elegant shoes she had worn to lunch with Martha Torrens were soiled as the thin heels cut into the ground. She wondered how long it was since she had been by the lake alone—years perhaps. It was grey and still, lightly hazed in rain. The silence rested on it absolutely and completely. In the distance she could vaguely distinguish the outlines of the Downside Seminary. Her footsteps echoed hollowly on the wooden jetty. She stood for a moment looking at her wavering shadow in the grey water, then she sat down on the jetty steps, indifferent to the wet on her dress.

Jeannie's cry of pain and anguish had touched off a response in Harriet that was keener than any emotion she had experienced for a long time. It had the sharpness of regret, the finality of a dead hope. She saw herself at Jeannie's age—she saw herself the night that Josh had walked out of the cabin, and her father had waited angrily here on this jetty. She had had her chance for revolt then ; she had gone halfway only. Looking back, it seemed that the events of that summer night long ago had foreshadowed the night in the desert with Mal—twice he had been the instrument of her revolt, and twice she had turned back. She hadn't had the courage to keep the freedom that had almost been won. She had returned both times to her father, and in that return she had been on her way to a complete acceptance of his world —the world of Burnham Falls, the world of the factory and the tradition of holding on to the small spheres of identity—this cabin, the house, Burnham Falls itself. It had engulfed Steve, and this world had in turn been engulfed by the corporation. All the wonderful potential of that summer had come to nothing but this wishing and remembering by the lake, contemplating the limitless monotony of days that ended as and where they began.

Jeannie knew what she had not known—that when you could control this small world it had its own excitement ; when it controlled you, you were lost. So Jeannie was leaving it behind. And she was right.

It was hardly a surprise, then, to hear the steps on the jetty behind her. A few minutes back she had heard the sound of a car moving slowly on the dirt road. It could have been a visitor to one of the other cabins, but unconsciously she had sensed that it was not. Someone came here with purpose on a rainy Monday afternoon. She glanced expectantly over her shoulder.

Mal had left his jacket behind in the car, and he walked bare-headed in the mist. His step was unhurried as he came towards her. Slowly she rose to meet him.

They stood and looked at each other for a long moment without speaking. Then she said: "Why did you come?"

"I come here whenever I get the chance. Just about every time I come to Burnham Falls. It's always been empty—until to-day."

"But *why*?"

He shrugged. "Who knows? Why does anyone ever go back? It doesn't do any good. . . ."

But she knew—looking at his face she knew utterly and without doubt why he came here. She knew that the memory of the talks they had had that summer on this jetty were as alive for him as they were still for her. The question that had hovered between them since that day on the train was removed now. Through all the years and experiences in between, they still retained that much of each other—that memory of freshness and hope.

With a jerky but almost involuntary gesture she opened her arms towards him. Then she felt his own arms about her violently, and she was clinging to him. When they kissed there was no strangeness about it. It was the same kiss, only warmer and deeper, as the one with which they had parted that morning in Los Angeles after they had come back from the desert.

They sat on the jetty steps and talked for more than an hour. Harriet's hand lay in Mal's confidently; occasionally he stroked the back of it, and exploringly touched her rounded fingertips. They didn't talk of the present or future; they both knew that lay before them, yet to be examined. They filled in the gaps of the thirteen years, not the restrained, tactful talk of strangers treading warily and eyeing each other —as it had been until then. They talked like lovers, frankly and easily, not afraid of blame or reproach.

"I've been in love twice since then," Mal said. His grip on her hand tightened a little. "One of them was a married
249

woman, and she never meant it to come to anything, and the other—well, we would have been no good to each other. She was an obsession I knew I was going to resist. These were the only two who were important."

She looked at the still stretch of water ahead of her as she talked. The mist was rolling away somewhat, but Downside had not yet emerged clearly. But she seemed to be looking at this scene differently. A sense of aliveness and satisfaction that Mal's kiss had wakened in her had taken away its sombre chill. It was not dead, but only peaceful.

Quietly she told Mal anything that seemed important during those years, and she was aware of what little telling it took. The births of Gene and Tim had been the only great things of those years and that he already knew. She told him how entrapped Steve had been by Joe's pleas, and Joe's debts, and how she had never understood why he had chosen to remain with the old man. It was harder to express the monotony of that time, the slow loss of expectancy and waiting.

"I've had no feeling of being special or particular in all this," she said slowly. "I don't fill any special need—a special function. I don't think I'm very important to Steve personally—but he would deny it, because he doesn't really know it. Sometimes I think he almost regards me as my father did. If I were not here he would miss me because I'm part of the pattern of things."

"All marriages are patterns—chaotic or orderly, they all make patterns."

She gave a short laugh. "Then perhaps I'd like some chaos in my orderly life. It seems I've never *done* anything—never driven a car too fast, never broken a law. I might almost wish for the sort of chaos that Jeannie's in—and out of which she's finding the strength to determine what's best for her. She's not just accepting things, as I've always accepted them. Yes . . . I might like a little of that chaos."

He looked down at her hand in his. "Are you sure this isn't chaos?"

"It might be," she answered. "Yes—it might be that."

She walked back to the car with him. Before he touched the ignition he looked at her, one final, questioning look. "Will you see me again, Harriet?"

Many times she had heard him ask this question, and in many different ways—all of them had existed only in her

250

imagination. Now she heard the words spoken for the first time, in the damp, still air.

"Yes, Mal."

They made no specific arrangements, and it was better that way. When they parted they each had the feeling that their next meeting would be as unplanned as this one, and it held the same promise of freshness and spontaneity. As Harriet walked back to the lodge, she could almost believe that if she never saw Mal again she could still be content. She had a strange sensation of being cherished and treasured because Mal had held an image of her close through these years.

She smiled often to herself, a secret, quiet smile, as she sat and waited in the lodge for Jeannie to stir and finally waken.

11

Jeannie left Burnham Falls that same week, despite Ted and Selma's protests. She refused Harriet's offer to drive her to New York. Instead she caught the bus in Main Street, defiantly outstaring the people she knew who glanced curiously at her and at Ted, standing unhappily beside her, the shabby suitcase at his feet. She clung to him a moment before parting.

"I'm going to be fine, Dad. Everything's going to be fine!"

She hadn't told him that she had accepted Harriet's offer of a loan of two hundred dollars until she could get a job.

"I'm not so sure that I know it all now," Jeannie had said. "And I can't afford to be proud about taking the money . . . I intend to hold out until I get the kind of job I want."

"What kind of job?" Harriet asked.

"Oh . . . I have a few ideas," Jeannie had replied vaguely.

When she reached New York she took a room at the Barbizon Hotel for Women. Harriet had told her to go there —it was a good address, without being too expensive. Jeannie studied the streams of women in the lounges and corridors; she didn't like a world that held nothing but women. She decided that she would leave it as soon as it was practical. In the meantime, it would be comforting to Selma and Ted to know she was there.

She spent the first day in New York simply roaming the

251

fashionable streets, and wandering through the expensive speciality stores. At the end of the day she had a firm image in her mind of what was accepted as the ideal of the smart woman. They all looked somewhat like Laura Peters. In the next two weeks Jeannie dieted off five pounds, had her hair cut to the fashionable length, and had bought some crisply tailored, dark cotton dresses. She also bought hand-bag, shoes and gloves. They were not the most expensive, but they were not cheap, either, because now she was really gambling. Paying for them and the hotel used up all her own savings, and she had to dip into Harriet's money. She told herself that by the time it would be necessary to buy a fall suit, six weeks from now, she would have to be earning enough money to pay for it. None of the clothes she had brought from Burnham Falls would do—and she didn't want them, either.

After the first week she started having interviews for jobs. Some, which she didn't want, were offered to her immediately; others that she did want, were harder to get. After two and a half weeks of being called back for more and yet more interviews, she was finally hired into the manage-ment training department of the country's biggest selling, high-priced cosmetic firm.

The pay was low, and Jeannie hesitated about accepting it. But most of the girls training with her had college degrees, and they all knew that certain ones among them would even-tually succeed to executive jobs. So Jeannie put on the smart grey uniform, and went to sell the product behind the counter at a Fifth Avenue store, which was the first six months of the training. She wrote to Harriet that it would be a little time before she could pay back the money, and she wrote Selma that it wasn't very different from selling the same product in Carter's drug store, except that the amounts that some women bought at one time totalled more than her whole week's salary. Management trainees were not allowed commission.

What she didn't tell Selma was that many men stopped to buy perfume, and that a lot of them didn't want the per-fume, but only to talk to her.

252

CHAPTER TWELVE

It was still warm, but the September days drew in, ending sometimes with a little chill in the air, and sometimes in the mornings a ragged mist hung about the trees, and each day the sun took longer to burn it away. Laura noticed it on Tuesday mornings as she drove to New York. She counted out the summer's end on these Tuesday mornings. Once in the city, the heat and humidity would again close in, and it was easy to forget that it would soon be fall.

Goodman was away on a visit to Europe. Strangely, Laura missed the old man. What she felt for Phil was reaching out hesitantly now to touch other people, and Goodman had sensed her love, and was close to it. She did not tell Ed that he was gone; she still needed him as an excuse for staying overnight in New York. She had grown bolder in her dealings with Ed, but not to the extent of flaunting her relationship with Phil before him. She supposed it would have to come sometime—but later, when she was more confident of Phil himself.

During the long, idle Tuesdays, after she left the hairdresser, there was nothing to do but wander through the stores. She bought clothes extravagantly—dresses, shoes and gloves, lingerie, robes. She was greedy for clothes in a way she had never been—even in the days when Larry had first started making money. She knew that Phil admired beautiful clothes as he admired beautiful women. It was a mark of her insecurity that she wore something different each time she saw him, because there was always the fear that he might grow bored looking at her face alone.

It was a terrible thing now to sit in front of the mirror and stare at her own face, wondering if it were possible that Phil could grow tired of it. She had a panicky feeling of having nothing else to fall back on. It was an experience of poverty that the lovely clothes and the skilful hairdresser couldn't take away. She lived with the fear that once he had grown used to the way she looked, he would discover that she was ignorant and stupid.

Because of Phil she was thinking more often of Larry now than she had done for years. Larry had known her ignorance, and had helped her cloak it; he had even changed

253

her from a pretty girl into an idea of beauty. He had known her flaws, and had been tender to them. From the viewpoint of the stage she had reached with Phil Conrad, she could look back to Larry and know for the first time the extent of his love for her. And also know what she had let slip away.

She didn't ever attempt to deceive herself about Phil. He was selfish and self-centred, a ruthless promoter of his own ego. But he had the fascination of a handsome man who is also a clever one—and in his work he was sensitive and perceptive. All his creativeness, warmth and generosity went into his work. There was little left over for Laura. And yet what little she received was enough to tell her what the whole might be. She cherished the small hope that if Phil really fell in love with her he might yet offer her all the richness of his personality—the gifts and talents and success might be offered fully to her, not just absent-mindedly shared.

And she could tell herself, looking in the mirror, that she hadn't done a single thing in her life to deserve any better kind of man than Phil Conrad. Compared to Larry, he was not worth anyone's love—and yet she did love him, because he was all she had to love.

He quite often mentioned *The Other Kind,* which was scheduled for production early in spring, so as yet had no great urgency. He had given Laura the script, and she knew it by heart, but he had not named a date for the reading.

He was deep in plans for the winter series of shows for Amtec, as well as the opening of a play on Broadway early in November. Knowing all his activity, Laura was grateful that he would take every Tuesday night to see her, and she made no protest when it was only a part of the evening. Sometimes he was very late, and she waited for him, either in his hotel or her own. The hours of waiting were bad, and she was afraid that this time he might not come at all. And yet she could not risk a reproach. There was too much to lose in losing Phil.

On a few occasions Phil had insisted that they dine in a restaurant. Laura didn't like this because she was afraid of gossip. But Phil was not a man on whom she could place restrictions or limitations. He preferred to eat in restaurants. He was essentially a man of public places; he wanted people about him—people that he knew. He wanted the constant gossip of show business, the greetings from table to table, the meal interrupted half a dozen times by acquaintances stopping to talk. And through all this he wanted a beautiful woman seated by his side. Laura knew that the evenings she was not there, her place was taken by others. How far Phil's relationship extended with other women she didn't know, and she didn't ask him. She just lived with the hope that some day he might decide that she was enough.

Inevitably, they were reported once or twice by gossip columnists as dining together, but by then the rumour had gone around that she had a part in one of the shows Phil was producing for Amtec. Whether or not Ed had seen the columns Laura never knew. He never mentioned the subject.

Once she spoke of this to Phil, and he shrugged his shoulders and laughed a little.

" Of course he won't say anything about it. Aren't you doing a good public relations job for Amtec?"

" Yes, but . . ."

" What can he do? Order you not to see me any more? He wouldn't dare do that—not right now. At the moment he may be thinking that I'm more important to Amtec than he is, and if I wanted you I could bring a little pressure in the right places. . . ."

Laura listened unhappily. She had never thought of Ed as lacking courage. And yet there was a point at which prudence became cowardice. She shrunk a little inside herself when she considered of how little importance she was to either of them. So long as she was discreet she might do what she pleased, it seemed—or at least so long as what she did produced some good for the corporation. She didn't want to believe it. She tried not to. And yet Ed's manner seemed to bear it out—his lack of interest in what she did in New York, his seeming willingness to let her go her own way. He protested nothing, not even the increased size of her dress bills. As the weeks went by she grew almost desperate for some sign from him, but none came. She began to wonder what was wrong with a beautiful woman who couldn't rouse her husband to jealousy.

Not from Phil either did there come any reassurance. She did not easily forget the night when she had tried, for the only time, to question his feeling about her.

It was very late; he had been in a meeting all evening with the director of the play he was producing. They had been hours of loneliness and mounting tension for Laura.

255

When he appeared in the door she moved towards him quickly, impulsively. She embraced him with a fierceness and a hunger she hadn't known was in her to express.

"Phil—my darling, I've missed you so . . ." She put her arms about his neck and forced his head down to meet her lips.

After they had kissed he drew back, smiling and a little surprised.

"Well—what's all this passion about? I told you I'd be late. . . ."

She clung to him, standing on her toes to reach close to his ear. "Phil, I love you! I love you so much I don't know what to do with myself."

He patted her cheek, a little absently, as he might have done with a child. "Easy, lover . . . easy!" He tried to disengage himself from her arms.

She clung to him still. "Please be kind to me, Phil! Please!"

Now he pulled himself away without any tenderness, and walked over to the table where the drinks and ice were ready. He said nothing to her while he poured himself some brandy, sniffed it, and rolled the glass a little between his hands.

Then he turned back to her, raising the glass in a small salute.

"Here's to you, lover!"

As she opened her mouth to speak, he silenced her with a wave of the hand.

"Don't, Laura! Don't say whatever it is you're trying to say." He sipped the brandy. "You're very beautiful, you know . . . really beautiful. We suit each other—we're having fun. How much more can you have?"

He smiled at her. "Let's not spoil it."

CHAPTER THIRTEEN

Tom knew as soon as he entered the Humphries house that this party was a good deal beyond his depth in the corporation. As he hesitated in the doorway of the big living-room, whose sliding glass wall was thrown back to permit the crowd to overflow on to the patio and garden, the first people he saw were Harriet Dexter and Art Sommers, the comptroller.

Tom immediately felt that he had somehow stepped out of line; he had never before been to a private party where the higher echelon of the Laboratories were gatherd. He looked around hopefully for the bar, or for a maid with a tray of drinks. A drink in his hand would at least give him something to do.

Just then Mrs. Humphries caught sight of him standing alone. She excused herself from a group and hurried forward, her hand extended and a welcoming smile fixed on her face. At the same time he saw the second's flash of bewilderment, the struggle to fix a name to him. Arnold Humphries was the head of the largest department at the Laboratories, and the closest Tom had ever come to Jane Humphries was having her pointed out to him at the country club.

He took her proffered hand. " Mrs. Humphries—we haven't met before. I'm Tom Redmond."

" Redmond . . ." Suddenly the puzzled look cleared from her face. " Oh—Sally's husband. Well, I'm happy to know you at last. Such a dear girl, Sally, and such a wonderful worker! She's taken a load off my shoulders."

As she talked she was shepherding him, one hand on his arm, towards the patio. " Sally's out here somewhere. . . ." She gazed around the flagstoned area, dotted with caterer's tables and chairs, where the hum of conversation rose into the warm dusk. " Ah, there she is. . . ." She propelled Tom forward a little. " Well, you know everyone here, since you're one of the family, so there's no need for introductions. . . ." Jane Humphries released her hold, and vanished quickly back into the living-room.

Tom paused a moment before he approached Sally. She was standing in profile to him, talking to Steve Dexter. He noted the confident animation of her pointed, upturned face, with its white skin and dark hair, the smile that crossed her lips and face, and made her look pretty, even though she was not strictly pretty. She was seven months pregnant, and she held herself proudly and beautifully, and as yet there seemed no thickening of those lovely legs and ankles. She looked cool and fresh; her maternity clothes were smart, and he remembered then that she had made them herself. She had ignored the empty chairs about her. Sally never sat down at parties. Tom watched her for a few seconds longer in silent admiration. He had passed Steve Dexter many times in the corridors at the Laboratories, and he had never yet spoken to him. He had been in Burnham Falls eighteen months, and it took Sally's volunteer work for the local Republican Party to bring this meeting about. He experienced more sharply than before the feeling that he was out of his depth.

Then he went forward to claim Sally.

When he was introduced and began to talk to Steve Dexter, Tom underwent a sharp reversal of opinion about him. He had seen strength before in that handsome, worn face, now he saw the snap of humour as well, the sudden relaxation. Tom knew that the older man was enjoying talking to Sally. And yet it was a vague, disengaged enjoyment, as if he had come out of a solitary world of his own, and expected to return to it shortly. He would remember the smiling, happy face of this woman, big with her child, but when he encountered it again he would have to establish contact with it all over again. Tom knew the small legend that had grown up about Steve Dexter at the Laboratories, he knew roughly the outline of the work Steve had laboured with alone in the years before Amtec. Everyone at the Laboratories had enormous respect for Steve Dexter's ability, and yet no one approached him very closely or intimately. He had the detachment of a scientist, and yet with it the anxious, frustrated air of the scientist who is unwillingly being turned into an administrator. The frustration seemed to fall from him a little as he talked with Sally, and a rare, gentle smile in turn lit his own face.

Steve proffered a cigarette to Tom. He lit his own from the stub of the last one. " You're in Alan Taylor's department, aren't you?" he said.

"Yes, sir," Tom answered. "How . . .? He cut off the question. It wasn't his business to ask Steve Dexter how he remembered such details of men he'd never met before.

Steve nodded, inhaling the smoke deeply. " Some fine work coming from Taylor's department. It even looks as if one of your products might turn out to be saleable to the public . . . so that keeps the Military and the Amtec Board happy. That's the hell of being a scientist—you don't know where the ends are pulling." He suddenly looked fully at Tom. " You—Redmond, you're young yet. Don't *you* think it's hell being a scientist?"

Tom wondered if Steve Dexter hadn't had too much to drink. He was faintly embarrassed. Men in Steve Dexter's position were supposed to make pronouncements, not ask

258

opinions from their juniors—especially about a subject as sacred as their work. He wished he didn't have to reply.

"I've never questioned it, sir. I've always thought . . ."

Steve cut him short, nodding, losing interest. "You're quite right. It's better not to ask questions. You make the hell for yourself if you do."

Ignoring Tom, he turned back to talk with Sally, and Tom felt that he had made a poor showing, that he had disappointed Steve Dexter, who had somehow hoped for better from him —or if not better, then different. The party, which should have been a good opportunity for him to talk with his superiors on more equal terms, suddenly went dead on him. He wasn't interested any more. As soon as he decently could he extricated Sally, and suggested that they leave. She looked at him with some surprise, but she made no protest.

As he started the car he said. "Well—let's forget the Republican Party for a while, shall we? Let's go out to dinner. What about Guido's, over on Route 40?"

Sally looked at him doubtfully. "That's awfully expensive, Tom . . . and I left a meat loaf all ready at home."

He started to pull out of the line of parked cars. "Oh, to hell with the meat loaf! Let's live it up a little! If I try I might even be able to act like a rich Republican!"

"Oh, Tom——" Then Sally gave a gasp as Tom suddenly braked sharply. A light-coloured Cadillac swept by them, and up to the Humphries' front door.

"Well, well," Tom said. "And to think I just missed the honour of busting Ed Peters' right headlight!"

II

When Sally left him, Steve Dexter drained his martini, and got another from the tray as it went by. A few minutes later, when it came round again, he replaced the empty glass, and took a full one. He wasn't listening to Art Sommers, who was trying to talk to him, and he didn't pay any attention to the small stir that went through the room when Ed and Laura Peters arrived. He just beckoned the waiter with the serving-tray.

Steve got drunk that night—not loudly or too conspicuously, but enough so that those who talked to him knew it. No one had ever seen Steve Dexter drunk before. He

259

started to tell rambling fishing stories that bored those around him. He was reluctant to leave the party, and he and Harriet were almost the last ones there.

He had driven from the Laboratories with Art Sommers, and Harriet was driving him home in the Rolls. It was sluggish in starting, and she murmured with impatience.

"Well—I suppose we've had more from this car than anyone can expect. It's time to get rid of it."

"No!" Steve laid his hand on her arm with some urgency, snapping out of the happy vagueness of his intoxication. "No—don't do that. Have it patched up. It'll last a bit longer if you don't let Gene and Tim fool with it."

"I thought you didn't like it."

He shrugged. "I've come to think of it as one of the nicest things in our life. I wouldn't like to . . ." His words came stumblingly, and slurred. 'I woun't like t'walk out t' a parking lot one day an' not know which car was ours."

After that he was silent all the way home. Once he started to hum, and then stopped abruptly, as if he didn't like the sound.

Only when Harriet had run the car into the garage did he speak again. "They're all the same these days . . . y' can't tell the difference."

"What are you talking about . . . cars?" Harriet was tired and impatient.

"No—kids! They're all alike. None of them ever has to think any more. Scientists who don't think." He opened the door and half-stumbled from the car. As they walked down the path he held on to her arm. "These kids think science is a job with a pension at the end of it. They never think of what they're doing."

Harriet opened the kitchen door, and Steve leaned against the jamb for a moment, blinking in the strong light, facing the rather startled expressions of his sons and Nell.

III

At Guido's, Tom raised his glass to Sally. "Here's to the big wheel in the Republican Party!"

Sally wrinkled her nose at him, but drank the toast good-humouredly. "I'm a very small wheel . . . but that doesn't say I won't get bigger."

He broke a breadstick on the table, and crumbled it

260

between his fingers. "Well . . . you've just about got Mrs. Humphries in your pocket, and that's not a bad start." He suddenly looked up, cocking an eyebrow at her. "Have you told your father that you've gone over to the enemy?"

Surprisingly she blushed, and sipped her drink quickly. "It isn't his business."

He laughed at her. "So you haven't told him! Well, the roof should fall when Mike Brennan hears you've deserted the Democratic cause."

"Why should the roof fall in? I've never belonged to the Democratic Party. Dad just *supposed* I did . . . as a matter of course."

"He'll still be hurt."

Resentment flared a little now. "I don't care if he is! I've got the right to make my own decisions about politics. And about everything else!"

He looked at her carefully. "Are you sure you didn't make that decision because most of Amtec is Republican? Are you sure you weren't playing politics yourself?"

She set down her glass with great deliberation. "Listen to me, Tom Redmond! Has it hurt you even a little bit to have me working for the Republican Party? Would you have been where you were this evening if I hadn't taken all the clerical work away from Jane Humphries?"

"Sal, you sure are a talkin' woman!" He shook his head. "No, I certainly couldn't have been there. But I wonder if it matters?"

"What do you mean? Of course it matters! You're not going to pretend you don't know that!"

He sighed. "No, I can't even pretend . . . I know I've got a working wife, even if she's not on the payroll. But the boss is always there. . . ."

"Tom! . . ." Suddenly she stretched her hand across the table and touched him, closing her fingers about his own.

"Please don't let's fight! I didn't mean this to be anything to fight about. After all, is it so wrong to want to help you if I can? We live here—we're part of this organisation. If there are easier ways to the top, why shouldn't we take them?"

In return he squeezed her hand, and his face relaxed a little. "We're not fighting, Sal. I just . . . just don't want to see you get mown down by the Jane Humphries of this organisation."

She shook her head. "Believe me, no one's going to mow

261

me down. I'm learning my way. As long as you stick by the rules you can't lose."

"But after the baby's born?" he said. "You can't go dashing about to meetings with the baby on your back."

"A good deal of it can be done on the telephone and typewriter. And I'll be joining a baby-sitting pool." She picked up her glass again. "It can be managed," she said firmly.

He shrugged. "It'll sure be a great Amtec baby."

In silence then, and growing tenseness, they studied the menu. Around them the room was quiet, the conversation of the other diners muffled by the carpet and heavy drapes. Tom and Sally were subdued, very much aware of the isolation in which they had placed themselves by their quarrel. To dine out in a place like Guido's was a rare occasion for them both, and they were resentful of each other because it had been spoiled.

Sally looked suddenly at Tom across the top of the menu. "It's very expensive," she said. It sounded like a reproach.

"So—what of it? I've a right to celebrate, I suppose."

"Celebrate?" she said, uncertainly. "What are you celebrating?"

"A salary raise," he said. "Since George Leonard moved over to Humphries' department, I'm Alan Taylor's assistant."

"Tom!" Her voice trembled a little. "Oh, Tom! And you let me make all those pompous remarks about helping you get on in the company, and all the time you'd got a promotion up your sleeve." She looked at him a moment, then gave a nervous little laugh. "I feel like a fool," she said. And then she added. "But it's wonderful—it's really wonderful!"

He grinned a little. "Yes . . . it's O.K."

"O.K.? Is that all? It's——" She frowned, leaning towards him. "Tom—what is it? What's the matter? Aren't you pleased?"

"About the raise! Yes, I suppose so."

"Not just the raise! The promotion . . . that's what counts!"

"Well, Taylor owed it to me! He damn' well owed it to me! That son-of-a-bitch knew he'd better come across with something."

"But why . . .?"

"Because he let that paper I worked up from the side-data on fluids be published under his own name. *Only* his

262

name! Do you get it? He told me that if I cared to work up a paper on the stuff we'd publish it jointly. That's why I've been working late, and stewing over the figures on the weekends. It would have been the first paper I ever got my name on!"

He shrugged. "Of course he's well within his rights. He *is* the director, and everything that comes out of his department is technically his. He kept looking over my shoulder and making suggestions, but some of it was *mine*, Sal. There were some angles in it he never thought of. The least he could have done was put my name under his."

She looked at him miserably. "What can you do?" she said softly. "Is there anything you can do? Any way to make him give you some credit?"

He drained his glass, and angrily motioned the waiter to have it refilled. Then he turned back to her.

"If there ever was a way to make him share the credit, I've lost it now. I've accepted his lousy job, and from now on I'd better keep quiet."

"But that's bribery."

"No, it isn't! He's perfectly within his rights, I tell you. He needn't have done a damn' thing for me. I could have made loud noises if I thought I'd got a case, but I don't really. Just a few ideas I put on paper mixed up with data from his own project. But if it came to a showdown I don't know half as much about the whole project as he does, and in the end I'd look plain silly!" Beneath his hand, the breadstick snapped loudly. "Who am I to run and tell my story to? Dexter? Or Ed Peters? A lot of good that would do. No, it was either a choice of keeping quiet or resigning."

He sloshed the whisky round against the ice in his glass. "Well, supposing I'd decided to resign? What about the mortgage on the house and the instalments on the car? What about the baby and the hospital bills? It could have taken me six months to get a job at the salary I'm getting and doing the kind of work I'm used to. I'm nearly a specialist, and specialists don't mix too easily . . . and the field gets narrower as you get farther on. In fact, Sal, I need Amtec much more than Amtec needs me. That's where the shoe pinches."

Suddenly he was aware of her distraught face across the table. "Sal, I'm sorry! I'm sorry I said that about the baby . . . and the house and everything. I led you into this, and it isn't your doing. It's my own! It's been my own doing

263

ever since the moment Amtec recruited me straight off the campus. I didn't even have to look for my first job—it was handed to me right on a plate, complete with pension plans and insurance. I took the easy way, right there in the beginning, and I've got no business to cry over it now.

" Sal, try to forget what I've said . . ."

The waiter bent close to him, pad in hand. " Would you care to order now, sir?"

Tom didn't even glance at the menu again or refer to Sally. " Yes—we'll have two prime sirloin steaks—rare. And a bottle of champagne."

IV

On the strength of the salary raise Tom applied next day at the First National Bank for a loan. It depressed him a little to realise how easily it was granted. George Keston simply evaluated the information he offered—his salary, his position with Amtec, his house in Amtec Park, the length of his employment with the company. Then he gave instructions for the loan to go through immediately.

As he shook hands with Tom he beamed at him paternally. " Always glad to do business with any of the Amtec people. It's been wonderful to see all these young people coming into our community—I hope you'll be with us a long time in Burnham Falls."

Tom went away with the uneasy knowledge of having committed himself even further, and yet knowing that there was no other way for him. All over the country he would find a duplication of his own pattern, and the pretty houses and the bounding, healthy children of Amtec Park were ample proof that the pattern was not necessarily a bad one. He had no alternative to run to; he didn't know where to go to be free.

He felt better when he went to spend the money from the loan. It was good to deliberate in the used-car lot, with the cheque hot in his pocket. He chose a light-blue convertible. Then he parked his own car at the garage and drove back to the house. He gave three loud, childish blasts of the horn as he turned in the drive-way.

Sally came to the kitchen door. She looked cool in her pink checked smock, with the radiant serene beauty of a pregnant woman about her. Her eyes opened in wonderment at the sight of the car.

"For you, Sal," he said as he kissed her. He smiled teasingly. "If you're going to run this community you'll need transportation." He kissed her again, on the ear. "I'm sorry there isn't a chauffeur—but that'll come later."

CHAPTER FOURTEEN

Laura didn't acknowledge fully that she had intended to walk in the direction of the Music Hall that Tuesday in October. She knew, of course, that the film based on Larry's *The Leaven* was playing there. She could remember too well the sickening lurch of her heart, the bitter pang of envy when she had opened the *New York Times* and seen the advance advertising—the bigger-than-life profile of the Hollywood star who was playing the role which Larry had written for her, Laura. She had read the reviews, all of them, and they were good. She thought that she couldn't bring herself to see the film, that even if she went only to criticise what the other woman did with her, Laura's, role, the experience would still be too painful.

"Treat yourself gently for once, Laura," she told herself. "Don't be a fool."

The day had been of interminable length and emptiness. It was empty because it contained no promise of seeing Phil. Two days ago he had flown to London unexpectedly to see a play with the possibility of bringing it to Broadway. Laura had had a telephone message from his secretary.

She had gone to New York, maintaining the fiction that it was necessary, but still knowing she hadn't a thing to do. Goodman had come back from Europe, and had been immediately taken ill. He had put himself in hospital, and enjoyed a procession of his friends and students coming to visit him. Laura had dutifully gone, with flowers and a book, and spent an hour listening to him tell her what was wrong with the theatre. He had refused to discuss the part in *The Other Kind*.

"I'm too weary to think about it now," he said. "Next week I'll be hobbling about at home and we'll go through it then. After all, Laura, it's only *television*."

265

After she left him she lunched alone, and halted for a few minutes to admire the flowers in Rockefeller Plaza, and watch the crowds. She had perched, rather self-consciously, on a bench, knowing that this was only a moment's pause, and that she had nothing to do but go back to the hotel. She left the bench soon; it would be unbearable if someone she knew should walk through the Plaza and see her. No successful New Yorker had time to sit on a bench in the October sunshine and watch the crowds and the pigeons. She couldn't place herself so obviously in the role of having to kill an idle afternoon.

So she got up and walked through the Plaza at the same brisk pace of the people about her. Once out of the sun, the ceaseless wind that blew among the skyscrapers was chill; the flags about the skating rink snapped and danced. She wouldn't let herself pause to watch the skaters, even though that had always been a legitimate occupation for a New Yorker. She hurried past, and then found herself outside the Music Hall, still without acknowledging that she had meant to go there in the first place.

She stood in line for a few minutes to buy her ticket, miserably aware that she must have seemed like all the other women about her, in from the suburbs for the day and sporting their new fall hats—a morning's shopping, lunch at Schrafft's, and then the afternoon matinée at the Music Hall, with the stage show always more important that whatever film happened to be playing. Laura hurried into the dimness of the vast lobby with relief. Then she sat and smoked one cigarette after another until the feature was due to start again.

The film was over, and Laura was walking back through the lobby when she saw Larry. He was pushing open a door into the outer lobby, and she had almost to run to catch up with him.

" Larry! "

Still with his hand on the door he glanced around. Behind his glasses he blinked for a moment in the dimness. Then his hand dropped off the door.

" Why, *Laura* . . ."

She began to speak rapidly, afraid he might move on. " Isn't it strange? It's an odd kind of chance, isn't it—seeing each other here? " She rushed on, " I just had a few hours

266

this afternoon. . . . I was afraid I might miss it if I waited for Ed to have an evening free."

Larry grinned. "It's no chance at all seeing me like this. I get such a kick out of seeing *The Leaven* up on the big screen that I'm willing to drop in any time I'm passing. I guess I'm a real hick at heart."

"But it *is* strange," she insisted. "We haven't run into each other for so long . . . and now here, of all places."

As he didn't respond she added, "Well . . . I mean, *The Leaven* was both of us, wasn't it?"

For a second he looked absolutely blank; he covered it quickly, as a polite man always covers a social gaff, but she had time to realise with great finality that he had completely missed her meaning. He had failed to remember, even when she prompted him, that *The Leaven* had been written as a vehicle for herself. He had forgotten why the woman moved a certain way, and spoke certain lines—because he hadn't remembered that the lines had been tailored to her, Laura.

"Oh . . . well, yes! Of course!" He fidgeted. "Well . . . it's hard to remember the old 'Leaven' from this version. This is pure Hollywood." Then he shrugged. "And who's to quarrel with that? This baby's raking in money, and they'll love it in Des Moines. It's going to run another three-four weeks here. I don't mind taking those cheques at all, even if it isn't art."

She made herself smile, although she felt a freezing coldness within her. "You don't sound like a Pulitzer Prize winner—not with all this concern about money and be damned to quality."

"Since when haven't I been concerned about money? I tell you, Laura, a Pulitzer is a great thing, and I'm proud as all hell of it—but better not try to pay the grocery bills with it for long."

He pushed open the door for her, and she passed by him to the outer lobby. He went on talking.

"You see," he said, "I haven't changed all that much with the years—still as commercial as ever."

She softened a little, because with his mention of passing years he seemed to be recalling their own time together. She glanced sideways at him as they walked together towards the glass street-doors.

"You never were as commercial as you make yourself sound, Larry."

267

He laughed. "Well, keep quiet about it, won't you? It might not go well with me next time I make a contract."

The laugh sounded genuine, as if he were comfortable with her. She was grateful for it, grateful for even this slim evidence of closeness and contact in the horrible loneliness of the day. Larry knew everything there was to know about her—in a sense he had created her—and she wanted to feel that he thought well of what he had produced. It would be something to have Larry think well of her. She permitted herself to smile at the thought.

He must have caught the smile, brief as it was. Suddenly, before they reached the doors, he touched her arm and turned her gently towards himself.

"How goes it with you, Laura? All right?" He added, as a kind of afterthought, "You look wonderful."

She wished he didn't stare at her so directly, a stare that didn't allow her eyes to waver from his. "Things are fine, Larry—just fine!"

"I heard somewhere that you're doing a show for Phil Conrad. Nice work!"

"Not yet!" she told him quickly. "It isn't final yet. It's an Amtec show . . . there are a lot of angles involved."

He nodded. "I know . . . there are always so many things before the real job can be done." He paused, frowning. "You know, I——" He stopped again, searching for words, but he seemed to want to go on talking.

Impulsively, rashly, she broke in. "Larry, what are we doing standing here talking? Let's go find ourselves a place to sit down—let's have a drink. I'm staying at the Plaza . . ."

Her voice trailed away as she realised she had said the wrong thing. At once his air of friendly preoccupation left him; the brisk, Larry-manner slapped back into place. She had presumed too far, had pushed her loneliness on him—asked for companionship—and he was instantly wary and suspicious, not wanting to be dragged, through pity, into a kind of one-sided emotional involvement.

"Say—I'll have to take a raincheck on that one, Laura. I'm kind of late for an appointment right now."

It had been very one-sided, she saw. She had been guilty of a grave error in judging his attitude towards her. She had mistaken friendliness for a much more personal concern. Larry didn't regard her with bitterness or dislike; he was simply indifferent to her. So far away from her was he in

268

thought that he had been startled and a little shocked when she had revealed the residue of her attachment to him, the desire to recall things that were past. For him the past he had shared with her was not just dead, but forgotten.

He bustled her through the glass doors and out on to the sidewalk. At the kerb he whistled into the passing traffic for a taxi.

"In fact, I'm on my way home right now," he said, speaking quickly as if he had to find something to say. "I have just about all my business meetings at the apartment now because Mary's on the verge of giving birth."

"Mary . . .?"

"Well, sure," he said, grinning broadly. "Didn't you know I was about to become a father? Isn't that a kick? Can you imagine me with a kid? It scares the hell out of me, and yet I'm tickled pink with the idea. I'll bet I'll make a terrible father—poor kid!"

A cab drew up, and Larry reached over and opened the door. Before she got in Laura turned back to him.

"Funnily enough, I think you'll make a good father. It will be a fortunate baby."

"Well, thanks!" He raised his hat as she settled herself. "Good to see you again, Laura. You're looking wonderful. . . ."

The words were said with the heartiness of indifference, and he probably didn't know he had said them before—and wouldn't care if he did. Glancing back as the cab moved away she saw that Larry's gaze did not follow her. He was whistling for another taxi, and in his impatience she saw that he had forgotten her already. She huddled back in the corner of the cab, feeling the chill of the October evening.

She bought all the late edition newspapers and carried them up to her room, intending to order dinner there since she didn't want to eat alone in a restaurant. It was while she was drinking the first martini that she saw the item in one of the columns. *Phil Conrad in London to catch the new Sherman play, is currently being shown the town by actress Katryn Franklin.* Laura choked for a minute on the liquor, and then swallowed the rest of it in a gulp.

269

CHAPTER FIFTEEN

Mal's call came early on one of those clear, bright autumn mornings when the blueness and clarity of the sky over the lake and hills was almost harsh. The fierce tide of fall colours had swept over the countryside, too spectacular not to hold the gaze unless you have seen it many times, as Harriet had, and when it seems nothing of itself—only a herald of winter, and the spring beyond holds little of hope or expectation. Harriet felt only its sadness. Mal was going to South Africa the next day; he would be gone for three weeks or a month. He had called to tell her that he was coming to Burnham Falls that day, not on business for Amtec, but for the sole purpose of seeing her.

He had said he would call for her about noon. She went through the morning routine with outward calmness, but the familiar excitement and disturbance which Mal always brought with him had possessed her already. Heaven knows, she thought, their times together were rare enough. He had been on the West Coast for two weeks, and there had been, in fact, only one meeting since the day they had sat and talked by the lake—the day they had kissed. And even that single meeting had been frustrating and futile; they had met for lunch and talked across a table in a fashionable and crowded restaurant in Manhattan, and afterwards, in an effort to break through to the mood of freedom that had been theirs on that other day, they walked for a while in Central Park. Harriet was glad Mal hadn't suggested going back to his hotel. They would have gone to bed together, and it would have proved nothing. They had much farther to go in their journey backwards through time before they would again reach that point. Only once Mal had possessed her, strongly and beautifully, that night in the desert. He had won her then, mind and body, for the rest of her life. To use each other physically now, casually and as yet uncommitted, in the anonymous atmosphere of a hotel bedroom, would be to risk what had been gained then. Theirs would have to be a permanent relationship, exclusive and single-minded, or it would not exist at all. They were too far gone for flirtation, and as yet neither was ready to say in plain words what the alternative was to be.

270

This knowledge had been with them when they parted, and Harriet knew it was the reason why Mal had not called her for more than a week after he had got back from the Coast. Steve had mentioned that Mal had been at the Laboratories, but he had not come to see her. Now there was this call, and the calm, purposeful tone of Mal's voice. He had reached some decision during this absence, and he was coming to tell her.

She dressed herself in a skirt and sweater and flat-heeled shoes. Mal had said, "I'd like to eat out of doors somewhere. Don't worry about food—I'll bring everything." She paused to take stock to herself a moment as she dressed, wondering if she didn't still look a little too much like the image her father had made her into—the cashmere sweater, the matching skirt of beautiful, subtle tweed. This was how she had dressed when Mal had first known her. Then she shrugged. It was also the day-time uniform of the executive's wife—discreet, understressed, and expensive. She flipped a comb through her hair, which crackled with vitality, and in the sunlight which fell across it, even caught again the old red tints which seemed mostly to be missing of late. She was glad they were going to meet out of doors. She wanted Mal to see the red still in her hair, the fine complexion that glowed when she applied the vivid lipstick, her slim figure that in the sweater and skirt didn't look so very different from the younger Harriet's. Then, with her hand still holding the lipstick, she suddenly sobered. Whatever they felt about each other, they could not deceive themselves about the true facts—even for a few hours. She leaned closer into the glass and examined herself carefully. Let Mal also see the part of her that was not so young. The strong sunlight would seek out and reveal the faint lines that had come under her eyes and those grey hairs running back from her temples. They should not pretend, either of them, that they could go back to that other time and pick up where they had left off. The years in between counted, and there were marks in both their faces to tell them so.

She grabbed a handbag and ran downstairs when she heard the car in the drive.

Mal was mostly silent during the drive—not grim, just silent, as if he didn't want distraction from his own thoughts. He answered her questions about the South American trip briefly. He was going as a consultant for an American firm

271

which was opening branches in Caracas and Buenos Aires. Though he spoke of it lightly she sensed his pleasure in the thought of movement, the readiness to pack his bags and for a time become part of another scene. He had not changed so much, she thought. He would always be something of the boy who had walked away from Burnham Falls in such a hurry.

They drove on Route 40 for about five miles, and then on 211 for a while. He didn't say where they were going, and Harriet wondered if he had any definite plan. She didn't ask him because it was more pleasant to just sit and leave the decision to him. He had put the top back on the rented convertible, and the sun fell warmly on her bones, and the wind whipped her hair across her eyes. She loved the feeling of youth and irresponsibility that came with driving in an open car on these empty roads on a weekday when everyone else was working.

She was startled almost when Mal turned suddenly off 211 on to a winding dirt road. It was many years since she had been here; she couldn't consciously have remembered its existence. This road ran along the back of the Farmington Reservoir, and came to a dead end; it was a service road that led to the sluice gates, and was travelled only by the odd workman, and the local people who came to fish. Mal parked the car where the road ended near the sluice gates.

He smiled a little as he looked down at her shoes. " I'm glad you came prepared to walk," he said. He took a small canvas grip out of the trunk of the car, pulled off his jacket and slung it across his shoulder. " Can you make it up there?" he said.

She saw that he meant the high point of the hill above them, a grey tumble of boulders that stood out with stark bareness from the brilliant colour of the woods about them. There was no road there; they would have to fight their way through the tangle of timber and brush. " I'll make it," she answered.

He didn't say any more, but started off ahead of her. They walked in silence all the way. She followed closely in his path, watching how he found the easiest way through the woods, skirting the places where the brush was almost impenetrable, zig-zagging up the slope to ease the climb. Although they were completely surrounded by timber he never hesitated about the direction. He was so sure and quick that Harriet, following, thought it might have been possible

272

to believe he had been here only last week. She was breathless when she gained the top a little behind him, but he wasn't even breathing deeply. He put down the bag and his coat, and turned to look about him. The view of the reservoir and the valley was superb—the colours of the woods dramatic and strong, the water the deep clear blue it had at no other time of the year. Mal stood looking at it for a few moments, nodding his head a couple of times as if he were pleased with what his memory had told him was here. Then he put his arm about her shoulders, and drew her slightly in front of him; the gesture was encircling and protective. She pressed against him, firmly, confidingly.

Mal's New York hotel had prepared a picnic lunch for him, and it was elegant, and wryly out of place. He laughed as he unpacked it—the thinly-sliced chicken, the crisp rolls, the half-bottle of good bourbon. "They don't want you to rough it," he said as he took scrubbed salad vegetables out of plastic containers.

Harriet examined her torn stockings. "No—they don't," she said.

While they ate they were a little distant with each other. It was a time of waiting. Harriet knew Mal would choose his own time to tell her why he had come. She accepted the waiting.

They finished their meal with cheese and apples. They sat within the shelter of a tall boulder where the sun was warm and the wind did not reach them. Occasionally a little collection of cloud drifted across the sky, and for a moment the sun was lost. The shadows of the clouds were a deeper blue on the lake.

Mal offered her a cigarette, took one himself, and lighted them both. He frowned over his first draw.

"I suppose you know why I've come?"

She shrugged. "Should I?"

"You might know." He looked at her quickly. "You've always been so damned patient. You always look as if you could afford to wait half a century before satisfying your curiosity. I can't think of any other woman who could have waited all this time without asking a single question."

She shrugged. "I've found that people usually act in their own time—they do their own deciding. Especially Mal Hamilton. So what's the point in being impatient?"

"That's your trouble," he said with a touch of annoyance.

273

"You always wait for other people to act, and they end up by not expecting you to have any power to act on your own."

Her voice grew a little tense. "What exactly do you mean?"

"I mean it would have done your soul good if you'd called me in New York and given me hell for not writing and not coming to see you. You ask for too little."

She was shaken. "I'm afraid to ask for anything. I'm afraid . . ."

He put his hand over hers, lying on the warm rock. "What are you afraid of?"

"Of you—of myself. Afraid of reaching out to grab in case you might decide to shake me off. Afraid to make any move because it might be the wrong one. If I left things to . . . drift, perhaps you might stay a while. If I pushed—or demanded, you might go."

He put his hand up and touched her shoulder, shaking her with rough impatience. "But you must know that you and I can't drift, Harriet. The time for that is long gone."

"What else is there?"

"We could get married."

He spoke the words very firmly, very calmly. She drew in her breath sharply, her eyes widened.

"Do you mean it, Mal? Do you mean . . . married?"

"Of course I do!" His tone was terse, as if he were dealing with someone who was stupid and obstinate. "We'd only be doing what we should have done a long time ago. When I let you go back to Steve I thought it was what you really wanted to do. I know now that if I'd insisted—if I'd made myself stronger that Steve, you'd have stayed with me. You were just following a blind habit of obedience. You were waiting for someone else to act. It was Steve who acted . . . he came back to life, and you went to him as meekly as you've always done everything."

She put her hands to her forehead, blocking out the sight of him, the sun, the lake, the woods about them. "Stop it, Mal! Stop it! You're being cruel and mean. You know there was no other choice for me then—nothing else I could do."

"There *was* something else you could have done. But it was harder than the way you chose. You slid out of it, Harriet. You just accepted what came."

She took her hands away from her face. "Don't go on talking, Mal! There's no point to it. What's the use of the

274

regrets, the blame, the accusations? What use? I haven't anything to offer you, Mal. I haven't anything to offer except the tangles and problems of a woman too deep in marriage ever to get out. A woman with children . . . with responsibilities and obligations. I have nothing to offer but trouble."

"I might take that offer," he said. "I just might take it. Try me."

She gestured to silence him. "Don't taunt me, Mal. I can't take it now."

There was silence between them for some minutes. In the woods below them somewhere a pair of crows called harshly, and rose up suddenly from the trees—great black birds, ugly, whose plumage flashed briefly in the sun before they disappeared back into the foliage. Harriet saw them, and shivered.

Mal drew hard on his cigarette. "I'll tell you what's going to happen, Harriet," he said. "To-morrow I'm on my way South, and I'll be gone the best part of a month. During that time Amtec will be told that I'm no longer available for consultation."

Startled, she turned to him. "But why——?"

"The first step of the way out," he answered. "Whatever your answer is to me, Harriet, I want you to know that I won't be working for Amtec again. I won't come to Burnham Falls again."

She said slowly, "You can do it . . . just like that."

"That's the kind of freedom I've won for myself," he said. "At one time I damn' near lost my shirt for that kind of freedom, but it's mine now. I've the right now to say where and when and what I'll work at."

She drew in a long breath. "Oh, God! How I envy you, Mal!"

He touched her again, touched her arm urgently. "And that's what I have to offer you. You'd be free of Burnham Falls. You'd be free of everything you thought you had to be—your father's girl, your husband's shadow." He paused. "Is that saying it too roughly? Well, it's needed to be said for a long time."

Then he added, "Naturally, freedom has its price. There are few stabilities, and very few plans. There are no mortgages, either."

"I have children . . . there's Gene and Tim. And Steve . . . what about Steve?"

He squashed out his cigarette. "Look, Harriet, I'm not

275

interested in figuring out how many obstacles we can remove before you make your choice. If you want to do this, you make your choice and then you figure out how it can be done. *This* time you have to act for yourself."

"Gene and Tim——?"

"There's no reason why you shouldn't have them with you." Then he gestured with annoyance. "I wasn't going to make your arguments for you, Harriet. If you really want this, you'll know that the obstacles can be overcome. If you don't . . ." He shrugged. "If you don't you'll find plenty of reasons for saying ' no '."

"I don't want to say ' no '," she murmured, almost in a whisper. "I want this more than I've ever wanted anything in my life."

"Then say ' yes '," he urged her. "Commit yourself to it, and go after it! Want it, and go after it, and it will be worth having, I promise you it will be worth having."

"You can say that . . . because you've never had anything to lose."

He swore softly. "God damn it! That's true—and how lucky I was! I was drunken Charlie Hamilton's son, and I hadn't got a nickel's worth to lose. But you, Harriet—you were born in the Carpenter place, and it must have seemed that you had a lot to take care of, a lot to look out for. I guess I was luckier than you—the way things turned out."

She pressed her hands together, closing her eyes and for a moment blotting out his face, the sternness, the hardness. It was possible to see why he was so strong—why he had gained such freedom. He was still ruthless with himself, as he had always been. He never permitted himself the luxuries of wavering and indecision. He had always gone straight to the heart of the matter, and now he was demanding the same courage from her. She shied away from it violently.

"Mal, you sound as if you hate me! Why do you have to talk to me like this?" She turned to him wildly, "If you had ever said you loved me . . . if I had ever heard one word of love from you . . ."

A look of wonder broke on his face. "You crazy idiot! Do you imagine that I could ask you to do this if I didn't love you? I've been loving you since you were seventeen years old, and your legs were skinny and you didn't know how to talk to a man."

"Since then? I wanted you then, Mal, but you sent me away?"

276

"What did you expect me to do? You were a kid. You didn't know your own mind, and it would have been too easy. How was I to know you were never going to know your own mind? By the time we met again in California I knew I was ready to make it up for you."

He reached out and touched her hair, stroking it back from her forehead gently and rhythmically. "I've thought about you so much since that time—more than you'll ever understand. Little Harriet Carpenter with the tender brown eyes and the wide mouth—always asking questions and wanting to learn. And I was aching to teach you."

"I didn't know, Mal. Oh, God, I was such a fool that I didn't know."

He drew her into his arms and kissed her, a long kiss that had the expectation for further time behind it.

"I want you, Harriet. But I won't take just acceptance from you—I want more from you than that."

"It's much more than that—*much* more." She lay back on the rock and pulled him down towards her. She felt his weight close over her, and again the sun was blotted out.

Their love had not the urgency of the first need and knowing in the desert; it was more thoughtful, and fuller.

II

When Harriet opened the front door Nell was seated on the chair by the telephone. She got to her feet immediately. Her bony face had a pinched, greyish cast.

"I've been calling round town to see if I could find you," she said. Her voice was quiet, but sounded on the edge of desperation "I just called the Laboratories for Mr. Steve."

"What is it?" Harriet took a step towards her, but her body seemed suddenly weak. You always paid, she thought —you never got away without paying. A bitter feeling of guilt was upon her already. She said unsteadily, "Has anything happened? Gene or Tim?"

"No, it's Ted's girl—Chrissie. She was with him at Downside to-day. And now they can't find her. She's wandered off somewhere . . . into the woods. She's lost!"

Abruptly Nell sat down again. "She's lost," she repeated. She twisted her hands together. "—And there's going to be a frost to-night."

CHAPTER SIXTEEN

The word started to drift through Burnham Falls later that evening. At first it went only to the local people, the ones who had known the Talbots all their lives and to whom the news that Chrissie was lost had a sense of real and personal tragedy. The word was passed by telephone, and the men went off to join the search with no more hesitation than if it had been one of their own children who was wandering in the darkness somewhere in the Downside woods. The women began to prepare sandwiches and put coffee into vacuum flasks, and they were more patient with the noise and wilfulness of their own children as they thought of Chrissie.

As the hours passed the news went farther. It reached the strangers in Burnham Falls—the construction workers in the bars and the poolroom who had come into town with their Friday pay cheques in their pockets. It was talked about at the cash registers in the supermarket; people talked about it in low voices and then stared out beyond the bright lights and the big windows to the darkness of the parking lot where the cold autumn wind tossed the dry leaves before it with a noise like the scurrying of feet.

There was no organised movement among these people —the ones to whom Burnham Falls was only one town among a string of towns where they had built a plant or factory and then gone on to the next job. They knew the Talbot name well enough because of what had happened to Jeannie; they remembered the police and the questionings at the trailer camp. All they knew beyond that was that Chrissie Talbot was five years old. They were not woodsmen, any of these people—they had arrived at the Amtec construction camp out of every possible environment—and very few among them would walk with familiarity among the heavy underbrush and the granite outcrops of the woods. But at the bars along Main Street, they finished their drinks and didn't order a second round; most of them left quietly without attempting to recruit any of their friends. Cars started pulling out of the parking spaces along Main Street and heading in the direction of Downside; soon there was no one left in the diner. The men who had gone to the supermarket with their wives cut down the shopping list drastically and drove back

278

to the camp with more haste than usual. They checked the batteries in their flashlamps, slipped on a sweater under their jackets, and set out for the seminary. Most of the men didn't know the way to Downside; they fell into small convoys following the lead car of someone who did know.

It was getting late before the news finally spread through all the houses of Amtec Park. Here there was less certainty about what was the best thing to do. There was more telephoning from house to house than there had been in the town; more consulting with one another, more advice given. Some men set off alone for Downside, but most of them waited for a signal from authority. There were those who pointed out that if they choked the narrow dirt road leading through the Downside estate with their cars they would hinder the police; they talked of the need for a properly organised search instead of a haphazard, hit-or-miss one.

Steve finally located Ed Peters at a house on Long Island where he and Laura were week-end guests. Ed's voice was noticeably impatient when he was finally brought to the phone.

"What is it, Steve? . . . I'm in the middle of a game of bridge."

Very briefly Steve told him about Chrissie Talbot. "I want your authority to go all out on this, Ed," he said. "She's got to be found, and quickly. A kid about her age wandered off over in Hale County a couple of years back. It took them four days to find him, and that was just about a day too long."

"Isn't this a job for the police?" His voice was still impatient. "We haven't gone into the rescue business yet, and I don't see that we can do any better job than they can."

There was silence for a few seconds on the line between them. It seemed to carry a suggestion of all the windy distances of that October night. Finally Steve spoke again. "It isn't a question of taking over from the police—they need *help*. They're getting the kind of help they can do without at the moment. Everyone in the district seems to be converging on Downside and they're about as efficient as a flock of sheep. If someone doesn't organise this thing properly we'll have half a dozen other people lost as well as Chrissie." Suddenly Steve's tone rose with exasperation. "For Christ's sake, Ed—you *know* what the Downside woods are like! They'll have to be combed. If the kid's asleep or

279

unconscious you could pass a yard away and not see her."

"So!" Ed said irritably. "You don't need my O.K. to go ahead and organise. This is supposed to be your own back-yard, Steve. I don't have to tell you what to do!"

"It's going to need more than that. There should be search parties tackling the area from the back way—possibly based on the country club and the Laboratories. We'll need a lot of food and coffee. The club could provide all that, but they'll want to be paid. As soon as it gets light we should be ready to really move into those woods. I thought about those walkie-talkie sets and the mobile units Amtec used at that Civil Defence show at White Plains. We could use them . . . and the company helicopter from Newark. . . ."

"Just a minute! Isn't this carrying things a bit far? I don't see that all this is going to be necessary! How do you know the kid isn't found now? I'll look a damn' fool if I ask for all this equipment and then it turns out it isn't needed. These people aren't going to relish being pulled out of their beds and told to get themselves to Burnham Falls. . . ."

Steve cut in. "She isn't found, and she's not going to be until someone gets moving! The county police and fire-men just don't have the kind of equipment Amtec has just sitting about waiting to be used. If you give the word we can get behind them and really do a job."

"I still don't see . . ."

"I suppose I don't have to remind you," Steve said. "This little girl's name is Talbot—got that! *Talbot.* Just forget that she happens to be a sweet, pretty little kid who's only five years old. Just forget that her parents are nearly out of their minds. She's also the kid sister of Jeannie Talbot."

"*Talbot*—I didn't . . ."

"Amtec earned itself a fair share of bad feeling in this town over that affair. If you can't think of it any other way, just see it as a chance to win back something."

"Yes—I see," Ed said at last.

"O.K.! Then I'll go ahead. . . . I'll get on to White Plains and Newark right away."

"Never mind that!" Ed's tone was sharp, the edge of impatience had disappeared. "I'll attend to that from here. Get things moving on your end, and I'll be back in Burnham Falls in about three hours."

"You're coming back?" Steve said in surprise. "Well—I didn't mean to pull you away from . . ."

280

"Skip it," Ed answered shortly. "You just do what you have to do, and don't worry about me."

He hung up decisively, cutting off whatever Steve had been going to add.

In his host's panelled library, Ed looked down at the telephone and swore softly.

"Son-of-a-bitch! Don't think you're going to shut me out of this. If you're looking for organisation, I'll really give it to you!"

He spent the next twenty minutes on long-distance calls, and fifteen minutes after that he and Laura were driving away in the Cadillac, leaving behind a dinner-party that was both bewildered and impressed. Laura in her silk dress and fur coat, sat slumped on the seat beside him, angry at the way the week-end had come to an abrupt end. She would have preferred to have been left behind, but their hastily packed bags were in the trunk, and they were not going back. Instead she was faced with Burnham Falls again. On the journey Ed hardly talked to her except to tell her what she was to do when they arrived, about coffee urns and supplies of food that she hardly bothered to listen to. There were always people like Harriet Dexter who managed those things so much better. She was sulky and unresponsive when Ed stopped for five minutes at a diner for coffee. It was hard to think that Chrissie Talbot had anything to do with her, or that any act of hers could help. She thought of Selma Talbot. Selma would understand that she, Laura, couldn't be of much help. Then when they were back on the road again, and midnight was long past and the drive had taken on a wearying monotony she realised that it had grown colder. As she pulled her coat closer and turned up the heater, she was suddenly much more aware of Chrissie. She remembered her more clearly—a slight, golden-haired child who had occasionally accompanied her mother to the Peters house when the weather was too bad for her to go with her father. Laura remembered her as docile and quiet, busy with her own secret games; she was sensitive, and talked only rarely, but she was also trusting and confident with strangers. She looked as if no one had ever hurt her, and she had not learned to be suspicious. As Laura remembered these things she felt ashamed that she was not more eager to go back to Burnham Falls and help look for Chrissie. But she knew that whatever she tried to do would have very little effect. What

281

was going to happen would happen whether she was there or not. Nothing or no one depended on her.

II

The telephone was ringing as Jeannie turned the key in the door of her apartment. It had a lonely, urgent sound in the semi-darkness. The glaring neon sign from the night club across the street threw bars of light across the room. As she hurried towards the phone she glanced at the clock. It was twenty minutes after three. Behind her, her companion closed the door softly.

"Hallo?"

"Miss Jeannie Talbot?" the operator asked.

"Yes."

"Long distance calling. Burnham Falls, New York. Go ahead please."

"Jeannie?" It was Selma's voice. "I've been trying to reach you all night."

"Oh! . . . I've been with a friend who's sick," Jeannie lied swiftly and unoriginally. "I had to wait . . ."

Selma didn't seem to hear her. "Something terrible has happened," she said flatly.

Jeannie listened, and one part of her mind seemed to refuse to grasp what was being said. The words sounded false and theatrical, just as the words printed in newspapers never carry a personal and intimate sense of tragedy. "Chrissie . . ." she murmured unbelievingly. "*Chrissie?*"

But as her mother started to repeat herself all over again like a lesson she had learned, Jeannie's senses began to function once more. Her first stunned reaction over Chrissie changed to concern for Selma. The distant voice was strained to breaking point. In the dull tones repeating the words for the second time there was the warning of hysteria. That in itself was part of the strangeness. No one had ever expected Selma, who was so calm, to break. She had faced the horror of her daughter's rape and beating with such strength that she had held the whole family together at that time. Jeannie wondered desperately, as she stood holding the phone, if her mother hadn't borne too much of the load then, and that now she lacked the endurance for the waiting period, the hours and perhaps the days that must pass before she learned the final truth about Chrissie.

Jeannie spoke quickly. "Mom, I'm coming right away! Do you understand? I'm leaving here immediately and I'll be with you in a little while. Just try to hold on and I'll be with you . . ."

When she replaced the receiver she turned to the man, who was still wearing his coat and scarf, as if he had anticipated her request.

"Charles . . . will you drive me up? I must go at once." He nodded. "Of course."

The big Lincoln moved easily and silently along the northbound parkway; the traffic lanes were clear and empty. The October night was cold, but within the car there was warmth and luxury. Jeannie talked a little about Chrissie as they sped along. Charles encouraged her—nodding, asking a question occasionally. It eased the tension to talk of Chrissie, somehow Charles' speaking her name gave Jeannie reassurance that she was still alive, not lying somewhere in the wood or in the Downside lake. In the moments she spared from thinking about Chrissie and Selma, Jeannie had to acknowledge again that Charles was the kindest of men.

Occasionally she glanced sideways at the thin, handsome face. If it were not for the lingering thought of Jerry she could have been in love with Charles. As the situation was, it was fortunate for her that she was not in love with him. Right from the beginning it had been understood that there would never be any more than what existed now.

The beginning had been less than two months ago, but Jeannie knew that because of Charles she would eventually go a long way in the cosmetic industry. He would discreetly open doors for her at the right moments, and from there on her own energy and initiative would do the rest.

Charles had been married for fifteen years to the woman whose famous name was on the products Jeannie sold; he was president of her company. It was more than twenty years since his wife had started manufacturing in the States, and by that time she was already rich from her European salons. She was twice divorced and in her third husband she was looking not for money, but a man with a sense of business and the right social background. Charles gave her both these, and she never asked for more than that. They were amiable and friendly with each other at the times they were together, which wasn't very often. Beyond that, they went their separate ways. After fifteen years their financial affairs

283

were too entwined ever to permit a divorce—unless Charles was prepared to walk away from it with no money at all. It was obvious that he would never do that.

Jeannie knew well enough, as other people did, that she was not the first woman with whom Charles had sought to lighten the loneliness and boredom of his marriage. He had stopped at her counter at the department store early one morning before Jeannie's supervisor had appeared on the floor, had questioned her about sales, and then invited her to dinner. A week later she had moved from the department store to a job in the promotion department of the company. It was a relatively minor job, and in the course of it she never caught even a glimpse of Charles, but it meant a good rise in salary, and an immense rise in prestige. Charles never directly mentioned that he had been responsible for the change, but she knew it was meant to indicate that the way was open to her to move steadily upward. She was learning that the way upward was going to require toughness and patience and staying power. Charles could be an invaluable guide on the way.

He knew the harsh and rapidly moving world of New York, and he loved it; his experienced hand smoothed Jeannie's path, and pointed the pitfalls before she reached them. She needed him, too, in a desperate, frightened way, as a haven and a respite from her own fears and loneliness. Just with him she could relax and forget her homesickness—though she never called it by that name. Charles made her feel secure and warm; he made her forget that sometimes she woke at night sobbing Jerry's name. But he also strengthened her and taught her not to permit her fears to show; he taught her the ways of his world, and the world that was to be hers.

She knew that in time the small-town attitudes would be stripped away from her one by one; that in time she would be polished and honed and hardened to the point where she was indistinguishable from any other successful woman of this city—where she would not need Charles as a refuge but would be able to meet and challenge this world on its own terms, with all the shrewdness and toughness it demanded.

These were the things she thought as the empty spaces of the parkway swept by them. The powerful headlamps of the Lincoln probed the darkness, picking out single trees, startling, paper-like clumps of grey birch, massive outcrops of granite. This was the road back to Burnham Falls. Her heart ached to think that it was her world no longer—she would touch and experience it again for only a few hours, a few days, but she would not be a part of it, she would not belong. The foundations of her life had slipped that Saturday night with Patrino and Reitch, and no rebuilding was possible. The situation with Charles seemed to her a poor substitute for what she might have had in Burnham Falls. But leaving it behind had not been her choice. Other people and other attitudes had taken it away from her for ever. In this case the city was not the despoiler—the spoiling had been done already. And Charles was not to blame because she had come easily to him. There had been no other person to whom to go—no other place. She felt only gratitude towards him, and she already knew enough to hope that gratitude would not turn to love, because he might be hers only for a short time, and never that wholly and completely. But the thought of having him to return to in New York would sustain her through these next days in Burnham Falls, would help her not to care because she no longer belonged.

So she sat close to him in the warm softness of the car, and smiled faintly when he looked down at her. It seemed important to let him know that even in the midst of the fear and worry she was glad to be with him.

The light had started to appear in a cold grey sky by the time they reached Burnham Falls. Jeannie directed Charles down past the shellac factory to the Talbot house. They kissed urgently for a moment; she felt herself clinging to him.

" I'm afraid to go in," she whispered. " I'm afraid of what's waiting."

" Don't be afraid," he said. " My Jeannie's never afraid." Then he touched her softly under the chin. " I'll come if you need me. All you have to do is call."

She slid out of the warmth of the car and met the cold morning air.

" Thank you," she said.

She stood watching the car as Charles turned it and headed back towards the town. Soon he would be speeding down the parkway, and the seat beside him would be empty. He would return to the brownstone house in the Sixties that was just an address to Jeannie, and he would bathe, shave, and change; and then he would be off again in the Lincoln, heading this time towards Idlewild Airport. His wife was arriving on an early plane from Paris. Possibly in Sunday's papers there would be a photo of them together, smiling like two friends. After the meeting at the airport they would drive to the house on Long Island where they had a dozen week-end guests expected. For two days they would be together before his wife set out on a tour of her salons in California and Texas.

Jeannie knew it wasn't much of a life, even if what there was of it was wrapped in luxury. But she felt desolate and alone as she watched the car move off. For the first time she felt a stirring of jealousy and envy.

A light had gone on in the front room of the house. Jeannie picked up her bag and turned towards it. The door opened and Selma's figure was outlined against the light. Jeannie started to hurry down the path.

"I heard a car . . ." Selma said.

"A friend drove me up," Jeannie answered. "Is there any news . . .?"

Selma shook her head. "None."

Inside Jeannie dropped her bag and closed the door. "Where's Dad?" she asked. She could hardly bear to look at her mother's stricken face; it was a reproach for all the thoughts she had had of her own affairs during the drive, the anxieties and fears that had not been for Chrissie. She was shamed by her own selfishness. "What can I do?" she said.

Selma shook her head. "I don't know." A spasm of pain crossed her face; her lips started to quiver. "I don't know what I'll do," she said, transferring the words suddenly to herself. "I can't bear to lose Chrissie . . . too."

For the first time in her life Jeannie saw her mother weep. But as she put her arms about her she knew she could only offer the outward symbols of comfort. There was nothing in her own empty heart from which to give her mother strength.

CHAPTER SEVENTEEN

The full force of the movement into the Downside woods began as soon as the light was strong enough. Until then, through the night, there had been sporadic searching—little groups setting out from Downside itself and beating slowly through the underbrush, missing some places, and twice

286

searching others, and unable to say, when they returned, exactly what area had been covered.

By dawn the search was preparing to move out from four different centres. The groups from Downside would search the area between the lake and the highway, the groups from the Carpenter fishing cabin would search the other side of the lake. Parties would also set out from the Laboratories, and from the country club. Listening to Ed Peters explain it again, with frequent reference to the maps on which he had heavily outlined the various areas, Steve couldn't help thinking that it sounded for all the world like someone planning a blanket sales campaign. But by that time Steve was weary, and the awareness of Chrissie Talbot as a child had slipped a little; she had become an object—a prized and desired object for whose finding a whole giant corporation had paused in its stride and was pouring out its energies and resources.

Nominally the police were in charge of the search, but they were far outnumbered, and somewhat bewildered by the swiftness and smoothness of the organisation which offered to help. They watched the chain of command operate with practised efficiency; they could only nod in agreement as Ed oulined his plans, and then take over the leadership of some of the groups that had been formed from the construction camp personnel, the factory workers, and the research men from Amtec Park. It was no longer a matter of volunteering. The word had gone out to everyone even indirectly connected with Amtec. They were expected to, and they did, turn up in full strength.

There was no golf played that day from the country club, and the restaurant served no meals. Every member of the staff, and every catering facility was strained to provide the sandwiches and coffee that Ed had ordered was to be on hand at all the centres. He had stationed doctors at Downside and the Carpenter cabin, and by six o'clock two company doctors from the Newark factory had arrived to take their places at the Carpenter cabin and the Laboratories. The Civil Defence mobile units from White Plains stood ready.

The Downside lake, which never before had heard the sound even of an outboard motor, was noisy with the high-powered hum of Ed Peters' launch which he had had brought over from Lake Burnham. The police were using this to ferry the parties of searchers to various points along the curving

287

lake-shore. There was a student from the seminary in every rowboat as they inched along the shore searching the water line. For the first time the calm of Downside was gone. All about it, on the lake, in the woods, along the narrow road, were the sounds of feverish, urgent striving. Men's voices reached across the water.

Everything, just everything, Steve thought, had been reckoned with, organised, and finally put in motion. What remained now was the heart and guts and imagination to find the child. The incalculable entered here, and it seemed to defy the organisation.

One of the incalculables was the fact of the people of Burnham Falls themselves. They did not belong to Amtec, they were unused to the chain of command, but they had suddenly, the old and the young, become invaluable. They were the ones who knew the woods and the lakes. They were the hunters and the fishermen. They emerged as the leaders of the groups.

The search now had everything that could be given it, Steve thought. And as the skies lightened on the horizon it even had the promise of a fair day ahead, a day when a child might awaken in the woods with the sun on her face. He did not let himself think too much of the possibility that it had been the lake, and not the woods, which had drawn her. But as his eyes sought Ted Talbot's drawn face among the crowd at Downside he knew that that possibility had been well examined, and had been faced.

II

Steve held out a mug of coffee towards Ted. The man stood by himself at one end of the great ornate entrance hall of Downside. He was deliberately apart from the other men and the students who moved in and out of the refectory where breakfast of a kind was being served to those who had just returned from a night in the woods.

" The bastards!" Ted said simply. " The stinking bastards!" Mechanically he took the mug from Steve but he just held it without drinking.

" She'll be found, Ted," Steve said. " Everything's working for her now."

Ted made a motion as if to spit, and then restrained himself. " D'ya think I like knowing how it is?" he demanded.

288

"D'ya think I like the idea that these stinking bastards are going out to find Chrissie? If I could do without them I'd spit in their faces!"

He clenched the mug tightly between his hands. "Look at them! That scum from the construction camp. Just look at them! And they're the ones that're goin' out to look for my little girl. After what they did to Jeannie, I have to stand here cap in hand and be grateful to them."

"Take it easy, Ted. There's no question of being grateful —no one expects that," Steve said quietly. He knew that in Ted's mind he wasn't remotely connected with the activities of the Amtec people; Ted still thought of him as Joe Carpenter's son-in-law.

Ted went on as if he hadn't heard. "If I could do without them I'd tell them to go to hell. If I could search every inch of these woods myself I'd do it rather than have any of them lay hands on one of my family again."

Then he looked at Steve, and the agony in his eyes was very real. "But I keep thinking of that kid over in Hale County a couple of years back. It took too long to find him. I haven't got that kind of time for Chrissie, and so I have to let these bastards go ahead."

He jerked the mug angrily, and some coffee splashed down on the polished wood floor.

Steve didn't try to argue against Ted's conviction. Ted wanted his scapegoat and Amtec would have to serve.

"Just try to remember there are a lot of your friends among the searchers, Ted—and Chrissie's friends too. Every last one of the students have turned out, and every man in Burnham Falls. Chrissie will be in good hands. She'll be all right, Ted."

Ted took a swallow of the coffee at last, and he seemed to be reflecting on the other's words.

"I still can't figure out," he said, gloomily, "why she decided to wander off in the first place. She must have been here a hundred times before with me. The Fathers were all very nice to her, and the lay brothers in the kitchen made a sort of pet of her." A bleak kind of smile flickered across his face. "You know, Brother John was just joking with me the other day that she's gettin' too grown up to be around a monastery. Of course she *is* gettin' grown up. She'll be startin' school next year."

He spoke the words with a kind of defiant hope. Chrissie had been missing less than twenty-four hours. There was still

C.W. 289 K

plenty of reason to hope if you forgot about the lake.

"Brother Matthew was her favourite," he went on. "He's young—a real nice boy, he is. He always takes Chrissie to help feed a couple of pet racoons they've got out back of the kitchen-garden. Well, Brother Matt's sick in the infirmary, and we figure Chrissie probably went to see the racoons by herself. The woods come in close to the kitchen garden there. We figure maybe she saw a deer, or a rabbit, and maybe followed on in . . . and couldn't find her way back. These woods are awful dense—no one ever cut 'em over."

"Dense or not, we'll find her. There are just too many people searching now to miss her."

He finished his coffee, and reached out and took Ted's mug from him.

"I'll drive you home, Ted. We both can use a couple of hours' sleep."

Ted looked at him, frowning. "I couldn't leave here. Supposing they find her? She'll need me . . ."

"They could just as easily find her and bring her in to one of the other places. As long as you're at home they can reach you quickly."

"But she'll expect me to *be* here."

"She'll expect you to be standing on your feet and able to give her a smile." For a moment, gravely, Steve rested his hand on Ted's arm. "I'm sorry, Ted, but it's possible that she won't be found to-day. Selma will need you at home, too. Jeannie just called here, and she's with her mother now. She'd like you to come as soon as you can."

"But Jeannie *knows* I've got to be around when they bring Chrissie in," he persisted.

"They need you at home, too, Ted."

The other man shook his head. "I'd rather stick around here and wait." He spoke more slowly, with less conviction. Then finally his gaze wavered from Steve's; he shrugged, with a gesture of defeat. "Well—I guess I don't want to go home. I can't face Selma and tell her Chrissie's not found."

III

It was Sally who suggested searching the porches and garden of the deserted summer cottages on the hill above Lake Burnham. The idea came to her as she brewed one of the count

290

less cups of coffee she had made since Tom had left early that morning. He had been with the first party which had set out from the Laboratories at daybreak; she did not expect to see him again until evening—or until Chrissie was found. When he was gone she went through the usual round of housework, slowly, moving heavily and with care because the baby was due soon—in a little more than two weeks. The chores were too quickly performed in the shiny efficiency of the house, and she was back again in the kitchen drinking coffee and smoking continuously. The thought of Chrissie did not leave her; she pictured the child too vividly although she had never seen her—a yellow-haired child of five, they said, dressed in a brown skirt and yellow sweater. Inside her Sally felt her own child stir and kick, vigorously claiming its own hold on life. She gloried in the feeling of strength and passion there, and yet she clutched on her swollen belly protectively, as if to shield the unborn child from danger. She found herself praying silently. " . . . the Lord is with thee; Blessed art thou . . . and the fruit of thy womb . . ." She rested her face in her hands, bowing forward over the kitchen table. "Holy Mother, let them find her . . . please let them find her soon."

It somehow seemed that the fate of the unknown little girl, Chrissie, was in a sense bound up with the safety and well-being of her own child. She was praying for them both, with real desperation.

When she thought of the empty summer cottages on the hill she went to the phone immediately to call the Laboratories to check whether they had already been searched. The possibility that Chrissie had travelled so far from Downside without being discovered was fairly remote, but the Laboratories agreed that there was no harm in trying.

Sally spent the next ten minutes on the phone, and soon afterwards a little caravan of four cars left Amtec Park, loaded with Sally's near neighbours and the children who were too young to be left at home. Sally felt her heart beating with an absurd, unfounded hope as they drove through the town and on along the lake front towards the colony of summer cottages.

The little gardens of the boxy frame houses were blanketed under drifts of leaves; blown by the wind they had collected in dry heaps around the steps and along the walks, they clung about the rose bushes and the lilacs. When the wind

291

touched them they would lift and move tentatively, erratically, the rustling sound had the quality of light soft voices in the empty gardens. The maples and oaks with which the hill was bespattered were all the shades of gold and scarlet, a dazzling sight with the sun shining fully on them.

They did not find Chrissie. She was not on any of the porches, not lying in the shelter of any of the garages or the little tool-houses. As Sally moved heavily down the porch steps of the last house she could not quite believe it. The premonition had been so strong, the hope so wild and apparently foolish that it had almost seemed to prove something by itself. She felt again her moment of strong faith as she had prayed in the kitchen, but it had only been the hopeful, trusting prayer of a mother wanting her child to live. It had not meant anything for Chrissie. She was disconsolate and more troubled than before when they drove down off the hill.

She dropped Marcia Webster at her house, and went on to the Laboratories. She knew very well that they would already have all the help they needed, and that there was something rather ludicrous about a woman as heavily pregnant as herself hanging about all day just to serve a few cups of coffee. But her need now was for some reassurance of action, a knowledge that other people beside herself cared what happened to Chrissie Talbot.

She made her way into the cafeteria of the Laboratories, whose glass walls gave a view over the whole valley. Women sat about at the tables, smoking, knitting—the talk among them seemed only fragmentary, as if they had long ago exhausted their conversation. Out in the parking lot she had seen one of the Civil Defence mobile units, but the driver had sat in it quite passively. She guessed the real action was taking place upstairs in Ed Peters' office, and at the switchboard off the entrance foyer. Here in the cafeteria the lack of activity was anti-climax ; they were all just waiting.

Suddenly Alan Taylor's wife, Barbara, got up from one of the tables and came towards her. Sally watched her approach with confidence. Since Tom had taken Alan Taylor's offer and become his chief assistant, and since she, Sally, had taken over the bigger share of the clerical work for Barbara's Cancer Fund Committee, there had been no lack of graciousness from the older woman. The hostility over the luncheon she and Tom had backed out of on the day of the golf tournament had been put in the past.

"My dear," Barbara said. "What are you doing here? You shouldn't really have come . . ."

Sally shrugged. "Oh, I knew there'd be more helpers here than you need, but I've had enough of moping about home worrying. I just thought I'd come here and wait until Tom came in . . ."

Barbara laid her arm about Sally with a gesture that had just a suggestion of gush in it. "Why . . . you poor thing! Of course you must have been feeling blue . . ." Her voice had risen enough so that the small groups of women about the tables glanced over at them. She led Sally forward. "Come and sit down—you don't want to be on your feet too much just now."

Someone thrust a chair forward, and Sally found herself at the table where Barbara Taylor had been sitting. Barbara leaned towards the others confidingly.

"Mary, Nancy . . . have you met Sally Redmond? Her husband, Tom, is Alan's assistant. This is Mary Sommers and Nancy Harvey."

Mrs. Harvey smiled. "Are you the Sally that Jane Humphries raves about—the one she says does so much work for her Republican committee?"

Sally smiled demurely. "Oh—I don't do anything important. Just address some envelopes—that's about all it amounts to."

"Sally's a very good worker," Barbara Taylor said, with a proprietary air. "I don't know what I'd do without her now on this Cancer Drive. You know, our latest figures are going to . . ."

As Barbara Taylor launched into her favourite topic, Sally sat back and prepared to listen. She knew that suddenly something important had happened. She was seated at a table with the wives of three of the most important figures in the hierarchy of the Laboratories; it was true that they were treating her with the faintly condescending air of one very much their junior, but yet definitely one of them. They were acknowledging that she belonged—even if only by reason of the fact that she desired to belong, and was willing to work for her place. Although they wouldn't be prepared to acknowledge quite so much, Sally knew that the line of succession started right here.

But there was one other thing that was also important. A

293

little away from the group, but still attached to it, on a chair that had been half-swivelled to the view of the valley, sat Laura Peters. Sally felt a sense of excitement as she became aware of the other woman. It was possible that she would be introduced. In the eighteen months of living at Amtec Park, this was the closest she had ever come to the wife of the president.

The thought of Chrissie slipped further from her mind as she stared at Laura Peters. Finding Chrissie had ceased to be such a personal, individual responsibility. She was reminded by the sight of all these women sitting in this room that her single effort was insignificant beside the combined one. She could permit herself now the wonderful distraction of her first close, long look at Ed Peters' wife.

She was truly as beautiful, Sally decided, as she appeared on television—but somehow the quality of this face was altered. It was graver, a trifle more hollow-cheeked. Then she reminded herself that it was some years since Laura Peters had made her last television appearance. To Sally, the face she looked at now seemed more human, more aware; it had come to life in an odd way even though it was less youthful. Her figure, in a sweater and skirt, was lovely—slim and pliant; her hands were graceful and tapering—and of course exquisitely manicured. Sally was a little in awe of the perfection of the whole turn-out, the attention to detail that made the whole. For the first time it occurred to her that being a beauiful woman must be a full-time job.

Laura was reading a fresh copy of the *New York Herald Tribune*, and so Sally was free to study her without any embarrassing meeting of their glances. She seemed completely absorbed in the paper, as if the rest of the room, and the low undertone of conversation didn't exist. For the president's wife, Sally thought she seemed strangely solitary; she didn't pay the least attention to Barbara Taylor's talk about the Cancer Fund, and no one seemed to expect her to. That was perhaps strangest of all, Sally thought; the women who saw her most often expected nothing more from her than they got now. It was as if they were used to having her physical presence, but of receiving no contribution from her. Then Sally realised that it didn't matter now whether or not she was introduced to Laura Peters, because, good or bad, Laura would remember nothing about her. Deciding that, Sally gave her full attention back to Barbara Taylor.

It was only about a minute later that the interruption came

—the sharp scraping of the chair as Laura Peters stood up, the slap of the folded newspaper as it hit the ground. Immediately those closely by her turned to look. Her face was twisted and savage, it had turned a chalky white colour on which the careful make-up for the first time looked garish. Without a word she strode past the women at the tables and left the room.

Mary Sommers glanced at her companions. She said in a low tone. "Well! What's the matter with her?" She looked towards the blank glass door where Laura had disappeared, and then back at Barbara Taylor and Nancy Harvey. Her eyes moved a little self-consciously to Sally, as if she wasn't quite sure that it was right to speak this way before her.

"Do you suppose she's not well? She *looked* sick. Do you think one of us should go out and see if there's anything . . ."

Mrs. Harvey interrupted her. "I'll tell you why she looked sick." She indicated the entertainment page of the *Tribune*. "Listen to this item. . . . *Phil Conrad back from London with beauteous Katryn Francis, whom he will star in* The Right Kind *for the Amtec Playhouse.'*"

Outside in the parking lot the driver of the mobile unit straightened with a little show of interest as the blonde came out of the building almost at a run and headed for the white Thunderbird. He expected other people to follow her—it seemed as if there must be some news of the kid—but nothing happened. The Thunderbird roared into life and came out of the line of parked cars at a reckless speed. The tyres squealed as it took the bend outside the parking lot.

The driver shook his head slowly. "You sure are going to get nowhere, lady, in as big a hurry as that."

IV

Harriet stayed at the fishing cabin all day Saturday. It was the least busy of the centres because it was the smallest, and there was no telephone to connect it with the other three. But one of the young doctors from Newark and a mobile unit stood waiting—from the truck she could hear from time to time the garbled voices on the walkie-talkie sets. There was still much traffic on the road to Downside, and every few hours fresh supplies of food would arrive from the

295

country club. There were a few other wives from Amtec Park with her; they came and went as the day wore on. The ones who left were always relieved promptly by someone else. Others, who had no children to tie them down, had arrived early in the morning, dressed in slacks and warm jackets, and joined the searchers. The waiting seemed endless, and as the day wore on, no one seemed hopeful enough to talk much about Chrissie. As the early October dusk came down, a young woman, only married a few weeks and a newcomer to Amtec Park, started to cry, with gentle, timid sobs, as if she wasn't sure how everyone else would take the disturbance. Some one of them patted her on the shoulder, soothed her for a few minutes, and then drove her home. When she had gone someone else wondered aloud if she were pregnant.

The silence after that seemed worse than before. Harriet wished that one of the groups would come back, even to report lack of success, because there would be the bustle of giving them coffee and sandwiches, and then sending someone to report to Downside that another area had been thoroughly searched.

Beside her on the sofa the young doctor stirred, produced the pack of cigarettes which he was chain-smoking, and offered one. Then he lighted them both.

" Must be a lovely spot here—when it's normal," he added. He indicated the lake. " I'll bet that's great fishing."

The lake was still dotted with small boats, and it seemed unfamiliar to Harriet. She nodded. " It is," she agreed. " Very good fishing. The trouble is that we don't get time to use it much."

The doctor nodded understandingly. " It's always the way . . . the thing you like best you hardly get to. I like to go fishing along the Jersey shore, but it's surprising how few times in a season I get there. My wife always needs something done, or the kids have to be taken some place. I tell you its the greatest thing when I'm there . . ."

Harriet let him talk on, let him think she was listening, because it was a blessed cover for the silence, and it let her pursue her own thoughts without anyone noticing that they were disturbing ones. She felt ashamed and guilty that so few of them were directly concerned with Chrissie. The inner, private part of her mind saw nothing but Mal, the beloved shape and image, the voice, the words she heard

296

again, she felt the passion and tenderness. And all the time her heart was crying bcause to-day Mal was on a plane flying towards Caracas.

She looked out towards the lake, to the jetty where she and Mal had kissed for the first time, when it was many years too late. Mal, you fool, she told him silently. You fool—it should have happened the first summer. You should have taken what I was offering, you shouldn't have mistrusted me. You shouldn't have mistrusted youth, nor believed your own toughness. We should have been together all these years; they shouldn't have been missed and wasted—because it is probably too late now.

He had left the choice to her—as hard on her as he had always been, demanding honesty, not sentiment. He had told her to choose first and then together they would solve the difficulties—not to ponder the difficulties and by them decide that what they wanted was impossible. She wondered if it took more courage than she had, more strength. Did Mal see her as a different kind of woman from the one she really was? The thought struck her that by one single action she would become the kind of woman he wanted her to be, or at least he would help her to become it. But the first choice was hers, and she had to make it alone. If she did nothing, if she allowed the passive acceptance of all these years to hold and keep her, she would never see Mal again.

It was very simple. All she had to do was nothing.

The young doctor realised at last that she wasn't listening to him. He didn't mind, really. He kept on talking, so that he wouldn't break the reverie that made her calm face a quiet study of beauty.

v

In the end Laura didn't even see Phil Conrad. All that passed between them was a telephone call.

She had had no real plan in mind when she sped down the parkway to New York. All that mattered was to see Phil and hear directly from him a denial of the item in the *Tribune*. It was as simple as that, but the thought that urged her to a frenzy of speed and reckless driving was that he wouldn't deny it at all. But she couldn't permit herself to believe that even Phil, for all his casual ruthlessness, would

297

choose to break with her in this fashion, and in doing it would snatch away from her the last chance to get back into the only world she knew or wanted. She couldn't believe that it would be as brutal a rejection of love as this.

She checked in at the Plaza. The desk clerk, who recognised her, seemed surprised at the absence of luggage. " My husband has it with him," she said. " He's checking in later."

The man nodded. " Oh—I didn't expect to see Mr. Peters to-day. Not with all he has on his hands. Been reading about it in the paper." From under the desk he produced the newspaper and showed her the small item on the bottom of the fourth page. It was a short account of Chrissie's disappearance, and mentioned that the state and local police had received valuable assistance from Amtec Industries. Edward Peters, President of the Research Division, was personally organising and directing the operation.

" Oh, but they'll find her before night," Laura said quickly. " There's no doubt at all about that."

" I guess so," the man said. " Seems like they got the whole state out looking for her."

Laura took the key from him and almost ran towards the elevator. It was no use letting herself think about Ed now, or to wonder what his reaction would be to her absence at this time. She didn't pretend that it would affect the organisation at all ; she was useless, and most people knew it. Chrissie wouldn't be hurt; all that would be hurt was Ed's prestige.

Once she was in her room she started telephoning. Phil wasn't at his hotel, though they had confirmed that he had returned yesterday from London. She called his office, but no one answered there. After that there was only the dismal attempt to locate him at one of the restaurants he used frequently. She drew a blank at all of them.

There was nothing to do then, but to wait, telephoning his hotel every fifteen minutes, because now she didn't trust him to respond to the message she had left asking him to call her at the Plaza.

It was a very long afternoon. There was no call from Ed, and she didn't think there would be until very late. If he missed her at the Laboratories, he would assume she was at Downside or the club. It would be a long time before he learned that she was not in Burnham Falls at all.

About five she rang room service for some gin, vermouth, ice and a pitcher. She mixed the martini very carefully, letting

298

the glass chill well. It consumed some time, gave her some little distraction. But eventually she had to start drinking it, and eventually it was finished and there was nothing to do but mix the second one. About this time she started calling the restaurants again. At seven she ordered some dinner. That, too, was more of a distraction than a need, for when it came she ate hardly any of it. She had asked for the evening newspapers, but it had become an enormous task to concentrate; the only nerves that seemed to function for her were the ones that strained towards the telephone, that pleaded for the silence to break with its ring. All she wanted to hear was Phil's voice on the other end.

At eleven she began to debate going to Phil's hotel and waiting for him there. But she was afraid to—she was afraid of his cold anger at what he would regard as an invasion. Between her and Phil love had no privileges.

It was almost one o'clock before she reached him.

"Phil? . . . It's Laura." Her own voice surprised her; it was weak and pale. Phil's was light, easy.

"Why, baby! Nice to hear from you! I've just got in—just got your message."

"I've been calling all day." She rushed on. "Phil, it isn't true, is it?"

"What isn't true? What are you talking about?"

"You didn't give *The Right Kind* part to Katryn Francis, did you?"

There was a short pause. "Oh, now look, baby—we talked this thing all through before. I said I'd like you to read for the part. Nothing else. Even with that I was straining because you know very well it wasn't exactly your sort of role. Katryn Francis happens to fit it perfectly. I'd be a fool not to cast her."

Laura licked her lips desperately. "Please reconsider it, Phil. Please do it, for my sake."

"I'm sorry, Laura. I never compromise with my work, you know that. For no one's sake. Katryn is best for the part, and she'll play it."

She hesitated for a moment in silence, trying to adjust to the brutal reality of the words. She had to tell herself that this couldn't mean the end of everything; this was only one part of their relationship, and that so long as there was Phil, she could manage to get past this. And she would find other parts, even without his help. Just so long as there was

299

Phil. He was all the more necessary now, to give her even a reason for going on.

"All right, " she said. The words were an acceptance of his decision. "We won't discuss it any more." Then she added, lightening her tone with deliberate effort, so that he should not feel reproached. "I can come to see you, can't I—now?"

"Now? . . . Why, Laura, it's late!"

"Does that matter?"

"Well, I mean . . . I'm still short of sleep from that flight. We were delayed . . ."

"Please let me come, Phil. I promise you I won't talk any more about the part. I just want to see you. It's very important."

"Can't it keep?"

She said slowly, "Phil—I love you. I love you very much. You're the only person I've ever been able to love in my whole life. You've sort of . . . made me come alive. Please don't take it away now—please don't!"

He gave a short laugh. "You're improving, Laura. Those are pretty strong lines . . ."

"They're not lines. I'm just telling you what is. You're the only person I've ever been able to love, and I suppose it's my misfortune that it happens to be you. It would have been much better for me if I'd been able to love Larry, who deserved to be loved. But it *is* you—no one else. You probably don't know what you've done, but you've done it, and there it is. I have to accept all the conditions you make because I need you."

He spoke harshly. "Sweetie, don't pretend about what we are to each other. You don't love me. You don't love anyone. You just love an identity you think can get you back on the stage, or in front of the cameras . . ."

"No, Phil! It isn't true! If you would just believe me. . . . Oh, God—don't hang up, Phil! Don't!"

She looked with frightened eyes about the hotel room, which was so lifeless and barren; desperately she sought for something which seemed missing—she dug inside herself for some spark of truth and integrity which might be produced now to save Phil for her. This was playing for the real thing; if she had any truth left, it had to come out now. But behind her there was only the long line of compromise—the compromises of her two loveless marriages, the compromises of the easy, mediocre acting jobs, the television commercials

300

selling appliances—all the compromises for ease and comfort and implied security. Inside her there was no truth to fall back on—nothing with which to convince Phil.

She wet her dry lips. "What can I say to make you believe me?" she said in a hoarse whisper. "How can I convince you that I don't care about the part—but I *do* care about you, Phil. This is the one good thing I have. And I have to convince you of that. Just let me come and talk to you, Phil. I know that I . . ."

He cut her short. "I'm sorry, Laura. You can't come. I have company. This isn't Tuesday, you know."

And then he hung up.

VI

Small groups of men kept on the search all through Saturday night. They did this without much hope, because in the darkness the chances of missing a sleeping child were very great, but with the onset of Chrissie's second night in the open the odds on finding her alive grew shorter. The pressure was on, and the need to make even a futile gesture was strong. Some of them searched because Ted Talbot was their friend; some of them had never seen Ted Talbot but they kept on searching because of their own young children asleep at home, or in the trailer camp. The wiser ones got some sleep to be ready for the first light of the dawn.

Ted Talbot spent the night crashing through the woods he had known all his life, feeling suddenly now that he did not know them, that this was an alien place, an unfriendly place. He was hoarse from calling Chrissie's name, and he was filled with a terrible sense of helplessness.

VII

The small bubble of publicity on the search for Chrissie Talbot which had started in the Saturday noon editions expanded rapidly. One of the television networks ran a short clip of an interview with Ed Peters on its seven o'clock New York newscast that evening. The local stations carried it more fully. The Sunday newspapers, hungry for news, gave it much bigger coverage. All the special facilities which Amtec was using in the search were reported.

301

" We are part of this community," one of them quoted Ed as saying, " and whatever happens here is of prime importance to us. We are not only an organisation ; we are people.'

In New York, E. J. Harrison, Chairman of the Board, looked pleased as he read the story. He tapped the newspaper for a few seconds reflectively. Then he looked across at his wife.

" Ed's doing a good job on this," he said.

She barely glanced up from the fashion section. " Yes . . .' she said.

After a few minutes he spoke again. " I think we'll just take a run up to Burnham Falls. Tell Garson to have the car round in about half an hour."

She snapped to attention then. " We can't go to Burnham Falls. We're having lunch with the Waterses."

" Call and make our apologies." He got to his feet briskly. " This is public relations." In the doorway he turned back towards her. " Oh . . . and don't wear anything too elaborate, will you?" It was a statement, not a request. " Simplicity is the note here . . . simplicity."

When E. J. Harrison arrived in Burnham Falls he was very displeased to learn that Laura wasn't available to pose with him for the photographers—that in fact she wasn't in Burnham Falls at all, but in New York. He thought that Ed's muttered excuses were indadequate.

VIII

They found Chrissie early on Sunday afternoon. It was a brilliant, sunlit day, with the autumn woods gone mad with colour, and at first, to the man who saw her, it seemed that the golden hair and the yellow sweater were only more of the colour. Then an exultant shout ripped through the woods.

" It's her! It's the little girl!"

Twenty yards away, Tom Redmond heard the shout, and came racing towards it. The woods were alive with the sound of crashing boots as the men from all around started converging on the place where the red-jacketed construction worker knelt beside the child.

Chrissie's eyes flickered a moment ; she saw the group closing in about her, and then started to cry—a thin cry of terror and exhaustion. The men stood there watching her momentarily helpless.

302

"She don't look too bad . . . she looks as if she's O.K.," someone said close by Tom's ear.

She was scratched and bruised; her sweater and hair were full of burrs. But her cry held more of fear than pain. The construction worker had slipped off his jacket and wrapped it about her, then very tenderly he lifted her in his arms.

"Easy on there!" another voice said. "Should you move her—she might have injuries. Better wait for the stretcher."

The man shot a look of furious scorn towards the speaker. "Listen, bud, I ain't leavin' this kid lying here on the ground another minute. I'll carry her out nice and easy-like, and there won't be no harm done."

He loked down at the child in his arms. "There, sweetheart —there ain't nothin' to hurt you any more. We're goin' to get you to your mommy right away."

Tom stayed beside the man for the mile or so walk back to the Laboratories, finding the easiest path through the brush, holding back the low branches. Chrissie had turned her face inwards towards the man's shoulder; occasionally Tom heard her muffled little cries. They were faint, feeble cries—a whimpering almost.

Someone had already been in touch with the Laboratories by walkie-talkie. The doctor and the mobile unit were on the way to the nearest point by road. A strange hush lay over the men who walked back in that procession. The big construction worker bent over his burden jealously, tenderly, murmuring to Chrissie now and then, reassuring her, trying to share his own great strength.

Sally saw it in Tom's face as soon as he entered the kitchen. There was a kind of radiance in it, a joy that he couldn't hold back.

"We found her! She's going to be O.K.! She's fine! The doctor said she'll be right as rain in a few days."

"Oh, God!" Tears came into Sally's eyes. She put her arms about Tom and drew him down close to her. "Oh, God, that's wonderful."

Tom said softly. "I guess it was one of the best moments of my life. I didn't realise until I saw her how much I wanted that kid to be alive. I wanted her so badly to be alive, Sal."

Sally's baby was born that night. It was two weeks early, but the birth was easy and swift. She bore her child as she

303

had always wanted to—with joy and a sense of completion
with little pain. Listening to its birth cries, she knew why
Tom had so much wanted the other little girl to be alive

CHAPTER EIGHTEEN

All day Sunday Laura stayed in the hotel room. She had
taken off her skirt and sweater, and lay in her slip huddling
between the sheets, cold even in the heated room. She had
watched the daylight come, and the hours of the day pass
away, and now it was the early October dusk again. She
didn't want to move, or think—just lie there, and by refusing
to think to hold at bay the pain and the terror of her alone
ness.

Through the day the telephone had rung twice, and she had
known it was Ed, and had not answered. She did not even
hope that it could have been Phil; there was no more hope in
that direction. She had sent away the maid who had come
to clean the room. She hadn''t eaten any food since dinner
the night before, and that didn't seem to matter either.

At some time during the day she had counted the money
in her handbag. It had totalled eight dollars and twenty-
seven cents. Then she went back to bed and lay waiting for
something to happen.

About six o'clock it did happen. The telephone rang, and
then some minutes later she heard the rapping on the door.
She recognised Ed's quick, almost peremptory knock, and
she knew the waiting was over. She got up wearily, and padded
across to the door in her bare feet. She hadn't bothered to
switch on any lights, and when she opened the door the
light from the corridor was strong, and it hurt her eyes. Ed's
figure was outlined against it.

For a few seconds he just stood and looked at her. In that
look she saw many things about herself—her bare feet, her
slip, her uncombed hair and what was left of yesterday's
make-up still on her face. She let him look, and didn't try to
turn away.

Then he brushed past her and closed the door, flicking
on the light switch at the same time. She saw him as
from a great distance, detachedly, but even so the impression
of his mood came through strongly, because it had never

304

been possible to ignore Ed, whatever happened. He looked weary—very angry. It was not a passionate anger, or an impetuous one. It had the sustained, even quality of all Ed's emotions. He had recently shaved, and his clothes were fresh; his weariness had dulled nothing. He was alert and efficient.

"Well," he said quietly, "perhaps you'll be interested to know that we found the Talbot child. She's all right. She's quite unharmed."

Laura licked her lips. "That's—that's good," she said. "I've been wondering . . ."

He walked before her into the rom. Then abruptly he turned back to face her. "Oh—you've been *wondering,* have you? That was noble of you, Laura. You were wondering so much you couldn't even pick up the telephone to satisfy your curiosity. Well, your wondering helped a great deal. It made a big difference to things in Burnham Falls."

She took a dep breath, but she didn't try to answer him.

"It made a big difference," he went on. "Essentially when E. J. Harrison showed up this morning. I was able to tell him you were very concerned . . . but not enough to stay behind and help."

"Harrison . . .?" she said dazedly. "I didn't know . . ." She shook her head. "I'm sorry, Ed. I'm truly sorry. But my being there wouldn't have made any difference. I wasn't *doing* anything—I was only getting in the way."

"I know very well you're useless," he said. "But your sole job was to *be* there. Even that shouldn't be past your capabilities."

She winced, and then with the last of her energy, she tried to force a protest, to make some gesture to stem the tide of his anger. "Please, Ed—no more now! I'm sorry I didn't stay. I just had to come. I couldn't help myself. That's all there is. I don't want to talk about it any more."

"Well—*you* don't want to talk about it any more! I don't think I've got much reason for caring about what you want."

He strode to the window that looked southwards towards all the brilliance of the city, the lighted skyscrapers against the blackness of the sky. His profile was sharp and clear against it. His face had assumed the look of coldness that she hated.

"You came running down here to beg Phil Conrad to give
305

you *The Right Kind* part, didn't you. You had to make a spectacle of yourself before everyone in Burnham Falls because you hadn't got enough control to do anything else. You're a fool, Laura—and a weakling."

"I had to try . . ." she said.

"And it didn't work, did it? Conrad not only threw you out of the part, but out of his life as well. That's what happened, isn't it? And you've been lying here ever since like a sick cat without guts to pull yourself together."

She didn't answer.

"Well?" he demanded. "Haven't you anything to say? I had hoped you weren't quite such a fool as to imagine that your little romance with Conrad could mean anything permanent. That's one man who doesn't give anything for nothing, least of all a piece of himself. If you were angling just for the part you might have made it—but trying for the man himself was just plain foolish."

He came back towards her. "Well, now, that episode's over, isn't it, Laura? It's time you got to know exactly what you are about."

"Ed, please——"

He cut her short. "And in case you're tempted to make a fool of yourself again, let me just tell you a few things.

"From now on," he said, "I am the one who will make the decisions. I don't want to hear any more of this nonsense about lessons with Goodman, or anything else like it. You're not an actress, Laura, and you never will be. Forget it."

"I can't forget it . . ."

"You'll have to, because I don't intend to subsidise your failures any longer. And I certainly don't intend to stand by and watch you become a laughing stock. You'll come back to Burnham Falls with me and do the job that you were meant to do in the beginning—which is quite simply to be the wife of the president. It's not a small job, and I expect you to give it at least as much energy as you've given your abortive efforts to be an actress. Only real talent has the right to make demands on other people, and you haven't got it. From now on you can just be glad you've got me—*and* Amtec and Burnham Falls. If you haven't got the brains to be anything more than decorative, then you'll damn' well be decorative—and charming," He added, "After all, I have the right to expect some value for money."

Dumbly she watched him take out a cigarette and light

306

it. The lighter blazed, shadowing the furrows of his tight, concentrated frown. He snapped the lighter shut, and drew on the cigarette deeply. She could feel herself going down before him, drowning in her own shattered confidence and the force of his will.

"That's about all, I think," he said. "Except for one thing. There isn't going to be a divorce. I hope you understand that. I don't intend to go through another divorce and you might as well know it now."

He sat down in an armchair, and stretched his legs before him.

"You'd better make the best of it, because there isn't any alternative for you."

He leaned back wearily, closing his eyes now as he drew on the cigarette.

"And now I'll wait for you to get dressed. We're going back to Burnham Falls to-night."

With a kind of numb, petrified obedience, she showered, washed her face and dressed. She had no cosmetics with her—nothing but a comb in her handbag. When she was ready to go the face that stared back at her from the mirror seemed scarcely her own. Without make-up, it was not beautiful, but plain, with hungry-looking hollows in her cheeks. The skin seemed to have shrunken back against her skull, and the veins at her temples stood out. Against her colourless, featureless face the gold of her hair turned drab, and her eyes were without depth or meaning. Without a pencil to darken her plucked brows, her face had the shiny, bald look of an egg. For a moment she glimpsed the face of an old woman in the mirror.

She had to wait in the lobby while Ed signed for her bill, and while his car was brought around. She wondered if he were enjoying the knowledge of her humiliation to stand there while groups moved through to the various dining-rooms—to stand there, dull, and even ugly, among the bright faces and brilliant gowns about her. She endured it because there was nothing else to do.

"Charlie Connors is coming up to Burnham Falls in the morning. I'll have him drive your car back." These were the only words Ed addressed to her during the whole journey back to Burnham Falls.

Jeannie left Burnham Falls on the first train Monday morning.

"I still can't understand why you have to leave now," Selma said as they kissed and parted at the station. "Surely they'd give you just one day off from your job—in these circumstances. You haven't had any sleep since Friday . . ."

Jeannie broke from her mother's arms, and stretched up to kiss her father's cheek. "Oh, they'd give me a day off," she said quickly. "But I can't afford a day . . . every day I'm not there someone or something gets a little ahead of me."

"I wish," Selma said, "that you weren't in such a hurry—with everything." But she did nothing else to stop her daughter from climbing on board. The whole lighted coach was empty except for Jeannie and the conductor. Jeannie pressed her face against the window to get the last glimpse of them as the train pulled away—her mother and father with their shabby clothes and handsome faces sharply revealed in the light that streamed from the waiting-room. Then they were out of sight and the town was left behind.

Jeannie tried to sleep during the long, slow journey, but sleep eluded her. They stopped at each station on the way down, and passengers straggled in, on their way to early jobs in the city. Their faces looked sleepy and pale, and vaguely resentful. Jeannie stared wakefully out into the darkness and saw nothing but the reflection of the other passengers in the coach. She thought about Chrissie, mostly. She had been given treatment at Kempton General for shock, and ordered a few days of rest in bed. Selma had fed her her first light meal, and then she had slept. She woke briefly to be fed again a few hours later, and then she had gone to sleep holding Ted's hands. Her need for reassurance was plain, and Jeannie had known that it must come from Selma and Ted, not from herself. In Chrissie's childish world, Jeannie was already someone distant and vague. She had smiled at her, but turned quickly away to her mother.

From that moment on, Jeannie had wanted very badly to leave Burnham Falls. Even her short absence had sharpened perspective, and the agony of waiting out these hours had added a great deal to her growing disillusionment. She had seen her father, frustrated and sick because he had to accept help from Amtec; she had seen the generosity of Amtec's action being high-lighted with the glare of publicity. And she knew, also, that it was not merely her own hardened attitude she was bringing from the city; these things had always been here, but until the episode of Patrino and Reitch she had ignored them. What she had won from that and from this forty-eight hours while Chrissie was missing was a little honesty, and much enlightenment. She knew now that her thoughts and regrets for Burnham Falls had been tied up with the improbable hope that somehow Jerry would come back to her—that any encounter with the town would be an encounter with him. Now she knew the falseness of that hope. What she had been searching for was mostly the lost innocence, the sweet enthusiasm of the young years—the years of dreaming before the age of reality and responsibility. She didn't want Jerry any more. She had grown past him at the moment she had given up dreaming. And she didn't need Burnham Falls.

So she could leave Selma and Ted and Chrissie behind to live on in the way they had always lived. There were good years ahead for Chrissie, and if Chrissie were lucky she could always stay in Burnham Falls without feeling any need to leave it. But Jeannie felt no sense of loss now in her own departing. The peace and security and love she had had would always stay with her; she no longer felt it was necessary to stay tied to the source of it, she was not dependent on it any more. What strength these years had given her would not diminish.

Finally she fell into a light sleep, and didn't waken until the train had pulled into Grand Central.

The early morning streets appeared washed and clean, and the light was breaking into the deep canyons. She rode home in a taxi to her apartment on Second Avenue with the windows rolled down, feeling the wine-sweet October air on her face. There was a wonderful sense of familiarity about the city, a sense of welcoming, of returning. She felt no longer a stranger, and alone. She read the name on the driver's licence mounted on the glove compartment—Abraham Cohan. She had not exchanged a word with him beyond giving him the address, and she would probably never see him again,

309

but quite suddenly, in these moments, he was her friend—as the city was her friend.

Back in the apartment she showered and lay down on the bed. There was still an hour to sleep before she need get up and prepare breakfast, and press the blouse she would wear to the office that day. She fell into a deep sleep almost immediately, and it was the telephone that aroused her. Before she picked it up she knew.

His voice warmed her. He was calling from Long Island.

"Good morning, Charles," she said. "Everything's fine." And it was.

CHAPTER NINETEEN

It rained all that Monday in Burnham Falls. It rained almost continuously through the day, a light rain which fell with a monotonous dull sound on the carpet of leaves. Laura lay in bed late, listening to it, hating it. When at last she got up, close to noon, she stood at the window for some minutes, looking out. It was an ugly, sad day; the frost had come sharply last night and now the leaves and bushes were withered and brown. The whole scene had a sodden, mournful look. It seemed that the winter was very near. Laura clutched the draperies as she stared out, and shivered. What she saw seemed to be an immediate projection of her life—routine monotony of days that dragged by, and were the hue of the brown matted leaves piled in the flower-beds.

Jane Humphries called, reminding her of the P.T.A. meeting the next day. Laura promised that she would be there, and hung up abruptly, not wanting any more of Jane Humphries' discreet probing. They could all think what they liked about her week-end absence; she had no intention of making any explanations.

After that call the real depression of the day set in. Laura wandered about the house, picking up a magazine, then a book, leaving them both down again unlooked at. To-morrow was a P.T.A. meeting—and to-morrow was Tuesday. There would be no more early morning rides on Tuesdays down the parkway to New York. There would be no more sense of excitement on waking in the mornings—of counting off the days. From now on the weeks could be without end, and it would not matter. Phil Conrad had closed the door on her, had taken away that lovely, shining world. There was no one else to show her the way back into that world. If she wanted it, she had to go and get it for herself.

Thinking of this, with a kind of desperate hope, she went swiftly to her dressing-room, and opened up the closets. There were the two mink coats hanging there, a mink jacket and a chinchilla wrap. In the little safe were the jewels both Larry and Ed had given her. She laid her hand tentatively on one of the coats. There was money enough here to keep her for quite a long time if she wanted to go back to study in earnest with Goodman, if she wanted once more to start the rounds of the producers' offices. It would mean living in a walk-up, probably in Greenwich Village, or somewhere on the upper West Side. It would mean watching her money, riding in the subway instead of taxis, of noticing the price of food in the supermarket. It would mean being all the things she hadn't been since those days before Larry had taken over her life, before he had started the process of coaxing into being and nurturing a creature that hadn't existed before. It was possible that she didn't know how to be once again that early Laura. She wasn't used to doing things for herself any more; she wasn't used to asking —for parts or for anything else. She didn't know if she had the courage to enter the producer's office and sit meekly waiting.

But worst of all, she didn't know that when she was given a part, she could play it. She hadn't ever been sure, and she wasn't sure now, that she was an actress. Without Larry to bolster her, without the cushion of Ed's money, was she able to tackle the grim world that was part of the shiny one? She didn't know that, either. Larry had created a thing of fragile, spun-glass beauty—and without talent none of it mattered. She let the sleeve of the coat drop limply; she was afraid to take the chance.

At mid-afternoon Clare and Elizabeth came home from school. Laura was conscious of their presence in the house in a way she had not been for a long time. It seemed an impossible burden that she was partly responsible for the way they grew up; she realised that she hadn't the slightest notion of what they thought, or how they felt. They were also a part of the world of Burnham Falls that she had kept steadily at bay, refusing to admit that it had reality in her

311

case, or that she could be expected to be a part of it. Now she knew that Ed not only expected it, but he could demand it. He was demanding that she reach out and embrace this alien world.

Hesitantly she went towards Elizabeth's room, cherishing the meagre hope that perhaps in this one contact she might find a beginning. The very violence of Elizabeth's bewildered adolescent emotions might make a starting place. But the steady loud beat of the rock-and-roll music greeted her. She stood before the closed door for a moment, and then turned and went away.

It was after four o'clock, and it was still raining. The only words Ed had addressed to her that morning were a reminder that Handley Parker and his wife would be joining them at the country club for dinner. She remembered Handley Parker; he was from the Budget Department of the Amtec head office. He and his plump wife spent their lives in an almost perpetual tour of the Amtec plants all over the country, and Laura had once thought that he looked a little like the long twist of paper from a cash register. Unwillingly she started the motions of preparing to meet them.

This routine was also familiar, the act of creating the face, the look that she wanted. But to-night it had no magic; even with no trouble she would be the most beautiful woman in the dining-room of the club—probably the only one. There was no challenge to meet, no excitement. Mechanically she went through the ritual—the careful removal of the make-up she had worn through the day, the shower, the splashing with cold water, the talcum, the lotion on heels and knees and elbows. It was all done as before; it had very little meaning.

She zipped herself into a foundation garment, and put on stockings and high-heeled satin bedroom slippers. Then she slipped on a terry robe and called Gracie on the house phone to bring her ice and pitcher and gin and vermouth.

"Wouldn't you like me to mix it, Mrs. Peters?"

"No, bring it all here. I want to do it myself."

She drank two martinis sitting at the dressing-table staring into the mirror. It was last night's face she saw there, the one that had looked back at her from the mirror in the hotel bathroom. It had faint cracks running down from each side of the nose; it had the smallest of lines under the eyes. That wouldn't have mattered if it had possessed life or eagerness. But there was no life in it at all. It was the face she would have to take to dinner with her to-night, the one that would appear at the P.T.A. meeting to-morrow. It was the dreary face of the suburban housewife that she was now going to be.

She drained the second martini down, and went to the phone. It occurred to her that Harriet Dexter could be the contact she needed, the person who might help her bridge this gap. At least she could talk to Harriet. It was always very easy to talk to Harriet; she listened so well. Larry had said it was the rarest of gifts to listen well; he had said almost no actress ever possessed it.

Nell Talbot answered the phone at the Dexters'. "I'm sorry, Mrs. Peters. Mrs. Dexter won't be home until about seven. Can I take a message?"

"No—no message."

As she put down the phone she was crying a little, the tears welling silently and slipping down her cheeks.

"I can't do it alone," she whispered in the stillness of the room. "I can't do it alone. Someone has to help me."

She went back to the dressing-room and mixed herself another martini. It was a long one, and she drank it too quickly—not for enjoyment. Then she rose, a little unsteadily, and went to the wardrobe to look for a dress to wear. She ran her hand along the dinner-dresses, a loving reverent touch; the feel of silk and chiffon was still real and beautiful. And then her hand fell on the olive-green jersey.

She had worn it that first night at the Plaza when she had dined with Phil. In her mind she called it the first night because it had been the first night that she had felt Phil's special interest, the night she had known he was attracted to her in more than the usual way. As she touched the soft folds of the dress she experienced again that triumphant sense of power, the excitement of an encounter that was about to begin. Then the feeling went dead. This was not a beginning, she told herself.

Almost absent-mindedly she mixed the next drink, and sipped it slowly this time, thinking of Phil. Somewhere with him she had gone wrong, she had made the false move that had taken away that first power she had held. If she could have waited a little longer, if she could have held him without revealing how vulnerable she was. Her mistake had been far back, right in the beginning, on that night she had been with

313

Phil in the Carpenter's fishing cabin. She had been stupid and naïve then; in her loneliness and insecurity she had blundered, and after that there had been nothing about her to excite or challenge Phil. Larry had warned her that she must never let down the spun-glass mask. But she had with Phil, and that had been the mistake. If it were just possible to go back, she thought . . . if it were possible to go back to that moment, to be what she had been before it. There was something of herself back there, that might still be retrieved, a sense of identity before it had been lost in Phil, a sense of hopefulness, perhaps.

Her shaking fingers put the empty glass back carefully on the tray. Then she wrapped her robe tighter about her. At the doorway the heel of the satin slipper caught in the rug, and she almost fell.

She found the Thunderbird in the garage, as Ed had said it would be, and the ignition key was in place. As she touched the starter she thought for a second of Ed, who always knew that the orders he gave would be perfectly carried out, who never made mistakes—except possibly the biggest one of having married her. The engine came to life with the familiar, powerful sound that she loved. She took off the brake and the car moved out quickly into the rain.

No one understood why she had been on the road to Downside at all—much less at that time of day, and wearing only a terry robe and slippers, her face bare of even a trace of make-up. The Thunderbird had crashed through the guard rails above the lake, leaving heavy skid marks in the soft shoulder. She had died from the impact when the car hit the rocks, not from drowning.

Laura had not known any of the priests at Downside personally, and it was hard to believe that she might have been headed there to seek advice or counsel. Some people remembered that the Downside road also led to the Carpenter fishing cabin; but the cabin was deserted, the electricity and water shut off. There seemed no reason why Laura Peters should go there late on a cold rainy October afternoon.

CHAPTER TWENTY

By the end of January Burnham Falls had been tight in the grip of a freeze for more than three weeks. Two days ago the temperature had risen a little, and it had snowed heavily; then it froze hard again. This afternoon the sun had shone fitfully, but the snow still lay like iron on the ground. The countryside looked stark and bare. There were very few birds.

The cold was intense. It seemed, Clif Burrell thought, to possess a stubborn force of its own, a physical thing that you could not ignore. He moved his feet a little to try to keep the circulation going, but he had already stood there too long, and old Cy Richards, the Episcopal minister, always took his time with burial services. Clif glanced across the open grave towards his secretary, Milly Squires, whose mother was being buried. She was weeping in an unrestrained way —as if, Clif thought, she hadn't been expecting her mother to die for the last three years. And then he frowned at his own thoughts. You're a cynical old bastard, he told himself. A woman has a right to cry at her mother's grave if she wants to.

It was over at last. Milly was surrounded by people, and she was being led down the slippery path towards the cars by a tall man in his late thirties, on whose arm she lent with an air of possessiveness. Clif knew he wasn't needed, so he searched about in the crowd until he saw Harriet. She signalled to him, and he went to join her. They started down the path together.

"Well," Clif said, "there's another one gone. She's had a bad time these past two years—I expect she was glad to go. She was a lot younger than me. It's a pity I can't die before I get too old and boring. No use hanging on, Harriet, when there's nothing left to do. I'll be seventy soon."

"Don't play for sympathy," Harriet told him. "You'll be ninety-nine before you're boring, and I think you've been old since you were five—so what's there to change?"

He laughed, a dry cackle which caused several heads to turn in his direction, and people remarked that Clif Burrell grew worse with age. He not only drank, but he was disrespectful, too. It was unfeeling to laugh at the funeral of his secretary's mother.

315

They had reached the parked cars. Harriet glanced up and down the line. "Where's yours?"

"I'm walking," Clif answered. "It wasn't far, and the snow's still a foot deep in my driveway. I wasn't planning to go anywhere, so I just thought I'd let the car sit until the thaw."

Hariet touched his arm. "Then come home with me. We'll get some whisky into us to take the chill away."

He nodded. "Thanks, I'd like to." One of the good things about Harriet was that she never pretended he didn't drink, and she never lectured. He thought it was smart of her to know that he wouldn't give up drinking just because someone told him to. He followed her along the line of cars. She stopped by a new Oldsmobile, and pulled open the door.

He looked at her in puzzlement. "Yours? Where's the Rolls? Did it fall apart at last?"

"No, it didn't fall apart. I just decided I'd had it long enough. Time to change."

He didn't say anything. He felt rather lost inside the new car. A little resentful, too. He had never thought of Harriet without her father's Rolls; he missed it.

The roads had been ploughed, but the drifts were piled high in the ditches and against the stone walls. The land had a naked, barren look, stripped of leaf and shelter; the hard hand of winter was on it, cruel and harsh. Clif remembered how he had loved snow as a boy, but he didn't love it any more. Harriet drove cautiously, slowly; the snow chains on the tyres made their rhythmic whirring sound.

Clif said, "Well, Milly isn't leaving Burnham Falls after all."

Harriet looked across at him, lifting her eyebrows. "Oh?"

"I suppose you didn't know. For years she's been hell bent on getting herself to New York, and living in the Big Town. Of course she would have been miserable, but she didn't know it. Milly hasn't the stamina for New York. Well—everything's changed. She's going to marry Jeff Haggens—he's a chemist who came here for Amtec about six months ago. So now Milly's discovered there's nothing she wants so much as to set up house right here in Burnham Falls. I guess that's one you can chalk up to Amtec's credit."

"You sound reluctant."

"Why shouldn't I be? For every Milly Squires who stays there'll be a Jeannie Talbot who leaves. If Amtec hadn't come to this town, I don't doubt that Jeannie would still

316

be here. And, by God, Harriet, we need the Jeannies. . . . Now *there's* someone whom New York won't beat. That girl's got guts . . ."

"We need the quiet ones like Milly, too," Harriet cut in. "And we need the ones that Amtec brings here."

"But some of them we're never going to keep," Clif answered quickly. "The ones like Laura Peters. You could tell right away she was never going to stay."

"But Laura's . . ."

"I know," he said. "I know she's lying there in the Episcopal graveyard, which is about as permanent as anyone can be in a place. But she doesn't belong here, and she never did. She's one of the ones Amtec moved here who should never have been made to move. I think she died because of that—whatever way she died."

"It was an accident," Harriet said firmly.

"You can believe that if you want. I think she was killed in the accident, but I think she died before that."

"I *have* to believe it was an accident."

He shrugged. "Maybe it was—but whatever led up to it was no accident." He looked across at Harriet. "And damn it, you know I *miss* her. Yes, I miss her! I suppose I never spoke more than six words to her, but she was always a sight to see. I liked the way she moved. You know, Harriet, there's too little style left in this world. I'm sorry when a piece of it goes."

"I wish Laura could have known a few things like that—I mean, what Burnham Falls thought about her. It might have made her want to . . . stay."

He shook his head. "It wouldn't have done any good. We were not what Laura was looking for. You can't just tell people what's good for them. They've got to know it."

There was silence between them for a while. He glanced at her, but she didn't seem about to speak, so he broke the silence purposefully.

"Well—I suppose there will always be those who go, and those who stay."

They drove on without speaking again.

Harriet looked at the dead winter landscape, and wondered where Mal was now, whether it was winter with him too. There was nothing left for her to do now—except to wonder.

317

CHAPTER TWENTY-ONE

The announcement of Steve Dexter's appointment as President of Amtec Laboratories did not cause much surprise, either in the corporation, in the industry, or even in Burnham Falls. In the corporation it had been hinted and guessed at ever since he had taken over on a temporary basis when Ed Peters had gone on leave after his wife's death; in the industry his original work on solid fuel was remembered, and it was recognised that Amtec might be trying to correct an earlier mistake by placing a scientist instead of a pure administrator at the head of the Laboratories—the era of the Russian sputniks and rockets had suddenly made the scientist an important man. And in Burnham Falls it was regarded as a natural thing, an appointment that was long overdue to Joe Carpenter's son-in-law.

Clif Burrell was thinking of these things as he sat in the bar of the country club on the Saturday night after the announcement. He had been present at a dinner the heads of the departments at the Laboratories had given to Steve —a relatively informal, sprawling affair which had seemed to include about half the staff of the Laboratories and their wives, as well as anyone else Steve and Harriet had wanted to invite. When the dancing had started Clif had headed for the bar; he sat over his whisky thinking that everyone had behaved with perfect composure—there had been nothing at all to recall Laura's death and Ed's sudden departure.

Ed was going back to the parent Amtec company as a special assistant to E. J. Harrison, and everyone knew that could lead anywhere.

"That's pretty close to the top," Clif mused to himself as he circled the whisky slowly round the ice in his glass. "There could be only one way left to go—out!"

And he thought that Steve himself would be staying only as long as skill and ingenuity and the ability to play politics would permit it. He hadn't been handed a franchise along with the presidency of Amtec Laboratories. They were trying a man of science in place of a lawyer or an accountant; if he could get the product and the results out of his researchers, he would be given the lawyers and accountants with which to hedge himself about. If he didn't, there was

318

nothing. On the face of it, it seemed no more hazardous a game than many men played in their lives; only here the stakes were higher. It was a desperate game, but how did a man—or a woman—stay out of it? How was it possible to turn back? He pondered the question as he circled the whisky more and more slowly around the melting ice in his glass.

Then the face of one of a small group farther along the bar suddenly stood out. It was a familiar face—the face of a young woman both friendly and quizzical. She was staring at him, her eyebrows raised a little, inquiring, waiting for recognition. He reached back in his memory and brought out her name. It was Sally Redmond, and the time had been about two years ago in this same place.

As she saw his expression change she broke away from the group and came towards him.

He took her hand in his. "My dear," he said, "it's nice to see you again."

"And you," she said, smiling. It was the same eager, warm smile he remembered. There was also something else he remembered particularly.

"And how is the novel?" he said. "Finished yet?"

She looked startled. "The novel? You mean I *told* you about it? I must have ben more excited than I thought, that day. Tom's the only one who's supposed to have known . . ."

"I assure you I regarded it as a secret. And I felt privileged you'd shared it with me. Is it finished?"

She shook her head. "No—and it won't be."

"Oh . . .?"

She shrugged. "Perhaps it never was worth finishing. It was starting to get in the way of the things I should have been doing to help Tom along—you know the kind of things a wife can do for her family, Mr. Burrell."

He nodded. "I can imagine . . ."

"You know, Mr. Burrell, you can't be half-committed. As in everything else, the half-way people never make it. If there's any help I can give Tom, he's got it. All of it."

Pushing her glass towards him then, she said, "Would you order me a stinger, Mr. Burrell?"

Clif visualised the forces at work. The pattern of the corporation life was there if you wanted to see it. He thought of Laura, who had come to it unwillingly, and had left it; of Harriet who had had it thrust upon her, and who would live with it gracefully and you might never suspect that she might

319

have wanted anything different. And then there was Sally. She saw and accepted the challenge of the corporation; she knew the rules of the game and played them with intelligence and skill. If it were left to Sally she would one day have Harriet's position—but not unwillingly or half-heartedly. Perhaps not in this town, or with this corporation. But somewhere—sometime.

THE END